kickländ

kickländ

A Novel

Kevin Hayes

HAYES AND HYDE PRESS
St. Johns, Michigan

Published by Hayes and Hyde Press
1210 W. Hyde Rd., St. Johns, Michigan 48879
Additional information: page 287

Publisher's Cataloging-in-Publication Data
Hayes, Kevin.
    Kickländ: a novel / Kevin Hayes.—St. Johns, Michigan:
    Hayes and Hyde, c1997.
        p.   cm.
    ISBN: 0-9654903-0-0
    1. Cross-country ski racing—Fiction. 2 Skiers—Fiction.
    I. Title.
    PS3558.A84K5   1996
    813.54 dc20   96-94813

PROJECT COORDINATED BY JENKINS GROUP, INC.

99   98   97   ❖   5   4   3   2   1

Printed in the United States of America

To Bernadette

In memory of Garret and Ketil

ACKNOWLEDGEMENTS

The author thanks the people of Thunder Bay, Ontario for their warmth and kindness during the Nordic World Championships; the North American VASA volunteers for their selfless devotion each and every February; and my family, friends, and so many others who assisted and encouraged me in writing this book. Finally, a special word of gratitude to all those with whom I have shared the trails for the past seventeen years. You have kept the sport pure. May it continue to be so as long as snow shall fall from the heavens.

"The wind of His grace is always blowing; what you need to do is unfurl your sail."

–Swami Vivekananda

Chapter One

Prologue

IN THE DISTANCE Tim Keagan knew one more arduous climb stood in the way of consolation. Contrary to habit, he paused and looked behind himself. Exhaling heavily, he grinned, self-consciously stifling a good laugh. Had he ever just stopped to see, to hear, to touch all this beauty? He remembered a time when so many others did, or at least seemed to, drinking wine from their flasks, moving so slowly in raucous bands celebrating this new craze, taking forever to cover the same distance he did in less than an hour.

He was never like them, he supposed. Not that he condemned them whatsoever. To ski alone was one thing; to be alone was quite another. As long as they obeyed the greater code, their presence was not only tolerable, it was welcomed. That was the way it was meant to be. It was the way of cross-country. It was the law of winter.

It was a positive sign that he could smile about it now. Things had changed a lot, but people hadn't. Not really. Oh, they didn't drink as much. And they didn't seem so hell-bent to save the world and destroy themselves in the process. At least not for now. A good ground war would change all that.

He remembered the American who started it all in that bicentennial year. The twenty-year-old with that look of determination, with all that snow secreting a young, bearded face. Only twenty! It happened at the 1976 Winter Olympic Games at Innsbruck, Austria, when Bill Koch – "Cokie" – stunned the Nordic world by winning the silver in the men's thirty kilometer cross-country ski race, introducing an entire nation to the sport.

Koch had actually led the 30K at one point, yet as he crossed the finish line not one American film crew was on hand to record the historic event. But who could blame them? Koch's feat was unthinkable. As ABC scrambled to atone for its sin of omission, young Koch endeared himself to the nation with his unassuming New England wit. When asked by a reporter to comment on their absence, he replied, "They'll be there next time." Another wondered if he had lived in Vermont all of his life. His answer? "Not yet." When the media wanted to know how he felt about the whole thing, he informed them, "To finish in the top ten was my goal. Of course, I'm even happier to medal." And remember, this was all before Mark Fidrych.

Unfortunately, it ended with Koch as well. He remained the only North American ever to stand upon an Olympic podium to receive a medal in cross-country skiing. Though Koch won the overall World Cup title in 1982, and led until the final day in 1983, he never came home with another Olympic medal. As the years since continued to grow into a new century, more and more of the few who cared wondered if there would ever be another.

Yet all of Koch's accomplishments paled to the one enduring legacy he left to the sport the day he stepped out of the centuries-old dual tracks used in the classical diagonal stride technique and touched off the skating revolution. By 1985, it was clear the skating technique was undeniably the wave of the future. The diagonal stride technique was on the verge of extinction as a racing style. In the following year, the International Federation of Skiing – the FIS – moved decisively to preserve the time honored technique by segregating Nordic races according to the two styles, calling skating "freestyle" and the traditional diagonal stride "classical." Ironically, years later that decision breathed life into another American dream, that of Tim Keagan's. But Keagan knew it could not be his alone. Not this time.

Tim got high on speed. There was no bigger rush than charging up to a group of stragglers at about twenty-five kilometers an hour and seeing their amazed reactions. That hadn't changed either. Nineteen years had passed, and Tim, at age forty-three, had reclaimed the magic, if not the past.

He pushed away from his brief respite, into the present. The precipitous descent gave him the verve he relished. The feeling was medicinal, therapeutic.

He hunched over, forearms resting across his thighs, his long poles awkwardly angled out to his sides. He wasn't racing today. He was thinking. Not about the hill up ahead, but about the mountain he had to scale. His life had been full of them it seemed, and he was ready to come home. If only everyone could be there to welcome him when he did.

Chapter Two

* * *

DISAPPOINTMENT ARRIVED AGAIN, borne upon shoulders of valiant mediocrity, weary and weak, legs spent rubber. America's best. Another Olympics. Another hopeless case. Another time. Yes, another time.

"We need more Kochs!"

"There are more in the 'fridge!"

"Not Coke! Koch! K-O-C-H! We need more Bill Kochs!" Simply by her misunderstanding Nikola exponentially added unto the ordinarily benign rage spelled out in a frustrated twenty year-old Timothy Keagan.

"What's your problem!" she retaliated, sudden confusion accelerating toward open hostility. She did not care for his condescending tone. As she wandered into their apartment's poor excuse for a living room, she got the picture. She glared at the television set and let out a knowing huff.

"Oh."

She must have married the only man in America who was a cross-country ski fanatic. The Winter Games. The men's 4x10K relay. Oh, that's right, he liked baseball too. That pretty well took care of the rest of the year.

"I don't have a problem, hon. They do. I'm the solution!" he replied flippantly, with that awful arrogance and cockiness only a man – only a husband – can convey to a woman, to a wife.

It was time to put him in his place. A place he had never been before. Well, nor had she.

"Well, if you can't do it, maybe this one can," she announced, way too early, patting the little surprise gently, and not in a manner that she hoped would convey her own brand of self-assurance.

Tim rose up immediately. Instinctively.

"You're pregnant?" His attitude took a sudden about face. So soft. In awe, without sex as a predicate. She couldn't remember the last time...was there ever one?

She nodded, as he leaped into an embrace. It was a long, peaceful interlude, but she could not see his face. This is not like Tim, she thought. What is he thinking?

"So what do you want, a boy or a girl?" she asked. What else could it be?

Tim chuckled. A preference was the last thing on his mind, yet he paused in anticipation of a clever response.

He glanced back at the screen. Black and white. Everyone should be so poor for their first. There would be special strength that way. It was his father's way. It was his grandfather's way. Now it would be his way, too.

"It really doesn't matter, Nikola. The women's team needs a Koch just as bad as the men's team," he answered, amused at his own wit.

She playfully slugged him. "So, this is how you propose to solve your problem?" she demanded, referring to the relevant subject growing within, giving only the slightest convex form to her shapely body.

Tim just continued to laugh, until she joined in. He wanted the baby! And it didn't matter! He would be a good father, she was sure. Now she was sure.

Chapter Three

THE SUN WAS just setting over the east arm of Grand Traverse Bay. It should have been dead still silent, as there was no wind this clear Michigan evening. But a rhythmic sound faint in the distance rapidly approached. It was in no way curious to three-year-old Phillip Keagan sent out to play by his harried mother, nor did the -10° Celsius chill seem at all foreign to him this January night.

"I'll be around again in ten minutes," said his father, as if Phillip could actually understand time.

But Phillip knew his father would be back, of that he was sure. Therefore, there was enough light this darkening evening for more play in the snow. His baby brother Jerry had been born only a month earlier, and it seemed like he was always sleeping. Phillip's eyes widened as he watched his father quickly disappear back into the woods, and he resumed sledding when the sound merged into the silence of the north.

Ten minutes later his father's promise was fulfilled, as always.

"Okay! Time to go in Phil!" he called. "Are you cold yet?"

"No, Daddy. I am not cold. Are you cold, Daddy? Is that why you want to go inside?" replied Phillip, applying logic to his world.

"No, I'm not cold, Phillie. But, I want to go see baby Jerry, okay? Don't you want to see your baby brother? I bet he is awake by now! Let's go inside!" he said with inordinate enthusiasm, hoping to spark motivation in his three-year-old.

"Okay! He's my little brother, huh, Daddy? Mommy said I'm his big brother!"

"He sure is, Phillie. You'll always be his big brother and he'll always be your little brother."

"Yep!"

"Okay! Let's go inside now!"

"Daddy?"

"Yeah Phil, what?"

"Can you teach me to ski fast like you?"

"How would you like to ski faster than me, Phil?"

"Faster than you?"

"Yeah! I'll teach you to ski a lot faster than me, Phil. You just wait and see. Someday."

"When is someday?"

"When you get bigger, bigger than me, you will be faster than me. A lot faster!"

"I bigger than you...someday?" Phil asked, as perplexed as a three-year-old can be at the revelation that something beyond childhood loomed ahead.

"Yes, Phillip. Someday you will be." He unhitched himself from his 210cm Fischer race skis.

"Dad?"

Tim looked at his little boy. Not 'Daddy'?

"I can hardly wait for someday!"

Timothy Keagan just smiled, wishing for the moment that his biggest admirer might instead remain three forever. But, don't all parents know too well the paradox?

Eternal childhood would require eternal parenthood. An earache here, a wet bed there, and throw in a couple of temper tantrums and you're ready to see them off to college.

As they were going inside, Phillip asked, "Daddy, why do you ski so much?"

Tim hesitated. How does one explain an addiction? Like candy? No, let's not bring up candy.

"I just like it, Phillip. Do you think you might like it too?"

"If I get big like you, I ski too!"

There we are, growing up again, thought Tim.

"Well, okay, Phil!" he said, hoisting his three-year-old up on one broad shoulder of his 190 centimeter body. He checked his watch and saw that he skied thirty kilometers of laps in under ninety minutes, which was flying. To any Norwegian, however, he was just an anonymous skier, just as he was in his own country. In a sports crazed nation, this Olympic hopeful, husband, and father of two, existed as little more than an uncirculated rumor in an impassive court of considerable apathy. And now with his arrival there would be one less American viewer, for he was a man who thought himself ready for all things.

He had but one more firm definite statement to make. And his teeth ached to smile at the conclusion of his next race. It was America's second largest ski race – the 50K North American Vasa – held right there in his own hometown of Traverse City. For surely now the Games were within his grasp. At long last and none too soon. He was getting old. He was twenty-four.

Chapter Four

BEFORE DAWN, ON the morning of the Vasa, he woke up Nikola asking her if she had made arrangements to come out and watch the race. Perturbed that yet another dream of sleeping in some Saturday morning was destroyed, she scoffed at his implication that the scenario was remotely possible. It was becoming more and more common for her to do so, and now in this new situation, on the precipice of a dream of his own, Tim came to acquire a shorter and shorter fuse of his own with his wife of four years. Other options and possibilities were discussed, to put it mildly.

"I can't find a sitter on a Saturday morning at 7:00 a.m.!" she insisted.

"Well, you should have thought about that last night! Just bring them with you then!" His voice raised a notch louder.

Her husband was so dense. As if she could find a sitter on a Friday night. But she had a dig left.

"I'm not bundling up two infants and carting them off to another one of your stupid ski things in this kind of weather."

He fumed inside. Who was this woman he married? Sure, she had given him two beautiful, strong, healthy sons, but what had she done for him lately? And to top off his day, he read in his own local morning newspaper an article fawning all over some high school senior from Minnesota, who was allegedly rewriting the record books in the American heartland of Nordic racing. In it, the teenager proclaimed himself the favorite, and "regretted that Koch could not be there to give him some real competition." The columnist was kind enough to note that "our own Tim Keagan was expected to finish high."

"Well, do whatever you want to do then. I'm outta here!" Outside the bitter cold only increased his contempt for the entire situation. "Bitch," he muttered, as he entered the frozen vehicle. Other expletives emanated from him as his car struggled to turn over. All of this anger and anxiety funnelled into desire. The desire to leave everyone and everything behind him. And this morning the cure would come. He would defeat all comers and stand alone at the top and it would not go unnoticed. Not this time. Here, on his home turf, in the big race, his arrival would be heralded. His day had come.

He quickly dismissed the altercation as just another with the wife. His desire to make the Olympic team placed a heavy burden on Nikola. His training required what seemed to her to be an inordinate amount of time. The kids didn't help, and neither did Tim Keagan's still meager law practice. It hardly provided for the realization of any of her fantasies or dreams. Still they were young and most of their friends were not yet outpacing their economic lifestyle. But Nikola did not possess hope that cross-country skiing was her ticket to his promised view of the Bay. From high atop a hill. In a nice neighborhood. Where lawyers, doctors, and such are supposed to live.

Tim would not hear of such negativity. Skiing was his paradise. Her complaints and nagging seemed incessant to him, and no response from him, however articulated, seemed to bridge the impasse. It was a broken record.

"Honey, look at Bill Koch," he recalled telling her again and again. "Don't tell me it can't be done. No one thought he had a chance and he takes a silver in the 30K. The Americans are just starting to compete. I'm telling you, next time we're going to get gold. Koch's still young enough and there is no reason the rest of us can't compete with the best in this sport. Plus, look how many more people are cross-country skiing now!"

"Well, you tell me how Bill Koch is going to feed our boys."

"Oh puh-leez. Like we're really starving."

"You know what I'm talking about!"

"Yeah, I do. Unfortunately you can't see where I am going or what I am all about. You married one of the best skiers in America and all I get is your complaints. No wonder I like it on the trails so much – to get away from this crap!" he howled. "If you could see where I am going and where the sport is going, you would take all of this in stride."

"Look at today, Tim. Look at where we are. You don't respect my wishes. How do you expect me to care about yours? What happened to our dreams? Our plans?"

"I get all the respect I need out on the trails, Nikola. Out there I don't hear about your carpeting, your kitchen, your this, your that. Your universe is this damn house. Mine is the world. And you think I'm making the wrong choice?" he emitted a scornful laugh.

Nikola began to cry. It was clear she was going to lose again today. Maybe she had become a rag, but didn't Tim promise to be her husband? What was he but a selfish ogre? He gave great deference to his boys when he was home. Yeah, right, when he was home. If he wasn't skiing, at least he could be working, earning thirty-five dollars per hour in his so-called law practice.

Despite all her misgivings, there was a time she encouraged his addiction by actually skiing with him. She too was an excellent skier, but then came Phil, then Jerry, each with another five kilograms and had never found the time to take it off. Her child bearing days were over now, but she never intended to ski competitively. Not that that mattered to Tim. He was on his own ego trip and the thought of victory intoxicated his being. At home his two boys, especially Phillip, who was just now exhibiting the athletic prowess he prized, gave him the emotional high Nikola once provided, but now lacked. The novelty of intimate prospects and the empathy which existed between them as young lovers were coming to their crushing, final end, and neither of them really knew how precious a commodity they had mutually forsaken in the pursuit of alternatives peculiar to themselves.

On balance, Tim felt no loss. He was skiing with authority, and with confidence – beyond that – with expectation. He did not need

Nikola to recognize each level of accomplishment that was his. Now, he had assured himself more than a spot on the US team; he may even be that person to finally do more than achieve the incredible silver of 1976, when Koch surprised the world; to be the best of the best, and let the alarmed world know that America had arrived without question once and for all. Keagan's name, not Koch's, would be in the minds and on the lips of American aficionados of the sport. He would be the one who finally brought home gold. This was his goal, and if he was to be stopped short of it, defeat would not come from within his own home. He would leave her if that is what it would take.

As he prepared for the 50K North American Vasa ski race, with the Birkebeiner a fortnight off, and the Olympics a year away, the stage was set, once and for all, to solidify his preeminence on the North American scene. But Tim wanted more – to dominate so fully that the Soviet Union, Finland, Sweden, East Germany, and all the rest would be compelled to take notice. And so on this day victory would not be enough. He intended to bury his rivals.

In those early days of the skating revolution, it was not uncommon to see an individual engage in a combination of techniques involving classic and skating styles, and Tim was no exception. Tim was the consummate classic skier, but even he added to his technique elements of skating, such as the marathon skate, by which one ski is kept in the diagonal track while skating with the opposite ski, pushing off simultaneously with the poles. His bread and butter style, however, remained the traditional form of cross-country skiing, and until someone beat him at it, he would delay making the switch in styles so many others were resigning themselves to do.

Excepting Koch, the best in America were represented in this Vasa as it did not conflict with World Cup competition. Also on hand were several Norwegians, Swedes, and Finlanders, who anticipated the event to be a race among themselves. Next to the "Birkie," the penultimate American event, a 55K race between Cable and Hayward, Wisconsin, was this one held in Keagan's own backyard. And as the gun sounded, he quickly found himself forced to hold back just to remain grouped with the elite Scandinavians. It became apparent almost immediately after the adrenaline rush quickly subsided that he could easily ski a faster pace without compromising the endurance required for this marathon. So, at approximately the 2K mark, at the wooden bridge crossing the crystal clear waters of Acme Creek, he sought to take the pace to a higher level. For the next nine kilometers the racers would engage a series of tough climbs and quick downhills. Many a novice skiing this course for the first time is beset by awe and panic finding this first section so taxing of anaerobic conditioning.

Of little notice to Keagan, the wind above the tree tops began to torque violently counter-clockwise from a benign southwest breeze to the inevitable beginnings of a winter storm. In the woods the wind was a fraction of the gale blowing over the still open waters of Lake Michigan. The snow was beginning to fall silently, but in increasing tempo, on the path before him. It was a wonderland, and his skis waxed for fresh snow responded beautifully to every demand he made of them. He took the lead at the ascent of "The Wall" – a damnable climb – at the 10K mark. A Finlander and two Swedes followed close behind. A Norwegian was now falling back of the pack. By the time they reached "Lombard's Luge" at 12K, the Norwegian was out of sight. The closest American was an incredible two kilometers behind. He was the eighteen-year-old so-called phenom from Minnesota. Tim would leave no doubt to whom Koch's cup would one day pass. He would abort him.

At the 13K mark, the path splits at a point called "Big Rock," which separates the 25K trail from the 50K. Here the land was flatter for a couple kilometers and Keagan was anxious to see if the pack of three following him would pursue a faster pace. He snapped off a couple powerful classic strides, followed by several alternating kicks in the double-pole mode, then double-poling for five hundred meters more. He was pulling away with thirty-four kilometers remaining. It seemed too good to be true, but it only got better. He threw in a few marathon skates just to apportion muscle load and then resumed double-poling until the hills inevitably rose again, which now found him all alone. The snow and wind intensified while he skied in that open stretch, but soon the woods reappeared and a more benign terrain prevailed until the split rejoined with the 25K trail just before reaching the tortuous Jackpine Valley. From there up to the sprint at the finish, the course is dominated by a series of uphills and downhills, but at Jackpine one encounters two serious ascents and descents in rapid succession. It was specifically included in the system to reward the conditioned athlete, and to test the mettle of the mediocre. But Keagan was fully aware of the terrain, if not the weather.

The day started out cold – very cold at -17°C – but when the breeze turned into a gale half way into the race, the windchill dropped to -40°C. That, coupled with the biting snow, whipped and stung the exposed flesh of the skiers' faces. Tim had skied in colder. In snowier. In windier. But never in this combination. For most it was not a race at all, but an exercise in survival.

The fine snow stuck like klister to Tim's eyebrows and lashes, while his thick four-day beard collected ice and snow like a vacuum, sticking on him like glue.

It was snowing harder yet as Keagan reached the 30K mark, and this fact could do nothing but inure to his benefit. He ran in herringbone fashion up the second incline at Jackpine, feeling strong. After the downhill segment he resumed a diagonal stride technique. Heading to the 38K mark, his hamstrings began to tighten. He skied on, hoping to kick out of it. When that failed, he double-poled to rest his legs, but soon the hills reappeared and up he climbed. It required him to utilize his triceps to an exhaustive extent, as double-poling and uphill ascents stressed those muscles in particular. Soon lactic acid build-up was a physical reality which Keagan endured. He massaged his muscles mentally, and with every movement he sought to acquire maximum glide. Every downhill now was an answered prayer for rest. Indeed the elevation profile of the course showed graphically that he would encounter many more meters of descent than ascent from there on, even though that was of little comfort after nearly two hours racing at near maximum heart rate.

As he passed a dormant campground at 40K, signs of the end became familiar, but one could not anticipate the end even yet – twenty minutes of the most difficult part remained, because at this point one paid dearly for any strategic error regarding pacing. And Keagan was feeling it in every meter unsupported by downhill gravity. His feet, calves, gluteus, abs, pectorals, forearms, wrists, hands, and neck were near exhaustion. His hamstrings and triceps were spent. Yet he persisted despite the pain keenly piercing his primary means of propulsion, because he knew with each pole and kick, he would overcome and win. So despite the discomfort manifested in his face to every observer at the aid stations along the way, his pace remained fluid and even. His head was totally in the race, not even glancing to acknowledge their exhortations of approval.

He loudly demanded "Wa'er!" at the final aid station, not able to articulate his intense thirst, frozen lockjaw having set in. He threw the wasted cup violently into the storm, still skiing, disregarding the volunteer who handed him the drink. Thank-you's could come later – maybe – if he bothered to remember. He was anxious to be crowned victor.

Only 5K remained. A huge uphill. A long steep downhill. 4K. Another uphill. 3K. Acme Creek again. 2K. A slight upgrade. Out of the woods now, he rounded the final turn to the finish and suddenly into a blinding white-out snowstorm. The forest had concealed until now the raw intensity of the blizzard. The snow continued to accumulate everywhere on the trail and on Keagan. His heavy respiration produced a micro-climate all its own. Icicles formed below his nostrils into his mustache, and on his stubble formed a well-defined icy beard. His lycra suit was frozen stiff in front where he took on the brunt of the storm. As he headed into the final sprint he had more the appearance of an ice-clad ghost than that of a living man.

He looked up and could just make out the finish line. He looked back one final time – only white. His eyelids were almost frozen shut by wind-driven snow and ice. Can't quit now! He double-poled on the slight decline, determined to finish strong in an incredible sprint to the finish. He had conquered both man and beast. It would be a race its participants would never forget. Of the thousand who registered, only half would finish, and most of those who did suffered frostbite in one degree or another – a reminder of the toll the sport exacts upon those who would dare to "manage the elements" as the great Vegard Ulvang once observed.

When the banner became clear, only fifty meters ahead, he rose from his position to glide in, and claim his due reward, raising his hands. But, where are the cheers? For a moment he dreaded the impossible. Had someone somehow passed him? Where? Who? The assembled mass of spectators were more silent than the whipping, driving sheets of white. They looked on with an eerie reticence. He looked for a familiar face. No one. What was happening? He checked up to see if his bib was still pinned to him. There has to be a mistake! Ten meters, and across. "Tim Keagan, Traverse City, First Place." Subdued, polite, discomforting applause. No joy. No enthusiasm. "Good God," Tim thought, "is this a practical joke?" His greatest achievement, but where was his victory? People moved aside as two volunteers approached him to aid in the removal of his skis. A Grand Traverse County deputy grimly appeared from the blizzard.

"Tim – "

Keagan looked up at the burly officer, bundled up like the Michelin man. Something awful had happened. His adrenal glands were commissioned into service yet again. They ached and pounded.

"There's been a terrible accident. Your wife is in critical condition. Would you come with me?"

In a daze, he was led off, leaving a vacuous feat with his skis and poles and change of clothes.

Fifteen minutes later, just as he was entering the emergency room at the Traverse Memorial Hospital, the second American crossed the finish line, a man who would come to be known as America's best Nordic skier for the next sixteen years, eighteen-year-old Mitchell Henry Plank.

And for just about as long, Tim Keagan just quit caring.

Chapter Five

"**D**ADDY, WHERE'S MOMMY?"

"She isn't here any more, Phillip."

"When is Mommy coming home?"

"She is not coming home anymore. Never ever."

"Anymore? Never ever?"

"No, Phillip. She's all gone. She died."

"Died? What is that?"

"She's sleeping and she can't wake up."

"Why won't she wake up? Where is she?"

Tim was tired, but kept answering, "She is still here, Phillip, but we can't see her."

"I want my mommy right now! I don't see her!"

"No, Phillip. She is in heaven. Do you know about heaven? It is where you came from."

"I thought I came from Mommy's tummy like Jerry!"

"Before that, you were in heaven waiting to be born." Got to change the subject, he thought. It was two days after his wife's funeral. Despite his understandable tantrum, already three-year-old Jerry wondered less and less about Nikola's absence. It wasn't his questions so much that bothered Tim, but the realization that his two sons slept, ate, played, and grew in spite of their unthinkable tragedy, totally unconscious of the fragility of life and of their father's commission of responsibility in all that had befallen his family, past, present, and forever. A week prior, his heart, strong as a lion's, could withstand any obstacle in its way; now it beat feebly in a chest laden heavy; suffocating.

He weakly rolled a ball to Phil. "Bring it back to Dad, Phil."

"Daddy, I want to go outside and play! You can ski while I play!"

"Daddy's a little too tired, Phil, just like Jerry. Come up here and sit next to me."

Jerry was sleeping. He lifted Phil up on his lap, seated upright in the recliner. They just sat there together, Tim staring, eyes drier, at a blank television screen. Phillip did the same. It was the most comfort he had felt since the news of the accident. He closed his eyes. He tried to make his mind blank like the screen. And he was able to blot out everything except for the one pervading reality. Darkness. His greatest achievement he would gladly forfeit for a minute with his wife, so that a gram of his despair could be lifted, if only for that minute. He would spend that minute begging for eternal forgiveness, pouring out his grief to the one that mattered more to him now in death than he ever allowed her to mean to him in that last day of their life together. He had done nothing more than what hundreds, thousands, even millions of spouses do every day, every week, every generation in the last days of the travails of a marriage gone sour, but the proximity of her death to his sins was especially poignant. His conscience would not allow him to forget any, either of commission or intent. Nikola had proven her point better by dying than she ever could have in life. What the hell was he thinking when he thought he could have it all? That his wife was as expendable as his promises? That having an affair would be all right as long as it remained his secret?

He must punish himself, and suffer a self-inflicted impotence. And this ultimately is why he became a mother and father instead of a house guest and child; why he became an advisor instead of a lawyer; why he held hands instead of kicked butt. This was not his penance. He believed that this was his just punishment, and it would last for his lifetime.

Chapter Six

TIM NEVER HEARD a single war story from his father. Not one. Oh, he heard he was stationed in New Guinea. There was something about three weeks in Australia. The Philippines. Even Nagasaki after the bomb. But where was the glory? The victory? He longed to hear of conquest, and though opportunity abounded, his ears were never to hear of any. Not even one. And now at age forty-three, Tim understood. His father was but seventeen years old when he volunteered. Seventeen! By the time Tim was born, all victory ceased to have meaning. War was not about construction. It was an ugly and empty vessel. In it was contained no glory, only the screams of the dead and dying weighing heavily against the propaganda of those well back of the ranks, fueling absurdity with platitudes and...and yet, not once did his father ever suggest that any of it was unnecessary. Not even the Bomb. It was right for its time. It must be left there. When Tim turned seventeen, his father was fifty. It is funny how few things sons learn about their fathers, and how much they do know, notwithstanding.

So when the time came that Phil and Jerry first asked their father to take them skiing, they expected to show him what to do. Phil had no memory of his father in the backyard; Jerry had even less reason to think otherwise. Their father grew eerily quiet as they drove near the trailhead at Camp Hayo-Went-Ha, a YMCA camp on the shores of Torch Lake, an hour north of Traverse City. Tim nervously informed them that S.S. Kresge donated the expensive tract of land.

"Who?"

"Kmart."

"Oh."

Charity just does not have the same ring when it passes through corporate hands first.

After renting the necessary equipment, his sons were about to learn the first of their father's secrets. With his first kick and glide on the easy terrain, his sons gawked in awe of their father's effortless speed. He was the best they had yet ever seen. Still, another two years passed before they heard of his Vasa successes, and yet another before some half-drunk trail bum, upon learning of their identities, informed them that their old man was once a sure bet to make the Olympic team, and that next to Tim Keagan, he himself was the greatest skier in these parts. They didn't think so, but the inevitable question formed in their minds. What happened to their dad? Why did he quit if he was so good?

When that winter was drawing to a close, Phil persuaded Jerry to ask the inevitable question. Was it true?

Tim laughed. But the look in his eyes showed more serious reflection. Maybe.

"Were you really that good, Dad?" Phil asked.

"For that time, I guess I was pretty good, Phil." But I'll never know how good, he thought. He hated contemplating the impossible past. That war, like his father's, belonged to its time.

"What happened? Why did you quit?" Jerry wondered.

"I don't know, Jerry. I don't even know," he lied.

That night, before retiring to bed, Tim scrutinized his thirty-eight-year-old body. His face. Lines. What happened to his stomach? He was not a skier any longer. He was a lawyer. And he did not like what he observed. He repeated his sons questions to himself...what happened...why did you quit? He looked at himself once more. I don't even know you Tim, I don't even know you. It was a man of twenty-five speaking.

The next day, on crusty snow softening in the March sun, a lonely figure snapped into a pair of Kneissel klister skis, newly purchased at half price. Breathlessly, he struggled, climbing the rolling hills on his oh so familiar holy ground. At the top of the third climb, he had to stop. How did his sons become so strong without him? Sweat was raining from his body, his face reddened, temples pulsating, forearms quivering.

He leaned over his poles – abdomen, chest and head parallel to the ground. God, I'm going to get sick, he thought. He refused to submit to the urge though, catching his breath instead. He thought to look behind him and look down upon the hill he just climbed, but he stopped mid-turn. Nothing there. It was time to go forward. Yes, he would have to come back, but not without a heavy debt. The abandonment of purpose exacts the highest of levies for its reclamation. There can be no redemption in running away. It is known as starting over.

As the next several years passed, he felt limited absolution. Some days he even felt a smile appearing in his mind, and slowly, skiing again brought smiles to his face. He had slowly become a different old man, one who could at least temporarily believe in conjugal love again, so he skied, and skied, and the more he did, so did his sons, until they were like a family of alcoholics where no one could refuse a drink from the well, and no one could talk the other out of one either.

Chapter Seven

TRAVERSE CITY, MICHIGAN, located halfway between the Equator and the North Pole at the base of the Old Mission peninsula on the eastern shores of Lake Michigan, is a town for all seasons. A vacationers' paradise, having countless azure lakes, unsurpassed summer boating and sailing, and home to magnificent freshwater dunes, state and national parks, it was initially peopled by the Peshawbe Indian tribe who remain today, operating one of the ubiquitous gambling casinos dotting reservations throughout the State and the nation.

Farmers came in the 1800s, planting the many orchards which flourish thanks to the micro-climate produced by the beneficent moderating effects of the great freshwater lake lapping at its shores. In the fall spectacular vistas of the season's foliage inspire massive hoards of visitors to pass through, taking in panoramic views of the wooded and rolling hillsides the highways transgress.

The spring brings the bursting forth of trilliums from among dying leaves and melting snows of the previous fall and winter. Sharing the hillsides of the north one may easily find thousands upon thousands of wild onions, and the more celebrated hunter will chance upon the short-lived and inconspicuous morel mushroom. Despite its well earned reputation for unpredictable weather from day to day, viewed objectively in a general sense, Michigan may well be one of the most clearly defined four-season sites anywhere on earth.

When the buds of the maple, oak, beech, and birch explode in the midst of a warm May rain, the fresh greens blending with eternal verdancy of the great variety of pines interspersed among them, every woodlot becomes a dense forest.

But when the sun again becomes low in the sky, and its color becomes pale, a light grey cloud brings with it a cold front and snowflakes. From that point on, until winter arrives resolutely upon a storm, a sense of suspended animation prevails. Halloween arrives for the children, and then Thanksgiving and the Lions' football game. After that, the guns of autumn fall silent and the entire north soon becomes locked in a thickening blanket of white. Every distant sound is heard, the trees stripped bare of leaves. This was the land Timothy Keagan called home, and as his children grew into men, once again it became his winter domain.

Others found comfort in the theatre, or in the lodge, or upon a snowmobile. Some simply cocooned, preferring television, videos, and telephones over any social intercourse. But in twenty years time, Phillip and his little brother Jerry, both now as tall as their father, put more than enough snow under their skis to circle the globe and then some. Their time had arrived to graduate from the North American Vasas and the White Pine Stampedes, from the Birkies and the Finlandias and the comforting victories they shared in such races together. They were on the verge of making the national team in a big way, something their father narrowly missed nineteen years before – something their father was not about to miss this time. Whether their standing in the sport related to training regimens, good genetics, or simply the dearth of gifted, quality skiers in America couldn't be of less importance to the national sports media. And when the three of them quietly arrived in Anchorage for the final Olympic qualifier, they handled their own baggage, carrying it up to the room from their trusty Ford Club van – nine thousand kilometers more to its credit.

Chapter Eight

THOUGH CROSS-COUNTRY SKIING developed thousands of years ago as a practical means of transportation through the Scandinavian woods and over the frozen tundra and marshes of the north, the sport of cross-country skiing is of relatively recent origin. It is no older, in fact, than baseball. Organized Nordic ski competitions began as late as the mid-1800s at Holmenkollen, Norway. Although the late Soviet Union certainly earned its share of Olympic gold, as have Italy and Russia in recent years, the sport was and remains so dominated by Scandinavians and Finns that it is referred to as "Nordic skiing."

And well it should. One could hardly overestimate their devotion to cross-country skiing. Undoubtedly, it is rooted in the fact that they would not have survived as distinct peoples without skis. Norway takes credit for having within its borders the site of the oldest ski ever found. The Birkebeiner race recalls the dramatic rescue of the infant boy Haakon Haakonson by soldiers on skis in 1206, who was later crowned King of Norway. The modern nation-state of Sweden was founded in 1523 because military leader and eventual king, Gustav Vasa, escaped certain execution at the hands of King Christian II of Denmark by retreating eighty-nine kilometers on skis from Dalarna to Salen before organizing an army and driving out the Danes. Finland, at least in part, remained free of Communist despotism because troops, led on skis by Carl Gustav Mannerheim, held the Russian forces at bay for the entire winter of 1939-40 during World War II. But today their heroes do not shape wood or bone, wage war, or sit on thrones. They ski, and they have set the pace from the first Olympiad on.

A cross-country racer lives and dies resigned to conditions of snow and forces of gravity. Downhill segments on skinny skis at international Nordic venues can be every bit as dangerous as its more popular alpine counterpart. Yet, in order to ascend the steep mountain trails there are no tow ropes or chair lifts; it is of course only accomplished by the will and the power of the competitor alone.

The legends of the game include a list of names left better printed than spoken – Sixten Jernberg, the great Swedish skier of the 1950s and 60s. The incomparable Russian, Raisa Smetanina, the greatest female skier of all time, having earned twenty-three World Cup and Olympic medals. Gunde Svan, of Sweden, who best bridged the era of the traditional diagonal stride method to the skating technique, unquestionably the greatest male skier of the 1980s and perhaps ever. There are others as well: Vladimir Smirnov, the muscle bound Kazakhstani; Harri Kirvesniemi, the durable Finnish classic specialist; the ageless Maurilio DeZolt of Italy and his younger teammate Silvio Fauner, whose matchless sprint to the finish line in the 1994 men's 4x10K relay, remains etched into the tablets as one the great Olympic moments of all time, silencing a quarter million Norwegian fans on hand whose team was just edged out. Two Norwegians who raced that same day are deserving of equal or greater mention as all of the above – Bjorn Daehlie, Olympic multi-gold medalist, and Norway's, indeed the world's, beloved "terminator" Vegard Ulvang, from tiny Kirkenes above the Arctic Circle, who, with Daehlie, earned three golds and a silver at Albertville in 1992. Daehlie and Ulvang took part in every gold medal awarded that year in cross-country.

In the States the Europeans are respectfully received, with their strange names and their graceful skates and strides, every Olympiad in the course of the televised spectacle, between the figure skaters and the bobsled and the luge. Their names are quickly forgotten, if ever learned, and thoughts of spring and losing that winter's spare tire soon commands the more urgent attention of the nation's viewership. Still, from the herd of those exposed to the sport, a few dare to dream. And from that few, some act upon their desire. And among those still fewer who act, only a handful remain who may live the ultimate dream. And from this great inequality comes a chance, comes the very thing, that had made this nation, this sport, all competition, great. It is the very thing that Ulvang and Daehlie, Hamalainen and DiCenta, Fauner and DeZolt, Jernberg and Svan, and all the others learn of when they step onto the highest of podiums and become recognized as immortal, those whose spirits overcame flesh, whose faiths dominated doubts.

Chapter Nine

TIM SPECIALIZED IN the classic style of skiing, and though he was a good skate-skier, that was all he was, which was not good enough. Though certainly he could defeat any man his own age in a freestyle event, skating had become the far more preferable technique for the generation of racers following Koch's development of the technique in the early 1980s. But he could still hold his own with anyone in classic racing. For men, one competitive event employs both methods – the 4x10K. The event provides for two classic skiers and two skaters to represent each nation in a forty kilometer relay race, with each participant skiing ten kilometers in his particular style. As a result, Tim came to believe a possibility remained to make the team, and to make the same team as either or both of his sons, in this, his final attempt. Tim scolded himself many times during training: Why do I ever allow myself to even think this way! He above anyone else should know better than to speculate on such an absurdity. But still, here he was, with each double-pole and kick, doing all he could to see it come about. He felt best just being in the tracks, with all in life reduced to one destination and one desire – to get there before anyone else, which he often could.

The men's 10K Nordic event is a sort of hybrid long distance sprint, if one can think of ten thousand meters in any sport as a sprint. It is the shortest of the men's Nordic races. One must not hold back too long; in less than twenty-five minutes it will be complete. The beginning of any mass start cross-country race is as critical as any stage in the race, because once behind a train of skiers, precious seconds, even minutes can be lost trying to pass others on the narrow trail systems. On the other hand it is a dangerous race tactic to get out in the front of skiers too early in a race. Besides all of the drawbacks of establishing pace, it is the lead skier who absorbs all of the wind resistance. Even more salient, the pacesetter loses perspective on the psychology of the race itself. In essence, the pacesetter is not racing at all, he is engaging in a kind of time trial. The sport of Nordic racing does not lend itself well to looking back at what's happening behind you. You listen and learn from the sounds of the athletes and from the crowds. A leader may escape punishment by utilizing a sixth sense of instinct or by becoming especially astute to collateral indicators, or by simply just being too good and feeling too good to hold back.

Vegard Ulvang's leg, the second of the 1992 Albertville 4x10 relay remains the classic example of proper implementation of the rarely successful strategy. With a Swede and a Finn on the tails of his skis for the first six kilometers, Ulvang refused to acknowledge their presence. When the Swede slipped just for an instant, Ulvang sensed its occurrence and increased his pace ever so slightly. The Finn, upon passing the exhausted Swede reduced to a stumbling unrhythmic mess, valiantly attempted to fill the vacuum for a time. But he had seen the writing on the wall, and wisely opted to position his team for a medal. It was the last any competitor saw of Norway's red, blue, and white lycra that day. In the final leg Daehlie mercifully ended the rout, skiing backwards across the finish line. The bronze medal was awarded that day to Finland who beat Sweden by a blink of the eye. It all had begun with a seemingly innocuous moment twenty-four kilometers earlier. It cost Sweden the bronze, maybe a silver. But in Anchorage, the world did not watch, nor even care. The Finns, the Swedes, the Italians, and the Norwegians were flexing their collective muscles testing each other often in World Cup races. Already they were computerizing pairings against each other's teams in preparation for the Olympic relay. America was not included in their programming.

Tim's sons had guaranteed themselves positions on the US team.

They had risen to the national level two years before, winning more often than not and never placing out of the top six skiers in any field composed of North Americans. Although they briefly sampled World Cup racing the previous year, neither finished in the top ten in any race. But then, no other North American did either. In Anchorage though they walked about with justifiable confidence that they were the best of their countrymen. They were respected as well, as they often took time to give encouragement to those they defeated.

They purposefully avoided competing on the international level since last season's end. They knew what they were up against – why bother to try to out-sprint a cheetah or to out-endure a husky? More pressing to them now was their hope to have their father qualify along with them for the team. They knew their father's ability better than anyone, and indeed of anyone they would like least to face in competition was their father.

It was their father who consistently rose before sunrise to ski twenty kilometers before work. At lunch, if his schedule allowed, ten or fifteen more. In the evenings, at least another fifteen. On weekends he would routinely ski fifty or more kilometers. Yet he never referred to it as training, for it was pleasurable to him that he skied, or so he insisted. If on Saturday he raced a 50K freestyle, two hours later he was back on some trail, gliding and double-poling into the woods for an additional fifty kilometers of classic, just for the fun of it.

There was, of course, that time he abandoned his passion. But after a sabbatical, like a train gaining momentum out of the station, he steadily returned to competitive form. And as his sons grew and strengthened into two of the Midwest's and then North America's finest skiers, he did not lack for training partners who could push him to his limits. If the weather was nice, he took it for all it was worth; if the weather was bad, he had surely experienced the worst years before. No condition was too poor if there was enough snow to cover a trail. Such is the way of cross-country. All is not predictable by nature in the temperate regions; if one yearns to ski, he must be about his business, like fruit being about growing in its season.

His sons heard as pre-teens, and now saw for themselves, his fierce competitive nature. He was always content to train and race at his own pace, and if someone passed him, however rare its occurrence, he bided his time. The inevitable uphill would arrive when he would power by his opponent and at the peak of a climb, get into the tightest tuck imaginable, and literally pick up seconds on the downhill, step-turning, then quickly and rhythmically double-pole into the next climb, his abdominals and triceps propelling himself like a human sled, kilometer after kilometer, feet and skis parallel to one another. When a skater once complained that his double-poling was not classic skiing at all, and that a real skier should utilize the diagonal stride throughout a race – i.e., the kick, pole, and kick technique – he retaliated that skaters should apply grip wax to their pockets or stay out of his tracks on downhills.

Tim fully realized this was to be his last attempt to realize a long suppressed desire. It took no genius to figure out that by the next Olympics, at age forty-seven, he would only watch from the sidelines, if at all. As much as he desired to make the team, in this, his final effort, he was rather complacent about the politics and the collateral malarkey that concerned the internal decision making process of those who went along to Thunder Bay. He should not have been.

Tim Keagan remained faithful in all that he regarded as holy and sacred to the sport. It was a religion; what, with its waxing rituals, the vigils and solicitude given to snow conditions – and what woods and high places as temples to worship in! It had its holy days, its high priests, its pilgrimages. One felt the thirst, the hunger, the fatigue of the aspirant and of the sadhu. With walking sticks and staffs, with foot paths to each holy mountain top, inspiring vistas and peerless silence, one communes with his own innermost spirit. Beyond this, evidence of a common creed exists among one's fellows on the trails. For year after year, decade after decade, century after century, there has developed a code of ethics, of morality, of virtue, and goodness. There is no racism on the trail. There is no theft. There is no deception, no lust, no envy, no gluttony, no sloth. If someone is in need of assistance, all commit to that aid. If a glove, scarf, mitten, sweater, or jacket is lost or left behind, it shall remain on a signpost for months at a time, waiting for its owner to return. Every hill can and will be climbed and descended.

Everyone on the trail shall make it back to safety, whatever the weather. Worry not. You will not be abandoned to the elements. You will know warmth. You will not only survive, you will prosper.

To Tim Keagan, however, it seemed those involved in racing were beginning to go a little insane. High altitude training was one thing, but every year there were reports of further inanities and encroachments upon the purity of his sport. Newer, more advanced and tremendously expensive glide wax and grip waxes, ski base compositions, fluor waxes and compounds, stone-grinding, special wax and structuring brushes, rillers and a multitude of other accessories for ski base preparation became the norm. Wider and wider trails, which now looked in some places like super highways, were being constructed, mitigating the role the forest plays on the psyche of the cross-country mind. All of these things complicated his penchant for the simplicity and the affordability of the sport. Things had come a long way from three pin bindings and bamboo poles. Or had they? Occasionally he wondered if he were to start all over again as a youth today would or could he commit to it? Could he afford to race?

These changes were minor compared to physiological advancements in the so called field of "sports science." Tim Keagan loathed the thought of this development. He had an abiding belief that champions could not be formed from molecules, nor could they be described utilizing objective science terminology. He was in agreement that the body could be thought of as a machine, if those people so desired. But if bodies could win races, why not just hook them up to their sensors and their gadgets and give them all medals based on DNA and heart rate reserve? And if you want to throw a little more science into it, configure in snow structure, ski base preparation, grip and glide index, and reward the technician as well. Were the Finns really asking their skiers to sleep in specially sealed dorm rooms, breathing specially formulated air, all in an effort to win cross-country races? In many ways the American team by contrast remained so pure, so innocent. But they too were on the verge of exalting data over experience. A few experts were beginning to try to explain Tim Keagan, now at age forty-three. How do you measure heart and soul?

How do you figure in commitment? Would it be meaningful to explore his guilt, his painful pilgrimage to a sought-after redemptive state? Does praying on one's knees nightly to an invisible God really help to overcome physical limitations, to stem the tide of the aging process? Or would he have turned out to be a better man if he just listened to them telling him to grow up and get a life?

The venial sins of the European powers notwithstanding, Tim remained somewhat content that America had not broken through and attained supremacy or parity with them. Because he knew what that would mean. To Tim, the creeping commercial exploitation of his sport had not yet advanced to the degree found in Europe, and it was certainly far more subdued than that observed in American alpine skiing. The American media, in conjunction with their corporate sponsors, seemed determined to rush the nation into oblivious stupefaction. Inevitably, the time would come where they would produce and televise parodies of the sport itself. Eventually some diversion developed by some hung-over college dropout would someday be added to his sport as an Olympic event! How else could one explain the inclusion of aerials and moguls into alpine competition? Skiing should be about racing and distance; points regarding "style" do not belong in the true heritage of the sport.

The holiness of his sport was not found in the expanse of downhill clearings. He did not regard downhill skiers or snowboarders as his "alpine brothers." They, to him, suffered all the sins of excess. Their boots were far too sadistic; their poles stunted; chairlifts, a needless and ridiculous submission to the cold. His answer to the latter complaint did not include the notion of heated gondolas. Their lodges could not match his forests. Their trees did not serve as wind breakers like his, but as obstacles. Their sport's glamour came from without – it must – because only time and discipline could draw out beauty from within. In short, they became co-opted. They sold out. Nature was embraced only when convenient. More often than not, it was abandoned or destroyed or "tamed."

The longest event in Olympic alpine skiing takes about two minutes to complete and its winner is idolized, especially in America. The two hour Nordic marathon, even though it is the last event of the Winter Games, is disposed of summarily and understandably. Americans are just too busy. Besides, close up shots of the world's best conditioned athletes agonizing in pain just do not play well to a sedate television audience. The exhausted finishers are truly unpleasant to observe: an awesome, permeating, collapsing pain. Tim both knew of it as a competitor and as a spectator, and there was little difference between the two. The empathy one feels for them is total, as if the viewer had stumbled upon survivors of a dreadful disaster. The Winter Olympics are supposed to be nice games, when we can all be happy as a world, admirers of grace and art and ballet. The 50K is not the short program of ice dancing, where forced smiles deceive and befriend.

As he secured his boots to his racing bindings, and his hands nervously adjusted the straps to his poles – poles reaching to his armpits – he could not help but rethink for the umpteenth time the circuitous route that brought him here: his poignant life and the paradox that accompanied the very thing that gave him both desire and despair. As the "crowd" was warned to remain absolutely still in that last minute before the start, he winked at his sons lined to his left. Once the gun sounded, all extraneous thoughts must disappear. There would be no time left to adjust strategy. There was no yesterday, no tomorrows. Either a vision was actualized or it was destroyed – there was no middle ground. Any compromise ensured defeat. At bottom, this is what he learned best in forty-three years.

Chapter Ten

ANCHORAGE WAS JUST edged out by Thunder Bay, Ontario – the Land of the Sleeping Giant – for the Games. Both locations provided the best Nordic facilities North America had to offer. Anchorage's Kincaid Park was the best maintained, most challenging, and final of the six race sites among the US qualifiers.

Temperatures are surprisingly bearable in Anchorage throughout the winter, and contrary to supposition that the earth there is covered by tundra, the trail system is wooded throughout. Cook Inlet is within arm's reach and Denali seems a dream on the distant horizon.

An infinite variety of trail systems confronts and confounds the visitor, some flat enough to accommodate the novice, others taxing enough to exhaust the Olympian. Homage is paid to the area's Nordic missionaries via nomenclature granted memorable, if not damnable places like Mize's Loop and Folly, and Elliot's Climb. Trails turn, twist, and tumble in a serpentine maze, rising then falling, south, north, east, and west, doubling back on one another in rapid succession. Eventually one finishes, chewed up and spit out.

The US Nordic Ski Team invited twelve skiers for the final Olympic qualifier. Earning a position on the four man team involved separately formulating the results of three races in each technique. By this final event – the third in the classic style – Phil and Jerry had already assured themselves to be the first two American representatives on the team due to their one-two finishes in each of the three skating races. After two of the three classic events they were third and fifth respectively. They did not have to race in it – essentially it meant nothing to them, but they agreed on the way to Alaska to race in it no matter what and wanted to show their "old man" how to really ski the "old style."

In pre-race braggadocio, together they informed the other nine competitors, including the "old man" once again, they were going to "whip up on them" and move up to one-two in the classic category as well. The others, whose fates as participants in the upcoming Games depended on the Keagan clan performance, laughed somewhat nervously. In fourth place in the classic category was thirty-five-year-old Mitchell Henry Plank – "Hawk" as he was known for four Olympiads so far; his best finish was thirty-first in the 30K freestyle ten years earlier. He had developed over the years a seemingly effortless technique in both racing styles, never appearing to struggle or strain. Graceful though he was, he consistently lacked the will to step up the tempo at the international level, or in the big race.

In first was twenty-seven-year-old Cane Paulson, Jr. of Mercer Island, Washington. Cane was everything the Keagans were not. He arrived in Alaska via his father's allowance, flying first class. He was diffident to his American colleagues, preferring to associate whenever possible with the meager array of media representatives, and in other venues with international legends of the sport who might tolerate his presence for a season, or for a beer together. His great desire for the sport was to please his father. Perhaps one day he would be satisfied when Cane atoned for his spoiled rotten upbringing by winning something big, somewhere big. Unlike the Keagan boys, he only knew *of* his father, he did not *know* his father. He knew what might please him, but success eluded him. He remained dependent on his father; he knew of no other life. It seemed perfectly natural to him. His father carefully kept abreast of his son's annual progress in the sport, and even though there was none, what else was he remotely competent of handling? Notwithstanding, Cane was a very good skier – an excellent skier – and a fine athlete as well. In spite of noteworthy examples to the contrary, he did not lack competitive spirit. Cane had a strong and athletic classic technique and was equally adept in the skating tech-

nique. He finished third overall to the Keagan brothers in the sum of
the skating qualifiers, and if not for the Keagans he surely would have
remained the fair haired boy of the American team. As it was, nothing was guaranteed. The biggest rap on Paulson, aside from his silk
stockings upbringing, was his incredible ability to snatch defeat from
the jaws of victory. When a race tightened, as it inevitably does in
cross-country, Cane skied in a desperate hyperactive state, often leading to a fibrillating breakdown of rhythm and glide. Soon not only
would he relinquish the lead, but dreams of medalling would totally
fade, as skier after skier would pass him as if standing still. In the big
race he always skied scared. Tim Keagan knew Paulson in this regard
all too well. Whether its origin began with fear of failure, or fear of
success, it was a self inflicted form of punishment which went straight
to the heart of his father, who suffered unspeakable disappointment in
his son whenever it occurred. As much as Cane Paulson might be dis-
liked, no human with compassion could take comfort observing him
self-destruct so regularly and at such inopportune times.

This was the day for Cane's traditional choke. He was primed for
Olympic sacrifice with the veteran Plank eager to feed on his carcass.
Yet, Keagan saw something in Paulson that Plank could never acquire.
Even though Cane was psychologically ill he did not lack ability. Just
as Keagan could beat the complacent Plank on will alone, so too could
Paulson, if he were rid of his self-induced paralysis, somehow.

It takes four to race the relay. In his subconscious mind Keagan
had picked this team months before. In Paulson, he would lay down
all of his chips, but not because he had any justifiable confidence in
him. Rather, he knew that Hawk Plank in no way could or would
meaningfully compete. Oh, Plank would finish and he would be
respectable. Plank would never be shamed or embarrassed in a
newsprint pose, huffing and puffing, derisively scorned by lesser tal-
ented teammates passing him just meters before the finish. With
Plank as a teammate the Americans would finish eighth, tenth, or
twelfth, as usual. To Hawk this would be cause for celebration. But
sure as Keagan knew he had but one more spin of the wheel left to
play, Paulson, the victim of his father's indulgence, the one bearing

extreme capacity for folding in the clutch, could redeem all his losses and then some in just one day. For all of these reasons, just before the minute of silence began Tim Keagan wished Paulson good luck. Paulson looked quizzically back at him smirking, and cynically laughed as he replied, "Yeah, right." Keagan just shook his head. In silence, he wondered what could ever get through to that guy. There was no forthcoming reply. He prevented himself from a retort, but his adrenalin skyrocketed. The announcer called for silence.

"Sixty seconds...thirty...ten...." BANG!

All twelve shot off the starting line. The first fifteen meters or so they skied the diagonal stride and as soon as momentum was established, the abs, shoulders, and arms powered them like pistons in the formidable double-poling technique. At this stage of the race while the energy level is still high, extra momentum is acquired by raising and lowering the heels with each upstroke and down from the ridged bindings. With each downstroke their breaths vaporized together in the frigid Alaskan air, filling their chambers with oxygen on the upstroke. Within two hundred meters they encountered their first of many uphills and already the group of twelve was split in half. As they began to ascend the hill they began to add an alternating kick to their rhythm and as the climb steepened, back into a striding method. Soon the glide became nonexistent and they were literally running uphill, with the grip wax acting as a glue beneath their feet, covered by shoes over two hundred centimeters long. Some already found their grip insufficient and opted out of the tracks on the steep uphill and began a herringbone run on the packed outside portion of the trail. It was going to be a horse race. In ninety-eight hundred meters Tim would know if he belonged.

As the three Keagans, Plank, and Paulson descended their first hill, each racer learned valuable information about one another. All things being equal, a downhill segment will accurately determine whose skis glide best. Since gravitational forces are constant, if a skier gains on another in front of him it is obvious he enjoys a better glide. It may be due in part to aerodynamics of course, but a skier knows the difference between that factor and the real advantage provided by proper waxing and ski selection. The proper stiffness or "camber" of racing skis is all important as well, and different conditions demand proper selection. Before a race a skier may likely test three, four, or even more pairs, before settling on the pair to race on. If conditions change during the race itself, Nordic rules prevent a change of mind or a change of skis. The flip side of great glide may be poor grip. On the ski's base, in the camber of the ski, is the wax pocket, where grip wax is applied. Too much camber and the grip wax will not adhere to the track, inhibiting kick and hill climbing. Too little camber and the glide will be impaired. Finally, outside of the wax pocket, a racer must saturate the tip and tail of the base with glide wax, which is melted, cooled, rilled, scraped, buffed, and otherwise excessively pampered. Proper waxing is an essential element of racing performance and is about as exciting a topic as improper waxing. Though ski companies and wax manufacturers derive tremendous sales boosts via victory stand poses, with product names plastered all over a champion's clothing, in the end nothing comes close to matching the importance of the actual performance of the racers themselves.

Topping the next hill in order were Jerry Keagan, Hawk Plank, Phil Keagan, Tim Keagan, and finally the overall leader Cane Paulson, Jr. One more skier had been eliminated on the ascent. Tim was within easy striking distance of Plank, who was the only threat to move onto the team in his place. Screaming downhill like freight cars in a train, Tim arched his neck up and back several times to observe those in front of him. Plank was right on top of Jerry's skis and had to get out of his crouch and pick up wind to avoid contact. Next he saw Plank shuffling his feet up and down in the tracks in an effort to slow even further. He clearly had superior glide. Despite all of Hawk's efforts to slow himself, Tim Keagan got no closer to him. Paulson was right there behind him and as the descent flattened out at the 3K mark he began to pass Keagan on the next slight incline.

"Look out old man!" he yelled as he passed Keagan, slipping quickly and legally in a brief skate to the right-set lane of tracks, instantly resuming a diagonal stride technique.

Keagan ignored the insult for now, and found himself in fifth.

With seven kilometers left, it would not be wise to engage in a duel yet. Soon all five were in unison again, employing alternative double-pole and kick rhythms, followed by the diagonal stride again as the hill steepened. Keagan was breathing fully and his heart rate was extended to its maximum, but the feeling was common to all and he attached no thought to it. After passing Phillip, Paulson skated quickly back into the common lane, in behind Plank. They ascended a second hill. On the way down Plank's glide advantage wasn't quite so obvious as the decline was gentler, but it was still there. Soon all five were double-poling and Keagan moved to the right, passing his son Phillip. As he pulled even in the tracks opposite Paulson to pass him as well, Paulson suddenly darted ahead of Tim, blocking him in the passing lane! Keagan raised his arms, and slowed to avoid contact, but Paulson's move was clearly unwarranted. Keagan slid back into the common lane, now behind Plank. Inexplicably, Paulson immediately slowed down and slid back behind Keagan in the lane he had just come from. The move made no sense whatsoever. Keagan, not wanting to lose momentum or have his effort wasted, again darted right to double-pole past Plank, but by now the trail steepened again, and he could not do so without expending more effort than he desired. His son Phillip had dropped far enough back that he was able to get behind Paulson for the ascent. He had accomplished little at a point he felt he should have had taken the lead, but still the majority of the race lie ahead. They took on a steep but brief ascent followed by a bodacious descent, having an acute turn cutting sharply back to the left before dropping suddenly, like off a cliff. This was immediately followed by an acute right turn with an equally fearsome fall. No one could do anything here but employ all of their downhill skills and hope to come out of it in an upright condition. There would be no passing here. They all survived it to find at last two hundred fifty meters of flat ground leading back into the arena where they began. Keagan went back into a smooth rapid double-pole. Plank utilized the stride, and Paulson the double-pole and kick. Jerry relinquished the lead to the pack of three.

Now the group of five was reduced to a trio. In order to make the team, Plank had to win and Keagan would have to finish third. Anything else and Plank was history. With his own sons already on the team, Tim was well aware that only a Plank-Paulson one-two finish could upset the family plan. Paulson's way was paved to the games with anything better than a fifth place finish – a choker's dream. Even if the Keagan family finished one-two-three, Paulson would not be denied a place on the team. As they left the arena, Plank now reluctantly led the pack. Keagan remained in third behind Paulson. Now Plank slowed the pace, strategically confused. Plank wished it was over, because this is exactly how he wanted the race to finish, but one five kilometer lap remained.

Keagan, if he had to, would simply follow Hawk all the way into the arena. He had yet to see Plank even once apply a burst of energy at the conclusion of a race. It was hard to judge Paulson, but it was clear he was skiing strong today. But why? Maybe because there was so little pressure on him now. They covered the first lap in thirteen minutes. It was a demanding pace, faster than any of the prior qualifiers.

The next half kilometer was easy, too easy. Keagan darted into the right set of tracks to see if Plank would pick up the pace. He could not afford a third place finish. Suddenly Paulson cut him off again! Keagan swung back quickly behind Plank, and Plank slowed purposefully. Paulson skated back in front of them all. Still in third, and at a pace not suiting him, Keagan moved out once more. Paulson moved with him yet a third time to cut him off. Now Keagan knew something was very queer.

"What's the matter Keagan? No sons to help you out?" Paulson mocked, in heavy breaths and emphasis.

Keagan, skiing now alongside Plank, in a quick glance engaged eye contact. He returned a glare that told all. It was now obvious that for whatever reason Paulson and Plank were working together against him. For a moment he could not understand why they would not let him take the lead and let him bear the brunt of being their windbreaker, but they knew that he needed to expend great energy each time he moved back and forth between the dual sets of tracks. His efforts to pass were to no avail, and it had upset his rhythm many times already in the race. Plank on the other hand was doing exactly what he did best – conserving energy. Not once did he unnecessarily move from his position. Plus he had that good glide today.

They are worried that if I get in front, knowing their strategy, I'll pick up the tempo to eliminate Plank. But why is Paulson helping Plank, he thought. At least now he knew exactly what was happening. Yet Paulson was right – he had no sons to help him out. Below him, five hundred meters back, his sons were oblivious to the drama above, content to let their father destroy Plank on his own, like they knew he would. Their father was skiing strong, and his finish was his forte.

Paulson's actions were illegal, but did not appear as such. One must allow a faster skier an opportunity to pass. But each time Keagan moved up, Paulson's response was to temporarily pick up his pace just for the duration and purpose of keeping Keagan in check and blocking both lanes. Only Tim was privy to their conspiracy against him. They were trying to throw the race.

Keagan remained in third, and saw no way he could move up now. Plank chugged along ahead of him, after allowing Paulson to conveniently take the lead.

Keagan yelled ahead at Plank. "What's the deal Plank? Afraid to race?" It was the first time in twenty-five years, since he began racing, he had ever verbalized anger at another in the course of a race.

"Pass me if you can Keagan, or can't you do it on your own?" Plank retorted.

"That's a laugh Plank! So when did you two come out of the closet?"

Plank rose his stick high and whacked Keagan's pole behind him, trying to break it. Keagan avoided the effort just in time. "I'll be waiting for you at the finish line, Plank!" Keagan said as he purposefully dropped back even further. Only three kilometers remained, which included the monster descent before one last opportunity to sprint to the finish.

Keagan's conversation with Plank ceased by his own accord. This was neither a debate nor an aerobic workout. He needed oxygen – bad. As they ascended the final climb all three employed a herringbone run to the top. Their grip wax no longer adhered sufficiently to make the climb in the tracks. They edged their skis into the incline, jabbing their poles at their heels as they lifted for another step. Still, Keagan could not begin to pass. Worst of all, it became apparent Paulson would not hyperventilate today. He had found a friend and a co-conspirator and he did not have to win.

Jerry and Phil remained thirty seconds behind their father.

The three leaders were exhausted as they topped the final summit. Normally a downhill is an opportunity to recoup, but not this one. Plank followed Paulson, right on his tail, both snowplowing heavily on the descent and back to the left again, now skiing seventy kilometers per hour! Paulson's effort to switch back on the sudden right turn following it was choppy. As he leaned hard into the left bank, his outside ski edged out, well up onto the bank. His weight shifted solely over his right ski, which he attempted to edge back inside. It happened so fast, too fast to compensate! Instantly he was sliding on his back, his skis pointing into the path of Plank! Plank tried to step-turn around him, but it was impossible. A tremendous crash ensued. As he too slid down the hill now just ahead of Paulson, a locomotive was bearing down their path. Tim Keagan, Olympian! Their falls had cleared the wide turns for Keagan as they laid out together in the straightaway. As Keagan approached the two of them struggling to their feet, Paulson, then Plank, made vain attempts to detour Keagan into a fall, but he was able to skillfully step over their skis with his left ski, balancing on his right. The race was his. The Olympics were a *fait accompli!* He could barely help but let out the biggest war whoop of his life as he sped down the hill alone, unobstructed, unimpeded at sixty-five kilometers per hour, with no strategy left to employ. But instead all the satisfaction of the world was left inside for now. In the end no double-poling was necessary. Employing the diagonal stride classic technique, he raised his hands high waving his right pole above his head. As he finished he turned to await his confrontation with Plank and Paulson. Instead he saw his two sons coming in behind him. He hugged both sons as they came across, but the reunion was short lived. Paulson sheepishly approached the finish line and the Hawk, a broken man, skied in behind him, gliding in fifth.

"Sorry to spoil your coming out party lads," Keagan snapped, letting out his anger in a quick breaths.

"Prick," Paulson muttered under his breath. He stooped over to check his soon to be badly bruised leg. He didn't get that far. With a lightning-quick flip of a wrist, Keagan lifted the exhausted Paulson upright by the torso with his pole, its sharp carbon steel tip immediately at Paulson's underchin as he lectured.

"Look Paulson, or should I call you Junior? I'm going to forget what happened out there, mostly because I don't have much choice now. But you don't have a clue as to what the word 'team' means. But you're stuck with us, and if you don't like it, get over it before you choke big, in front the whole world next time!" He jabbed his pole under his chin just ever so slightly for emphasis. Then he turned to the wheezing Hawk. It was easy for the rapidly recovering Keagan to monopolize the airways.

"Nice glide today, Plank. A little too fast for the last hill, huh? You know Plank, what you just did out there?" Keagan waved a pole back toward the trail. "I just want you to know how proud I am that someone like you almost got to represent America again. Isn't that what we are all about? What you did out there? Winning's everything, isn't it, and if you don't get caught, hey, why bother with the rules? You're a loser Plank and you've always been a loser and you've proven it again today."

Plank hadn't been through four Olympics for nothing. He spat out a rebuttal. "You should talk about rules. Let's see how good you and daddy's boys do."

"Speaking of sons, Plank, where are yours? Are they still in your undescended testicles, or did they just get flushed down the toilet with all your other great achievements?"

"This ain't over, Keagan," Plank retorted.

"You're wrong, Plank. And you know I'm going to miss passing your sweet butt in those pretty tights."

Keagan's sons stood by absolutely stunned, as if they had been transported to the Twilight Zone – or worse – to the Outer Limits. They had never, ever heard or saw their father come close to such talk or behavior, especially while skiing.

They skied to a quiet corner of the arena and Phil asked their father if something happened on the trail they weren't aware of.

"Yes, Phil. I'll tell you all about it. But there is something I've waited to do with you guys for about twenty years I want to do first."

"What's that, Dad?" asked Jerry.

"It's time to buy you both a Guinness back at the hotel. I'll tell you all about it then."

"Dad, I'm only twenty." reminded Jerry.

"In Alaska, I'm told that's old enough to be a man, and I figure they are right," he responded.

As they left the corral, Jerry and Phil looked back to see Plank huddling with Cane and his father, Cane, Sr. Suddenly, Cane suffered a cuff upside the head from his father! Late in joining them was a man who winced at the severity of the blow, Coach Leonard Franz, whose next task was to figure out what happened out there, once he got out of the cold.

Chapter Eleven

MERCER ISLAND DOESN'T get much snow. That didn't concern Cane. His father had the means to plant him in the Snowy Mountains of Australia for a month of Sundays if he so desired. That Cane took up Nordic skiing at all could only be attributed to fate or to misfortune.

The Great Northwest does not lack for precipitation, and in the mountains comes a tremendous abundance of winter snow. Cane enjoyed great natural balance, and this fact was recognized even in infancy by his father who, like so many others, began to assume his son's athletic skills existed to enhance his own ego. Cane possessed a temperament remarkably dissimilar to the other children on the island. Although he was neither pampered nor spoiled any more than his classmates born of auspicious circumstances – wealth and privilege being common denominators to most – from the beginning instructors noted of him an aptitude which fueled superlative performance. But there was, even then, a flip side. He was the boy who could construct a castle of building blocks, but come the first obstacle, an overwhelming frustration would consume him. Soon the whole work came down with flailing arms in a tantrum of rage. He would not ask for help. Perhaps he never learned to ask; his father provided before need arose. Maybe it was his nature.

Mercer Island is a paradise for families who can afford to be neighbors with executives of Boeing and Microsoft. About twenty-five kilometers in circumference, fifteen kilometers long, and five kilometers wide, it packs a population of thirty thousand, yet retains much of the natural beauty of the dense forest that once covered it entirely. Interstate 90, which makes a bee-line through the north end, not only provides access to Seattle, but atop the freeway one can find tennis courts, playgrounds, and carefully manicured gardens and lawns. It is a haven for bicyclists who can escape the busy streets found elsewhere in the urban surroundings. There, one may enjoy a perfect hour long aerobic workout riding the circuit of Mercer Way. The loop consists of scenic vistas and hills, which add the amenities necessary for pleasurable and serious training. East Mercer Way consists of several hairpin curves which provide evidence of the aboriginal beauty of the local environment, and homes constructed alongside are built among the giant evergreens, ferns, and thick green foliage. At the south end of the Island one can easily observe the majesty of Mount Rainier on clear days. It rises like the glacier covered volcanic king that it is, and cannot help but induce awe and sometimes inattention to the road. On the west side appears the ever-higher skyline of the Emerald City, a city of exuberance and life, day and night. Pike's Place Market, the Space Needle, and Puget Sound are all familiar names to the world, and indeed it can be argued that it is Seattle which shall have far greater meaning in the twenty-first century than New York City, or other metropolitan areas in the United States.

In its ports, trade with the nations of Asia abounds. The resources of Alaska are deposited there and shipped elsewhere. Canada's burgeoning west finds a special alliance with its neighbor across the border. And all who come to visit wish to return and many others find an easy way to stay.

Tourists the world over flock not only to Seattle, but to Mount Rainier and close by Mount Saint Helens. The latter site instills in all who experience it not only awesome respect, but visceral terror. Yet hope peeks through the graveyard of ashes, and life has returned from the gray earth. Then there is the Olympic Rain Forest. Further south, Oregon's Cannon Beach; north, Vancouver, British Columbia; west, Victoria and Vancouver Island. There seemed to be no end to the wonderland encompassing the world Cane Paulson, Jr. abided in. He introduced many of his European adversaries to this country, and they were only too happy to travel, explore, and guest at his expense. Still, they would not accommodate Cane when it came time for him to move up a notch on the world circuit. When it came to racing, winning was their meal ticket. And Cane was never hungry enough.

Cane downhill skied for about as long as he could remember. But it wasn't until he was in the eighth grade when his entire class had their annual winter excursion to Paradise at Mount Rainier National Park, when he for the first time observed real cross-country skiing. The sky was a deep azure, and the ground as pure as white could be. The evergreens were gently draped with heavy snow, as if caked with a thick white powder. The only sound was that of their own excited voices, and with the mountain itself towering so high above them, it was as close to a cathedral as Cane would ever see in his youth. The temperature of -2°C in the sun-kissed, fresh-scented, quiescent air rivalled any summer day on the Island. He observed several groups of young adults playing in the snow. Some were actually skiing over the top of the Inn, which, with over fifteen meters of snow each winter, remained closed through April. Several skiers, enjoying a break, were copiously sharing a flask of wine. Cane split from the control of his chaperones; a junior high student would be remiss in failing to avail himself of such an opportunity, and he approached the jovial bunch. They were students from University of Washington, he quickly learned, and he impressed them as the precocious street-wise rich boy he, in fact, was.

One of the happier of the lot didn't think it wrong to allow Cane to share in the festivities. What a coup! thought Cane. He would be so cool! But first, a condition had to be met. He had to ski to Alta Vista and back before he got some. They all laughed heartily, because it had taken their contingent a whole morning of skiing and drinking and stopping and talking and groping and making out to get back to their van. A coed offered him her equipment and without hesitation he accepted. After a brief lesson in three-pin bindings, off he started up the trail, set in the Nordic track for classic style skiing.

This was Cane's first exposure to the aerobic sport, and indeed his first race as well, for he knew his whereabouts would soon become of concern to someone, sometime from the class outing. The climb from the Henry Jackson visitor center to Alta Vista is allegedly less than three kilometers, but it is all tough uphill, rising a couple hundred meters along the way. After one hundred meters of walking, one is often found breathing uncomfortably, as the beginning point is already at a fifteen hundred meter elevation. The students fully expected Cane to give up the attempt within five minutes, maximum, and return with the skis. They watched him for a few moments and then it was back to the wine and beer and the inane talk college students find so gratifying. After a few minutes the promisor excused himself to the back of the van to relieve himself. He casually glanced up at the trail in the course of his duty. Where did that kid go? he thought. Must have returned around to the front. He finished the call and rejoined his giddy friends. Such a beautiful day. No one minded cutting classes. What classes?

"Has anyone seen the kid?" he interjected. "I can't see him."

Slowly his comment weighed in on the group one by one and a few others gave a casual glance toward the trail. There were some skiers out there, definitely not the kid. Finally, almost simultaneously, the party was temporarily doused with concern. Where was he?

Their eyes were forced to follow the trail higher and higher although they knew a thirteen-year-old kid couldn't possibly be up there yet. Finally a pair of eyes spied a lone distant figure nearing Alta Vista.

"Man! Could that be him?" she asked incredulously.

The happy one had grown very somber and very near sober. "God, I sure hope so," he said. "But it can't be him, could it? It took us almost an hour and a half to get there!"

By then a pair of binoculars were produced from the van. "I'll be...that is him!"

"No, dude, that's impossible!"

At age thirteen, his first time on skinny skis, Cane had become a legend in the minds of eight preppies. He climbed – no, he sprinted uphill – no, not uphill – up a mountainside for three kilometers in less than twenty minutes!

Cane did not admire the vista at Alta; he had completed the hard part of the deal. The downhill was cake, just like the alpine slopes.

"Look at him coming down!" the coeds cooed, reflecting respect. He entered a new stage – young manhood. He had easily out-skied their boys. Cane made it back in twenty-five minutes and the small assemblage was aghast, marveling at the phenom in their midst. They had forgotten the deal, but Cane hadn't. On his approach, Cane sensed their amazement.

The coeds ingratiated themselves to him. And he basked in it. These young adults, as he saw them, were making such a fuss over his little side bet. But he didn't ski up there and back just to impress them, he wanted to find out how it felt to laugh and be happy – like them; to socialize, party, and feel good. So he enjoyed the brief adulation while he drank as much wine as he could coax from their flask, as fast as he could.

Before its effects hit him, his other search party had spotted him.

"You have quite a skier here!" extoled the supposedly more learned bunch to an unamused school official. The crisp air concealed evidence of Cane's wine consumption for now, and by the time his entourage arrived, the flask was safely, if not prudently, being passed around among the other "adults" again. "He's a natural," another said, hoping to divert Cane's chaperone from learning of their misdemeanor. "Yeah, he's really something."

Cane felt proud of himself. He had actually earned and acquired something on his own. And his head felt wonderful, and it was feeling better by the moment.

As he meandered back to the school bus the collegians kept encouraging him, "See you in the Olympics someday! Great skiing! The new Gunde!"

It was the origin of something bigger than school or home. But what was a "goon-dah?" Whatever, he wanted more of that which impressed his admirers. He didn't even know what he had just done was called Nordic skiing. He figured it was just skiing without chair lifts, and thought their praise of him concerned his downhill technique. But those tracks were weird. And the bindings and shoes must have been from the old days. And he made it a point to make sure his dad got him some and find someplace to ski with those funny trails, because he really did better on them!

On the bus returning to Mercer Island it was not difficult for the adults to discern Cane had engaged in some pre-teen apres-ski, and the least restrictive disciplinary measures were meted out. The now staggering, swearing, belligerent, cocky brat was ostracized and placed in the row opposite the commode, and soon the wisdom of such a placement was evident. Upon their return, his instructor was duty bound to inform his parents of the episode. On Monday, before she had even so much as unfastened her seat belt in the school parking lot, his teacher was threatened with a hefty lawsuit and was being verbally admonished by the enraged Cane Paulson, Sr.

"Leave my son alone!" he said with his omnipresent attorney Frederick Gannon IV at his side. After their assault, they continued on the offensive, breaching the school doors. Their display of force sent the school administrators scrambling for cover and writing letters of apology. This "act of love" by daddy set them both on a course of co-dependence, sailing on a sinking ship of irresponsibility.

It was the first time, the last time, and the only time Cane's father showed interest enough in his sons "education" to set foot on school property. And what a lesson Cane learned that day. The threat worked. He immediately discovered the value of the immunity granted him acquired by his father's blitzkrieg.

The irony of the episode escaped Cane's father, who, on behalf of Washington's manufacturing community at a state legislative hearing the very week prior, railed against "the unsatisfactory performance and general apathy of new hires at his industrial compound" and about "the need for the return of real discipline to our schools!"

Mr. Paulson was proud of his newfound concern, acting just like the father who bails his son out of jail again and again after years of inordinate neglect. Shocked, he improvidently proffers the entire bank of emotional and financial resources miserly withheld from appropriate occasions, and in one conflagration of ultimate blindness, tries to redeem all with lawyers and motions and letters to prevent the reign of justice from taking hold in his child's life. But above all he does all of this to show his love. This attention was called quality time. Tough love.

Cane got his funny new skis, with better bindings and the best equipment the very next day. And his father found him those funny trails that kept his skis together. And he got to go whenever and wherever he desired. This was his reward for getting drunk just days before. It kept him "out of trouble." Above all, this was his punishment for fatherlessness.

Chapter Twelve

"WELL, WHAT DO you want this time?" Franz asked the senior Paulson in a terse voice after the dust settled, inside the trailer brought in to serve as US Nordic Team headquarters at Kincaid Park.

"The way I look at it we have several good options," Cane's father proposed. "A, I suggest we clarify the rules. Plank finished fourth overall when you look at both the freestyle and classic results combined. He deserves to be on the team. That would be the easiest thing to do. Then if that doesn't fly, we try plan B. We go to the committee to discuss the Keagan family's flagrant abuses in the process of selection, and as a remedy disqualify them, or at least Tim Keagan, for what happened today. Or we can do C. We remove Tim Keagan in that he obviously fails to possess the requisite Olympic ideals of sportsmanship and universal brotherhood. Or D, we go to court and enjoin him from participation."

"Okay." Leonard replied. "A – How? B – What? C – Why? D – When? But most importantly, E – Who?"

"Who?" asked Mr. Paulson.

"Yeah, who is 'we'? Who told you I would be party to any of this? What's it to you? Your son made the team."

"You forgot to ask 'F', as in 'where.' Where is this program heading without financial support from people like me? No one had to tell me to come to you, Franz. And why do I care? Well, I don't like anyone putting a knife to my son's throat."

"Oh c'mon, Cane! Keagan didn't put a knife to your son's throat! You played sports at one time didn't you? It was in the heat of battle. And what about you? Is slapping your son for making the team your way of expressing pride?"

Paulson slammed his hand on the table so hard the paperweight cube tumbled aside. "I'll handle my son! You handle Keagan or I'll handle him myself!"

"So I get rid of Keagan. Will that make you happy? Then what? Back to the Hawk? Oh, that's a real improvement. Tenth place, here we come!" Franz retorted, his index finger circling in tiny orbits near his ear.

"You just think real hard on it, Franz. This team of yours isn't going anywhere anyhow and you know it. But with me, you got a future. The program has a future!" he insisted, as he stomped out the door.

Franz chuckled silently as Paulson scrambled out of the office. "The future good of the program..." he shook his head. How many times has he heard that phrase the last four Olympics? The last thing Franz wanted was controversy. He had a cake job. No one expected much of him or of his team. His teams have always been easy to manage; upon reflection, maybe too easy. He, at the age of sixty-three, was not intimidated by the senior Paulson's tirade, but like Keagan ninety minutes earlier, he had not an inkling of what really was going on. "For the good of his team" though, he knew he had to speak with the Keagans. They must know something, he thought. And why did Keagan do what he did to Paulson after the race? But not tonight. He had an awful headache. Just as he was about to leave the race headquarters he heard a gentle knock on the door. A pleasant request to enter followed. "C'mon in," he called, in the most civil voice he could muster, figuring it wasn't Paulson II.

A miraculous apparition of stunning beauty appeared, four hours behind her expected time of arrival.

"Hi. Coach Franz? I'm Lisa Nelson of *Sports Unincorporated* magazine. Uh, you may have heard of us, uh, *SU?* I understand you have quite a team heading to Thunder Bay this year."

"Yes, it's quite a team, Ms..."

"Lisa. Lisa Nelson."

"...Lisa."

Two plus two would soon add up to three.

Chapter Thirteen

The purpose of Lisa Nelson's visit with Franz originated with an unanticipated large advertising account barely a week old. *Sports Unincorporated* was the nation's fastest growing magazine. It quickly found a niche competently reporting on the large variety of competitive sports outside the bankrupt mainstream of those utilizing balls, bats, and pucks. Its circulation already enjoyed one and a half million subscribers, representing a coalition of rollerbladers, runners, triathletes, explorers, and rock climbers, mostly between the ages of twenty to fifty-five. They were slow to engage in coverage of the Nordic sport of cross-country skiing, until a Seattle-based entrepreneur indicated a desire to become a long term supporter of the magazine's objectives, as they had a mutual affinity for promoting the ideals of under-appreciated young athletes. But of course they had to "talk" first. And when a Mr. Cane Paulson, CEO of ForesTek, Inc., a Fortune 500 company, walked in the door, a checkbook and a lawyer accompanied him.

And when Mr. Paulson left, less one corporate check later, ForesTek, Inc., was elevated to a "green" company. So was its much younger Emerald City business associate *Sports Unincorporated, Inc.* Much greener in fact. All Mr. Paulson asked, aside from a guarantee to "allow him" to purchase a full page ad on the inside front cover – and on alternating months the back cover – for the next twelve months, was that they consider, with a wink and a handshake, having Cane

Paulson, Jr., and soon to be five-time Olympian Hawk Plank grace
their February cover. He had even gone to the extent of providing them
an "excellent article about the upcoming Games, written by Hawk
Plank himself." In it, Cane Jr. was prominently featured. The Keagan
brothers were allotted one line. Tim Keagan was not even mentioned.

"Well, we certainly don't have a policy against publishing an article not written by our staff," Paulson was assured by *SU* President Stu
Weinberg. He looked around the table to his associates. "I can hardly
see a problem with a five-time Olympian giving our readers some
insight into the sport, can any of you?" Several of his male associates
were nervously tweaking their beards. It was all happening so fast.
Without question, unspoken suspicion hung in the air. But no one
was concerned with a cover or an article. That seemed reasonable, but
why the rush?

Paulson informed them, "The only time we can get the attention
of America in this sport is at the Olympics. When February's over
we'll have to wait four more years. Besides, the relay race is the one
cross-country race people remember best from the last two or three
Games. It exposes Americans to all of the Nordic skiers in the world!
And Plank has been at all of them."

Lisa Nelson spoke up, "I guess I don't see anything wrong with it.
But if we're going to publish the article, don't you think we should follow up with coverage at the Olympics? I volunteer."

Laughter.

"You just love those big, blue-eyed blonds," said Stu, reaffirming
the Nordic stereotype.

"Why deny the truth?" she admitted with a question.

"And in tights, even," another male observed.

"All the better. But I don't think its all that big a deal when it's
twenty below outside."

Knowledgeable groans issued from the otherwise male audience.

"Okay," said Stu, "enough aspersions on the male anatomy as it
relates to the law of thermodynamics. I think this sounds good. We'll
go ahead with the cover. Why not? Plank is who he is, and Paulson is
ostensibly an up and coming star. But I think it is the fair and respon-

sible thing to send Lisa to cover whatever she can up to and through the Olympics. We will print Plank's article, and Lisa can do an updated insert for the March issue. Personally I like cross-country skiing. Most of us here have tried it from time to time, and the sport lends itself to our range of coverage. One thing for sure," he said as he accepted the check, "we certainly can afford to send Lisa now."

The meeting broke up with laughter and handshakes.

As the room emptied Weinberg caught Lisa's eyes. He raised his hand to his waist, palm up, signalling her to remain behind.

"Should I feel like I've just been had?" he asked her.

"Is it their environmentally conscious spiel?"

"No, it's not that obvious. No one expects anything less of an advertiser."

"Is it his son on the cover?"

"Yeah. There is something about that. Have we – have I – sold out?"

"It can't be any worse than our first cover, 'Monkey-eaters of the Amazon'."

"No," he winced a smile, remembering the old days, "but no one could say I sold out on that one!"

"Don't worry, boss. What does Paulson have to gain? He is already a near billionaire. I'm sure it's for his kid. And Plank's been around long enough. There is credibility."

"It isn't the facts Lisa. It's the vibes."

"Whatever, boss. You can count on me. If there is a problem we'll work it out. It's not like we can't survive a mistake."

"I'm not worried about that Lisa. No, no, we'll be bigger than ever this time next year, no matter what. It's the trend I'm worried about. You know what I mean. The trend we set." He thought for a moment. "We stepped out of our track today. It is always just a little scary whenever we do. I'm sure I'm just being nostalgic."

"That's why I like working here, Stu. We might not always know where we're going, but we can always get back home."

"In any event, find out what this Nordic business is all about. There must be something to the sport. God knows they don't do it for the glory."

Chapter Fourteen

L ISA WAS ILL-INFORMED, or so it seemed to Franz.

"You mean to tell me that Hawk Plank is not on the team?"

"Well, no. Not officially," hedged Franz. A short hesitation followed. "Well, no. Actually he is not. He might be an alternate to the team, but I haven't decided, yet."

"That's strange. My information was that he was already selected."

"You must be confused."

"No. I was specifically informed that Plank was on the team."

"Well, that's funny. Where did you hear this?"

"Back in Seattle, a week ago. It came from Plank himself."

"Apparently he is not clairvoyant, because two hours ago he got his butt whipped by Tim Keagan. He's the other member of the team. The team was not even filled out until today."

She shook her head slowly, brunette locks brushing her shoulders. Well I'm here, she thought, I might as well find who these other people are.

"Who is Tim Keagan? Jerry and Phil's other brother?"

"No. He's their father."

"Father!" she exclaimed. "How old are these guys?"

"Let's see. Phil is the oldest son – he is twenty-three and Jerry is twenty. Tim is forty-three, I believe.

"He had 'em young, huh?"

"I guess. They're good kids. Real easy to coach."

"How good are they?"

"The best in North America. You don't know that?"

"What about Cane Paulson? I heard he was key to the team."

"Yeah, you could definitely say that. If he raced an entire race to his potential, we would have a fair team, maybe even a better than average team with the Keagans skiing like they have been."

"But the Keagan boys are better?"

"Ask Paulson himself. He'll tell you. Well, let me correct myself. Paulson did win a classic qualifier. But then the Keagans were concentrating on the skating qualifiers. And the Keagan boys can and did beat Paulson today in the final classic."

"And who won today?"

"The old man, walking away with it."

Jeez, what a story. Her hands were already busily typing away in her mind. Even if this was nothing but an insert article, it had to be of equal or greater interest than Plank's ruminations.

"Well, just to wrap up, did something happen to Plank so that he did not make the team?"

"That's what I don't understand, Lisa. A week ago he didn't have much of a chance to make the team. The skating legs were owned by the Keagan boys and Plank was behind Tim Keagan and Paulson for the two classic legs. I mean it was possible in theory I guess that he could've made the team. I have seen stranger things, but for him to come right out and tell you he was already on it just isn't the Plank I've known for sixteen years."

"Well, actually he didn't tell me that. He had written it in an article he submitted to our magazine."

"Now Lisa I know that wasn't him. He was he in Anchorage all last week. Someone's putting you on."

"No – he didn't give it to us personally – "

"Oh, he mailed it, I see..."

"Cane Paulson brought it in to us."

"Cane Paulson, Sr.?"

"Yes, you know him, don't you?"

"Better every day, Lisa. Better every day." Franz paused.

It was obvious to Lisa that Franz suspected something sinister. So did she. She began to share with him some of the details of the meeting Cane Paulson, Sr. held with *SU.*

Franz clearly saw plans B through D on the horizon. Paulson had to be stopped.

"You can write this: Coach Leonard Franz of the US Men's Nordic Team is pleased to announce that Tim Keagan, Jerry Keagan, Phil Keagan, and Cane Paulson...leave out the Junior...will comprise – strike that – have earned positions as America's representatives at the Games. As to whether any of them, with the exception of Cane Paulson, will actually compete at the Olympic games is subject to whatever influence Cane Paulson, Sr. may peddle with the US Olympic Committee, and if failing that, the unpredictable courts of the United States."

"Whoa! Excuse me for being so dense, but I detect not all is copacetic here in the great white north."

"You know I like that word 'copacetic.' I haven't heard it for a coon's age. Lisa, you don't know what you've just walked into. I know this because I didn't have a clue either until you walked into the room. But print that quote. I guarantee you it is all true. I stake my life on it. If Tim Keagan doesn't lead off the 4x10K relay in Thunder Bay, something really insane is going on."

"Why should Paulson care if the Keagans make the team? It seems like more media attention would be focused on his son then. It's quite a human interest story to have an entire family on the team, even if they don't contend for a medal. Besides that, why would he go to bat for Plank?"

"All I know for sure is that if you're in Alaska and you hear the thunderous sound of hoofbeats coming your way don't look for wildebeests. Certainly there is no logical reason. So to solve the riddle you have to look at it illogically, I suspect. Personally I don't really care to solve it. I got a team to field in six weeks time. Why Plank? Paulson suspects that the Keagans might be winners and that scares him to death. You see, Plank is his son's parachute. Correction, Plank is his guarantee. Plank would ski the first leg and by the time he finished the US would be battling Belarus and Slovenia for twelfth place. It wouldn't matter if Cane stinks if the whole team stinks. But Tim Keagan's got some fire in his eyes, and his sons are what we've been hoping for here since Bill Koch. Junior's leg might actually matter. And so far, whenever the game has been on the line, he has yet to come through."

"Can you give me an example of what you mean?"

"An example? How many would you like? Take today for instance. He is leading the race with one and a half kilometers to go, on a downhill. Now Cane has been here all week. I've watched him ski down that hill twenty times. He never so much as rose from a tuck, and today he loses it, comes in fourth. Other times when a race gets tight, he just starts walking up hills, out of breath, or just hanging his poles to his side, like he is exhausted, even in the flats when everyone else is sprinting to the finish."

"How can someone like him make the team?"

"Since the team was determined by the results of three races, the pressure was not so great. But at Big Thunder, we're back to one big race at a time. You know, I would like to see Cane ski without choking. He really is good. But I've yet to meet a coach who can teach an athlete to perform in the clutch. You can't teach faith. It is the one thing in life that comes from within."

"Maybe you're right, Coach..."

"Len."

"Len. But it sure can be inspired."

Franz's ears perked up, and he rose his head. "Say that again?"

"Maybe you can't teach faith, but it can be inspired," Lisa repeated nonchalantly, oh-so catholically.

"What is its antonym?" Franz quickly asked in succession.

"Ah...ah...disinspire, ah, to take away..." she struggled at the unexpected turn of topics.

"No, no...expire! Maybe faith can be infused, and maybe it can expire only from within. When someone loses faith...like when someone quits believing in himself." He was thinking, of course, of Cane.

"You know, you have a surprisingly good vocabulary for a coach," Lisa complimented.

"It pays to increase your word power." Len admitted.

"And if I can be so presumptuous, you seem to have a good read on human psychology."

"Coaches are the best psychologists on earth, Lisa. And now if you'll excuse me I have some patients to schedule appointments with."

"What about my article, though? What should I do about all this?"

"Make an appointment. Or to save time, print what is true."

Chapter Fifteen

MEANTIME, A SLIGHT wind slackened, like a fishing line snapped free of its catch. The sky was already gray and blackening further. Some lighter clouds beneath the darker ones piled above, and began to conspire with one another. From the four winds, they began to circle, ever so slowly, hesitating at times, but never repeating. The air stilled, but above, the four clouds independent of the silence, cavorted seditiously. Their movement organized and the pace quickened. The space between them lessened, the clouds extended vertically. Now circling faster, now together, now one, longer, now twirling, thinning, spinning, sinuous, no control, no destination, no shelter... air consumed into it, can't breathe! can't breathe! choking, choking...!

The bottle slammed down... can't swallow, can't breathe! Swallow! Swallow! Bottle up! Up! More rum, mon? Get a grip! Have ganja, mon? No guts! X-tas-see? Familiar feeling. Nirvana! Ha! Ha! Ha! No guts again! Co-Bain, mon! Keagan! It can be over! Cut it! Choking! No! – your wrists, stupid! Stop it! Stop it! Can't do it! I feel it, it's here! Today! Today's the night! Today's the night! 27! 72! 27! 72! You're going to die, mon! For your sins, mon!

Who's here? WHO'S FREAKING HERE! Jesus! Jesus! Jesus! I don't want to die! I don't want to die! I don't want to die! Oh God! Oh God!

Then the sheets of rain came, followed by thunder. The bottle of overproof rum dropped to the carpet spilling the one hundred milliliters remaining. The knife followed, still open, falling to the side. Finally a crumpled sobbing mess of twisted emotions, still clothed in lycra and nylon, reeking of despair and alcohol, dropped to its knees. Another thud, by the lamp stand. Then finally face down, into a ball. It's so cold. So cold! Why is the pillow so hard, so wet? Oh my head! Jesus! What is that hard thing on the floor? A brick? A book? Slow motion. Tired. Over for now. God! God! Sleep with God! Sleep with God tonight. Warmer. Softer. Softer. Warmer. 27. 27.

Into blackness.

Jesus! With fumbling fingers the knife was folded and pocketed carefully, silently. He turned off the dim lamp. He carefully lifted Paulson's hand from a page of... a book? He turned on the light. He read now with deliberation, finally with incredulity. He looked around him. He shivered, and goosebumps grew over gooseflesh. He contemplated for a moment in the light and wrote a note, crumpled it and pocketed that too. He managed to lift and drag him into the bed, and removed his boots and tucked his boy in. Should I even let him know I am here? He rewrote a note, and started to crumple that too, then stopped. He flattened out the note and placed it like a marker in the book, where Paulson's hand previously lay. He tossed the book on Paulson's bed next to his numb and outstretched arm.

At first Franz could not help but wince a twisted smile at the irony of the whole damn blessed day. He sat in the chair at the table near the foot of the bed staring blankly at Cane. For a brief eternity he sat and tried not to ponder further, but eventually his chest began to heave slowly, with great force, which gathered momentum to his lips and mouth, and finally to his whole anguished face, as he began to sob as quietly as a man could hope to, in an attempt not to disturb his guardianship over Cane.

"Oh God," he sobbed, praying quietly through repressed emotive instinct, "Oh God, let him know it's not so important as this! Let him know it's not about winning. It's not about losing."

Ninety minutes passed as a lot of opposites and extremes, and meaningless scenarios of pressure and failure and praise came to mind. All paled to the power of love, to the lack of judgment, to forgiveness, to simply life itself. He gradually became silent again, and in stages reversed the entire range of emotions he endured. He approached Cane's bedside and stoked Paulson's thick blond hair and kissed him on the forehead, whispering, "Don't ever remember. Don't ever forget." In the ambient light Franz could swear a slight smile appeared as Cane half rolled over in a drunken stupor. As Franz prepared to leave he hung up Paulson's phone which had been busy for six and a half hours. He closed the door behind him, which he had earlier so delicately pushed open to schedule an appointment with his client. Franz knew only one thing. It was time to get busy. And he wouldn't wait for the day to dawn.

Way too soon an awful beeping split Cane's dark night in two.

"Paulson? Time to work. Be at the trail in twenty-five minutes."

It was 6:35 a.m.

"Ah, okay...Coach?"

Click.

Cane slammed back into bed and his head hit something hard. What? Quite obviously I got drunk last night. Too drunk again. What stupid thing did I do this time? A Bible? Seems like, seems like something about a knife. No knife? Was it a dream? Oh, another stupid Gideon's Bible. Must have read something. Can't remember. Twenty minutes. Gotta go. Shower. I got five minutes.

He turned on the water. Yeah, I'm going to be real productive out there. Yes sir. Yessiree. He began to laugh at himself. And dance stupidly in the shower, singing obnoxiously. Oh, my freaking head....

IDIOT! He scolded himself. Get ready! Sober up! He finished his quick shower. His brain felt like a pin cushion. Finally it dawned on him. Practice at seven! It's dark here until almost ten o'clock! Something's up. Did he find out about Plank and me? My stupid dad! Anyhow, I can't deal with it today. Just do what you got to do and come back and sleep. I don't care who I ski with now. Never did. Who cares? I don't know anything. It's not my problem.

He threw yesterday's clothes into a corner and hurriedly put on a clean outfit. As he forced his right arm through the tight sleeve, he picked up the Bible still on the bed, and with a shaking hand, went to place it back on the lamp table. What's this? A note? He opened the book to the mark. It was simply an arrow, and it pointed directly to some passages, which where recorded underneath. No time for this now, and he slammed shut the book and exited the room, following Franz's command like a zombie.

He arrived at Kincaid's trailhead and found Franz standing all alone in the dark, waiting. "Where are the Keagans?" asked Cane, still shivering from the freezing ride to the hills. The cold air seemed to numb his pounding headache ever so slightly.

"Oh, I didn't ask them to come. I'm not sure I want them on my team. You better try skating today, Cane. You never know. Phil and Jerry might have a problem."

"Well," Cane said, "they made the team, didn't they?"

"Maybe. But you know Cane, after talking to your father yesterday, I think it would be wise for us to reconsider just what our objectives are. But I want to assure you that you're on the team no matter what happens. Anyhow let me talk to your father some more about it and we'll decide that later. I just wanted to go out skiing with you today for twenty to twenty-five K's. I saw something yesterday that I think I can help you with. Just an easy pace, okay, so I can point some stuff out to you as we go. Remember I'm over sixty."

Franz activated the lighted 10K trail system. They had the trails to themselves. "You know," Franz said, "I used to hate skiing this time of day, but the older I get the more I appreciate it."

"Well, Coach I don't think I can possibly appreciate this any less than I do today."

Franz laughed heartily. "At my age sometimes I say I'm just glad to be here at all."

They started up the hill at a moderate pace, and an easy downhill followed. Ahead of them was the biggest hill on the lighted track. About halfway up, the turbulent forces in Cane's stomach rumbled toward an eruption. "Coach, I gotta....!" Out came exorcised demons. His stomach felt like it was being expelled from his body. Three times, a pause, hands shaking, too tired to fall on his knees, he bent over, squeezing the handles on his poles like a drowning man's grip. Rapid

shallow breathing, more contractions. Another pause. Stunted coughing followed more regurgitive attempts. The contents of his insides
soon wrung out, yet the disgusting performance went on, with dis-
jointed attempts at spitting and breathing in between the wretched,
abominable convulsions. The dry heaves finally subsided. Pale and
drained, Paulson humbly looked upon his coach.

"Sorry. God, I'm sorry, Coach."

Franz smiled broadly, "What do you guys like to say? Been there.
Done that? I know the feeling. You'll survive." He chuckled, not in a
mean spirit, but at the accuracy of his plan. "Only twenty-four more
kilometers to go."

They continued the climb.

"Stop!" called Cane to Franz who was now about to descend.
"Wait!"

"Okay. I'll wait."

Cane herringboned up the slope. "Coach," he said breathlessly,
leaning on his poles, "I don't think this is doing me much good. I'm
really sick. Can I come back out later today?"

"Yes, you could, but what good will that do? Cane, don't you see
what this is all about this morning?"

"Punishing me for getting drunk last night, right?"

"Cane, I have no desire ever to punish you. Let me tell you what
is going on here. Just relax for a minute or two."

Paulson started to unfasten his bindings, stopping to massage his
bruise on the way down.

"No! Leave them on. Once you put on your skis they don't come
off until you're done." He paused. "In the old days we called this
building character. Now we're not leaving until we ski twenty-five
kilometers. Why? It has nothing to do with making you faster or a
better trained athlete. It is not punishment. In fact, I'm glad you got
totalled last night. Because today skiing is tough, and the fact that you
want to quit is precisely why we are here. When we're at Thunder Bay
in two months, you might think you'll remember this practice and
that will inspire you to ski hard. Forget it. It won't happen that way.
That is not why we're here."

"Then why are we?"

"Because you need to become someone you not yet are. Right now, this very moment we begin." And down the hill Cane followed his guru.

At ten o'clock, they completed twenty-five kilometers. Paulson stopped and smiled in self-admiration. "How was that, Coach? I did it."

"Yes. I am very proud of you Cane," he said, even though it was at the pace of an amateur.

Paulson started to unfasten his bindings.

"Ah-ah-ah-ah!" exclaimed Franz, wagging his finger. "We're going another fifteen. You're looking too good. I wish I was only twenty-seven like you!"

"No! You can't be serious," he begged.

"Yes. After we finish I'll tell you who's on the team, okay?"

"You're going to make me do it anyhow, aren't you?"

"No, you are. And yes, I am, so let's get on with it."

It was a comfortable pace, but at this point it became obvious to Paulson that his Coach was beginning to struggle. "Hup! Hup! Hup! I'll lead for a while," Cane called, and slowed his pace for Franz. "You know Coach, it was awfully hard to hear anything you said to me while I was skiing behind you, did you know that?"

"Huh?" Franz yelled back.

Another hour and a quarter later the end was in sight: five hundred meters of glorious flat earth awaited. "Okay, push it!" Franz screamed.

They both began V-2 strokes, sprinting to the finish. Paulson won easily, and panting, uttered, "Now what – another ten?"

"Nope. That's all I care about, Cane. Next time you're going to have a lot of help doing forty. You looked like Fauner out there today."

"Yeah right. Silvio in mud." Cane was starting to feel alive again. "Hey, so who's on the team?"

"I don't know." He lied again. "Like I said. I have to talk to your father."

"But you told me fifteen kilometers ago that you would tell me." he insisted.

"Okay – after you tell me who you want on it. Who you really want on it."

Paulson looked toward the trail, now bathed in daylight, thinking against the obvious answer which would have included Plank prior to this outing.

"We both already know who belongs, Coach. One thing I realize is that my father should not be a part of it! Please do me a favor and keep him out of this. He is too worried about me and every time I see him everything gets screwed up. I can't even win for losing with him around."

"Is that what happened yesterday?" Franz did not know how far to go. Did he even remember last night?

"You mean why I got drunk or why I fell? Why do I ever get drunk? Why do I ever fall?" Cane laughed a little. "There's a lot more to it than that. He told me a couple of days before the race to do all I could to let Plank win, and hold off Keagan for second. I couldn't even do that right."

"Well, why? That doesn't make any sense."

"That way Keagan and Plank would've been tied for second over-all and he figured the Olympic committee would name Plank to the team. Probably thought he could influence their decision somehow. Anyhow that's what he told us."

"You and Plank?"

Cane nodded.

Franz continued. "What is the deal with Plank? Why is your father so determined to keep the Keagans, especially Tim Keagan, from ski-ing on the team?"

"He doesn't like Tim. Keagan doesn't kiss his butt. Never asks for his money. Wouldn't accept a sponsorship. Drives his van to events. Plus he is always with his two boys who have stolen the spotlight from guess who's son as our team's best skier. Because of them he can't go around work bragging to all his suck-ups about how his kid is best. He can't buy them. Plank is someone who will gladly take his money and suck up to him, because he knows he is about all washed up. Has nothing but praise for the 'up and coming' Cane Paulson. A true sycophant."

"Well, how about you? What do you think of them?"

"I thought I got along okay with Jerry and Phil. I mean they're nicer to me than anyone else out there. We don't hang with each other much, since they're from Michigan and I'm from Seattle. We don't see one another much. I know they've improved a lot in the last year or two. They're at a different level than anyone else in our program. I doubt I'll beat either of them ever again."

"What about their old man?"

"He doesn't seem very friendly. It is like he has a chip on his shoulder. Like he has old ex-jock syndrome or something. I mean what is he doing out here? How old is he, forty-five or something? It's like he's trying to prove something. He ought to kick back and check out his son's races. They're better than he ever was."

"So you don't like him then?"

"I'm not saying that. I have to admit he surprised me a whole lot. He has a lot of tenacity. Man, he's a double-poling machine, too. I just wish he was fifteen or twenty years younger. I just don't believe he can do the job. The sport has left him behind."

Franz admitted, "Things have changed from twenty years ago, but one thing hasn't."

"What's that?"

"If you won't be denied, you can move mountains. That old man was going to run over anyone who stood in between him and the finish line yesterday. And he is not done yet. The reason I brought you out here today is because when he touches off after that first leg at Big Thunder and the US is in first place, I don't want you messing your pants. I can't have you second guessing your ability, or even fate itself. You have to be ready. I've seen a lot of US Nordic Teams come and go. This one is special. This is what I've waited for since forever. I knew it would arrive and when it did, it would come as a family. The Keagans will ski in Thunder Bay until blood comes out of their pores. Why? With every meter their family name is on the line. What about you Junior? Whose name will you uphold? For what would you give your own life-blood?"

Paulson gently stroked his sore larynx. He was surprised. He didn't think Keagan had poled him so hard. No answer.

"Is it fame? A gold medal? Women? What do you yearn for that can equal the Keagans' drive?"

"I would like, I think, someone to tell me when all is said and done that I skied up to – no, beyond – my potential. Just once to be appreciated, in anything, actually. It doesn't have to be skiing. Skiing just happens to be what I do best, sometimes. What makes someone a winner, Coach?"

"Never giving up in the triumph of principle, Cane. The problem with so many people today is that what once were principles are equivocations. Or even worse, principles are never taught at all. I have never held it against your generation. It was mine who let it slip away. Generation after generation we've been given much more than what we have earned or needed. I'm not talking about material things only. I'm talking about earning. We have forgotten what it means. Some of today's athletes are better than ever, but how many are really tough? How many would fight for principle? Individual performances may have risen, but team standards have fallen. Records are broken and set, but all at the expense of virtue, dignity, and loyalty. The degradation in sport and in society in general hasn't affected cross-country skiing yet. But you're right, twenty years ago things were very different. But so far they are less pronounced in cross-country skiing than in any sport I know."

"So, what is the triumph of principle?"

"It is more than just doing the right thing, Cane. It is winning a race not because you're faster, but because you earned the honor through training and mental preparation. And if you lose, it is not because you didn't train hard enough or weren't really prepared. It is putting aside division for the good of the team and fostering unity. It is sacrifice, shared by all, so that later, when the harvest comes, all may be filled beyond measure."

"Coach, I've never heard this kind of talk before. Some words you use I'll have to look up. But if I could win or even do well, my father might feel justified by all he has done for me. And then maybe I'll get past what's bothering me."

"Do this. Get something to eat. Go back to your room. Get some sleep. From what I saw of you last night you need it."

"You? When did you see me?"

"Well, I came to your room to tell you about this morning's practice. Your door was left open just a crack and since your phone was busy, I just walked in. Sorry."

"Well, it didn't bother me as far as I know. The last thing I remember was buying a bottle of rum downstairs. Then I woke up this morning with one of those stupid Bibles they always leave in hotel rooms. Isn't it funny that no one ever steals them?"

"Well, that might have been your best move of the night as far as I could tell."

Cane laughed, but his head still ached big time.

Franz continued. "I don't know much about the Bible. I'm not an expert. Never figured I needed it much. But when I came in, your hand was on a real interesting point. Anyhow if you ever need me for anything call me right away. You're on my team now and I got to have you at your best. Anything. Anytime." He reflected a moment. "Something must have been bothering you last night to pick up the Bible, huh?"

"Yeah, but I don't know what it was. Something's missing," he answered, scratching his head. He knew he had blacked-out.

"That's good sometimes. Maybe you'll find something new to fill in whatever that might have been."

"Okay, Coach. Well, good night," he said. It was twelve noon.

Franz watched as his weakest link shuffled back to his rental car. Should I call a doctor? Am I in over my head? But what would Paulson tell a doctor except that he got drunk and woke up with a Bible in his hand? Of course, I could inform whoever about the knife. The big thing is that he is alive and I know his problem. I also know his remedy. And if I'm to succeed, it cannot involve doctors, priests or psychiatrists at this point.

There wasn't enough time to intellectualize his recovery. The easiest way out for Paulson would be to give up, get therapy inside a building, and get away from his problem. But that would not solve it. It would only delay facing his greatest fear – success. Undoubtedly, the best prescription for his patient would be proper training and preparation for the Games, and as Paulson said himself, to ski beyond his potential there. And the best of all, the next several weeks would involve little else but group therapy.

Chapter Sixteen

T HE KEAGANS DID not look forward to the long drive back home, especially given the dark, short winter days. But they had a lot of preparation left for the Games and did not care to stay in Alaska any longer than necessary. Phil and Jerry were jubilant at their results, and their enthusiasm to get back and get ready could not be restrained.

"Let's stop at Big Thunder for a couple of days on the way home, Dad," said Jerry.

"Let's see how hard it really is."

It didn't sound like a bad idea.

"Well I think we should have Franz and Paulson with us when we do. We are a team now," said Tim.

"Not from what you told us yesterday, Dad. I don't want to work out with Paulson. Let Franz and his daddy handle him. He should be kicked off the whole team, as far as I'm concerned. What are the Olympics all about anyhow?" said Phil in a huff.

"Believe me, Cane is not the problem. He's the solution. It's his father that is the problem."

"But didn't his company absorb a lot of the expenses of the Olympic qualifiers?" asked Jerry.

"Supposedly. But he is really just financing his son. Otherwise he could care less about cross-country skiing. If his son played tennis he'd be buying up television commercials and putting together tournaments for him."

"How do you know that?"

"Why would a fool back someone like Plank who is serious about being competitive with the world? People like us don't set well with the likes of Paulson. Two years ago he called and offered to sponsor both of you if I would let you go to Europe to train and race with Cane. As your agent and your father I turned him down. It was a tough decision. Looking back, maybe I was selfish, but a fantasy stuck in my mind ever since I started skiing again to do exactly what we are going to do at Thunder Bay. That is to be on the Olympic 4x10 team together. I needed you guys for my own training partners or I never would have made it. And just as you have made me a better skier, imagine where Cane might be now. But above all, I thought Cane would have been a bad influence on you. He was older and had all the money and toys a twenty-five-year-old shouldn't have. You were only eighteen and twenty-one and I didn't want you out drinking and partying throughout half of Europe. You have no idea how many Americans with potential go to Norway, Sweden, and Finland and come back totally ruined. You weren't mentally ready to ski at that level and the Europeans would have made sure you would never think too highly of yourselves again. They are nice guys, but not when it comes to racing. Those guys know every trick in the book and they wouldn't hesitate to break you down mentally and physically – the younger, the better. I think that's half of Paulson's problem. He learned to lose with regularity. He should have entered a lot of races back here, acquiring winning skills."

"I guess we'll find out if you were right, Dad," said Phil, not sure he was happy to learn of his father's unilateral decision as his "agent." That was a new one.

"It has worked so far, anyhow," said Tim.

"You know Dad, except for what happened yesterday, I kind of liked Paulson. He never hurt anyone and it seemed like he always found a way to let me win. Plus, even though he is rich, I feel sorry for him. He's kind of like a Kato Kaelin on skis."

Soon Jerry started to snicker at his impromptu analogy. Phil joined in and started to break into laughter. Tim threw an arm around both of them, laughing loudly at the remark which appeared so fitting. Say what you will about the once famous house guest, and probably most, if not all, is correct. But one thing is definitely true, no matter what, you just can't stay too mad at a child for very long.

As they headed east on the long lonesome gray ribbon of lifeblood and sanity, they saw the writing on the wall. Their mutual fate was inextricably intertwined with their Mercer Island misfit. Every time one was tempted to engage in the near blasphemous notion of winning the bronze, the image of Paulson, collapsing like a detonated skyscraper, ended the fantasy before it was given utterance. Even so, there was nothing else left to dream of, and their avoiding discussion in regard to it manifested to each of them that only a medal could make them stop thinking about it.

"We have no choice. We are at the mercy of Cane Paulson. Though I will never submit to him, neither can we subdue him. And we must learn to love the paradox. Our only hope is to create a friendship with him. He's not that bad of a kid, is he?" Tim said to break the silence.

After a moment's reflection Jerry insisted, "No, like I said, Dad. He's all right."

"Yeah, how come you didn't let us go to Europe with him? Jeez!" complained Phil.

Pretty soon Phil and Jerry were all but spending Paulson's inheritance.

"All right! All right! Let's not overdo it. We have to extend the olive branch," Tim said. "It is incumbent upon the more powerful and numerous to approach the weaker, and invite him into our camp."

They thought of turning south and seeing him right away in Washington, so boosted were they by their frondescence, but a forecast of a major winter storm in that direction kept them steady on course.

"Let's invite him to TC," meaning Traverse City, "as soon as we get home, Dad. I bet he would like it there. We can train there together for a few days," was Phil's alternate plan.

"Well, where we train will be up to Franz, but it sounds okay to me. We'll see what he says when we get back," Tim said.

As each day on the road passed, their highly conditioned bodies begged for a tortuous workout. They made it a point to maintain the fitness level they already achieved.

As fate would have it, Thunder Bay, Ontario, lay upon their path of travel. After 1,500 kilometers of fields and plains, the land of the Sleeping Giant was a beautiful skyscape to behold. The Olympic teams would descend here soon and the city was busily bracing for the onslaught. Without debate, their skis had to touch snow at Thunder Bay. As they stopped for gas just north of Kakabeca Falls, Jerry stepped inside the station for a much needed pit-stop. Relieved, he glanced at a newspaper as he was returning to the car. "Ah, what the heck, I'll take one of these, too," he informed the counterperson, handing him a loonie. As he scanned the sport's section, his hand outstretched for change, his heart sank as he read:

"CONTROVERSY SURROUNDS USA MEN'S NORDIC TEAM".

Jerry rushed with the paper to show his father and brother the unbelievable report. Their eyes gleaned the brief article hurriedly. Afterwards they shook their heads, stunned at the news.

"So now a person can be enjoined from lawfully pursuing his dream. And for this inalienable right to be sued without cause I desire to represent my country, and march proudly in honor of freedom and hypocrisy of justice and duplicity? And people ask why I would want to give up that crap?"

"What are we going to do, Dad?"

"I don't know, lads. Hire a lawyer?" He started to laugh at his own suggestion, at the frivolity of it all. At least it prevented the tears. "I should be able to walk in that court, belch, and collect a $1 million defamation award, but instead I have to hire a lawyer. And for that we pay, and for that we give Plank's claim credence to the jackals and hyenas in the press."

He thought to himself for a moment, trying to clear his mind, and find a logical way to deal with the threat.

"At least there is one lawyer I trust, but I know he's never handled anything like this. Come to think of it," he paused, "I don't know anyone who has ever handled anything like this."

"What about the Tonya Harding case?" reminded Phil.

"Great. Now we'll be compared to that bitch, Gillooly, and Eckardt. What an accomplishment," Jerry pitched in.

"Yeah, unfortunately I remember the case. It was the most cowardly decision ever rendered by an Olympic Committee."

Tim knew the comparison was inevitable as the allegations against the Keagans were that they "colluded and/or conspired with one another to impede Mitchell Henry Plank in the course of the Anchorage qualifier, and in so doing did cause Plaintiff, a four-time Olympian, irreparable harm thereby." Their actions were alleged to be "in violation of the rules of the US Olympic Committee, and contrary to the spirit of the Olympic games."

Plank's attorney was demanding that the Keagans be removed from the team due to their "egregious conduct, insulting to the concept of sportsmanship" and that Plank "and those others justly deserving to represent America's notion of fair play, be named in their stead."

One positive note was contained in the article. "When asked about his opinion of the charges leveled against the Keagans, embattled Nordic coach Leonard Franz laughed uproariously and left the aborted press conference with no further comment."

The article went on to say, "The Keagans whereabouts are unknown and all were unavailable for comment. Plank's attorneys speculate that they are avoiding confrontation with the press concerning the allegations against them."

"Isn't that special?" remarked Phil. "Every single one of them knew we drove to Anchorage, and all this happened while we were driving back through the hinterlands of Canada, knowing that we're not hearing a thing, knowing they would have five days to propagandize the country without a chance of our response. Avoiding confrontation – what a crock. Why don't we just settle it by racing again? I won't be so nice this time!"

Tim Keagan laughed, "That would be too much truth for any court. As a matter of principle we shouldn't have to. It would set the worse precedent possible. We earned our place and Plank and Paulson know it. They colluded and conspired, and we get blamed for it. Isn't that modern day America? But I would race again right now, just so I could have an even better time at the finish line than I had in Alaska. And to stick it in his attorney's face."

"What next?" asked Jerry.

"I suspect...well, forget that...Paulson's old man has to be funding all of this. Plank doesn't have the money or the guts to take us on alone," replied Tim. "And you can bet Paulson's got his best attorneys on the case. You know the kind – the ones who so easily weave the truth into a lie, and vice-versa, depending on who their john is."

"Oh, you mean 'good attorneys'," said Jerry cynically.

"I taught you well, didn't I, lads? And now you'll get to experience it in real life, too!" Tim responded, with mock enthusiasm.

"Bring 'em on." said Phil. "They can't be any tougher than that climb to Big Thunder's top," he concluded, peering at the table-top mountains in the distance.

"Yeah, let's go skiing anyhow," said Jerry.

Their problems would still be waiting for them when they got home. They concluded that for now they had about as much peace and togetherness as they were going to get until the press and pundits got their fill of the smorgasbord of decay and decadence back in the US. They could not afford to skip another three, four, or seven days of training and proper rest dealing with controversy back home. Fortunately, they remained totally anonymous in Thunder Bay, and soon they felt almost perverse pleasure knowing what lay ahead of them, and acting calmly indifferent to it. And the longer they enjoyed that feeling, the longer they resolved to stay north of Lake Superior in Canada.

Finally, when they arrived home, refreshed, clear-headed and confident four days behind schedule there was but one sole figure in the drive celebrating their return.

"Where in the good name of Jesus have you been?" came an exclamation of relief and consternation. A short and stocky figure ran to them, slipping as he did. He hugged all three Keagans in quick succession, patting their backs like a Russian diplomat. The Keagans were smiling broadly, and presented a portrait of complete satisfaction and happiness. It distressed Gavin Smith greatly to carry the cross of bad news, and he had a hard time tactfully presenting it.

"You don't know what you've been missing," he said in a wonderful understatement. The Keagans knew exactly, by his mere presence at their return, what was coming next.

"What, don't tell me they held a parade for us!" deadpanned Phil.

"I missed the Cherry Queen!" exclaimed Jerry. "Again! There goes my big chance."

Momentarily, Gavin was somewhat embarrassed by their remarks, because Traverse City, in fact, planned nothing to welcome their return. "Well, not exactly. But I guess you could say there was a parade of sorts." He formed a weird kind of smile, a little Steve Forbes-ish, almost convincing himself maybe humor is a good way to break the ice. "Right in the neighborhood. Lots of cameras, reporters, and people like that. You haven't heard anything about it?"

"No one told us about any parade, Gavin," said Tim. "We've been up in Canada for the last ten days and we drove straight through today from Marathon. Why? What did we miss?" Tim asked with feigned concern.

"You have no idea, then?" Gavin said in a low voice, hanging his head, his lower lip beginning to tremble. He couldn't bring himself to spoil their party.

The Keagans had taken their ploy far enough and rallied to lift up their friend's spirits. "What, Gavin? Is this about the team? Is Plank or Paulson up to something?" Gavin nodded, feeling lightened by Tim's cross-examination.

"I knew it! I knew it! I knew they were up to something in Anchorage. Gavin, we talked about them almost all the way back. So I'm not surprised. Not surprised whatsoever. Are you, boys?" Tim said with feigned alarm.

"No, Dad. Its just like you suspected. They were up to something," Phil answered.

Gavin looked stunned. "What are you guys talking about? Plank says you guys were up to something. And Paulson had nothing to do with it."

Tim ended the charade as the four entered the house. In a serious voice he told Gavin the entire story as it happened. Though there were many loose ends that Keagan could not explain, Gavin had absolutely no doubt in his mind that the Keagans were being mercilessly railroaded. He had suspected it long before they arrived home. He judged them under the standard he applied to everyone. The content of their character would not allow any of them to lie or cheat as their accuser alleged. Their consciences could not be saddled with a tarnished accomplishment. He had known this of Jerry and Phil all their lives. In the case of Tim Keagan, he had never met a man so tested by misfortune, and so resistant of temptation. He was a man upon whom he rested his faith that mankind can be good, and that virtue would not go unrewarded without a fight.

To see Tim fail now in his noble quest would cause Gavin to lose faith in that one Higher Principle, the One law that must remain after all present have turned to dust. He could not, would not, shall not, let that happen. And though he had no idea of how to proceed in a case like this, being a practitioner in real estate law, he was the one lawyer Tim Keagan trusted, the one he referred to a thousand kilometers ago. And the fact that he was the sole human awaiting their arrival confirmed with authority Tim's predilection.

"I'll do it, of course," Gavin assured them. "But I'm telling you it would sure be nice to have some help, guys. Besides Plank, the Paulsons, and Franz, would anybody else know anything?"

"Not that I'm aware of," Tim summarized.

"By the way, did I tell you that they amended their pleading and now they want to force Franz out, too?" Gavin told them.

"Let me guess. They want Cane's father to coach," Phil said.

"I don't know what that is all about. They must be saying he colluded too."

"Must be because he laughed at the press conference, eh?" Jerry noted. "So far he is the only one that had said anything sensible. Maybe he is the help we're looking for, Gavin."

"We may find out sooner than we think," Gavin said. "He left a message at the office earlier today to call him, but I wanted to talk to you first. Well, I've got to go home. It's been a long day...week, I mean. Meantime, stay in shape, guys. I'll get you up there somehow."

Chapter Seventeen

LISA WAS SUMMONED into the office by Weinberg. "We have a situation here, *n'est-ce pas?*" he said, sharing his rudimentary knowledge of French.

"Your guess is as good as mine."

"Not that I'm bound by your opinion, Lisa, but should we go with Plank's article?"

"I wouldn't."

"That's all? You wouldn't?"

"How can we print an article when we don't have a clue how this thing will turn out?"

"And by then, we'll have nothing in the magazine and the Olympics, if not the winter, will be over. Paulson's mad, cancels advertising, and we lose an opportunity to bring in more subscriptions."

"I can get an article-"

"By Tuesday?" Weinberg cut her off. "I have two whole days to either go with Plank's article or have a twenty page gap in our February issue. Not to mention what we'll come up with for our cover."

"Well, just print it then, Stu! Just print it. If that will solve your immediate problem, why lose sleep over it, okay? It's your magazine. And hey, if anything goes wrong, it's not our fault – Plank wrote it. We'll kiss and make up in the next issue. And you know something Stu? Our readers won't even care, anyhow. That's where American journalism is at right now. Live for today!"

"Whoa!" Stu responded. "Who stepped on your tail? Just answer this, Lisa. Can you tell me for a fact that what Plank wrote or what Plank is alleging about the Keagans is not true?"

"You know Stu, isn't it interesting that in order for us so-called journalists to sell a story, subscriptions, advertising, or whatever, that we have lately resorted to assuming the truth is established by the utterance of a controversial proposition, whether it is by a fool or by a saint, unless and until proved to the contrary? And we rush to publish it as fast as the ink can dry. We are in competition with the tabloids now, and we can't afford to be anything more than half-right about half the time, or be beaten to the punch. We're all sucker-punchers now, is that it? It's so improper!"

"Somehow, I'm missing your guilt trip logic, Lisa. There is nothing that is contained in this story that I can see as objectionable. If anything, it's totally current and newsworthy."

"You left out factual."

"What is unfactual about it?"

"There you go again. See what I mean? Like I said Stu, go ahead and print it. It won't be the last time virtuous behavior or the lack of it is dictated by the terms of a deadline...*n'est-ce pas?*" Lisa cynically mimicked as she turned on her heels.

"Lisa! Lisa!" The only truth Stu understood was the immediacy of a headache. "Catholics," he muttered in resignation. "Always desiring to convert or to be converted."

He looked at the proposed February cover. He again looked through the article. He studied the smart ForesTek ad.

He arose and removed himself to the washroom, his elbows on the sink, hands supporting his head, eyes looking into his eyes, thought searching for reason. A verdict was rendered, maybe temporary. Maybe not. The article must be printed with a disclaimer. As an insert. And the disclaimer must be worded so as to validate any later finding that the Plank article was in error. And it must please everyone, but above all, it must please Cane Paulson, Sr.

He shook his head, almost laughing to himself. It's just not that big a deal. Who even heard of these guys before Paulson walked through that door anyhow? Further justification, although unnecessary now, was amply supplied by his self-acknowledged ignorance of the entire matter. And Lisa, when given a chance to enlighten him, provided nothing but cryptic musings about the ramifications of a hypothetical error. But nothing concrete. Most convincing of all was purpose. Was not the major purpose of the article, of the issue, to expose his subscribers to this undistinguished sport, and in part introduce them to some – not necessarily all – of our nation's finest in that regard? Lisa, Lisa, he thought, come to your senses. There is no harm in this. He had employed every justification, and would continue to do so intermittently throughout the day. The money, already on deposit, was a thought of curious omission, if sin at all. How can one stand in need of absolution in the absence of knowledge of good or evil? And until man discovers evil, all is good, was that not our first lesson? Stu drummed his fingers on his desk as the day came to a close. It never occurred to him that the Keagans were humans who had invested more time in their achievement than he in his. Still, something was in the air. Something tugged at his conscience. He desired all the benefits of neutrality, but wished to escape all of the burdens.

Soon he grew disgusted with doubt. Does the apple Adam blindly tasted nourish still fantasy time wasted? The fruit hung delectably from the tree, but this Eve tempted him not to eat of it.

He went into the washroom a second time and looked again. He stared for a long time. It was so silent. He was the brink of whoredom, he knew it; yet he still loved sex. And he implicitly understood the trade off.

No such sufferance was found in Lisa. All the while in her purse she possessed, in the form of airfare, the currency for pilgrimage and for truth. From Sea-Tac to O'Hare to Grand Rapids, to the halls of the US District Court for the Western District of Michigan, she sojourned with mighty determination. Maybe the controversy spawned a journalist's dream. Maybe it was these unstudied men in their yet unsullied sport. Maybe it was Franz, the CEO, Cane, Plank, or the Keagans. Maybe it was all of the above. Whatever it was, a story cried for coverage. She did not expect such a challenge when she was given such an innocuous assignment, but above all, she knew beyond all shadow of a doubt that if Plank or the Paulsons, or both, were lying from the beginning, that the Keagans could not advertise their way to a fair hearing in the media. When Franz was added to the Plank complaint as a Defendant she knew something very insane was going on indeed.

Upon her arrival, she observed three men approaching the courtroom in the dimly lit halls in downtown Grand Rapids, Michigan. The Keagans? The old one sure didn't look very athletic from a distance. "Tim Keagan?" she inquired impatiently.

The three laughed.

"I guess I'm going to have to get some sun or something," Gavin quipped. "I'm Gavin Smith, his attorney. Hey, Tim!" he called.

"Yo, Gavin!" came a voice from behind her . She turned suddenly, to see a tall strapping man. A face as solid as his physique. Tim Keagan.

"Friend or foe?" he asked Lisa. He asked it with that certain smile. It was not a smirk, but it wasn't a come on, either. What was it? Whatever, she gave one right back. Their eyes locked and danced, and they both knew it. Even from that first moment she wanted to know Tim Keagan.

But a dance is only a question, not an answer. And as a reporter she knew where to find much needed information. Whenever possible, start with the person ethically bound to confidence. And she had yet to find an attorney who didn't like to talk.

Chapter Eighteen

GAVIN RE-CHECKED HIS appointment book. A typical day in court. The judge appeared, saw the number of contestants, and quickly adjourned the matter to "'the next available court date as today's hearing was not scheduled with the taking of testimony in mind." Now the courtroom was empty and would remain so the rest of the day. Gavin pleaded with the judge to expedite the matter, but to no avail. The judge didn't buy Gavin's cogent argument that this matter was strictly one for the US Olympic Committee to resolve internally. The court instead found "that irreparable harm to Plank would occur if the allegations in his complaint could be proved by a preponderance of the evidence." Though participation on the team was not a "fundamental right," he certainly "deserved due process and equal protection of the law in the determination of misfeasance by other Nordic Team members, in particular the defendants Keagans, and their coach, Leonard Franz."

"So, Judge," Gavin argued just minutes before, bordering on smug arrogance, "we have an Olympics about a month away. When is the last time you closed discovery, held pre-trials, scheduled depositions, exchanged witness lists, heard motions, granted or denied summary judgments or partial summary judgments, held a final pre-trial, notified and impaneled a jury, conducted a jury trial, allowed interlocutory appeals, or any of the above in a month's time? Or are you planning on enjoining the start of the Games, too? Do you think Canada and the

International Olympic Committee might have a problem with that?"

The judge was not amused by Gavin's sarcasm. "I'm in charge here, Mr. Smith, not the IOC!" he bellowed. "Of course, there will be no time for a trial! So I suggest you show a little more deference to this court as I will make the dispositive decisions on these matters. There will be no jury to decide this matter, Mr. Smith. Even a law school student knows that suits in equity are matters for the bench, not suitable for the whims of a jury. So you would be well-advised to acknowledge the authority of this Court." Judge "Big Bear" Griffey was in no mood to wrangle with this black fly from up north. He was also late for lunch and his racquetball game.

"Way to go, Gavin," said a bemused Tim Keagan. "By the time the trial starts you'll have him eating out of your hand."

Planks attorney was gleeful and Plank was smiling broadly. He shot a stare Keagan's way. He finally found a forum in which his arch-rival might be intimidated.

"Sorry about that," Gavin whispered.

"Don't worry about it. I've been here before, remember?" Tim assured him.

"For now this matter is set over for a week from today, gentlemen. Mr. Gannon, please prepare the order denying Mr. Gavin's motion for dismissal. The order of proceeding on Monday will be as follows: Mr. Gannon, you, having the burden in this matter, necessitates your offer of sworn proof. Any testimony or exhibits you wish to produce must be ready then. Mr. Smith, anything you wish to have the Court consider will follow. Mr. Gannon, your earlier ex parte request for a temporary restraining order prohibiting the Keagan defendants or defendant Franz from acting in any capacity relating to the upcoming Winter Olympics is denied at this time, as no irreparable harm can be established *eo instante*. They may continue as the apparent representatives of the US Nordic Team pending a full hearing resulting in a final decision on merits of your request for a permanent injunction. Mr. Gannon, let me remind you and your client, as your relief in this regard is equitable in nature, you must meet a substantial burden. Your interesting and novel claim that your client is a victim of 'unfair competition' is something this court has entertained heretofore only in a commercial trade law setting. But in a light most favorable to Mr. Plank, the verified complaint alleging the representation that his 'commercial value as an athlete, having contracted to endorse products of ForesTek, Inc., among others, will be seriously impaired, thereby causing him irreparable harm,' if not a tenuous claim, if successful surely would be precedent-setting, as far as I can ascertain. This is a matter I'll take under advisement. No case law has been provided this Court by Mr. Gannon which addresses this precise issue. Be warned gentlemen, if I do make a finding that something amiss occurred in the make up of this Olympic team, assuming I have equitable powers at my disposal – and I believe I do – anything may result."

As the parties marched out of the courtroom, no wiser in the law, Jerry muttered, "Oh great. Another Federal Judge doing as he ought to do. Or should I say as he wont to do."

"Blame it on lifetime appointments. Who ever Lord Acton was, he got it right. By the way, what is ForesTek, Inc.?"

Lisa, who witnessed the abbreviated proceedings, overheard Gavin's inquiry.

"The question you need to ask is not 'what', but rather 'who'."

Gavin looked behind himself. Her again. "And do you know the answer?"

"I know one thing, Mr. Smith. You and I need to talk."

Gavin would soon learn how good an investigator Lisa Nelson could be when motivated by the right pair of eyes.

Chapter Nineteen

"**A**ND SO SHE died, of course," Lisa concluded the tale for Gavin Smith.

"Not right away. She clung to life for three days. He never left her side. But, she never regained consciousness. My wife and I took care of the boys during that time. Poor Phillip. I'll never forget it. After Nikola died I spent as much time with Tim as anyone I suppose, being that we were sharing an office then. Tim was the strongest man I ever met...I mean mentally tough. That race that day meant everything to him, and then the accident proved how little it mattered. Everybody around Traverse City thought he gave up skiing right after that, but I saw him go out again right after the funeral."

"What happened?"

"I followed him in my car. Naturally I was worried about him. The big Birkebeiner race was a week away – maybe he had to know for himself if he could go on. Anyhow, I watched him from a side street above the trailhead. It was dusk, and the gray skies seemed so fitting. He skied only about one hundred meters, very slowly and finally he just collapsed to his knees, right on top of his skis. And he started sobbing. After several minutes he took off his skis and then heaved them and his poles into the woods. Then he just sat down right in the snow and stared until I couldn't even make out his figure. Who knows what he was seeing or thinking. All I know is that he did not put on skis again for ten years."

"What about Jerry and Phil?"

"No amount of depression can hold back healthy boys. They loved skiing. How can you live up here and avoid it? They had friends from school who skied and they were often invited to go along. Tim always allowed it. Eventually Tim went out to watch them. Pretty soon the boys were entering youth races. Tim couldn't stand the thought of his sons not reaching their potential. To do that, he simply had to put on his skis again, and assist in training them properly. But by then, the sport had changed so much. Tim was the last to win a Vasa race using the classic technique."

"When did he start racing again?"

"He gradually got back into it. He picked up the skating technique and was one of the best around here – but he knew the classic style best suited him. When his sons were both in high school, he started getting serious. When Phil turned eighteen and defeated the junior national champion here at the Vasa, something ignited in him." Gavin summarized, referring to the Olympic relay team.

"How did the accident happen?"

"Have you ever driven in a white-out?"

"A what?"

"A white-out."

"A snow storm?"

Gavin laughed. "There is no comparison. Imagine driving inside a dense white cloud, but then throw in a blizzard and add icy roads. Forget headlights, they have no effect, but turn them on anyhow. Imagine a coat of white paint covering the inside of your car windows. The outside too. Finally, close your eyes. And pray. Hard. This is what Nikola encountered at ninety kilometers per hour. No one knows how the accident happened. All anyone knows is that the vehicle left the road and flipped. No other car was involved. US-31 is no place to be in conditions like that. But up here, we've all done it, all too often. She had just dropped off the boys at a friends in Elk Rapids. She chatted there for a while before leaving to watch the finish of the race. By the time she got back on the road, the storm was unrelenting. She was lucky, I suppose, that anyone came across her car at all that morning.

But, I guess it didn't matter after all, did it?" he added reflectively.

"You know, Gavin, this is just an incredible story! Do you think Tim would mind if I wrote about it?"

"He would not want you to. At least not now. He wants to get this lawsuit out of the way first. And then of course the Olympics. That is the closure he needs. This is probably not the best time to bring it up."

Lisa thought of Plank's case and compared Keagan's tale of woe to his complaint.

"Could the Keagans have conspired to fix the results in the tryouts? You can't deny motive." Lisa reluctantly played the devil's advocate. But she had to be certain.

Gavin narrowed his eyes in a resounding emphatic stare. "I do not know this Plank man. But I do know Tim Keagan. I'll tell you this – Tim Keagan right this moment would drop everything, lace his boots, put on his skis and settle this – mano-a-mano. So what does that tell you?"

"Nothing that I didn't suspect already," Lisa replied. She learned all she needed to know for now.

As she began to dismiss herself with a good-bye, Gavin blurted out, "Wait, Lisa! Who is that person I need to know about?"

"I must call Stu." she said in a non-response, disappearing behind the foyer out of sight.

"Stu who?" Gavin muttered to himself, as he watched her scurry from the building into the busy lunchtime throng of pedestrians in downtown Grand Rapids.

Chapter Twenty

CANE FOUND HIMSELF alone at the massive home of his parents the Saturday preceding the hearings. He had been well coached by his father and the attorneys involved as to what they expected his testimony to be.

"So, you want me to lie?" Cane deduced in a monotone.

"No, no, no, no, no!" insisted Gannon.

"Just answer our questions truthfully and we'll draw the rational inferences from the proofs in the case," said the clone in the middle, Mr. Kenneth Kranwitz.

The senior advisor, Mr. Gannon, again piped in, "Cane, how many years now have I been a friend of your family? I would never do anything that would subject you to the consequences of perjured testimony. We just want to review with you what Plank is telling us and see if it can be corroborated. Okay? So chill out. Okay?"

"The Keagans didn't throw that race. That is the ultimate point, isn't it?" he summarized, arms folded across his chest.

"You may think that," rejoined the youngest attorney, Alexander Scarborough, who appeared to be about Cane's age. Cane looked upon him with disgust. "But how do you know what the Keagan's were actually thinking or doing? You can't tell us what was in their minds or what they planned together before the tryouts. The judge won't even let you anyhow! You're not competent to testify as to what they thought or did!"

"Oh, and you are!" shot back Cane.

Gannon was taken aback, but this exchange wasn't entirely unexpected. He knew of Cane's recalcitrance for as long as he knew him.

"Let's agree about what we know to be true. That would be a good way to start, wouldn't it?" he said, patiently, again.

After he concluded, the following points were firmly established, and summarized by Gannon.

"One. The familial relationship of the Keagans. Two. They travelled together to each and every event. Three. They roomed together each time. Four. They ate together each time, etc., etc., etc." He paused. "Those facts certainly support the foundation of a reasonable probability of a common purpose or plan – a conspiracy." The two other lawyers hastily nodded in agreement.

"Yeah," said Cane. "They wanted to make the Olympics. They just happened to be related. Jeez! You got them now!"

Gannon held his tongue. What a loser Paulson's son was! "Let's go on. We'll assume for now the Keagan boys earned their position for the – what is it called – the free skate leg?"

"Whatever," said a bored Cane.

"Freestyle, the skating leg, Mr. Gannon," said the recent admittee, Alexander Scarborough.

"So, why are they skiing in the final race at all? Well, we know why – to help their father make the team! What number are we on? Oh, six. Five skiers lead the race. Jerry Keagan leading the pace, Plank second, Phil Keagan, third. Right? Interesting. You pass the old man and now he's last."

"Last? There were twelve skiers!" Cane was miffed at the slight, remembering the previous slight about his "next to last finish."

"Yes, that's right. But last among the five." Gannon continued, "You pass Phil Keagan. And then Phil conveniently drops back so his dad can get behind you again. Then when the race is half way over, Jerry Keagan, exhausted, can't continue the pace – " Cane snorted, but Gannon carried on, not skipping a beat. It was good practice to do so. " – and without his sons aid, Tim Keagan remained in third place, and as I'm informed, cast, shall we say, highly improper aspersions toward both of you."

"Bigoted remarks," clarified Kranwitz.

"Shameless," added Scarborough.

Cane looked puzzled. "What are you talking about?"

"Isn't it true he made references regarding sexuality toward you and Plank?"

Cane laughed heartily. A homophobe he was not. "Are you guys really going to play that card? Give me a break. Let's see. Let's call off the Super Bowl, the World Series, the NBA finals, the Stanley Cup. Oh please."

"Okay. Okay. Cane, we understand. It only goes to show state of mind. The conspiracy against Plank," Kranwitz suggested.

"We're not saying he really is a bigot," said Gannon.

"Or that you are gay," explained Scarborough

"Oh, thanks," Cane replied. "So, how do you guys get past the fall on the hill?"

"That's immaterial. By that time the damage had been complete," said Kranwitz.

"Plank was trying to get up and Keagan stepped on his skis," chimed in Alexander the Great. "And so did the Keagan boys."

"That's what Plank will testify to," explained Kranwitz.

Gannon gave a final shot at convincing Cane of the merits of their cause.

"You see Cane, not all of what we think we know or see or experience is actually what really happened. If we break down this case point by point, frame by frame, we gather a whole new perspective."

"You know it's funny. Ever since O.J. everything is possible, isn't it?" Cane quipped. "C'mon, you guys. Don't tell me you don't know that it was me and Plank who tried to keep Tim Keagan out of it. If you don't know by now, I'm telling you, it's the truth!"

"Unfortunately, our client says otherwise. Besides, we're not the judge of that. That's Judge Griffey's problem. All we ask of you Cane is to answer our questions as they are asked. Don't add anything to any answer. Do I need to have your father speak with you to make our request any more clear to you?" threatened Gannon, holding the trump card. The truth was buried in the deck.

Cane slumped in his chair. "Whatever."

"And we've got a lot more evidence than just your word, Cane," said Scarborough. "Don't you worry."

"I'm sure you do."

The meeting ended. Cane understood his place. Under Dad's thumb. Living a lie.

As the pinstriped trio drove back to the firm across Lake Washington, they were laughing most heartily.

"Don't you just love this job?" said Kranwitz to Scarborough. "We make a case when there is none."

"We might have a problem with Cane, don't you think?" he replied.

"Don't worry about him," said Gannon.

They fell silent, only momentarily.

"Isn't it just an amazing world we live in – to be able to accuse someone of doing the very thing our client is guilty of?" laughed Scarborough.

"It couldn't be better. We have an incompetent, officious, perfunctory egomaniac for a judge and Keagan's attorney pal is already caught up trying to prove a negative."

"The truth is out there," Scarborough theorized, waving a hand toward the heavens.

"It's incredible, but I honestly think that judge will see things our way," said Scarborough.

"That's one hell of a pleading you drafted, Alex. I give you all the credit," said Kranwitz.

"...'unfair business practice' – you're a genius, Scarborough. And you're learning to do it all with a straight face. You're going to be a great one," interjected Gannon.

They all laughed, with a touch of pride.

"Wait until you have the truth on your side," laughed Gannon knowingly. "That's when it gets really frightening!"

"Well, one thing is for sure. There is nothing to be afraid of this time," Kranwitz assured his associates.

They pulled into the private lot and escaped into their magnificent quarters. The rest would be easy. They have photos and the testimony of two men. They had Judge Griffey. They couldn't have asked for more. After all, they lived in a country with the best legal system in the world, didn't they?

Chapter Twenty-One

THAT NIGHT CANE made his way downtown to Pioneer Square. Despite the early nightfall and cooler temperatures it was abuzz with activity. Reggae, rock, metal, grunge, jazz, and even the blues could be heard emanating from the various clubs.

Patrons wandered from club to club, their safety quite secure. The Seattle Police Department was one of the first to put officers on patrol using mountain bikes, an ideal mode of transportation in the congestion of downtown Seattle. It kept vibrant the many businesses dependent upon massive pedestrian participation, in spite of the presence of many homeless alcoholics who remain part of the city's fabric which began in the days of skid row.

Cane had a couple of wheat beers at Doc Maynards before heading to his favorite haunt, the Candlebox, famous for popularizing the sound of "grunge" for which Seattle became renowned in the nineties. Walking past the bust of Chief Seattle, he watched a goofy tourist kissing his cast iron cheek for a photo. He did not feel well, and sat down in the Square. He knew he should be training. But for what? His dad had screwed everything up this time. He had no desire to testify, or to race. He fulfilled his promise. He had done all he could do to help Plank along, but Plank was an even bigger loser than himself, he mused. He rose from the bench, dismissing any thoughts of going home in favor of the Candlebox.

He ordered whatever the waitress brought him. Some other microbrew. Standing room only. Again. He listened to the music and surveyed the place. For the first time in his life it looked as though the crowd was too young for him. He heard the singer, strung out on heroin or something bad, repetitively drone:

"Nothing left to live for, nothing left to live for, and on and on and on...AND NOTHING LEFT TO DIE FOR!" he screamed, as if possessed and insanely demented. He seemed to be looking directly at Cane with evil eyes. Cane's stomach dropped. Queasy, he took one more sip. "I got to get out of here!" he demanded of himself, saying it out loud. A strange, psychotic-looking punk turned his way. Shaking now, he walked from the club. His, rather his father's, Mercedes was four blocks away under a bright street light and hopefully police supervision. He had had enough. He was relieved to make it back to his car without incident, and made the quick drive home, which seemed a world away. He was so cold. He fumbled with the evening's change to throw on the dresser. He saw the post-it note from Anchorage. Oh, yeah, I remember. Was it from Franz? What does it mean? He tried to find a Bible in the home. He couldn't find one. Even so, he felt better now. He laughed and spoke to himself, "I wonder what it is like to pray?" But he didn't have the slightest clue how to start. He surmised it was possible anyhow. Start out with God, make a wish, and see what happens. And so before going to bed he got on his knees and said Cane's prayer.

"God, I don't want to testify." He paused. "And I do want to ski well at Thunder Bay." Anything else? He looked around at all the wealth encompassing him. After turning off the lights, he laid back in his ample bed. Resting his hands, fingers interlaced atop a pillow, he began to imagine what it might be like to actually ski at the pace of the world's best. Eyes open, he dreamed. He was not thinking logically; he laughed at himself; he rarely did anyhow. But as soon as the vision took form, it was doused by the worry of his scheduled court appearance.

Cane was a serious underachiever. He was spoiled. He was a Generation X grunge punk surfer dude, a lower middle class wannabe with an occasional yen for exotic dope that could help him pretend he was part of some struggle out there to survive. He didn't even crave alcohol that much, and he explained any excessive use of it as something that "just happens." At times he too could be a suck-up. But he wasn't a cheater. He had never needed to lie. Aside from the ill-fated duo with Plank, he went it alone and reaped what he had sown. Even then, he laughed to himself, he got justice. His conscience was a spare one; still he had rarely intended evil upon another. But the plight of the Keagans had not yet entered his decisional process like it had in Franz's. His prayer was to not testify, not that his father's scheme should not prevail.

Still, benign whispers were slowly swirling in his head. And in the morning he suffered no hangover whatsoever. His mother and father were who knows where. He shuffled to the kitchen to prepare a breakfast. He mussed his thick blond hair, cropped about seven centimeters in length over the crown, sticking straight up like a rooster's comb.

Cane Paulson, in spite of the gossip and abuse he suffered stemming from his classic meltdowns, was a powerful man. Standing just over 190 centimeters, he was well muscled, as are all Nordic skiers who achieve his level of conditioning. He was also a gentle man. To his credit he never engaged in moshing or violence as a youth or in adolescence, though perhaps dozens of opportunities presented themselves with his style of life – in the clubs and bars, and often intoxicated. Perhaps his lack of fighting instinct caused him to forego any offers.

Still, in a race situation, if his lead would go unchallenged, there was not a better American skier. But the Keagan brothers saw that those occasions became fewer and fewer in number. And Cane knew in his heart he was no longer the young American with promise. Others were justified in thinking he had probably reached his peak, whatever that was. If one can shoot ninety percent in practice, but deliver only twenty-five at game time, the sport itself dictates that you retire.

There was something about those Keagans he was utterly jealous of – their stubbornness, their comradery, their courage, their cockiness. They derived it all from a patriarch who would fight. Who would suffer a bloody nose. Who would take eight licks to get one good one in. Who would take on the best of Norway and Italy and Sweden and Finland and Russia and spit in their eye before he would give up. He was one of those rare and special athletes who give what is called a gutsy performance day in and day out. With a Tim Keagan, the odds makers always had to account. On any given day it was a given that he had a chance, however slim. In the opposite fashion, there were the Canes of the world, who were just as much an odds maker's nightmare.

Cane knew the difference existed, but did not know why. Those who should win on paper, but folded instead. He had found no resource to bridge the gap. Now, more and more, having securely made the team, he would buy it if he only could. Would Tim Keagan tell him the secret? Could he learn to become a warrior by watching him? Did Keagan pray? If he quit partying would his performance be improved? Or would abandoning his bad habits leave him with no self-made excuse?

"I need Coach Franz. I need him now."

Chapter Twenty-Two

Back in Big Bear's chambers, hypothetical settlements were about to spew forth like offerings at the bazaar.

Big Bear was well prepared to suggest his own wise solution. "Well, I'm sure we would all like to avoid the precious time these men could and should be using for training. Do any of you have some proposals?"

Gannon began. "Well, Judge, we're prepared to consider any reasonable option. By the way Judge, before we get started I meant to offer you a ride on our firm's yacht when you come out to the Great Northwest. Puget Sound is gorgeous and you should consider visiting the San Juan Islands. Have you ever been there?"

"No, but I have looked into it and I'm quite sure that I will someday soon."

"Well, make sure you remember to look us up."

"By the way, Counsel. I've been meaning to ask you, do you know Mike O'Hallohan?"

"Oh sure! Iron Mike! Oh yes, how do you know him?" Gannon had to fake enthusiasm, in that he despised 'Iron Mike' who all too often had more judges sucking up to him than he.

"We graduated from Notre Dame together back in '59." He paused. "I guess my age is finally catching up on me. There aren't many out there like Mikey, are there, Fred?"

"Yeah, Iron Mike is a tough one. A helluva lawyer, Judge. A helluva lawyer! I'll say hello to him for you, Judge."

"That would be great."

Uncomfortable silence. I hope he doesn't call Iron Mike, thought Gannon. Well, hopefully the judge didn't catch his deceit. He shouldn't, his skill at it being so enviable. Gavin, on the other hand, twiddled his thumbs. What did he have to offer Griffey? A invitation to the Grand Traverse Bar Association Pig Roast? So he just sat there in the silence. Keagan would be so proud of him, he thought. Studious. Quiet. Focused. Going about business. Not about to concede a step.

That would soon change.

The judge broke the silence. "How about if you two talk about a settlement?"

Finally Gavin spoke, "Well, Judge, remember it is the Olympic Team they seek to enjoin. What about Leonard Franz?"

"Judge, let me intervene. If we can agree that Plank gets on the team we can drop our suit against Franz. It's only fair. Besides it is a little late to get another coach, realistically. If we can get Tim Keagan off the team, and our client back on, we'll be happy." Gannon laughed without a trace of humor.

Gavin finally erupted. "What has Tim Keagan done to you guys! Why Tim Keagan? You have no idea just how good a man he is!'

"C'mon Gavin..." said Gannon, who was doing all the talking.

"Don't call me Gavin. I don't know you well enough, even though I think I know you and your ilk too well. Still, don't call me Gavin." His blood pressure leaped.

"Gentlemen!" Big Bear, the peace-maker, resurfaced. "Gavin, er Counsellor Smith, would not Timothy Keagan rather settle this so that his sons are assured a place on the team? These are serious allegations – against all of them."

"Judge, I know we can say things in chambers that we can never say in court. But there is no justice in compromise. There is no justice back here. Ask Tim Keagan." And he walked out the door, went to Counsel table and waited, his head weighing heavily in his hands. He had nothing but truth with which to proceed, but who cared?

Tim Keagan came to his side. "So, what'd the judge try to cram down your throat?"

"Your neck."

"What did you say about that?"

"I told them to kiss my big black butt, brother."

"I suppose it's too late to fire you, Gavin. Just make sure your butt's on the ship going down with me. I hate drowning alone."

"Don't you worry. If we're going to get screwed our names are going down in history, securely."

"This is not the way I had hoped for, my friend. It's a good thing you're doing this pro bono."

"Well, Tim, it's like you always said, 'you get what you pay for'."

They both started laughing just as the Big Bear sauntered in.

The judge saw them, thinking they were grinning at him. He adjusted his robe. Their time will come, those Cheshire cats. They'll know their place.

Meantime, passengers were arriving at Kent County International Airport. The great debate between money and truth had resolved itself. Stu Weinberg could not sit this one out.

Chapter Twenty-Three

THE BEAR DID not like to work under pressure, if at all. The lifetime presidential appointment, once an honor, soon became a feifdom, and all who appeared before him were his subjects. He rarely displayed any qualities of a beneficent monarch. He did, of course, respect one thing – wealth. And among judges that trait was hardly peculiar.

The plaintiff Plank however was a curious anomaly to him. He was not wealthy; indeed he did not even possess the air of the wealthy. Yet, Paulson backed him to the hilt. The judge was inclined to let both Keagan boys, Cane, and Plank ski on the team. He had already devised a dozen logical reasons why it was "equitable." Everyone got something. The fact that Tim Keagan would be booted would be balanced by his own sons still getting to ski the third and fourth legs. Plank should make the team because, objectively viewed, he was the fourth best skier on the team. Sure, Tim Keagan beat him in the classic tryouts, whatever that meant, but the plain facts showed when the two techniques – skating and classic – were combined and their times totalled, Plank came out ahead of Keagan. Franz's decision to base the results on each style could be artfully deemed "arbitrary and capricious." Support for his findings would be amply supported by the fact that the Keagan boys bothered to race the final classic qualifier at all. Query: if they had already made the team in the skating tryouts, what legitimate reason did they have to be racing in the final classic race?

His answer: either A) to improperly aid their father, or B) it demon-
strated a "constructive waiver" by Leonard Franz in regard to the rules
previously promulgated which segregated the results of the two racing
techniques. Either way, Plank came out ahead. His desire though was
to strong-arm this most reasonable compromise. He wanted everyone
to leave his courtroom happy at the result, and impressed with his
Solomon-like wisdom. Then a little vacation to Seattle later this year
would be of no more interest to anyone than last winter's cruise on
that restaurateur's yacht in the Caribbean. Ah, compromise and con-
cession can be so rewarding!

But this Gavin did not seem so affable. And Tim Keagan didn't look
like the capitulating type. When his backroom strategy failed to
impress a settlement, he came out of chambers with a bullying growl,
and began preceding in his standard gruff, abrupt, and demeaning
manner. Invariably the focus of his scorn centered on the party reject-
ing his self-generated proposal. He thus became dubbed "Big Bear."
His intimidating tactics usually succeeded and when they failed, rare
was the time this Bear could be treed by the truth. He was deft at
becoming hung up on the issue in controversy, and his rulings reflected that trait. His decisions were properly decried as "result oriented" by
attorneys who dared to grapple with the Bear. To Keagan's advantage,
however, even the Bear had to follow the form of justice, if not its substance. So, a hearing had to be held, regardless. The hearing provided
Tim and Gavin a "record", that is, the recorded content of evidence
produced against them at the hearing, that they would have to rely
upon in expediting an appeal, as was common from Griffey's court.

This was the hearing Cane prayed to avoid. It was the hearing
where nothing could be proven.

"Brief opening statements, Counsel," he huffed.

Gannon began, having the burden. "Good morning, your Honor.
This Court is well aware of my client's position, contained in our pleadings. I'm certain this Court has read the memorandums of law we filed
with the Court today in support of our well-founded theory to enjoin
the Keagans from further participation on this winter's US Olympic
team. And in addition, your Honor, to enjoin Leonard Franz from act-

ing as Coach in these same Games. Why? In a nut-shell, Judge," Gannon's voice rose to fill the courtroom, and with an accusatory finger specifying each to their crimes, "they have violated the spirit of the Games themselves, your Honor, by fraud and by cheat, through conspiracy. Unethical behavior. Unsportsmanlike conduct, including not only an assault, but actual battery. Not only using insulting language, but bigoted and slanderous remarks. Because of their attack upon my client, a four-time Olympian, Mitchell Henry Plank, he has been denied the right he earned to make his fifth Olympic appearance, unprecedented in American history. And his coach, when fully advised of the circumstances which gave rise to this action, did nothing. In fact, his response was to laugh, derisively. Well, we know this court will not scoff at the severe moral and pecuniary harm that my client will suffer should injustice prevail even one step further in this matter.

"Your Honor, we know that anyone can make an allegation. We know that. But we are not afraid of the truth. We are fortunate in this case because beyond the sworn testimony of my client, Mitchell Plank, we will call Cane Paulson, Jr., who is better than a witness, Judge. He too is an Olympic skier – a world class skier who not only knows the rules of the sport, but was racing in this particular event, and what's more, heard and experienced exactly what my client suffered. He will testify that, but for Tim Keagan's reliance upon a race plan supported by his sons in a familial conspiracy, Plank would be our nation's classic style representative instead of Tim Keagan.

"Finally, we have photos which will clearly corroborate the testimony of both my client and that of Cane Paulson. These photos were taken by none other than Cane Paulson, Sr., who was on hand to watch his son's competition. He observed something very unusual occurring in the second half of the race, and using a telephoto lens was able to record in photo form a sequence of events showing Defendant Tim Keagan taunting the Plaintiff, and generally obstructing his race performance. He also personally observed Timothy Keagan assaulting Cane, his son, at the conclusion of the race, while that Defendant's two other sons stood by for their father's protection. Cane Paulson, Sr., your Honor, is a major contributor to this Olympic team, providing not only his gifted son, but a large amount of financial support through ForesTek, Inc. He has no bias, no interest except that the sanctity of the Games be preserved. He tried to work within the system. He pleaded his cause with Leonard Franz from the moment the race concluded to no avail. Then with the US Olympic Committee. Now he – now we – beg this Honorable Court to hear our cause, so that the American way, so that our notions of integrity and fair play, are not impugned in the coming Games. And we ask that those who would allow it to occur be removed from any representation of our nation at Thunder Bay, and to replace them with those who deserve to carry and follow in the footsteps of our flag bearers and act according to all it stands for, the values that have made our country – and its legal system – the envy of the world."

"What a loser," said Tim to Gavin, just loud enough to arouse others in the courtroom to remark, Did we hear him right? Gavin placed a supporting hand on his client's shoulder and proceeded to the podium.

"Good morning, Judge." He refused to call him your Honor. He paused. "Judge, what do my clients need to prove? Do they need to prove anything more than what has already been established in the proper forum, in the snow and on the trails in Utah, in Vermont, Wisconsin, New York, Idaho, and finally in Alaska? That is, they have proven they are the best three skiers on the Nordic team. Now, are they also required to advocate this established fact as a legal proposition subject to the equitable revision of this Court? I hope not. I do not pray for my clients, nor will I beg anything of you on their behalf. They have earned their standing on this team, in these Games. No, I pray in this place for these participants, in this game in this courtroom. Because that is what is happening here, make no mistake. There is no equity in dividing the truth by a lie. There is nothing more anti-American than the Government, especially an unelected judicial bureaucrat, meddling into the proper affairs and administration of organizations like the US Olympic Committee when they have violated no law of this nation, this or any other State, nor any rule of their charter."

The Big Bear bristled, interrupting, "Unelected judicial bureaucrat, Mr. Smith?"

"Yes, Judge, that is my exact phrase. I would be happy to expound, if you didn't understand its context."

"Were you referring to me, perhaps?"

"I am referring to the third branch of government, Judge, with the implication that even you enjoy only limited review of the lives of my clients, and it is my fervent hope not only to direct you toward that notion of limitation, but to instruct you how to appreciate the relief it would provide those in your profession if you just quit interfering with people's freedoms."

The Bear was steaming. He was being condescended to! By such a miscreant!

"I see you Judge. I can tell you're not happy. But you know you have no business hearing this case. I tried to tell you..."

WHAM! The Bear's paw slammed the dais. Then he immediately grabbed his gavel. BAM! BAM!

"Mr. Smith, I find you in contempt! And I'll have your license, trust me. Five thousand dollars or ten days in jail, your choice."

"I'll take the jail time, Judge. Thank you." Gavin had about given up hope. He didn't care. He would have an emergency appeal ready for filing before the judge even rendered his decision, so certain he was of losing. "Shall we wrap this up before you have me disbarred, Judge? My clients would prefer to resolve this matter."

"You have my word, Mr. Smith. We shall indeed resolve this matter today. I'll hold your contempt penalty in abeyance until the close of today's session!"

"Thanks, Judge. That's all for now."

"Mr. Gannon," the judge turned toward Gavin's adversary. He forced a big smile, the tension in his face masked with a gracious affectation. "You may begin with your proofs."

"Uh-humm!" came a loud clearing of Franz's throat.

Everyone's eyes quickly turned to the risen Coach Franz. "Sir, do I not also have an opportunity to outline my position to the court as well? I believe I am a party to this lawsuit."

"Mr. Franz, I am so sorry I overlooked you." Now the Bear's face blanched and changed a different shade of red. "Why, of course. Let the record reflect Mr. Franz is representing himself, in pro per." Now it was the judge's turn to be condescending. "Mr. Franz, I apologize for the way Counsel Smith has caused this Court to deviate from its regular course of proceedings. You certainly deserve to be heard, Mr. Franz, and I will be delighted to be apprised of your position. Also, I recognize you find yourself unrepresented by counsel. I note that apparently this is your own decision, and after hearing from Counsel Smith who is representing the Keagans, perhaps it is not so unwise as I first took it to be. However, if you should have any questions about procedure I would be more than happy to elucidate. You may begin."

"Well sir, thank you very much. Is it kosher to refer to you as sir?"

"You may." Kosher? I'm not Jewish. Is he?

"Well, that is mighty egalitarian of you, sir." Tim Keagan bit hard on the inside of his cheeks to keep from laughing, as it was apparent that Franz was no more intimidated by the Bear than Gavin. But Franz grew serious. "I've been perplexed by this suit in so-called equity. Now I don't pretend to be an expert in recognizing or understanding what justice is, just as I doubt sir that you are an expert in Nordic skiing. But just as you can figure out that someone who can't stand up on skis can't be much of a skier, so do I know and understand beyond any question injustice when I experience it.

"I am sixty-three years old. I am not about to sacrifice my life savings to defend my name in this suit. I've participated in the sport of cross-country skiing for fifty years as a skier and a coach. I won't belabor you, sir, with the details, but there are two things no one here can deny. One is my love for the sport and the other is my commitment to its traditions. So sir, it is absolutely essential for you to know the sport and to value its traditions before this forum can possibly resolve the issues before you.

"I would wish that you would take the time and make the effort to know what I know, what Tim Keagan and his two fine sons know about the sport. I would be more than happy to help you find a way. But I feel here today sadness, a great sadness, that the things I treasure are no longer subject only to the elements, the terrain, and the human will, but to carefully articulated positions and artfully drafted lies, in a place sir, frankly, so cold and inhospitable. You are concerned about individual rights. I am concerned about a team. The men who will comprise my team representing the United States of America have been selected on merit according to clearly defined rules, published well in advance of the competitions. And I could not possibly be happier with the outcome. You see, sir, the very thing Plank maligns these men for is their greatest strength – which is unity and a common purpose. The Keagans do ski better when they ski together. Does this fact therefore prove a conspiracy? What it proves to this old haggard coach is that they have heart. They did not just win, they conquered, as a family, as a tribe, as a clan, whatever you want to call it. It won't be so easy at the Olympics because we lack a fourth Keagan. Cane Paulson, Jr. must fill that role somehow. If he can, perhaps one day all of us may say we finally conquered as a nation in the Nordic world.

"So it is in your hands now, sir. You may rewrite the rules. You may appoint another coach in my stead. In the exercise of your sound judgment and discretion you may deny our nation's finest skiers their just reward.

"I do not know what words or what amount of proof will convince you. Like Mr. Smith's clients – my three best skiers – I am here also, having committed no wrong. It did not happen in Anchorage as it is alleged. I eagerly await the opportunity to swear in the name of the Judge who knows all to tell you so. For I am at an age now where there is nothing more to fear but His judgment, not the one Plank or his bankroller would have you render.

"And sir, if you should allow injustice to prevail, you may advise the keeper of your cell to leave me a space beside Mr. Smith, and to provide for a longer stay on my behalf. I do not anticipate you desire to be any less than impartial, but I do not know this law of equity. It frightens me. My meager research of it reveals an inclination in the law to lower the mountains and to raise up the valleys. However honorable that may be in the proper circumstance, I beg you to appreciate the difference between equality of opportunity in competition which is good and proper, and the futility of competition if at the end of it all the winner is determined in this arena, based on notions of equity. Indeed we may well eliminate sport, if not life itself. However, one thing is indeed certain to be established. Whoever you determine shall represent America at the Games on this team shall truly reflect the State of our Nation, sir. And that is why if my team is not there sir, I shall truly be honored not only to lose this case, but to be imprisoned in the interest of justice, rather than grovel and beg or to pray to any man or woman for anything that has been so nobly attained. Still, I have much more work to do. I have three defendants and a witness named against them to somehow come together in four weeks time. My guiding principle of this day is not the triumph of justice, sir. As I said, it is already unjust that we are here in the first place. I am here to assist in the defeat of injustice. That is still possible today, here in this room. I only ask that you help defeat injustice today. And you let me and my team work on the triumph of principle. That is what the Olympic Games are about, not about this – this – this garbage dressed up in flowery language," he concluded softly, with tremendous effect.

The courtroom fell momentarily eerily silent. The judge tapped the top of his pen twice, softly but deliberately, and looked briefly at the ceiling straight above him. A minute passed.

"You may proceed, Counselor," he said, in an authoritarian command to Gannon.

"The Plaintiff will call as its first witness Cane Paulson, Jr.," said Gannon, in a confident voice. The momentum reversed with Franz's excellent diatribe. Cane's testimony would get everything back on track. The key was evidence, not impassioned argument.

A reluctant but fluid athlete entered the courtroom and proceeded to the clerk to be sworn, raising his right hand. "Do you swear to tell the truth, the whole truth, and nothing but the truth, so help you God?"

"No, I cannot," he said in the meekest of voice.

The courtroom, about a quarter full, rumbled and murmured, just like in the movies.

"What's wrong with him?" Lisa asked the newly arrived Stu Weinberg in a low voice.

The Bear's blood pressure rose for the umpteenth time. His breathing became shallow and a pain in the center of his chest suddenly prodded him to already consider a recess. The Bear wanted to go into hibernation. Not even Judge Wapner had to deal with the kind of day he was having. I need to make this case go away, he thought. Suddenly, a cruise to the San Juan Islands seemed like the last trip he wanted to make.

"Counsellor Gannon," he said, removing his glasses, "is this your witness?"

"Uh, yes, your Honor."

"I am going to give you a recess for ten minutes. When we return, we are going to get right at the heart of this matter. I have all the time in the world. These men," he said motioning to the five skiers, "obviously do not. Off the record!" he said emphatically. "Young man, you will tell the truth, or you will be wishing you had," he said, pointing a finger at Cane.

"Oh, Judge, I intended to tell the truth, and I would like to swear that I would tell the whole truth, and nothing but the truth. And I have prayed to God about all of this, but I have to tell you that Mr. Gannon has already talked to me and..."

"Hold on, Mr. Paulson! We'll cover that when we return." Griffey tried cutting him off, but Cane continued.

"Judge, if I only answer the questions the way he asks them then I can't swear I'll tell the whole truth!" he said in a tense but polite assertion.

"Oh, I understand. Well, Mr. Smith and Mr. Franz also get to question you, and that is how you get to tell us everything."

"Oh, gnarly, Judge. Can I talk to them now during the recess?"

"It's up to you. Court's in recess." The gavel came down once more. "Gnarly!" he muttered under his breath.

Smith followed Gannon out the door. "Want a lifesaver, son?"

"Don't be so sure, Smith. I've pulled many a case worse than this out of the fire."

Suddenly a confident voice of dissent was heard.

"Not this time, Mr. Gannon. Remember me? Stu Weinberg. I think you had better call Mr. Paulson right now and drop this thing before you lose a big, big, big client."

Gannon wheeled toward Cane. "What did you do this time? What did you tell him?" he said, nodding toward Weinberg.

"Nothing!" he held his hands up.

"Then what is he talking about?" Paranoia struck Gannon deeply.

"Does the name Rodney King mean anything to you lawyers?" Stu said, hoisting an imaginary video camera to his shoulder, peering through an imaginary viewfinder.

Gannon's forehead began to bead perspiration.

"And here it is!" He displayed his evidence. Every lawyer's dream. A videotape. "How many minutes left? Five? I sure think Mr. Paulson, or ForesTek, Inc., might be just a little upset if the CEO's son had to walk the 'plank' if you know what I mean. Do you hear me, Freddy?" he winked quickly at Cane.

Cane piped in on cue. "I'll be...you found that guy who had the videocam!"

"He wasn't too hard to find. Hey, Coach, come here!" Stu yelled.

Around the corner came a rotund clean shaven man of about fifty. "Gentlemen, meet Coach Hazlewood – no relation to the Captain – from Anchorage East Catholic. The Coach didn't think this video was of much value until he read something about this little thing here. It seems that your client, Mr. Gannon, and, uh humm! – another skier not of Keagan descent seemed to have an incredible interpretation of the rules of Nordic skiing. Something very much like a conspiracy, it appears. Isn't that right, Coach Hazlewood?"

"I saw it all," he agreed.

"Well, I'll leave it at that. You might want to discuss with Mr. Plank the penalties for perjury."

Stu turned to walk away. "Here, go ahead, take this," he said to Gannon. "I have plenty more. I'll be down in the lobby with Coach Hazlewood. Mr. Smith, when you're ready to wrap this one up, let us know."

"Your name again?" a stunned Gavin Smith tried to assimilate just what was going on.

"Stu. Stu Weinberg. You may have heard of me. *Sports Unincorporated.*"

"Oh, yes. Of course. Stu Weinberg." He hurried back to tell his clients the incredible turn of events. Then shook his head, and asked himself once again, "Who is Stu Weinberg?"

Outside the sands of time continued to crash down like an asteroid shower. Gannon nervously held the tape, labelled "Anchorage 1-12." The day of the race.

Cane nervously asked, "I'm still going to make the team no matter what. Right, Fred?"

"I need to talk to Plank. Or your dad. Go get Plank for me, will you?" He turned to Kranwitz who had already called for the CEO.

"What did the chief say?"

"Fold them. He said 'good try'."

"I've been aced!" he seethed. In a nanosecond though, he seemed to regain his composure. He turned to Scarborough and shrugged. "Now you're going to see us at our very best. How to be caught dead to rights in a total lie and escape unscathed. Like I said all along, we had nothing to lose. Therefore gentlemen, hold your heads high!" He pumped his fist at his side and laughed. "Man, how I love this country! Gentlemen, first class all the way. This is going to be a righteous billing!"

All three laughed, and then putting on humble faces, proceeded into the hallowed hall.

They didn't even bother to consult Plank as they approached the defendants' table.

"Mr. Smith. Mr. Franz. After consulting with Mr. Pauls-...er, Mr. Plank, we have decided to withdraw our motion. With our nation's best interests at heart, Mr. Plank wants to put aside the differences between us and get in the spirit of the Olympics. No hard feelings?"

"Let's get it on the record first, Mr. Gannon. Then we'll talk." Gavin replied.

Tim Keagan was not satisfied. "You keep Gavin out of jail. He keeps his license. No jail. No fine. No sanctions, or no deal. Got it? We'll have the hearing otherwise and the truth will come out. It's Cane, isn't it? He chokes even when it comes to testifying. I knew it!"

Gannon sighed heavily. "I'll try to convince the judge to reconsider, Mr. Keagan. I'll do my best."

"I'm sure you will."

"Mr. Franz. Mr. Smith. Let's go tell the judge about our settlement," Kranwitz told them. Their house of cards had detonated.

"Settlement?" said Phil to Jerry.

"Maybe Cane's not so bad after all," Jerry replied. "This must have been his idea."

"Maybe, but he's still pretty scaly if you ask me," Tim said.

"Maybe he's shedding his skin," said Phillip.

"I hope so. I really hope so," said Tim. "It is our only hope."

"Dad, just let Coach Franz handle him. All we have to do is tag and be tagged," Jerry said in reference to the relay team.

Phillip weighed in. "You know, maybe he didn't choke after all. What did he say to the judge? Something like if he couldn't tell the whole truth he wouldn't bother to testify at all? That's a positive sign."

"He did show more guts than usual," observed Tim.

"And he wasn't hungover," added Jerry.

"Plus he is a super skier. If he only figures that out in time," Tim continued.

"Oh, he knows he is good. Too good to have to prove it, he told me once," Jerry laughed. "And he was absolutely serious!"

"I don't think so, Phil. He wants to want to win just as much as we do, I'm sure. But first he has to believe it is possible, because until he does, we can't," Tim reasoned.

They all became silent. Tim's poignant remark hit home like a bullet between the eyes. It was a whole new ball game. And they found themselves on the same team as a man as impossible as their dream. Still, the Irish are so forgiving – provided of course, that absolution is preceded by a good fight.

In chambers the Bear compulsively swallowed a second aspirin, just in case the symptoms were indicative of a higher limiting force upon his measure in life. As Plank's gaggle of attorneys descended upon him with Smith and Franz in tow, the Bear's spirits suddenly lifted. "Gentlemen?"

"Um, your Honor, with all due respect we would no longer like to proceed with this case," Gannon confessed.

"And your client agrees?" The judge began to breathe a bit more freely.

"Absolutely."

"And," Leonard Franz chimed in, "there is one other matter we need to address, isn't there, Mr. Gannon?"

"Oh, yes. Your Honor," he cleared his throat, "in order to avoid further possible litigation, you know, like a counter-suit, we would like you to reconsider your position vis-a-vis Mr. Smith here. Not that I condone his remarks, your Honor. But I don't think he meant to direct them at you personally. He was speaking in more abstract terms, at least I think our mutual recollections should reflect that."

The judge choked on that proposal, but he desperately wanted to put this baby to rest. He obviously had nothing more to gain by exposing himself to further attacks on his role in this case. He sighed heavily. "I'll have the court reporter re-read his remarks in chambers. You may well be right, Mr. Gannon. Things do get said in the heat of battle, I understand. Heh. Heh. I'll take that matter under advisement. Anything else Mr. Franz?"

"Yes Sir, I have two more conditions: One, an unconditional surrender, i.e. a written apology to me and the Keagans and to the US Olympic Committee, signed by Plank and his attorneys. All of them. Two, they pay all costs and expenses incurred by me and the Keagans, including all legal fees in defending this suit."

"This is an anomalous request, Mr. Franz," the judge opined.

"As I previously stated, I am here to see the defeat of injustice and I will consent to nothing until my terms are met, and I am prepared to continue in a counter-claim."

"That would require you to file a counter-suit, and even then attorney fees are not allowable," the judge noted.

"I don't have any anyhow, but the Keagans do." He looked at Gannon. "Pay or we play." He stared at the tape bulging from Gannon's ample pocket.

Gannon cleared his throat. "Your Honor, we can arrange an accommodation in this spirit of, uh, our current understanding of the situation." His fingers rechecked the dimensions of the jacketed tape.

It was still there, intact as Franz's demand.

The judge sighed again. "So then, is there anything else?"

"Not at this time, your Honor. By the way, would you care to attend our twenty-fourth Annual Grand Traverse Bar Association Pig Roast, Judge?" Gavin asked. "It's really beautiful up there that time of year!"

Just to appear fair, the judge was constrained to ask, "When is it?"

"July tenth."

He quickly looked in his schedule book filled with pages full of plans. From the Fourth through the tenth in each individual box was written the letters S-E-A-T-T-L-E. "Oh, I'm sorry. I'm due to be in, ah, Toledo that day, on business."

"Toledo, huh?" said a smiling Gavin Smith. Yeah right, Toledo. "That's a great place to be that time of year! Reminds me of my home-town Flint. Are you going to take in a Mud Hens game?"

Scarborough and Kranwitz looked at each other. Scarborough emitted an abbreviated attempt to suppress a giggle and quickly covered it by coughing. Kranwitz turned his head away from the judge, smiling and wincing, stroking his cheeks hard with his thumb and forefingers of his right hand, to keep from chortling at the remark.

"Well, Judge, in any event I'll be thinking of you there. Maybe next year?"

"I'll certainly look into it, Mr. Smith. Now, Counsel, could you explain how this disposition came about? And why I had to endure this needless litigation?" He was getting testy and Bear-like again. The aspirin worked. "It seems to me Mr. Gannon you are coming out a lit-tle short here."

"Well, umm," he stuttered, "Mr. Paulson – Senior, that is – has agreed to compensate Mr. Plank as if he made the team, and there would be no pecuniary damage claim in that regard at this point. And also, Mr. Plank has a sincere desire to get this behind him now so he may concentrate fully in his post-athletic career. It was, ah, a mutual decision. Plus, Mr. Plank informed us that it would not be fair to Mr. Paulson's son that he be implicated in a suit taking sides against poten-tial teammates. In retrospect, your Honor, my client is now convinced that he should put his ego and hurt feelings aside for the good of

America's cross-country program."

"Really?" Franz exclaimed. "Then he should have nothing to apologize about." He stared again at the outline of the tape. "You know, Judge, it's too bad that when we have a case like this we just don't have a tape that tells us everything. Don't you agree, Mr. Gannon?"

"Uh, well, Judge, I did not mean that my client shouldn't bear some fault in this. We will abide by all the terms discussed here and we are prepared to place it on the record immediately so these men can start preparing for the Olympics right away."

"Okay. We'll do that. But first let me take up the contempt matter. I won't need the court reporter. Upon my own recollection and reconsideration, I'll vacate that order in the interest of closing this file. Gentlemen, this order will be prepared by this Court today for entry. However, Mr. Smith, I want to have a word with you alone. Counsel, Mr. Franz, you may repair to the courtroom where we will place this agreement on he record."

After they filed out the Bear attempted to get his slice of justice, too. "I could have had your license easily Mr. Smith. You don't have any idea who you're dealing with. I don't ever want to see your face in this courtroom again. Is that understood? And don't bother me about pig roasts or anecdotes about Flint or Toledo. Just avoid me like the Plague."

"Well, its like this, Judge. To cure plague sometimes you have to stick your face right in it. You know what I'm saying? And if I have to suffer a little quarantine as a result, I am comforted by the realization that perhaps I might save a few lives in the process. And Judge, I know what I'm dealing with, if not who. And you are right. You are the Plague, a black-robed plague."

"Tell me, are you boys up in Traverse City this rude to all your judges?"

"Up in TC boys like me are as thick as flies. Your kind probably would be well-advised to stay away. And Judge, before we go back into court, zip up, okay?"

The judge looked down, draping his entire front, his robe, unzipped.

"Gotcha! Heh! Heh! Heh! It was a pleasure, Judge. And about the

Pig Roast you don't want me to bring up – we don't need you there after all, we already got one on order! Heh! Heh! Heh!"

The Bear watched him saunter out. Three more aspirin. "Jill!" he paged his secretary, "Get me two tickets to Cancun...No, as soon as you can...Just do it!" Click.

The agreement was put on the record, and all were eager to leave the Bear's den.

As they filed out of the courtroom, "Coach" Hazlewood tapped Gannon on the shoulder. "Could I have my tape back, please?"

Gannon hesitated. "Why not? This case is over." He gave back the tape.

Hazlewood handed it over to Franz.

And around the corner the brunette reporter reappeared. "Well, Father Hazlewood! You made it after all!" said Lisa Nelson. "Good to see you again. And how is the new addition to the high school coming back in Anchorage?"

"Well, Lisa, I just so happened to bring you a video of it. I reviewed it this morning. It sure will be exciting to have all the kids in one place."

"But still no kindergarten?"

"No, not yet, unfortunately. Just grades one through twelve."

Gannon looked around himself. Scarborough and Kranwitz were well ahead of him. He had been had! Out of instinct, he started back to the court to cry foul, when Franz intercepted him.

"Give it up, Gannon. Don't even think about it!"

"You bastards!" he snarled.

"Only the truth hurts, right Gannon? Don't worry about it. Your case was going nowhere. I only did this for one reason: My team," Franz said, still blocking his path.

"You got to him, didn't you?" Gannon spat in reference to Cane.

"No, Gannon. He came to me. He told me everything. I saved his butt by going to Weinberg. It didn't matter to you that he would lie under oath, did it?"

"That was a good trick you pulled with that tape. Whose idea was it?" He asked with feigned admiration, changing the subject.

"Actually, Gannon, none of us can take the credit for it ... Stu!

Where did you get that idea again?" Franz asked.

"I read it in a book written by another lawyer, actually. A fellow from Seattle, too. Maybe you've heard of him, a guy named 'Iron Mike' O'Hana-something."

"O'Hallohan! I'll be ...!" Gannon stomped, fuming inside.

"Yes, you probably will," opined Father Hazlewood.

"Thanks Father. Go, and sin no more," said Stu. Hazlewood's laughter could be heard, while singing all the way to the exit, "It's a small world, after all."

"Well, you got me this round, guys. But remember I also represent ForesTek in a little contract with you, Mr. Weinberg. This might have some bearing on it."

"It might. Especially when y'all learn I nixed your article. Oh, by the way! I returned your check as well. But don't worry. Cane's picture is going to be on the cover. In fact, when we leave here, we're taking a new one. With the Keagans. And with Franz. And this time we'll print what we should have from the start. But that's okay, because this story is a little more current, I would venture to say. And ForesTek, Inc.? Well, live and learn. One thing I have been fully apprised of is that not too many hikers think their pine plantations are very sexy. And salmon fishermen think their spawning streams filled with your silt are more important than our advertising revenue. I finally remembered it's not always about money, Mr. Gannon. But you know what is funny? You work hard and strive to live by your principles and you make enough, more than enough. And another thing I'm learning? If you don't have any principles, no amount of money will ever fill the void."

"Spare me your morality lesson, Weinberg. I could buy out your lousy rag the moment it goes public, if I wanted."

"But you'll be the same old Gannon. With just another toy to break."

"You know you guys really flatter yourselves. Like I really care. I'm just a hired gun. So don't get too excited about all this. I sure don't. I walk out of here no worse than I walked in. And you guys are no better off either."

"That's where you're wrong, Mr. Gannon." Franz interjected. "Today was greater than great. Injustice was defeated on your own turf. It's a spiritual thing, Gannon, strictly ethereal," he said, as he tossed the tape repeatedly heavenward, tumbling back into his waiting palms. "You may go now. You served your role most perfectly."

Gannon departed stiff-necked as ever. One thing was certain, neither Kranwitz or Scarborough would ever hear about that Catholic school, nor would the senior Paulson. Truly, it was another victory! He kept his true client's son on the team and saved him from a perjury rap. He smiled at that thought. And Franz thinks justice was attained. What a moron! We should all be disbarred, but tomorrow we'll all be around to pick someone else's pocket instead. But being a lawyer, he couldn't stand Franz having the last word. Just as he reached the exit, he turned and called loudly in a distinct voice.

"Oh, Coach Franz! By the way, I'm really looking forward to watching your team in the Olympics. What do you think? Can you move all the way up to thirteenth place? Ha, ha, ha, ha, ha!" And off he went, laughing all the way to the bank.

Chapter Twenty-Four

GAVIN, TIM, JERRY, and Phil headed north together on Highway 131. It wasn't a particularly long drive, only a little over two hours, but it was like a world away. The snow cover literally deepened by the kilometer and they arrived in Traverse City free men far earlier and easier than they ever dreamed possible.

As Gavin was backing out their drive after dropping them off, he noticed a rental car pulling in. It was Franz and that blond kid from Court – the Paulson kid. He had yet to talk to Franz about what happened back in Grand Rapids. What was he doing here? After what Tim had told him, he must have a lot of guts or stupidity to come to his house without an invitation. Perhaps fences could be mended, but he figured Tim was not the most forgiving of people, since he couldn't even forgive himself. His wife's death left a bend in his life that no other had been able to repair. But it had been a strange day. Maybe the time had come.

There wasn't much choice otherwise. The Games stared all of them in the eyes. Three and a half days later, Cane did not yet feel part of any Olympic family. It was only the Olympics, after all. Yeah, only the Olympics. Every athlete on Earth yearns for such an opportunity as his, and here he was in Traverse City, or someplace. He had been in Traverse City for half a week, but not much had changed, it seemed. Twenty-five more days like these last three and I'll be in the nut-barn, he thought. But Franz was plugging in new data. Stuff like compression strokes, skiing like a piston in an engine while climbing uphill, working harder but maintaining speed. He's not talking about winning, but about skiing better. He's not talking about pressure, but about focus; not about expectations, but about self-realization. The observation that without the mind, the body would never get to the top of the hill, but with too much thought one would never try.

"It is all about balance, Cane, and you must especially be balanced in your mind."

"What are you talking about?"

"You must be prepared Cane, not to race the race of your life, but rather to ski the race of the day. Do you understand the difference?"

"You keep trying to make me think it's just another race. It's not going to work, Coach. I couldn't ski thinking that way in the tryouts. I can't even ski the Birkie and keep my cool!"

"Why not?"

"If I knew I would get you a medal in Canada."

"I know, but your offer is not good enough."

"A medal is not good enough?"

"Oh, I'll take it. But you can't get it for me. Even if you race the race of your life."

"There you go again. My best is not good enough. You keep saying that," Cane replied, frustrated.

"Let me repeat. To endure, you must ski the race of the day. Why did you lose the Birkie? Blow the lead at the tryouts? Fall on the hill? Have nothing left when it matters most? You know why? It is because every big race you ski in becomes the race of your life. You are always under pressure. You are hoping for a big reward, but you are both afraid to earn it and refuse to accept the fact you deserve it. But what is more important for you to remember is that there is no award anyone else can give you that will surpass the feeling that your spirit led you where you should be, and finding it all so unbelievably easy."

"Spirit?"

"How modern man has come to ignore his spirit is the saddest commentary on our time, Cane. The fact that spirit exists is as plain as life itself and is as obvious a fact as being born and dying. I'm not even sure that our spirits are even individual entities, it may be a force on loan from God. But I do know some people who have come to engage their spirit. Tim Keagan is one."

"How do you know?"

"Because he is not supposed to be able to ski like he does. But yet, a guy like Keagan does not throw in the towel. You have to knock him out or go the distance toe to toe. You should and you can, but he shouldn't. If you engage your spirit – if you just disengaged your negative spirit – who knows?"

"Negative spirits, too?"

"Cane, when a race is over, why does the winner jump and yell and dance and party until dawn the next day, and the loser collapse exhausted? Shouldn't the one who worked harder to win be the more exhausted of the two? It is so obvious. The body is a conduit for a higher energy source, which must be trained, even in a spiritual sense. Spirit is a force all its own and its greatness to its vessel is determined by how wide you open the door."

"Coach, I'm sorry. This is way beyond me."

"Cane, it's way beyond me, too. Don't worry about that. My understanding of what lies ahead is so poor. I have a shorter time left to learn more about it than you, but I say this Cane, if you have fear, fear only God. Don't be afraid of yourself or any other man. If you can do that you have made a beginning."

"How can I fear something I do not know?"

The Coach laughed. "It is the easiest thing to fear. Think about it. Let's change the subject. Do you know now what I mean about skiing the race of the day?"

"Not yet."

"Well, I'm going to break it down for you. Come with me."

Chapter Twenty-Five

"WHERE ARE WE going?" Tim recounted for the first time to a stranger his deceased Nikola's inquiry. It was said in a happier voice. When dialog was still civil. When everything he desired took a back seat to her approval of him.

His confessor, Lisa Nelson, who completely ignored Gavin's advice to refrain from the subject, listened intently. The trial was over. But this was the real story.

"You'll see."

He was confident then that was the day. His day. Their day.

In his cooler he had not one, but two bottles of piesporter. Some clerk at an Italian wine store told him the basics about the labels and "qualitatswein." He learned quickly about how many were enough stars on the label to impress his date. His dormitory floor "buyer" was surprised to receive such a particular order, but Tim Keagan was excited about this girl. She was nobody's fool, but then neither was he. As a student, however, Tim bordered on financial poverty constantly, but in order to acquire things that mattered, he was most resourceful. And for this one, meals were skipped, the heat turned down, and he hoofed it where he needed to go. His car, eight years old, showing prominent signs of rust, was meticulously cleaned inside, showroom clean, for a date with Nikola. And with the money saved by forfeiting things even welfarians took for granted, he was able to give her some small measure of due compensation in exchange for the priceless gaze of her green eyes meeting his. Indeed, Tim was in every respect a romantic; half-starved with a passion for exotic beauty. He was full of spirit, content to be poor and to live as a bohemian. If only a woman he loved could be so cool. Nikola? Who else had her skin, her body, her allure?

So what does a poor romantic do on a summer weekday afternoon date with a woman with whom he had played tag with long enough? Tim knew her venue well. Though she attended another university, Tim was no stranger to Mount Pleasant. And where else to take her, but among the flowers of early summer in the field, lay out a blanket, and muse of life? And best of all, spanning the Chippewa River, a covered bridge. If further enticement was required it could be found while traipsing along the path where they would encounter two swinging bridges. The plan was perfect. And so was the day. He had never been so right about everything, and humbled into submission, was fate itself.

Tim knew Deerfield Park better than did Nikola. Though he attended Michigan State University in East Lansing, one hundred kilometers away, he skied the same park the previous winter and was impressed by its attractive setting, and summer's effect was even better than he had hoped for. He had just completed his sophomore year, and was all of nineteen. Nikola was only a freshman at Central Michigan.

"Funny, I can't remember a word we said to each other. Not one," he continued. "Yet I remember being so happy. Everything was so new. You know, total independence. Anyhow, both bottles of wine were emptied. But I was intoxicated by her far ahead of the wine. I know it was the day I had made up my mind to be patient with her because I knew instinctively this could be serious fun. And it was."

"Within a year, we were married." Tim laughed, "And I thought that was patient enough." In two, he was a father. He was an adult. He had his degree. He was raising a family. His associates in law school seemed so juvenile and immature.

"Was it worth it? Bad question." Lisa knew better, and had corrected herself instantly.

"You mean was it worth it because she died so young?"

Lisa hung her head. "Sorry. I can't believe I asked that."

"That's okay. I've been waiting to have this conversation with a woman like you for an eternity. I've formulated a million different answers in my mind for such an occasion. So I might even be surprised by what answer I might give to some of your questions."

"And...?"

Tim looked straight through her, soul to soul. "It's always worth being patient, perhaps that is why I waited until now to allow someone to ask me about it all."

Lisa smiled, blushing like a school girl. He was attracted to me after all! What eyes! She wanted to look into him too, but she didn't, she couldn't. Not yet. She had business. Besides, this was not the first time she interviewed a man who captured her fancy – but his age, and his accomplishment at his age – most of her subjects were younger, far younger than her. Well no, it was just as much her age. She was thirty-four, almost thirty-five. She hypothesized: If I took out a personal ad would I answer this man's response? No contest.

Tim talked more of Nikola. Perhaps all courtship is idyllic. Well, of course it is. Why can't life be full of that feeling you have when you are young and in love?

"Well, I became impatient after all. In hindsight I guess I always was," he continued. "Perhaps I had nothing left to conquer but her ego. I don't know. But things were not good at the end, especially on the day that she died."

He told her all; well, almost all. She understood. That he would quit skiing made complete sense to her Catholic notion of penance. His practice of law? Gavin carried the ball for awhile. Tim, a natural competitor, could have and should have been one of the great trial attorneys in Northern Michigan history, but ironically he specialized in what, for him, must have been extremely tedious work in family law. He never had a case where his inclination was to do battle but, insofar as possible, to resolve disputes peaceably. Occasionally, he succeeded in reuniting families, instead of helping to divorce them. But for Nikola dying, there was little doubt he would have divorced her in the end, he told Lisa. It was so clear to him now, he said, that that would have been the only thing worse than her death; it would have been the triumph of selfishness, adorned with medals and shelves of trophies. But where would his sons be? Not likely competing in the Olympics. And of a hypothetical ex-wife? What sin did she commit? Gaining fifteen kilos by becoming a mother? Big deal. Experience in his practice showed the most successful weight loss program begins with the filing of a divorce action. Nikola would have lost it in a month. "She would not settle for less than love, but I would have, at that time."

"When did you realize you loved her? I mean…"

Tim laughed. "Lisa, do any of us know what real love is? As far as I can tell it is mutually consenting adults putting up with a lot of childishness, substantially."

"Not exactly 'Love Story' material."

"I said substantially. The rest is better than any story; anyhow you tend to forget the bad parts."

"Were you in love?"

"Did I love Nikola? Yes, even now. But it is an entirely different feeling. But as far as being in love? I love aspects of things, of people. 'In love' connotes an impossible relationship with another. To love and to be in love are two very different circumstances. Yes, I always loved Nikola, from the beginning to this very day. But I was only 'in love' with her when I learned I would never experience her again. There is nothing left to dislike; there never should have been in life either, but I found plenty – believe me. And it is the same now with me and other people. I try to be perfect, but I keep seeing me in the mirror. This is me, live and unplugged. How about you, who do you see in your reflection?"

"Hmm. Okay. Fair is fair. I see a story, incomplete, but going places. Working on another chapter. How's that?" she answered, inspired by her upbeat analogy.

Tim remained quiet, and gave it thought in the context of a relationship, stroking his chin. "Lisa, don't take offense. But what if your story ended right now? This is the thought I have lived with for almost twenty years. I had a chance to let someone in mine who gave me the youth of her life, something now I know is so precious. But Nikola's story ended in the middle of a sentence in the first real chapters of meaning. Yeah, I was in her book, to the very last word. I referred to her as 'bitch'."

"But what about now, Tim Keagan?"

"Skiing is the easy part of my life. Practicing law? After these Olympics I'm going to step on some toes. The Griffeys and the Gannons better think of retiring soon. There are too many lawyers around these days to put up with their way anymore. Like anything else, change starts at the bottom, and its coming, like a volcano on the verge of eruption. But that's another day. You know, this is a pretty strange interview for a story on cross-country."

"This is better than talking about glide wax and technique, don't you think?"

He looked into her eyes. Suddenly he realized what was happening. "Hey! Are you going to put all this stuff in your article?"

"Well, if I don't Mr. Tim Keagan, let's just say I'm just working on another chapter in my life's story," she answered, just provocatively enough that Tim allowed himself to ask what had been on his mind since their first encounter.

"So, do you have someone special, a boyfriend?"

"Nothing steady," she lied, but instantly it became the truth.

"Well, would you care to continue this over dinner?"

"Sure."

"I should find out what you skiers eat."

"Usually we search out buffets, if that is any clue."

She laughed. At last she may have found a man who could probably consistently out-eat her, but even that remained to be proven. "Okay, well you're the expert. You're the TC man."

"Well, I'm going to show you the Traverse City that once was, and still is, if you hang with me."

"I'll take you on."

"Sleder's. At seven. But don't keep me out too late. I would like to be home by two or three with the Games and all."

Sleder's is one of Traverse City's oldest and finest food and drink establishments. Located on Traverse City's southwest side, it is set apart from the busier downtown streets. Along with its white wooden slat siding, the interior decor meets with the approval of the curious visitor, being adorned simply, but invitingly: a bar with character, several booths and tables, and walls strewn with wildlife trophies of fur and fowl. The prices are reasonable, the food satisfying, and the atmosphere convivial. And they served Guinness Stout. Conversation abounds, and Tim and Lisa were no exceptions to the rule. Everything about Tim's seduction was conducive to trust, possessing the air of tradition and dignity, without pretense. There was nothing phony about the person or the place.

Over a dinner of lake perch, Lisa attempted to examine Tim's reputed psyche. She was well aware something haunted him, but it was just as clear that he somehow domineered, persevered, endured – if only one step ahead of it all. He was a man who appeared to her to have lived many lives – not all content – but in all refusing to submit to calumny. And now that he had made the team, was he satisfied at long last his ghosts were behind him? Would love follow? Could he allow for it? If so, when would that time be?

Tim thought nothing of the ambience, perch, or Guinness. He became transfixed by Lisa. Her smile. Her hair. Her scent. Her voice. Her skin. Her body. Her allure... He was in the midst of his deepest, most relaxed conversation with a woman, well, maybe in his entire life. Tim reached across the table and touched her hand, to hold it. He reached for her unconsciously, unintentionally, naturally, if you will. When he touched Lisa, he recoiled instinctively, as if suddenly awakened from a deep slumber.

"I'm sor-."

Before he could apologize, Lisa ran her fingernails lightly under his palm before taking his into hers. And they looked into each other like a mirror giving its greatest reflection.

She thought to herself. He knows. And he knows that I know. So what are we waiting for? But if he thinks I'll settle for a sip of wine less than Nikola he is out of his Nordic mind.

Chapter Twenty-Six

TIM KNEW THAT Cane should have been expelled from the Games. He, above any other, should not have been able to rest comfortably given the fact Cane was in *pari delicti* with Plank. Though Cane did in essence make a full confession, earning redemption in a spiritual realm perhaps, his Anchorage escapade remained an anathema to Tim's sanctimonious vigilance over the purity of the sport. The fact that it occurred in an Olympic setting only exacerbated his own sense of self-serving compromise.

But what other American was capable of rounding out the team? There was no one. He would live with Franz's decision to leave him on, but keep his distance. Still, he couldn't understand why Franz was so adamant about Cane's inclusion.

Tim's hypocrisy was grounded in the remote possibility of medalling in the 4x10K. Maybe Franz was thinking that, too. Even so, just as he told his sons on the drive back from Alaska, there was something about Cane that fostered – that evoked – his adoption within the Keagan fold. And so when Tim didn't dwell on the matter it almost seemed natural that they remain together until the end, moving through the sands of time with no chance of escaping a mutual fate.

Franz, though, was in his element. The four best American skiers since Koch, all of them half the time with more mental obstacles than physical. At least he thought they were great, and no one could persuade him otherwise. He had already predicted to himself likely finishes for them in their individual events. Jerry would finish in the top ten in the 30K free, and so would Phil; Cane just behind – a phenomenal finish for the Americans, but there would be no medal. But that would serve notice to the Nordic powers that the Americans had arrived. Finally.

In the 10K classic and 15K free pursuit however, he would have to be satisfied if even one skier could crack the top ten. The 10K is a timed event, and even if Tim Keagan chose to ski in it, it was not his forte. When skiing head to head, his stubbornness kept him in the lead packs, but the pursuit race is a different matter. Jerry and Phil were his best bets, but realistically they would be ecstatic to finish in the top twenty in classic and top ten in the pursuit. And Cane? All Franz hoped for was a strong finish. Most of all Cane had to convince himself that the 10K is a walk in the park, and get ready to go all out in the relay.

Phil and Jerry, from outward appearances, were the positive, stable competitors Franz needed. And they were just that, in fact. But as the day of the Games approached, Franz began to entertain an entirely creative approach to his 4x10K team – his dream team. Almost insane, actually. He had convinced himself a medal was possible, if he could convince the Keagans of his concept. He dared not present it until it would be too late to protest. He, at age sixty-three, had butterflies just imagining the scenario that he kept to himself. If it worked, his life's goal as a coach might be met; if not, well, it wouldn't be pretty.

Franz assembled the quartet of skiers in his suite at the Grand Traverse Resort. It was a marked improvement over the trailer in Anchorage. The Olympics were less than a month ahead.

"Gentlemen, as hard as it is, as impossible as it is, I need to lay it all on the line. Right now, while you all are present."

"Lay what?" asked Phillip.

"I need a team at Thunder Bay. I have to be honest with you. I don't think we're capable of winning a medal in the individual events. But there is no nation in the world that has four skiers who are as good. I would like to concentrate on the 4x10K.

The three Keagans and Cane all smiled awkwardly at Franz's supposition. How could a sixty-three-year-old man who knows better even utter such blasphemy? Franz took notice of their soft chuckling.

"Well, you might not think so, but I do. And you won't talk me out of it. You can prove me wrong if you want to. I can't stop you from that. But I'm telling you I won't quit on you until the race is won. All I ask is the same promise from all of you. Any objections?"

No one answered.

"Okay. Let's deal with Plank. I don't want him on the team as an alternate. He is off the team. We are the only ones going north."

"What if one of us gets injured?" asked Cane.

Franz laughed. "Then I'll ski. I have more desire." He paused. "What if two get injured? Three? Four? What if the snow melts like it almost did in 1995 at the World Championships? You four are my skiers. I can't engage in negative analysis. And neither can you. Now let me tell you why I believe in you."

Franz discussed with them the competition they would find in Thunder Bay. All agreed that this year no clear favorite for the men's 4x10K had emerged. Most likely it would be a tactical race throughout, albeit at twenty-five kilometers per hour. If they could just somehow become part of their slipstream...

They listened attentively. Even if it was possible, the end came down to guts. If only the last leg was to be classic instead of freestyle and Tim could be the anchor...

"All four legs are equally important. When it is all over you'll know why. But, I will tell you now." He described a principle known as synergy.

Franz knew Tim Keagan to be the perfect catalyst, but he was worried that Cane's performance might not carry his momentum into the all important third leg, but he dared not express that doubt here.

"Cane?" he asked, "Do you understand what I'm talking about?"

"I think so. It's like skiing out of my mind, right?"

Franz beamed. If only he would ski out of his mind. If only he did not think. But bad habits are such convenient roads. But he had heard the beginning of wisdom.

"Yes! We must all ski out of our minds. And in so doing, we must be mindful of one another. We must not think of our self, but of ourselves. If we do this, we can ski beyond ourselves and our own limitations. This is the essence of teamwork. We cannot win this race as a relay of individuals."

Franz needed one more development – unity. And what better way to bring together a disparate people than to coalesce against a common enemy and to declare war? Perhaps this is why it is said to pray for your enemies and thank God for them. But for now the biggest enemy was time and reality. And their biggest ally was fantasy. So he had decided to bring fantasy into fact. And Franz had the perfect recipe for dealing with the necessities of preparation. The next two weeks his team would train hard. Harder than any he had coached before. Finally, in the absence of an enemy you could put your finger on, could the Keagans and Cane become part of the same chain? Cane had made the necessary initial overtures and he sensed a thaw in Tim Keagan's attitude toward him. But he had to see more.

Franz's time tested solution would again be called upon – work. And he would not leave the Traverse City area. He smiled, almost sadistically, on account of the surprise he had in store for them. While the few American Nordic pundits would question the wisdom of his choice, it would soon be made apparent to his team.

The drive was a familiar one for the Keagans. Heading west on M-72 across the dormant cherry orchards and windswept fields that bisect the Leelanau peninsula, they were somewhat surprised Franz settled on this venue for their first practice together.

But as Franz drove the Club Van past each and every trail system, they began to question his destination. It had to be Shaugar Hill at the National Park. It was the only climb remotely comparable to what they would encounter at Thunder Bay.

"Coach, maybe we ought to train up in the Canadian Soo. It's not that far," Jerry suggested. Shauger Hill was tough, a very tough climb, but had too many switchbacks compared to the straight on power climbs Thunder Bay would demand of the Olympians.

"Oh I think we'll be okay." said Franz. "But if this proves too easy, we'll head north," he answered. "We'll see how we'll feel in the morning."

The Keagan boys snickered.

"What's so funny?" Cane whispered in back not to attract the ear of Franz.

"I know how I'll feel in the morning," answered Phillip in a low tone. "Like we wasted yet another day."

Franz heard it, but pretended otherwise. "We'll see," he muttered.

"Huh?" said Tim, oblivious to their secret quibbling.

"Uh, I'm sorry. Let's see. We're almost here." So it was Shauger Hill. The Keagans were not excited. Tomorrow they would have to move on. With or without Franz.

Shauger Hill was no huckleberry. It was a good interval training hill, one kilometer in length. When all five got to the top, Tim had to tell Franz.

"Len, this is a pretty good climb, but you know we – not Cane though – skied Big Thunder. Uh, this isn't going to cut it."

"Oh. I'm sorry I didn't know you considered that a hill." Franz played with him. "We're going over there." He pointed northwest.

"Thunder Bay?" asked Jerry.

"No. Just over there. Follow me."

The Keagans didn't know what Franz was talking about. He must have gotten bad information from some local. There was no trail of any significance that way.

The five skied together along the trail for a couple of kilometers, when Franz suddenly stopped.

"Where the hell are we?" asked a stupefied Cane.

Franz pointed due west. "There!"

Cane skied in that direction. Soon, he saw nothing but horizon. "Oh, my God!" he exclaimed, and not in vain.

Phillip screamed, "You mean we're going to ski the Mother?"

"Mother is right!" insisted Paulson.

The five lined up on the precipice of the massive bluff which rose one hundred fifty meters high out of Lake Michigan at an extreme forty degree slant, adding considerable distance to the heartbreaking climb. One could search the world and not find a greater freshwater dune. It is the biggest and was steeper than anything they would find at Big Thunder. The great lake had not yet frozen over and giant waves crashed silently into the ice forming along the shore far, far below them. As far as they could see was the blueness of the reflected sky, even in winter, though huge ice flows bobbed in the seemingly infinite sea.

Sleeping Bear National Lakeshore is a ten kilometer square system of dunes and bluffs rising out of the great freshwater lake. What they referred to as "the Mother" is the steepest and highest climb in the park, straight up the Lake Michigan bluffs. It was indeed worthy of the title; it is higher and steeper than the Great Sleeping Bear Dune located to its immediate north, overlooking North and South Manitou Islands. Many summer vacationers find themselves spending the better part of an afternoon negotiating the climb.

Perhaps the Canadian Soo would have been a more practical pre-Olympic training site. But Franz wanted a place that would inspire fantasies in their hearts – no, it was more than that – he wanted a vista of the eternal, of magnificence, of the handiwork of God Himself. No one could come to this location and walk away without a visceral understanding that a bigger force was operating, commanding all that we see, feel, and experience. In particular, he wanted Cane to know the beauty in great works, the reward of sustained discipline, and the interrelationship of each. And besides, they were about to do something no living being had done before, and they were about to do it over and over, again and again, until the snow and ice clad mountain of sand and gravel became a mound. Then there was time, too. Time. Especially time.

The Keagans had been here before, but it still inspired awe in them. They stood there, speechless, until finally they looked below them and saw a groomed trail going straight down disappearing into a point a few hundred meters below.

"Who was the sickee who groomed this?" Tim asked, astonished.

Franz cleared his throat. "Well, I did."

"They let you do this?" Jerry exclaimed.

"Yeah, it was a bitch finding cables and winches to secure the groomer, but that was nothing compared to the disclaimers I had to sign and the insurance I had to buy. You know they wouldn't want to, uh," he cleared his throat again, "get sued." After a pause he continued, "Well on alternate days this is where we'll be, as long as you find it tough enough."

Cane, still in shock, asked, "So, how do we get to the bottom of this mother? I'm not going straight down! No way!"

Mercifully, to the south Franz cut a long sloping switchback to the bottom. "Hopefully we won't have an avalanche," Franz comforted them. "Otherwise we should be okay. You know, they tell me you guys will be the first skiers to ever descend and ascend the dune," he said with the enthusiasm of a parent about to administer a dose of bitter medicine.

"Great," Phil deduced, "we're all about to defile the virgin muh–." He stopped mid-sentence and immediately looked skyward. His Catholic wit was sometimes too keen for his soul's good. "I was referring to the dune here," he told his friends in a low tone. He was not about to spiritually jeopardize his teammates.

It almost seemed a shame to Franz that his boys were compelled to hurry up the summit which took eons to form. But, in philosophical terms, Franz was not concerned with speed so much as accomplishment. He was yearning for attitude; for evidence of teamwork. It was simple to him. In a head-to-head race like the 4x10K, time only mattered if you couldn't keep up with the leaders. If you can, you are fast enough. Franz repeated this notion over and over, day after day. Time was ego; staying in the race was teamwork; winning was making it to the top. So, after one day he put away the stopwatch, and paired various combinations, one against the other, alternating classic and skating techniques.

They titled their nemesis "the Mother" with just cause, for indeed Indian folklore so dubbed the dune system centuries before. Nearly every Michigander is familiar with the tale – The Legend of the Sleeping Bear, after which the National Park is named.

Many years ago a great forest fire swept across Wisconsin's north driving an escaping sow and her two cubs into the great lake. The mother managed to swim the entire distance across to Michigan, and turning back, she awaited the arrival of her cubs. But they were not strong enough to go the distance, and drowned within view of the land their mother reached. The two cubs became what are now called the North and South Manitou Islands, and their mother became the dune known as the Great Sleeping Bear, who rests there forever, waiting reunification with her cubs.

A Washingtonian, Cane had never heard the story, and as Coach Franz related it to him, he couldn't help but think of the two islands he saw every other day as his younger teammates, and felt sympathy in his heart that they had lost their mother so young in life. Cane's mother was his one source of love, of comfort, of constant hope. His father was so domineering, considered by his peers as a man of great accomplishment, but his mother had always been the parent with the carrot, not the stick. Funny, it also was his mother who physically disciplined him, who punished him for misbehavior. But those occasions were rare in comparison to the nurturing she bestowed.

Franz listened intently to Cane. Unwittingly, Cane was describing the good mother in nature.

He told Cane his observations of the animal world. "Bears, lions, dogs, cats – all of nature – begin life with a harsh reality. The offspring of bad mothers do no survive to pass on their genes to a new generation. This rule is universal, excepting humans, of course. But what happens to children today who have mothers unfit by nature?"

Cane told him about his father. About how he bailed him out of trouble. Escaping punishment he deserved from institutional authorities. How, really, he has never had to work a day in his life. Hard skiing was the only challenge he ever knew.

"You know what you are, Cane?" Franz asked.

"What?" Cane answered diminutively, anticipating an unglamorous appraisal.

"You're an underachieving glorified welfare recipient. True, you're not on the public dole. But you're able bodied and minded and you're living off big daddy – aren't you?"

Cane assented, embarrassed by the analogy.

"You know, Cane, a little help is not a bad thing. A little assistance, a little advantage never hurt anyone – until it becomes a way of life.

Then it hurts the recipient most of all." Franz again pointed to the animal world for proof of his beliefs. "Look at them – even the wild animals. Sea gulls, bears, raccoons, squirrels, birds, chipmunks. If you provide feed for them, they'll come back everyday. Even at a garbage dump. But if you stop, they don't crawl off into a corner of a forest and die. They get busy, go out, and compete as God intended. It is no different with you or anyone else."

This information made sense to him. For the first time he was growing into a separation from his father. Every other day at that climb of climbs, he was looking down at his own two feet taking steps to reach the top. And he was making it on his own, but with the encouragement of his peers and of an authority figure with more credibility than his father.

Franz was pleased with what he saw, but what he couldn't see begged his reticent curiosity. They were no longer calling the bluff "the Mother;" instead they called it "Franz's little girl." But did they believe? Would they fight for one another? Would there be synergy after all?

Chapter Twenty-Seven

ANOTHER WEEK PASSED in Traverse City. Franz managed to ensure that all four skiers at week's end felt solid again. On alternate days they were put to the test in long distance training on the Vasa trail, which to them, after skiing the Mother, seemed as easy as gliding across a golf course. At Sleeping Bear National Park, Franz continued to demoniacally require them to repetitively climb and descend the one kilometer trail at Shauger Hill as well.

Then it was back to "Franz's little girl." Paulson, clear headed, sober, and relaxed was climbing the dune over and over impressively.

"Go at seventy-five to eighty percent, Cane!" yelled Franz.

"Okay, Coach!" he screamed back, as he continued his skate uphill.

Franz yelled back, "I said, seventy-five to eighty!" He muttered to himself that Cane's heart rate must be maxed out.

Cane purposefully slowed his pace, turned and yelled back, "How slow do you want me to go?"

"I want it aerobic this time, so you can converse!"

Tim Keagan laughed. No being in the universe could climb the Mother aerobically.

"What do you think I'm doing?" he turned and finished his long climb. He carefully descended where Franz met him at the bottom.

"Okay, now one hundred."

"No problem. Skate?"

"That's what you have on," Franz answered, meaning not to

change skis from skate to classic.

Up Cane went. Uphill skiing separates the out-of-the-medals skier from the bronze, the bronze from the silver, and almost always the silver from the gold. Sprints to the finish do occur, and so do downhill falls, but it's the technique on the uphills that provide the quick promotion to the elite level of cross-country skiing. Just as the Boston Marathon has its Heartbreak Hill, Nordic skiing also has many of its own legendary climbs.

Franz watched him go up in the freestyle form. Entire books have been written about the art of proper skate-skiing techniques. For a mass audience it is best to think of it as being similar to roller blading with poles. Skating when using simultaneous pole plants is called V-2 or V-2 alternate, depending whether the plants are made with each push off motion or on alternate skates. A V-1 skate is typically used in climbing hills where more power from the upper body is employed to assist in skating uphill. The pole plants are not necessarily simultaneous, but may be slightly out of sync in the V-1 technique. As the incline steepened, he changed from the simultaneous pole plants of the V-2 skate to the slightly out of sync V-1 plant, using a left hang arm. As the hill's elevation increased he shifted to a right hang arm, meaning his right arm hangs higher than the left where more force is generated from the push off. It is grueling work, and even the greatest can find all their energy sapped in a effort to keep an even pace. About two-thirds the way up Cane was compressing at the waist, bringing his hands well past his belt line, his rear end swinging back almost sitting on his skis. On the upswing he brought his free leg well forward, as if his feet and skis were attached to his hands and poles by a string.

"I've never seen anyone drive that low before. Where did he come up with that?" Franz asked Jerry.

"Why did he?" asked Jerry. The technique was just plain awful.

After his ascent, Cane came screaming down the alternate trail. Coach Franz asked him the same question.

"I just thought about how to get uphill faster. This technique seemed to be the only thing that would work."

"By persisting with the plant until you bring your hands past your knees?"

"It actually forces me to think forward, or else I would lose my balance. What I am trying to do is get parallel to the slant of the slope on every beginning stroke."

"Like throwing yourself uphill?"

"Yes, as I straighten out."

"But I don't see the advantage."

"It works for me as long as I don't force it." He paused, picking up on the fact he was convincing no one. "Well, how else am I supposed to climb a mother like this!" he shouted in exasperation. Everyone laughed. Cane did too. It was apparent to all of them what they were doing was insane to begin with.

"Well they definitely have more like her at Thunder Bay," Franz said as a sobering reminder. "It just looks awkward, Cane," he softly concluded in an effort to assuage him.

"I know, but for me it's easier on the steep grades. Easier and faster."

"Skiing uphill by leaning back?"

"No, by angling up and getting forward, with a low center of gravity at the push up phase, for more active power."

"Well, stay with it. Everybody thought Bill Koch was crazy too. Your improvement can't be denied." Franz tried to convince himself. Paulson looked like a monkey climbing a banyan tree. Somehow he just couldn't picture a racer like Silvio Fauner picking up the technique...Maurilio DeZolt, maybe, but this was a new generation, one that even the seemingly ageless "Cricket" could not bridge.

"Okay, let's try some classic climbs," said Franz, changing the subject as well as technique.

"More herringbones up the freaking half-dome," Tim mumbled. Keagan's heart and head were not in the day's training session. Perhaps it was the lack of real competition, or the after-effects of the aborted mini-trial, but he knew he looked mediocre in comparison to the others, and he seemed to slip often on the climbs. Still it was only one session. Even to Tim, Franz was a father figure, and the benevolent coach asked Tim to ride back to Traverse City with him when practice concluded.

"Was there something wrong out there today, Tim?" Franz's question snapped the daydreaming Tim Keagan back into the moment.

"No, Len. I guess I just want to get it over with. I think I'm just anxious."

"Well, I'm not. I'm going to bask in every second of it. I know I'm not coming back again, Tim. You know I even had a glorious time at that stupid excuse for a trial."

"I wish I could say the same."

"When you are my age maybe you'll have a different perspective. Anyhow, what's bothering you?"

"You know, being so close, so very close to a goal I had twenty years ago, and then realize how crazy a notion it was after all. Here I am, depending on my own sons, my kids. I changed their diapers it seems like only a year or so ago. Paulson's still listed as a dependant on his father's tax forms, I would bet. These boys don't know what they're up against. It is just beginning to occur to me, too."

"Well, I agree to some extent. But Cane isn't exactly a novice. He has more international experience than you, Jerry, and Phil combined. Sure, he hasn't done anything, but he has never skied in a relay. Maybe he'll catch on fire. He sure was looking good today. I think he's peaking just in time. I can't have any of you guys thinking negatively. If Jerry and Phil see you ski anything less than your best, it will ruin them. Do you know that?"

"Yeah, that scares me."

"And when you talk about them being so young, remember you're the weird one here. Everybody out there competing against them are closer to their ages than yours. Think about it. And another thing about your kids; they're not intimidated by the Europeans, or anyone for that matter. I think they picked it up from their old man."

"Well, not yet anyhow. I've kept them pretty naive."

"I don't think they're going to be. They know exactly what their mission is. They're not going to Thunder Bay to check out Mount McKay or Old Fort William. They want to bring back something heavy hanging from their necks. I feel good about this team. I feel it in my bones."

Tim thought about it. But Lisa was on his mind, too. She was going to the Games. The Games Tim promised to his wife; his ultimate redemptive act. Just getting to the Olympics was once enough, but now it meant nothing. He too desperately wanted miraculous intervention. Could his sons overcome any gap Paulson might leave them and still medal? Or could all four of them ski their greatest ten kilometers together and still come in ninth?

"Coach, I'm almost afraid to say it but..."

"You want gold?"

"Yes I want gold. That's probably one reason I skied so poorly today. I am thinking way too much. Here I am forty-three years old. My sons – I think – look at me like a tough old bird, and I suppose I am, but I really am beginning to feel pressure like I've never felt. I fantasize about winning the gold just about every moment of the day. How ignorant can I get? Then in the next moment I can see it collapse entirely and us finishing fourteenth, just like that shyster Gannon said to us after the hearing."

"Thirteenth. Anyhow the time to talk is now. So tell me what is on your mind."

"Well, we better find a place to talk. It could be a while."

"Your place?"

"No. It's not Jerry or Phil's problem. They don't need to be around."

"Well, let's send them off with Cane somewhere."

"Cane? He is the last person I want them to be with!"

"Tim, it's time for you to figure something out. Whether you like it or not, Cane has a lot more in common with your sons than you do, which is a lot more than you think. Besides, we are all on the same team. We can't have three of one and one of another. Give him a break. He's not such a bad kid."

"You sound like Father Flanigan or someone. Cane's half my problem. He's such a..." He hesitated, not calling him a loser. "He's just a rich kid who never had to make his own way. If he had the upbringing I had, he wouldn't be so nonchalant about biting it in the big races."

"He wouldn't? I think it's time for you to hear a little about what I know about Cane Paulson. You want to think that he'll be the one who screws up the Keagan family medal run, don't you? But I think you really aren't quite sure what he'll do, because if he skis his best then the pressure will be on both your sons, and then if they both don't come through, then who will you blame? So I just wonder if you have ever considered that should you and Cane finish the classic legs and we're still in contention, that only your kids can fail. That's your greatest worry, isn't it?"

Keagan's hairs stood up on the nape of his neck. Franz was right! When it came right down to it his greatest fear regardless of Cane's performance was seeing his sons get blown away in the last twenty kilometers by the legends of Europe.

"You must let me handle this team, Tim. You must set aside you worries. You must inspire confidence in the younger skiers. You must only concentrate on your leg as far as skiing goes. Don't ski Jerry's leg for him or Phil's either. Instinct will guide them on the trails. And Cane? I have a plan. True, the whole thing could blow up on his leg, but that's true of everyone in a 4x10 race. I'm not worried about any-one's condition physically. The victory is within each of us, but it is only possible if it is shared by all of us – even me. We must begin to believe. But first I hate to say it because it sounds corny, but you need to come to love Cane. The lack of unconditional love has made him fearful. He needs to know that whatever happens he has earned the respect of his teammates. To me that means more than gold, more than winning a race, even more than the triumph of justice. I've been in more sad locker rooms than happy, Tim. A champion's day is bright, but his glory lasts about one night. His teammates remain loyal friends forever though. It is the story of a common goal success-fully achieved that persists through the centuries, like the Battle of Stalingrad. Yet there is even a place for the courageous who come up short but give it their all. History is replete with them. Remember what got you here. And to change the subject, what is going on with you and Lisa?"

A boyish, but wide smile. He stuttered, not able to react verbally. Franz had never seen this look from his brash lead off hitter.

"Oh, I see. We overlook so many faults in a beautiful woman. But with Cane, we know him too well, huh?"

"Not me. I've been there. It's hard. Everything you think you have can be ripped from you, especially second chances." His smile turned to a quizzical philosophical frown. A fantasy of Lisa, and of wine. Of summer wild flowers, of a blanket on the grass laid out, embracing, tumbling, cavorting, laughing. Then of Nikola, not of thought, but an etched memory. "Why? What do you know about Lisa? There's nothing between us. Is there?" he asked.

They retired to a bar on Broadway for a beer.

"Why ask me? She definitely has a sense of purpose. Seeks facts, a good journalist. There is a lot more to her than that though. Beautiful? Yeah, you're right about that," Franz told him.

"What else about her?"

"I don't know. I just know from being an old man that you learn a lot in one night, Tim, but really not that much. Agreed? I know one thing. I'd like to have someone like her on my team. Another thing. She might be someone you need to take a vacation from until this is over. And then, when this is over, you will know, definitely."

The advice was wholly against Tim's natural inclination to proceed expeditiously, as in all things he desired.

"You know Tim...you must know. Sure, she's available, but you're not the first to call on her. Are you the best? Maybe, but let's keep things in priority. For now, be content with the challenge in front of you. Devote your attention to your team. Build them up. Then she'll see the goodness in you. She'll be there, but how is she going to feel if you cheat her from covering the event like she must? Let her talk to the Finns and the Swedes. Keep her away from the Italians though. Let her cover the Games. You train and you ski. Let her decide when you're worthy of another story, another day."

Tim's heart sobered. Was Franz telling him something between the lines? He was a fool to think she would be such an easy conquest. He was just an interview at a dinner. Yeah, she was congenial. Their eyes met often and smiled when they did. Was it all an act? She opened him up – big. Yeah, a good journalist, all right. He was indeed coming back to his snow-covered earth.

"So Coach, what do you think that lawsuit was really about? I'm a lawyer and it still doesn't make any sense at all." Tim asked. It was a more comfortable subject now.

"The bottom line is with Cane's father. Not Cane. But Plank is in it, too. All I know is that someone like Paulson does it for money, or at least money is part of it. To help out his son? Yeah, he would, but how did suing you help his son?"

A thought flashed immediately in Tim's mind. "Are they related somehow? Is that it?"

Coach Franz dismissed that hypothetical summarily. "No, that's surely not what it is about," he laughed. Cane didn't even like Plank. "But, I think there was some truth in their pleadings." Franz outlined some facts. ForesTek indeed had paid Plank an endorsement contract. ForesTek did underwrite him in a story in *Sports Unincorporated*. They were trying to bootstrap Cane to Plank's Olympic legacy at these games. The Hawk was on the verge of becoming a fifth-time Winter Olympian, a record not likely ever to be broken. Finally, Plank, although a mediocre cross-country skier internationally, within the USA he was the dominate skier for sixteen years, until the Keagan's arrived.

Tim's mind was still working. In fact, he thought he had thought of every possibility. Money? Plank? Cane? Paulson. ForesTek, Inc. Skiing...Plank. Anchorage!

"Coach, you remember that race, don't you?" Tim asked.

"Of course."

"What was different about Plank that day?"

"Nothing. Same old kick and glide."

"Wrong! He had a hell of a glide. He was picking up meters on us in the downhills."

"It didn't help him much when he skied into Cane," Franz laughed, then changed the subject. "So then can your boys show Cane around TC?"

"They're old enough to decide for themselves. Let them do what they want," he finally relented.

"Good, because I unleashed them about three hours ago. Well, I am their coach, am I not?"

Chapter Twenty-Eight

PHIL AND JERRY. Jerry and Phil. The Keagan boys. They were not celebrated by their peers in Traverse City. The youth of their city were the same as the nation over. Football players and drop-outs are the first to get the girls' attention, and everyone grows out of mountain biking the minute they get their driver's licenses. For all of its splendor, nature cannot compare with the back seat of a car.

But for the fact they attended St. Francis High instead of the public high school, they might have had a life. Unlike most Michigan schools, the public high had a cross-country ski team. Undoubtedly, they would have enjoyed at least limited acclaim there in that regard. But, St. Francis did not, and their social life suffered accordingly. Unquestionably they were the town's superior Nordic stars, but did not even have a letter jacket to show for it. They each recognized the injustice of it all, and when opportunities allowed, they would unmercifully crush the high school state champions in non-sanctioned competitions. To do less would have been un-Catholic, they were told by their father. And that anything less than their best "would upset the nuns." To which Phil would reply only half in jest, "Dad, what is a nun?" Yet, in spite of the paucity of a religious order in the classroom, they remained educated in a traditional Catholic sense. The parable of the talents applied especially to talent.

They lived in a man-child's world: athletic, over-disciplined, and socially limited. Neither yet had had a steady girlfriend; further, they were too humble to talk themselves up in the presence of the opposite sex. Cane Paulson would be good for them in that regard. Cane was over at the table with the best looking girls Traverse City had to offer before the band started playing. But Cane knew his younger teammates were looking for something special. Still, it couldn't hurt to develop style. Their girls would come by in due course. It could not be avoided; the Keagans, as boys, were already outperforming men. Plus, they were smart. They watched every move Cane made, and the reactions of the ladies. It was fun! Cane, who swore abstinence until the cork popped in Thunder Bay, was a riot to be with. And the women who thought Cane to be a little too much naturally gravitated to his...friends. Olympians? From Traverse City? How come they had never heard of them? Well, listen and watch, Cane told them, because they are going to be around a long time, and you can say you were among the first to know, he laughed.

Jerry was the best skier on the team, and only Phil could beat him. This was their fate as brothers, as competitors. Phil knew Jerry was better, but Jerry knew that Phil could and would beat him, if he wasn't on top of his game. If not for each other, they would not have known of real competition, except when their father forced them to ski "slow," that is, classic style. Those races were special, and the boy's skills in the classic style were second to none as a result.

When he found himself alone on the trails, Jerry's thoughts bordered on the mystic. The rhythms of skating gave him a kind of peace, like soft music. Happy, sad, light, heavy – all found space in the strokes of the technique. It was a conversation, granting complete empathy. Races were different. Always looking down, balancing on one ski, the toes, knee, and head in constant alignment. All of life rushed by too quickly, like downhill runs...like his mother's life.

Did he feel punished? No. He did not feel emptiness, but he did think life might have been fuller, at least different, if he had a mother to remember, if not to know. Jerry was always kind, in contradistinction to his unforgiving manner of racing. He provided lessons and advice to his competition, and urged them to do the same for those back home who were just starting to learn the art.

In a sense, because of Jerry's Nordic supremacy, Phil looked up to him. Phillip – the one whose moodiness presented itself in surly episodes of despair. Number two usually. Someone who could barely remember mother. Someone who barely knew he lost something; a relationship, a trust that she would always be there. Someone who was so very, very important to him. He was someone who thought what he remembered might one day provide an answer. But, as he got older, it only seemed to fade away.

Phillip was not unkind. Neither was he inclined otherwise. He doubted his own accomplishments, but would exalt his brother's. His protectiveness of his little brother was well known. No kid, Catholic or otherwise, dared utter the snide reminder of Jerry's mother's absence without an immediate physical response on his part. Not that Phil doled out gratuitous violence; he was simply not the type to turn the other cheek.

Though his passion in life seemed all too often the protection of his younger sibling, Jerry was far less sensitive to ridicule than Phil's presumptions. Jerry was well beyond his brother's ascribed diagnosis; in fact, he had never made its point of origin. If he had, it escaped him. His mother's gift was that she left him so young. He grew straight; perhaps fewer branches grew at the bottom. It didn't matter now. He was looking to the heavens.

Phil was reactive; Jerry, the calm assessor. Perhaps Phil's militarism allowed Jerry that luxury. Jerry was happy. Phil was not unhappy. Jerry believed in the intercession of saints. Phil wondered. When Jerry was but twelve a day arrived in which he would set his brother straight.

Tim had left the house to the boys overnight for the first time as he was required to try a case out of the area.

"What are you praying about now!" Phil yelled at Jerry. Phil, dog-tired and already in bed, had heard enough. Jerry was whispering a prayer, kneeling beside his bed in his room across the hallway. Jerry continued, oblivious to his remark. Phil got out of his bed and confronted him.

"I'll pound on you if you don't shut up!"

For the first time the younger, preadolescent, and still much smaller Jerry stood up to his older brother, with his underarm hair and all.

"Just try it!" challenged the perturbed little saint.

Phil feigned a punch to Jerry's head as a threat, but little Jerry had already set in motion a counterpunch, and struck Phillip full force in his midsection. He buckled to his knees, gasping for air.

"I'll...kill...you...punk!" It hurt Phil greatly to utter it, but it had to be said. It was just the Irish talking.

Jerry, amazed at his own power, became immediately concerned for his heavily gasping brother and felt extreme remorse. He did not think he could hurt his older brother at all, much less to this extent. Phil was not faking it. Finally, he got most of his breath back, and Jerry cowered in fear of his expected retaliation. Instead, Phil refrained.

"Are you okay? Should I call Dad?" Jerry asked, still worried.

"I'm all right," said Phillip, as angry at himself as Jerry, not wanting to admit further the pain his brother inflicted upon him. A new reality had descended in the blink of an eye. Jerry was no longer just a little brother. They each went to bed with the mixed messages the incident engendered.

The next morning as Jerry prepared to meet the bus, he thought to check Phil's room. Why wasn't he up yet? Their bus was to arrive within a few minutes. Dad would not like it if either of them skipped school.

Inside, he found Phil writhing on the floor, moaning, half-conscious. His appendix had ruptured. Jerry's quick actions saved his life. But Jerry knew only God or his mother or something above could have turned him around in time to check on his brother.

Phil had been too sick to feel fear, or even think of death. It was only after his recovery that the impact of the episode hit home.

He did not blame Jerry; he should not have interrupted someone who was praying. Jerry's role remained heroic to all who heard of the drama, as Phil refused to ever utter a word about that which precipitated his hospitalization. But, it was a lesson both boys took to heart. Nothing was a fait accompli. There are some secrets fathers never learn of their sons.

Thereafter, Phil lost count of the number of nights he heard Jerry whispering his prayers, always ending in thanks that his brother's life had been spared. And Phil's love for his younger brother grew stronger than ever.

Jerry was further immersed into the love of his Church; Phil remained Catholic by default. Jerry, convinced of miracles; Phil, a seeker of signs. One a doubting Thomas; the other, the faith of the centurion. One expecting; the other waiting. Both, the most awesome American skiers since one Bill Koch. Nikola provided her half of Tim's solution.

Chapter Twenty-Nine

IT WOULD BE on to Thunder Bay early the next morning, but Tim still had some unfinished business. He checked into his law office for messages, where he was happy to find an upbeat Gavin Smith preparing to call it a day.

"Well Tim, you are doing something in your life only a few out of a million ever experience. And you earned it. But, don't take it too seriously. The longer I live the more humor I see in everything. And I think it would be perfectly funny if you came back with a medal. I'd like to dangle it in front of that old codger Griffey, wouldn't you?"

"That's a fact. But what would really please me is to see us inspire the country to look at the sport, to understand cross-country skiing, to produce our own Bjorns, Vegards, and Vladimirs. Not to dominate, but to compete. The more I ski and watch and learn, the more I realize there is no champion in this sport who does not defer to the nobility of its traditions. This is the one – the only – sport of the Winter Games that celebrates the earth, the creation, the elements, and the weather in the way no other can. We are in the woods and forest, skiing in tracks in hip-deep snow. We belong. We are the essence of winter sport. And my desire is to give it its proper acclaim in America. I regret to admit you are correct, if we don't win we won't attract much attention. Then I guess I race for posterity, if nothing else."

"I don't know why you're telling a black man all this Aryan stuff. The only good thing about winter is basketball."

"Racist. I'd rather be puking."

They both laughed at, and with, each other. If only more of their countrymen could do the same...

"Well, Tim, my friend, I'm glad I helped you in some way to get you there. It's too bad all the negative coverage took away from your achievement of making the team. I guess the lawsuit wasn't the type of acclaim you sought for your sport, but I tried my best. Maybe if Gannon pays up in time I'll fly up to Thunder Bay for your race."

"You better," Tim warned, then turned more serious again. "I've been given a second chance. Of course I would like to win a medal, but no one is going to give it to me. Nobody's going to give up and say it's America's turn because it would be good for the sport. So if you see me and my sons return empty handed it is because someone else deserved it more."

"Tim, how are you getting along with the rich boy?" Gavin picked up on the omission.

"He scares me to death, but he has been skiing great in practice. He's putting in the effort and he hasn't smart talked me since Anchorage."

"Is he capable?"

"He's capable, but the question is will he become a part of the team or will he flake out as usual."

"Once in a while a miracle happens. Look at the 1980 US Hockey Team. Now that was an upset if there ever was one. And if you guys win, your names will be etched into the ages. And I think God has a lot to do with that."

"I just need to get it on and get it over. Life above all is a matter of time, Gavin. We all are invincible until our last sand falls in the hourglass. I worry only in those moments I feel unprepared. And I worry because I have to turn the reigns over to Ca – . Well, I mean if I was only twenty-five, I could win on my own."

"You cannot and you are not. You see Tim, your race is no different than life itself. All you can do is ski your absolute best. If it produces a result of which others take notice, then you may only hope that of those who do, that some may draw inspiration from it and try to exceed the standard you set. So quit worrying about Phil and Jerry. Don't think about what Cane's attitude will be. They seem so young, but they're not. They are men. Different? Yeah, they're all different. But, they didn't get where they are because they did not earn it. They did. The same as you. So don't sell them short. Not even Cane."

"Seems like I heard this before. Franz calls it 'synergy'."

"Well, it bears repeating. Anyhow, something tells me Cane is one of the few who has the strength to change course."

"You don't even know him."

"I don't need to. Day by day from the little I see of him, and the things I hear you saying about him after your practices, I believe he is becoming a man of integrity and a man of honor."

Their conversation drifted into a final good luck and good-bye, followed by Gavin's ridiculous rendition of the "Star Spangled Banner," humming it through his mouth and nose as if playing a bugle.

"Cut it out, you moron!" Tim exclaimed, laughing hysterically. "Just get outta here and go home. I'll see you up in Canada. See you later," he said, slapping the departing, still humming, Gavin Smith on his back as he paraded out the door. Tim watched, smiling, shaking his head.

Tim had but one more final obligation before leaving. Though Gavin left, his words remained behind. Tim was surprised that Gavin would go to bat for Cane. But certainly Cane did exhibit moxie at court. In fact, what he did was curiously, well, actually, kind of historic. Lawyers are so used to perjured testimony, they nary bat an eye; so much so that without hesitation they argue it to be the truth! Cane would not even participate in half truths. Plus, his skiing in practice was simply superior. He skated up Shauger Hill as if it was a gradual downhill. And up the bluff faster than Jerry or Phil. So maybe Gavin had reasonable grounds. For the second time within as many days, someone he respected and knew well spoke highly of Cane – not as a skier, but as a person.

What Tim didn't know was that Gavin's life was full of Canes while growing up in Flint. So many youths giving in and giving up before they even became adults. With so much potential wasted, in more ways than one – justifying living lies on the backs of others, even the deceased. The only difference was that in Gavin's old neighborhood they started at the bottom, and in Cane's at the top. But gravity works on dreams too, if you let it. It's a lot easier to fall and stay down than it is to get up and fly. And down there, losers of every race, color, and gender find no shortage of reasons why they couldn't make it. And for a while, like Cane, Gavin was one of them.

Chapter Thirty

TIM'S ENGINE WAS slow to start in the frigid air. As he waited for the van engine's reluctant process of warming, supplying heat in minute degrees, he huddled his arms together in front of him, elbows resting on his thighs, thighs wrapped in muscles like bound steel cables, he found himself staring down at his own hands clasped together as if in prayer. He began to shiver. Nineteen years. He looked up in the rear view mirror. In the darkness his eyes met his own reflection. Still him. Still just him. The van slowly showed signs of real warmth and Tim quickly reversed out of the lot.

"Nikola," he breathed heavily in a sigh, his words dispersed into vapors into the ages, just as his wife gave up her ghost, so long ago, only yesterday. And tonight, like every night, he relived the pain. The memory. The undivided guilt. Yesterday...

***

He stopped the car. Gotta hurry! Where's a quarter? A quarter! He punched in seven digits quickly.

"Are you coming out?...No...No, Nikola's not...Do you think I'd be calling if she was? Don't be stupid...Well, you will just have to wait...We've waited long enough?...Unless you want to meet me in the woods...Oh? You better hope I have a big, big lead, then!...I know, I know. But this time I'm sure...No, she doesn't suspect a thing...Yes, I'm sure!...Of course, I'm going to win the Vasa...that kid named Plank? I'm going to give him a skiing lesson. A big one...The forecast? No...Baby, I was born in a blizzard. Ha-ha-

ha!...I'll be there. Count on it...I can't believe it either, but hey! You're right.
Life is short...But I'm not? How would you know? Ha-ha-ha!"

***

"What a bastard I was!" he screamed into the night. "Is that why you killed yourself? How did you find out? Why didn't you tell me you were coming? God! God! God! Please tell me you didn't know, but if you did it was an accident! Honey, I was wrong but did it require this? Did you have to die in order for me to realize I loved you? Did you have to kill yourself to teach me that the other woman didn't love me? That she didn't even care? Well now you know. Nothing happened. Nothing happened. Nothing happened. Nothing, nothing...."

The sky, full of stars, was Tim Keagan's sole witness. He glanced up, searching the ethers for the soul of a woman buried beneath the snow under his feet. Rationality imposes limits in a universe of unknowable answers; there was no place to turn but inward. Keagan's God, above all, was the Master of Time. The Master had taken hers and now He had given back his. Nikola's death was his sin. What were her last thoughts? He had returned here to converse with whatever, with whoever told him to get on with it. No, it was a more precise message – to ask of Him the power to do One Great Thing in order for him to earn redemption, to grant Nikola an indulgence. There was only one path in front of him, and it led precisely to Thunder Bay.

"Honey," he murmured, almost as if speaking in tongues. Perhaps he was, for it was a voice reserved for utterances from the essence. "Nikola, I have come to realize who I am in life. Isn't it so simple?" He shook his head, like a drunken man, and took a very deep slow draw of the crisp clear air. "Oh, God, please be with us in Thunder Bay." He shook his head more and laughed. "We must move a mountain together, Lord." He looked skyward again, arms folded across his chest. He walked to the headstone, brushed some snow aside and rested his right hand upon it.

"Nikola, you gave me the greatest treasures. I am so proud of Jerry and Phil! They know the old man wants to win so bad. But honey, I'm not the skier I was. But, I have to show them it's still possible." He laughed at the irony. "Well, you know all this. You know why I'm here.

You knew I would come. So did I. I have come to tell you that I have come to believe in more than myself. I believe in the evidence of things I can't see. And that is my hope. That is our only hope." He laughed, again, as if still half drunk. Even his words were slurred, his jaw muscles having stiffened in the arctic air. "I must give back what has been given me, and more. There will not be another opportunity for me. The road I follow comes to an end. Lightning strikes at Big Thunder and my conversion will be completed there or I will have lost forever."

"What's that I hear? Lisa? Is she okay with you?" This was a life beyond Big Thunder. "Okay, okay, there is time for her after the Olympics. Have you been talking with Franz?"

He quit talking to himself. Now he stood silently for a minute. He looked upward again. No shooting star. No aurora. No special sign. Great. Same as it ever was. He would make his own way again. It was the only way he knew.

He walked back to the van. He turned and said more loudly, more distinctly, "Forgive me, Nikola! I was just intoxicated with my own self-importance."

Suddenly he was crushed to his knees, and began crying. His answer had come like a thunderbolt.

"...just like Cane...."

Chapter Thirty-One

LISA'S RETURN TO Seattle was unaccompanied by her usual anticipation. At her fashionable home in the foothills of Redmond, she dispassionately checked her phone messages before she unloaded. The parade of male voices began.

"Lisa, it's me. Just calling to see if you're in. Call me at Harborview or at home, whatever, when you get in," came the message from her soon to be ex-current most significant beau, Dr. Clifford Brandt. It did not bring a smile to her face, nor the typical hurried response call either.

The tape played on.

"Miss Nelson. Hi. Uh, this is, uh, Kenneth David, uh, Kranwitz. I was wondering if perhaps we might have lunch? Okay? Oh, I got you number from [unitelligable], when I met with you at the trial, [unintelligible], your magazine. Oh, remember me? I represented..." BEEP!

"Fat chance freaking schmuck," she muttered to herself. The idiot wasn't even competent to leave a comprehensible message.

Then another.

"Hello, Lisa, this is Benjamin Twofeathers. I just wanted to thank you for your fine article on our project in Yakima and see if you might make plans to attend our next Pow-Wow. I would love to see you again."

"Not bad," she observed. "A doctor, a lawyer, and an Indian Chief." But no Keagan.

Finally, "Lisa! Call me right away. It's Stu. Uh, it's 1:00 p.m. Today!"

She threw the carry-on from her shoulder and dialed him instantly. "Stu. It's Lisa. What's up?"

"Lisa! I deciphered the Rosetta Stone!"

"Congratulations. You're only about two hundred years too late."

He laughed. "No, not that Rosetta Stone!"

"What are you talking about, Stu?"

"What do you think? It's about Plank's lawsuit!"

"Oh, of course. How could I be so stupid? I've only been home two minutes and I couldn't figure it out. Luckily, I have you for a boss, Stu."

"Sometimes I wonder." he answered.

"Not as much as me, Stu baby. But what do you have?"

"I never would have figured it out in a thousand years, but now that I know it makes perfect sense. It's about wax."

"WAX?" she exclaimed in disbelief.

"Yes, wax. Well more accurately it's about super hi-tech hydrophobic ski-base products and materials. ForesTek, Inc. is on the verge of forming a subsidiary exclusively devoted to the manufacture and development of an entire line of extraordinarily high quality skis and ski products. The company was hoping it would 'take the world by storm' at the Olympics. The only problem was that they couldn't keep on schedule for any kind of mass marketing, so Paulson wanted to stage its appearance at Thunder Bay! But if the US Team failed to win anything he was willing to cover the whole thing up for next year's World Cup races. But if they pulled some upsets, can you imagine the publicity in front of literally one billion people, including Norwegians, Finns, Swedes, Italians, Russians..."

"I get the picture. Man, what an advertisement! And all for free! How did you find out?"

"Plank skied on them at the tryouts! The Anchorage race was its maiden voyage!"

"Kind of like the Titanic, I'd say."

"Well, why don't you ask Tim Keagan about Plank's glide that day, if you don't believe me," Stu insisted.

"How did you find out about Plank using it?"

"Come on into the office. I'll show you. I have the smoking gun right here with me."

"I'll be right over." Twenty five minutes later, she was in Stu's office.

"Well, let me have it." she requested.

He handed her a laminated layout. She scanned the document, a black and white print. On it was copied a rough pencil sketch of two skiers, one striding, one skating, and above them in bold letters: HOLD FOR SUBMISSION: *SPORTS UNINCORPORATED, INC.*

The ad read simply:

NEOTERIC TECHNOLOGY

For the Fastest Generation Ever

X-Tek Skis

Kickback Grip

Ultima Glide

Made in America

The superior ski and base preparations successfully introduced at Thunder Bay, against all odds.

X-Tek Ski, Inc., a subsidiary of ForesTek, Inc., Seattle, WA. USA

Coming Soon: The Downhill Sponsor of the US Olympic Ski Team

"Incredible! You know, I have to admit I like the ad! And what a product line! Those names are winners. But it's still hard to believe. How did this come about and how did you find out?"

"It is incredible, when you hear it all."

It started with a conversation with Franz, he said as he began to retrace the events of the last three days. Something that Tim Keagan had pointed out to him in passing.

ForesTek Inc., which had always been involved with the production of water resistant adhesives and repellants used in the timber and construction trade, began intensive efforts to develop technologies for products and materials to avoid the problem of icing on aircraft wings. It was a gamble, but the company had taken enormous profits over the past decade, and with its close proximity to Boeing, was eager to forge significant operations with the giant industry. And the airline industry was more than eager for the day to arrive when they could announce to the public that the de-icing of planes that is so incredibly time consuming, costly, and temporary could now be called a mere back up procedure. The day would come when de-icing would be rendered completely obsolete, once the public became assured of the performance of the new technologies. And there was no shortage of the price all were willing to pay. As a result of ForesTek's involvement in this research, Paulson himself directed a team to spin off these technologies into what would soon be known as X-Tek Ski, Inc. The molds, the core construction of the ski, and the base they developed were beyond state-of-the-art. It was a coincidental happenstance that American aerospace engineers and the monies they commanded would become pitted against an unsuspecting quaint bunch of dedicated sports enthusiasts that make up the European industries, who had up until now essentially controlled the entire market.

It would be nothing short of a complete transmutation of the way racing skis would thereafter be manufactured. He continued to describe the skis. Less than 650 grams, twenty-five percent lighter than anything presently existing. They were stronger, too. The base material is processed in the manufacturing stage to be frost, ice, snow, and water antipathetic, to the extent of virtual friction-free glide. Base application of the Ultima glide further enhanced performance in competitive racing. Unsubstantiated rumor had it that Ultima glide was so effective that several volunteers opted out of testing after just one downhill test out of sheer terror of the speed they achieved. Kickback grip "wax" tested to be effective and durable in all temperature ranges below five degrees Celsius, and its chemical composition allowed for unsurpassed forward glide. Indeed it gripped as well as a klister, yet picked up no snow or debris in the kick stage to act as a drag. The base required no saturation as did the current line of racing skis made by European manufacturers. Elite racers preferred skis waxed and worn dozens, if not hundreds of times, so essential to racing is base wax saturation. X-Tek's technology supplanted that hassle. Most compelling, X-Tek skis used synthetic materials that could be quantified with exactitude, meaning a skier, by knowing his weight alone, could literally buy or pick a pair of new skis off the rack the day of the race and find himself perfectly matched for grip for classic style, or glide for both techniques.

To those few who were privy to X-Tek's incursion into the sport, these advances were said to be no less revolutionary to the sport than the development of the skating technique itself. To Paulson, the only question remaining was whether the US team possessed the skiers capable of giving his products the blast off they deserved at the Olympics. Keagan's victory in Anchorage sobered him.

Plank was to have won that race easily. It was the perfect setting, complete with intrigue and subterfuge; X-Tek skis disguised as Atomics; Plank's Watergate-like theft of Cane's race skis, replaced by X-Teks and prepared with Kickback and Ultima. It would have been hard to suppress such a story until the Olympics had Plank succeeded, thought the X-Tek conspirators, but the Keagans botched up everything. Even more disastrous, when Paulson and Plank both fell, the Keagans finished one, two, three. With the slow wax. With Fischers. Paulson was convinced, had his son been aware of the super gliding machine under his feet, he never would have fallen on that hellacious S turn, and Plank would have made the team. His lawsuit was his parachute, but it didn't open. Now X-Tek Ski, Inc., was in a quandary with Plank off the team, and harbored understandable hesitation about approaching the Keagans for cooperation. Above all stood Paulson's greatest apprehension – putting his son in the forefront of it all.

"How did you find all this out?" Lisa asked, stunned by Stu's able report.

"Every chain has a weak link," he laughed weakly. "It was so easy." He paused, clearing his throat. "You asked 'how'?"

"How!" Lisa insisted, instinctively targeting Stu's evasiveness.

Stu hesitated, but finally relented. "Well, you're going to find out someday anyhow. Kranwitz wanted your phone number. He begged for it. I told him it would cost him. He spilled his guts." He laughed, raising an eyebrow in submission for what was sure to come, hoping she could find just a speck of humor in his methodology.

"You sleaze! You're as bad as him!" She started hacking and gagging – and spat on the floor right next to Weinberg's feet. "Now I've got to get a new unlisted number. And it's coming out of your pocket! You scum!"

"Okay! Okay! Jeez! How much is your phone number worth? I have to do one more thing. I'm supposed to recommend a date with him to you." He laughed, believing now that he would at least live to see another day.

"I can't believe this crap! No way!"

"We'll never find out what's next!" he said plainly.

"You know Stu. There comes a time when you know enough. Give me that phone!" She found the number and dialed. "Hello, get me Kranwitz. No, I do not ... Kranwitz, this is Lisa Nelson. The answer is no, nada, nyet. Got it? If you even call me one more time I'll have a stalking charge on your butt faster than you can perpetrate another fraud. Got it? I have a lot of cop friends who are just waiting for the chance to take a lawyer like you downtown. Understood? Good. No buts. Forget it. Oh, by the way thanks for all the information you gave my buddy, Stu. And if my threat isn't enough to convince you to leave me alone I guess you'll just have to figure out how much your license to practice law is worth to you. I think you know what I mean."

She slammed down the phone. "Chapter closed. New chapter please." Next she dialed Dr. Brandt. "Cliff. Lisa. No. No. I'm not coming over. No! You're not coming over either, Cliff. It's over. The patient is out! Got the picture?" Slam!

Next she dialed Mr. Twofeathers. "Chief? Lisa Nelson. No, I won't be at your next Pow-Wow. Why? Because I have other plans. What are they? I don't know yet, but trust me, I have other plans!" Slam!

Next she dialed Pacific Bell. "Sir, my frigging boss has forced me to request a new number, and I want it ..." She hesitated. She had given it to Tim! "Oh, never mind. I'll call back later." She gruffly hung up the phone.

Stu was cowering in the corner, covering his face with his arms, protectively, in a classic posture of submission.

She looked at him and shook her head. "Stu, you're so obnoxious. Now get me a plane ticket and a decent room in Thunder Bay."

She walked to her office and Stu marvelled. "She must have some Jewish blood in her somewhere," he said to himself with a trace of awe, as he rose to be seated at his desk. "Nancy? It's Stu again. Buzz Lisa, find out what she wants and get it for her, okay? Thanks." Stu smiled. There was no need to worry about Lisa's link in the company chain. She was that rare employee who needed no direction from above. She did exactly what she wanted to do. So what if she had a bitch from time to time? What is life if one is not about getting results? He reclined back, fingers interlaced covering his bald spot above his crown. "Chapter closed. New chapter, please," he laughingly repeated in a low voice, shaking his head.

Chapter Thirty-Two

CANE PAULSON, SR. did not need any more advice. His team of lawyers did not bring him an iota of good news. Now his focus shifted to his son, but not entirely. He did not personally underwrite a $7.5 million dollar subsidiary for nothing. Could he somehow salvage this mess in time for the Olympics? He had no choice but to attempt a negotiated peace. Plank, now banished from the Games, could not bear the olive branch. He would have to contact his son personally, if he could find him. He did not find out he was with the Keagans in Traverse City until the morning they left. Gavin Smith was surprisingly cooperative, even telling him the route they were to drive to the Games. There was only one anyhow.

The Keagans, Cane, and Franz began the long drive at 7:00 a.m. They bounded over the gently rolling hills of Michigan's lower peninsula, crossing the magnificent Mackinac Bridge spanning the straits before nine. From there they would travel almost due north into Canada for an additional three hours until heading west on Highway 17 from White River. Just before the International Bridge, Cane demanded they pull over at a grocery store. He ran in and came out in less than five minutes, carrying a cartful of Vernors Ginger Ale, his newfound sports drink. "Jerry turned me on to it," he explained. "They will let me bring it into Canada, won't they? It's not like I'm smuggling, is it?"

Once past the Sault Sainte Marie's of Michigan and Ontario it is a beautifully desolate drive. Traffic was nearly non-existent and soon so were radio stations that were of any value in alleviating the discomfort of such a long drive. But no one complained because the fantasy world permeating their sense of vision at every turn kept them from boredom. Even the Keagans, who had driven this road just weeks before, could not take in enough of it.

There were many vistas of Lake Superior through the Provincial Park having its namesake. True, Russia may indeed have Lake Baykal, whose extraordinary depth provides a greater volume of fresh water, but Superior is hardly a pond – having a maximum depth that would bury the World Trade Center. In surface area, it blows Baykal away, being more than twice its size. The circumference of Superior is a distance far greater then the Coast of California.

Out of this Great Lake and especially prevalent along the Canadian side is the Laurentian Shield, which accounts for the mountainous nature of the north shore. And in Thunder Bay it culminates in the Nor'wester Range where one finds the steepest and highest elevations between the Shield and the Rocky Mountains.

If one looks at a map, he will find precious few human habitations between Sault Sainte Marie and Thunder Bay. Before Wawa is wilderness. Between Wawa and White River is wilderness. Between White River and Marathon is wilderness. Between Marathon and Terrace Bay is wilderness. And what magnificent terrain! The topography around Marathon is inspirational; not quite what a Westerner would call mountainous, but darn near. The skyline, with hillsides tree covered and bare in February, still can mesmerize the traveller by its beauty, even in the austere season. There, one moment the big hills seem so distant and foreboding, yet in the next they appear to be in the palm of your hand. The Canadian cross-country team has a training facility there and its selection as such garnered the vanful's immediate appreciation. Off Highway 17 north of Marathon they made pitstops at the British Petroleum station. The Keagan boys and Cane were casually discussing the severe isolation the local youth must suffer with the young attendant. Traverse City, with a population of twenty thousand, seemed a cosmopolitan world class city by comparison. Franz approached them.

"Cane, they have a message for you to call your father."

"Why? Is it something serious?" Cane asked, somewhat worried.

"Don't know. Go ahead and call. We'll wait in the van."

Five minutes passed, ten, fifteen. Finally Cane dashed back to the van in the -15°C sun drenched air.

"Anything important?" Franz asked.

Cane laughed. "My father insists on meeting me in Thunder Bay and help me train for the races."

"Why are you laughing?" asked Jerry.

"I told him I already had a coach and not to bother." He looked away from everyone, staring at the hypnotic hills lying in front of them. Everyone picked up that there was a lot more to it than that, but respected Cane's decision not to elucidate further.

Tim changed the subject quickly. "You know, I forgot something in there. I'll be right back." A matter had been on his mind for a couple of days and he had to resolve it before another moment passed. He rushed into the store. Hurriedly he dialed Lisa's number. One ring. Two, Five. A recording. The beep.

"Lisa, this is Tim. Well, I'm in Marathon, Ontario. About four hours from Thunder Bay. If you get this message before you go, I hope to see you there. Bye." Tim returned, slightly depressed. But he was comforted by the thought that she might already be where he was heading. As the van lurched ahead, the five Americans were anxious to see civilization again.

Through quaint Terrace Bay and working class Schreiber. An hour more, then Nipigon and Red Rock. They continued until evidence of life steadily began to emerge with more consistency.

Suddenly, Jerry blurted out, "What's that?"

Franz looked up to his right. "The Terry Fox Monument? Never heard of it. Want to stop?" His highly trained athletes were fidgeting inside the tightly packed Club Van like caged tigers.

"Yeah, why not. I could stand stretching out a little," said Cane.

"All right," Franz said as he pulled over.

Phil whined. "It's probably some little statue of some voyageur or trapper."

"Just stay here then, baby," Jerry shot back.

"All right, I'll go up there and freeze my butt off just so we can say we did it as a team. Maybe I'll piss on his leg."

Up the stairs they sprinted. When they got to the monument and read of a courageous Canadian, silence befell them. They were all humbled by his story.

"Well, it looks like you won't have much of a problem choosing which one," Cane informed his teammate with the penchant for putting his foot in his mouth.

Terry Fox's final accomplishment in life was laid out before them. Dying of cancer, he attempted to run across the continent through his home country. Just before reaching Thunder Bay, he was forced by his illness to end his quest about half completed, very near the site of the monument. If only he had been given more time to do it in he would probably have made it easily, they surmised. Well, not easily, Franz interjected. He ran purely for the sake of others, to raise money for cancer research. On one leg and a prosthesis.

"I can't believe we never heard of him," mumbled Phil, in a voice seeking atonement. "What a man he must have been." He remembered the hellaciously long drive to and back from Alaska, a similar distance. "All on one leg. He must have been so lonely running out there."

The base of the monument was carved out of granite at a site near his collapse, his bronze likeness standing three meters high. The work marvelously captured the spirit of the deed he called the Marathon of Hope.

Then Jerry, who was the most visibly moved of the five by the memorial, asked Franz in a semi-serious way. "Coach. I have been wondering for three weeks now, if we prayed together before a race, would we be in violation of some Olympic rule?"

"Or will we get sued?" Phil asked.

"That's you father's domain," Franz answered, passing the buck.

Tim laughed. "As far as the Olympics are concerned I suppose you can pray to Zeus without fear of reprisal," came his cynical response in reference to the Greeks who started it all. "As far as United States Constitutional prohibitions, if any, they don't apply in Canada. So do what you want."

Franz shook his head, thinking to himself how sad it is that saints have become rebels. Is it really true that praying is on the verge of becoming a proscribed act whenever it implicated his nation in any public way? What would Terry Fox make of such absurdity? Wasn't his entire sojourn a prayer in the most public of manners? Afterwards, they all returned to the van. Thunder Bay was now only a short distance away and signs of human life increased with each passing kilometer. But the talk inside the van was its most subdued yet in the thousand kilometers traveled. Even Franz had butterflies in the pit of his stomach. There was no turning back.

"Here we are!" he announced, as if he was Columbus coming ashore the new world. "The place where we shall remain forever anonymous or forever remembered. This is not a land of middle ground."

"We came. We saw. We kicked butt," said Phil. "This shall be our legacy," he laughed.

"We'll see who kicks what butt," said Franz. "But it's okay to fantasize boys. All great deeds begin with fantasy, but you must believe in yourself, and you must believe in your team."

"Do you believe, Coach?" asked Cane.

He patted him on his shoulder. "Cane, if I told you, you would probably tell me to quit pushing you all. But because I believe," he hesitated, "I'm going to push you to the wall, so that you believe. Remember the morning after in Anchorage, Cane?" Cane nodded. "Don't forget. That memory alone will climb a mountain for you here. Phil, Jerry – you're as good as any pair of skiers on any team here, but the experts are going to tell you your time has not arrived. Don't believe them. There are younger Phil and Jerry's all over the world and four years from now they'll be in your face and in your way. So go for it this time."

He didn't say anything to Tim. Cane objected. "Hey, what about the old dude?"

Tim looked at Cane. Cane smiled back. Tim remembered the truth. He smiled back. Cane was so harmless. "Old dude, eh?" he said in deference to Canada. "It is true I have jockstraps that are older than all of you, but I am like leather that toughens with age."

"You're both out to lunch. Tim, you're just a lad too," said Franz. Everyone laughed.

"Don't laugh Jerry or Phil. I'm one of those young lads Coach talked about that is going to be in your face four years from now. So you'd best collect your booty while you can," Tim returned the volley. The butterflies were gone, temporarily. As they approached their hotel at Arthur Street, it dawned on them they were no longer just skiers, but Olympians.

Coach Franz led the way as they were welcomed by the hotel staff at the Valhalla Inn. They carried themselves like winners. They arrived a team. Cane fit in after all. And so did Tim.

After they checked in, Franz told them to get dressed immediately for a short ten kilometer practice. There was perhaps an hour of light remaining, and they had no time to waste. They assembled quickly, for they too were anxious to get their blood circulating. They drove to the Lappe Ski Center northeast of the city.

"Go ahead and just skate the course. Just to flush the system." Coach Franz knew Lappe. It was a perfect 10K course, having some very steep climbs. It was challenging but manageable terrain. The four set off into the faint light. Thirty minutes later they returned in unison.

"Nice course," Tim said.

"I knew you would like it," said Franz. "We'll do some more work-outs here. But for now, let's go back and check our practice schedule at Big Thunder." He started toward the van. "Oh! By the way, you guys need to pay the $8.00 voluntary fees inside." They all looked at each other. "It's an honor system," Franz explained.

At once they all looked at Cane.

"It'll be an honor, guys," he resigned himself to say.

"Cane, you know I'm starting to like you." said Tim.

Cane went in to pay the $32 Canadian. Jerry tagged along.

"You see, Dad? Cane is all right, isn't he?" said Phil.

"I just hope he got saved good this time," said Tim. "Because I doubt the devil is done with him yet."

Chapter Thirty-Three

L EONARD FRANZ GREW And matured in a time impossible for his team of skiers to understand. Born in the era of depression and war, he began skiing in the fifties on wooden skis. Cane poles were the norm for most of his life. Three-pin bindings were considered an advanced achievement. Wax was indeed wax, with no chemical additives, and tar was applied for grip. Few Americans skied at all, and skating, of course, was unheard of.

America's sole contribution to the history of the sport remained Bill Koch. In the heady days after his silver at Innsbruck in the 30K in 1976, literally hundreds of thousands of his countrymen took up the sport. Koch was only twenty, and it was hoped he could remain an international force for years afterwards. To some extent he did. It was no small achievement that he took the overall World Cup Nordic title in 1982. In addition, Koch also attempted to instill in young Americans the fundamentals of the sport by establishing leagues and sponsoring races for youth. Even so, as of late, the French, the Czeches, the Canadians, and Japanese had been defeating America in relays, and as Gannon cynically suggested to Franz, a thirteenth place finish would be consistent with the American norm in the event. Until now, Franz would have considered a tenth place finish an upset and would have been content to record it as a success. Ordinarily the Americans were out of the race by the 5K mark in the 40K relay. He felt otherwise this time; Tim Keagan would somehow, someway give the team a chance at least for a quarter of the race.

He was encouraged by Cane's redirection. He exceeded all of Franz's expectations. But who could say how he would perform with real pressure? If Keagan had a great first leg and Cane sputtered in the second, his two best skiers 10K legs would be run for naught. He decided it might be advantageous to reconfigure the team. Cane, his biggest question mark, would have to be considered as the team's leg man. If nothing else, if America could stay with the world for thirty kilometers that would be news in itself. If the team lost, at least the Keagan family would get their due. Certainly they had suffered enough through the lawsuit. Happily, by comparison to the Tonya Harding – Nancy Kerrigan fiasco, the media flap regarding the Plank suit was minor. If the *National Enquirer* didn't cover it, then it wasn't news. Maybe if Cane choked in the fourth leg America wouldn't notice anyhow. So if Cane blew up and folded down the stretch no one would be more devastated than Franz himself. He would absorb all the blame. He looked at Cane nearly as he would his own son, the son he never had, the son he wished could be right where Cane was now.

On Thursday the Olympics began. The day of the 30K freestyle race arrived. Tim would sit out both skating races. Franz's other three racers appeared to be relatively calm. It was a timed event where the poorer skiers begin the race in positions one through twenty-five. Bibs twenty-six to forty were good skiers. From forty-one to sixty were the best skiers. Above bib sixty ordinarily were other skiers capable of an upset. Eighty skiers raced. Cane wore bib twenty-one, Phil twenty-five, and Jerry twenty-eight. Only an incredible lobbying effort by Franz prevented his skiers from wearing lower bib numbers. By the end of the race, Franz's efforts were vindicated. Jerry finished thirteenth, 2:51 behind the winner from Sweden. Phil finished seventeenth, 3:05 back. Cane finished eighteenth, only one second behind Phil. Although Franz hoped for better places, their times were astoundingly good. Still, Jerry's finish of 2:51 back was the equivalent of being about twelve hundred meters behind the winner. Franz anticipated the10K classical and 15K pursuit race to learn more of their chances as a team in the relay.

All four raced the 10K classic two days later. Again it was a timed interval start, and again eighty skiers started out. Tim Keagan wore number seven. The others were accorded a higher ranking due to their opening day performance in the 30K. At the conclusion of the shortest race of the games, Franz was ecstatic to find one of his skiers, Jerry, crack the top ten, finishing ninth, :41 seconds back. Tim finished fourteenth at 1:04 back; Jerry and Cane virtually tied at 1:10 back. Tim Keagan passed his six predecessors by the 5K mark, skiing alone for the last five kilometers and without meaningful data regarding his competitor's times, perhaps he could have done better. With two races concluded all of Franz's skiers had placed in the top twenty. It was the greatest beginning by an American Nordic team ever! But no medals, no media.

Jerry, to no one's surprise, was emerging as the star skier of America's team. In Monday's pursuit, Franz was aware he had a skier in medal contention for the first time since Koch. Jerry was, as the Scandinavians were about to learn, a great skier. For the first ten kilometers of the pursuit Jerry hung with the second train of five skiers in the eleventh position. With five kilometers left he made a break to attempt joining the lead pack, which was now cresting the huge hill presenting itself for the next five hundred meters. By the 12.5K mark he had reached the skier from Italy in the fifth position. But the Italian was giving no ground. The first four skiers were not in sight. The youngest Keagan battled the feisty Italian stroke for stroke for the next two kilometers. His adversary seemed additionally motivated by national pride. It was easier to accept a Norwegian or Russian dogging him, but not an American. They had no business skiing at this level. But Keagan kept his tips on the Italian's tail. A one hundred meter decline kept them separated by a centimeter, Keagan rising to a vertical position to catch resistance to avoid contact. Finally the hill flattened out and without hesitation Keagan made his move to pass. The Italian furiously planted his poles in quick repetitive stabs, and picking up tempo managed to keep pace with the American, now immediately to his left on the hard packed snow. As they approached the stadium only four hundred meters remained, with a 180 degree turn over a pedestrian bridge halfway in between.

The gold medalist from Finland was just crossing the finish line to the roar of the multinational crowd and to the great delight of Thunder Bay's sizable population of residents of Finnish descent. More roars emanated as the Russian dueled a Norwegian for the silver, crossing just as Keagan and the Italian sprinted for the final two hundred meters, both amazed to find that only twenty meters ahead of them was the Swedish 30K gold medalist, exhausted, struggling, and obviously disappointed he was out of the medals.

The pace of the American and Italian was such that the crowd was in awe. They charged to the finish line as if the gold was at stake. They each passed the Swede like he was standing still. With twenty meters left Keagan's strokes exceeded that of the Italian's and the Italian assortment of fans were stunned to uncharacteristic silence as their team's greatest sprinter was outdueled by this unknown from somewhere in the US. They wondered if he was of Italian descent.

Jerry's fourth place finish was only seventeen seconds out of the medals. Catching his breath, he skated over to offer congratulations to the fatigued Italian with whom he fought so hard. Extending his hand, the Italian laid his pole in it and said in a heavy voice, "If a medal is win, it a different end, my friend. But good job fourth."

To which Keagan responded. "Hopefully, we both may see, *paesano*." He held up his gloved hand, "Five days more." He pointed to the path behind him. "See them?" The US uniforms worn by his brother and Paulson were clearly visible, entering the final turn. "They are the true sprinters on the American team." Indeed, they battled neck and neck in an equally furious sprint to the delight of the sparse American contingent, now turned on by the American upstarts. True Nordic fans knew that this day signified a major American breakthrough. With fifteen meters left, Phil glanced at his teammate, who likewise let up, and glided to the finish line together, holding up each others hands, finishing ninth and tenth, Cane crossing first.

"*Fastellos!*" the Italian spat. "No medal and think so fast. Italia tiny and beat you always."

"Really?" Jerry countered. "How many Italians in the top ten?"

"Ten only a number round. Gold. Seelver. Bronze. One. Two .

Three. Everything else..." he stopped and made obscene gesticulations with his right hand.

Coach Franz did not agree with the Italian's analysis. With tears of pride welling in his eyes, the relay did not seem so important to him at the moment. Though the US media was off at the Ice Arena, focusing on the women figure skaters as always, his boys were sending shock waves throughout the Nordic world. With America producing three skiers in the pursuits top ten, the established cross-country powers were left scrambling for answers. Their only salvation was that no medal had yet left the Club. But how long could they hold off the young bucks from Traverse City? What had gotten into their water boy Paulson? As their buzzing continued for hours, outside a lean, lanky expatriate lurked, pacing the corners of the credentials booth, cordoning off those who sought answers from he who had them.

Chapter Thirty-Four

CANE PAULSON, SR. was fit to be tied. Seven and one half million dollars into a project that might have been paying dividends by now. The American team was doing better than ever, but like a tree falling in the proverbial forest, no one was there to hear it. Why? Because his son, his suddenly insolent son, hung up on him at some God-forsaken Canadian piss-stop.

Only two cross-country events remained. He was so angry with his son he couldn't even bring himself to watch him at the Games. First he screwed up big at Anchorage. Then the fiasco in Federal court. Then he went AWOL, and the final straw, the unilateral, illogical, disobedient, rejection of his multi-million dollar effort to get his son a life, a job, adoration, an endorsement!

So what if the initial issue would run "just under three grand," five times higher than any other line of competition skis? Wasn't this twenty-first century technology? And weren't they worth every penny? He was doing nothing more than capitalizing on the insanity governing the world's sports markets. His skis could shave off two seconds per kilometer. In a 50K race, that amounted to a minute-forty. A 40K relay, a minute-twenty. So what if some could not afford them? The reality soon would be that no one could afford *not* to.

That Cane and the Keagans were turning heads without his skis, without his base products, only added salt to his wounds. They could be winning medals! The bottom line, however, was the bottom line.

Someone, sometime, somehow would soon learn of ForesTek's venture beyond his small cadre of sycophants. Ultimately he was not about to endure any humiliation that would accompany an untimely disclosure of his pompous scheme. Should X-Tek Ski products go unintroduced at the Games, his colleagues in the business world would scoff at the incredible miscarriage to the point of insufferable scorn. Of course the CEO did not come up with this likely scenario without the able counsel of Gannon, Kranwitz, and Scarborough.

Therefore, there was no choice but to act. Though only two events remained they were the biggest and most publicized of the Nordic events. The four quickly dismissed thoughts of approaching the biathlon team. They desired pure exposure. Alpine? It was impossible. They had not developed X-Tek downhill skis and it was necessary to publicize the total package, not just base glide products. Besides, all of the alpine teams were committed contractually to current manufacturers of skis and ski accessories. After these Games, they would come begging to him for his company to develop an alpine product line, and he would only be too happy to exploit their financial folly as well.

X-Tek had to act instantly. The men's 4x10K was going to be broadcast live in its entirety throughout all of Europe and it was rumored that due to the unexpected showings made by the American men, that ABC was strongly considering covering portions of the race. If not, it was still going to be broadcast live to millions of American cable subscribers. The race in Lillehammer gave the event a lingering sex appeal, and there was at least as much interest in this sport as the luge or bobsled.

Paulson left his attorneys in Seattle. Their advice was sound as usual, but this was a job only he could handle. He did not want witnesses to what he was about to propose. His company plane was readied. Accompanied by X-Tek's project manager, a technician and twenty pairs of X-Tek skis and a case of the hi-tech assortment of base products, the CEO called from the air to the Valhalla Inn to leave a message for one Coach Leonard Franz.

"Urgent. Extra urgent. Will arrive at 3:00 p.m.. Meet after clearing customs. Cane Paulson, Sr."

Franz saw the light flashing. The desk had a message for him. It
was 2:50 p.m. He casually dialed the front desk. "Who? Senior?" He
hung up the phone, perplexed. Things were going quite well without
him and his ilk. He threw himself on the double bed with the agility
of a teenager, lying back staring at the ceiling. He wanted to avoid
him, but perhaps it might involve Cane, he thought, as he remained
encumbered by the nuisance.

At 3:20 p.m., the distinguished CEO knocked on the coach's door.

"Come on in," called Franz in a monotone.

"Lenny! How are you? Your boys are doing real well. Real well."

"You obviously heard."

"Heard? You should see them back at the office in Seattle. It's exciting. But we have to get you some medals, Coach."

Franz laughed. "Well, if we do win anything at all, it will be no
thanks to you. If you had it your way, we'd be three skiers shy of a
chance. Have you forgotten that already?"

"Lenny, Lenny. Hey, I was wrong. I admitted it. Jeez. I'm paying
for it through my nose. I tried to make it right with you all, but if I
haven't, I brought something to you that will."

I can hardly wait, Franz thought. Instead, he flatly asked, "What?'

"The future of skiing."

"Well, your future better get here PDQ because I have many
things to do in the near, if you get my drift."

"Just have a seat, Coach. I think I hear it coming now." Cane went
to the door. "Ah. Good. Good. No, just leave them here with me for
now. When I need you I'll call downstairs."

The CEO personally wheeled in the cart of encased skis, and a box
of his base products.

"Coach, these babies cost seven-point-five million somolians. And
it'll be worth every penny to me if you'll have your team try them out."

"Gosh, Cane, don't you think we should wait a little longer?" he
answered in an air of disgust. "I mean we're only in the middle of the
most important two weeks of skiing these guys will ever do. Don't you
think you're just a little late to ask for favors?"

Cane let out a big CEO-sized sigh. "No, Lenny I'm right on time.

Right on time. Tell you what. Just take them out and give them a try. But I need to have an answer by noon tomorrow or else..."

"Or else what?"

"I'll find someone who will." The CEO stared into Franz's dark eyes.

"I'm curious. If these are so good, how would you know? Your own son is skiing on Atomics."

"Don't worry about Cane, Coach. He'll be skiing on these Saturday."

"I wouldn't bet on it. He's doing pretty darn good so far without them."

"What are you so indignant about Coach? If you don't like them, don't use them. But it wouldn't be fair to your team if you didn't give them a try. Here, hold these." He uncased a pair of the slick black skis and offered them to Franz.

Reluctantly he held one of the incredibly light classics.

"Wait'll you see how they perform. And you know where they are made? Right here in Americ-" he caught himself remembering he was in Canada now. "Right in Seattle! What could be better? How long has it been Coach, since an American ski company sponsored an American ski team? A winning ski team? You understand the implications don't you?"

"Well, I only have one problem."

"What's that?"

"Unfortunately I have to consider the source."

"Maybe you don't fully understand Coach. There would be something in it for you, too," he said, pulling out a wad of currency, bound in a money clip. "There is a lot more than this at stake." It was impossible to ignore a message full of Franklins.

"Like I said Mr. Paulson, unfortunately I would have to consider the source."

"Well, you are coach enough to understand you have the obligation to your team. Believe me Coach it would not look good if our boys get beat by our own skis. And guess who will be held responsible?"

"My men select their own equipment. That has always been my rule."

"Be that as it may Coach, after tomorrow you'll have to live with your decision."

"I make decisions every day, Mr. Paulson. And you know I haven't lost a minute's sleep over any of them for twenty years now. Let me let you in on a secret Paulson. There is something you can't invent, that you can't manufacture, that you can't sell, that you can't buy, and it guides me to every destination safely and on time. It's called principle. Ever hear of it?"

Paulson let loose a belly laugh. Nothing amused him more than the topic of ethics. "Okay, Coach. Whatever. Happy is he who believes who hasn't seen. But tomorrow you will see. Maybe that's what your 'principles' require."

It was hardly the first time someone opposed him on such grounds. But it was clear, as always, once facts become obscured by some code of morals, meaningful conversation becomes impossible. It was time to leave.

"Oh by the way, isn't it one of your principles to put the best onto the snow? Isn't that what you said back in Grand Rapids? Or does that principle apply only to men and not to equipment?" he sarcastically concluded as he whisked through he door.

Franz stared at the baggage at his feet. He smiled, bemused by the encounter.

"Wonder when his lawyers will arrive this time?" he said. He picked up he phone. "Keagan? Can you come up to my room and help me get rid of some garbage?"

Chapter Thirty-Five

LISA NELSON'S TRIP to Thunder Bay wasn't all peaches 'n Keagan. She was snowed in at Minneapolis and missed the 30K altogether. She caught the 10K classic and wanted to get with Tim afterwards, but since he finished early in the race, thinking she had plenty of time, waited instead, watching the others finish. By the time it was over, the corral of participants was a sea of European journalists, and the Americans were nowhere to be seen. Having missed Tim's message in Redmond, she didn't even know where he was staying, or if he was really even interested in her. Bad timing was becoming the story of her life lately.

But in her soul, she knew better. She checked the Olympic village and was a bit surprised to find that the Nordic Team opted out of it, as did so many others. Luckily, the excitement of the Games was infectious, and though disappointed, she was hardly bored. Besides, she justified the lack of a romantic interlude to the reality of her job and to the reality of his. What she didn't know was that Tim, all the while, was wondering where she was as well. But both knew the 4x10K was the real reason for being there.

Still Thunder Bay wasn't that big that she should never see him, even if only by chance. Or was it? She panicked for a moment. She suddenly remembered that, though she had been there four days and had made many superficial acquaintances in innocent conversations everywhere, she had yet to see anyone she recognized two days in a row other than the athletes she met. It was understandable. People were coming and going and going and coming. And no one had time to form any kind of habit or ritual in their daily lives. Oh! But there was that one exception! The dork chemist from Vermont. How could she forget him? He stuck out like a Southern Baptist at a Crown Heights Bar Mitzvah. Tall, thin, wearing zip up galoshes and wearing khakis pulled up to his chest, a sweater that he must have bought at the Thunder Bay salvation army – well, two sweaters, one over the other – well, maybe three, covered thoughtfully by the button up navy nylon jacket straight out of the 1970s. The horned rim glasses, the big nose, and crooked teeth made the absence of the white shirt and pocket protector a conspicuous fashion omission on his part. He probably had an acne problem as a teen.

He told everyone who would get near him about his ski waxes. "Yep. They ought to try them. Been working on them since November. Can't get through to the coaches though. I suppose they're a little hard to get a hold of though, eh? He, he, he."

After the men's 15K pursuit race, the Nordic women took center stage for their 10K freestyle pursuit, following their 5K classic held earlier in the week. Lisa covered those events as well, and sure enough the bespectacled Nordic nerd was present as always. He must arrive hours early every day, Lisa thought, because he was always right up against the rail, proselytizing his products carried in his omnipresent backpack.

Lisa finally realized he might provide her the humor necessary to get past her frustrations.

"Hey, Carol!" she called in a loud, but inviting voice.

Carol Fabiano, the number three American female skated over, smiling. She was in thirty-third place overall, and having no chance at a medal, was enjoying the Games without a hint of stress.

"Lisa?" she asked, not certain she had her caller's name correct.

"Yeah, from Seattle. Remember me from the interview Sunday?"

"Yeah, sure. *Sports Unincorporated*, right?"

"Yeah."

"One of my favorite magazines by the way. What's up?"

"Hey. I need someone to help me out. I have a good idea for a story. Do you see that nerd over there?"

"Who hasn't? Everyone is talking about him. What a geek, huh? He says he improved some ski wax or something. But, I don't see anyone lining up, do you?" She laughed.

"Why don't you try it out, just for kicks. I'll get a picture of you two together and I promise I'll include it in my story."

"You promise?"

"Yeah, you and him."

"Okay. That and one of me alone racing and you got a deal."

"All right. Done."

"Okay! Just let me run it by my coach."

The ruggedly attractive blue collar girl skated back to the corral. Her coach glanced toward the Burlingtoner, who was gawking back at them, his hands clasped together as if in prayer. Coach Simmons was nodding in approval to Carol's request, laughing. Fabiano skated back to Lisa.

"It's okay. Beth said the publicity can't hurt. At this point, it's only for fun anyhow."

"Great! It'll be fun I'm sure. Well, there he is," she said pointing at the isolated figure.

"Hey! I'm not going over to him by myself! You have to introduce me!"

"I don't even know his name," Lisa replied.

"He won't care. Trust me." Carol was confident the geek was starving for notice.

Carol skated slowly toward him, while Lisa paced quickly to meet her there. But Carol didn't wait, after all.

"Okay, dude. What do you got for me?" the short ball of energy demanded.

"Oh! Oh! Wonderful!" He nervously pulled out a program, looking up Carol's bib number. "You are um, um, Carol Fabiano?"

She nodded quickly. "And you're who?"

"Jules. Uh, Jules Dinkel," he answered, extending a handshake. "It's J-U-L-E-S, unlike the jewel I am. He! He! He!"

"You poor thing," Carol muttered underneath her breath in suppressed sympathy.

"Huh?"

"Nothing!" interjected the newly arrived Lisa. "Well, Jules. What exactly do we have here? Oh, by the way, I'm Lisa Nelson. I'm a columnist for *Sports Unincorporated* magazine. Mind if I get the story on what you're doing here in Thunder Bay?"

"No, no. Of course not." He was elated. His long trip had not been for naught after all. "Well, Ms. Nelson, I have developed some new ski base compounds. One might say I 'dinked' around with a lot of different formulas until I finally got it right. He he he."

"He he he," parroted the skeptical extrovert. "Well, Dinky, I don't have the luxury of time my friend Lisa does. I'm up in forty-five minutes, so fix me up with what you got."

Jules obediently complied, pulling his backpack around, unzipping it, exposing his wares for the first time on the wooden bleacher seats behind him.

"Okay. Give me your skis, Ms. Fabiano."

She looked at him quizzically.

"Where's the heat?" she asked, referring to the common practice of melting in glide preparations with an iron or a propane torch.

"Don't need it, Ms. Fabiano. Don't want those nasty vapors in the air or in your lungs. We want every molecule to stay right in the base."

"But my skis are cold!" she protested. She didn't mind going along with the charade, but thirty-third place still looked a lot better than eightieth.

"I'll be done momentarily. Just wait," he replied, showing a hint of displeasure with her needless concern.

Jules hunched over the skis working fastidiously. He spent only a few minutes on each ski applying his formula.

"Okay. Now give them a try," he announced confidently, with an uneven smile.

The brown eyed St. Paulian bent over and snapped back into her racing bindings. Before she even returned to a standing position, she darn near did the splits.

"Whoa!" she yelled instinctively.

Jules laughed. "He! He! He! Watch it, Ms. Fabiano. They're going to be pretty slippery."

She quickly regained her balance.

"I see!" She shot a glance over to Lisa and shrugged her shoulders.

"Go ahead, Carol. Ski up to that bridge and back," Lisa requested. "Let's see how it works."

Carol skated off, with an extremely conservative push. She felt the sensation of being on roller blades with directional force wheels everywhere underneath her feet. Gradually, she pushed off stronger, taking longer glides. Though the temperature was -9C, her glide was equivalent to a -1C to +1C day – optimal glide. It seemed as if the course had suddenly been transformed into perfect race conditions.

Her return was effortless.

"Dinky, what's going on here?" she asked, on the verge of conversion.

"Molecules, Ms. Fabiano. It is nothing more than molecular structure."

"Well, will your molecules take 10K of pounding?"

"Yes ma'am," he informed her.

"We shall see, Mr. Din-kell." She looked over to Lisa. "Maybe you better adjust your shutter speed for my picture." She laughed, but her cynicism had faded noticeably. Her skis glided. There was no doubt about that.

"Well, Dinky, I'll either kiss you or strangle you when I'm done. Okay, baby? *Ciao!*"

She skated back to the corral to see her coach. She could be seen shaking her head, pointing to her skis, shrugging her shoulders, and though she had poles strapped to her hands, kept gesturing all the while, true to her Italian heritage. Beth's muffled laughter could be heard all the way over to the bleachers.

Jules repacked his products and put on a look that professed Yankee pride in his workmanship. In fact, he appeared far more focused on the race than did Carol.

"Uh, Jules?" Lisa asked, trying to break through his trance.

"Yes, Ms. Nelson?" he responded, without turning her way – the only male not to do so in years.

"What do you do for a living, for employment, I mean."

He stroked his chin. "Well, when I'm not in my basement or my garage working on environmentally friendly compounds, I'm usually in the woods in my knickers hiking or skiing and taking photographs of birds and nature. He he he. And I have been pretty fortunate. I sold a lot of calendars last Christmas. But no one would buy my compounds. You know sometimes you just have to sell yourself first. He he he." He returned to his test pilot.

"Oh. Okay," replied Lisa. "I'll talk to you after the race," she concluded, with her subject just standing there, staring like he was spying an ivory-billed woodpecker. Methodically he put his field glasses to his eyes. The personification of the stereotype. The last fifteen minutes of the Games was her personal highlight so far. "I met Jules Dinkel. Who needs a medal now?" she convinced herself. Her trip was now justified. She had the perfect angle on the American effort at this Olympics. A low-tech Eddie the Eagle.

Soon the announcer called, "Carol Fabiano, USA!" A cheer of sorts emanated from the sparse but enthusiastic American and Canadian sympathizers.

She glided easily out of the stadium and temporarily out of view, into the woods. Soon she was visible again, taking on her first of many steep inclines. She skated in an easy, uniform pace.

The layout at Big Thunder is unique in several ways. Even though Thunder Bay is considered a Midwestern site, it is far hillier and steeper than most World Cup venues. Because what goes up must come down, races held here are among the world's fastest meter for meter. The course was designed with the fan in mind, and provides for unparalleled viewer participation. It is possible to watch the majority of a 10K race without the need to dash along the trail from one vantage point to another; however, doing so provides ultimate satisfaction for the fan. Best of all, in this particular race, the women were to make four separate passes in front of the assembled crowd, as opposed to the men's 10K, where only two passes are made. Since the course inside the arena is flat, fans are treated to a plethora of head-to-head sprinting, even in interval-start races.

Twenty-five hundred meters into her race, Carol cruised into the stadium. She looked over at Jules and gave him a thumbs-up signal. She had already passed six skiers, and was now in twenty-seventh place. Even so, it appeared that she was skiing within herself, at an even pace.

"Go Carol! Go!" yelled Lisa, who snapped her picture gliding into twenty-sixth place. She liked Carol's attitude. She had personality – streetwise, unpretentious – an urban Catholic. Like herself, Carol was unmarried, athletic, and could handle what came her way. Out of the stadium, she began her second lap.

At the 5K mark, she had picked off another four skiers, advancing to twenty-second place. Lisa was ecstatic. Jules was clinching his mittened hands in tight little fists whirling about his chest like a baby shaking a rattle. "Go Carol!" they each screamed.

Some of the other Americans picked up their enthusiasm as well, yelling their scattered support. This time Carol did not acknowledge them. With 5K to go and such an easy glide she knew it was time to get into a higher gear. She increased her tempo accordingly and steamed by an exhausted train of five skiers at the 6.8K mark. Down the hill she went into her tuck, and resumed skating as the hill flattened out. Three skiers were in front of her as she entered the stadium for the third time. She passed all three in the super-wide lanes there. Incredibly, she found herself in fourteenth place, and was now ahead of every North American in the field.

Jules removed his field glasses for the moment, hollering, "Go! Go! *Hei! Hei! Hei!*" picking up the popular Norwegian chant. Lisa was screaming still louder. Scandinavian fans looked at them askance. All this commotion for fourteenth place?

Carol was energized by their realization that she was skiing out of her mind, and the small contingent yelled even louder as she passed yet another three before exiting the stadium. Less than 2,500 meters remained, and in that space she had to conquer three more giant climbs and descents. She could hear Coach Simmons implore her to give it all she had. Now she skied with passion, reaching deeper down than she had since she first made the national team. She had forgotten about Jules and his wax; she was conscious only that she was in a race at a level she had heretofore only fantasized about.

Head down, she kept up her mantra. Balance, glide, pole, push, skate. Balance, glide, pole, push, skate. Over and over, faster and faster, and she was chewing up the meters in impressive fashion. At 8K she closed in on two more, but they managed to crest the hill before her. Lifting her head for a moment, she saw beneath her a third skier, struggling. She climbed furiously up the next hill to catch them, and passed two of them before she was halfway up, and for one hundred meters more did battle for eighth place. On the descent, Carol's glide proved supreme. Eighth place! Coach Simmons watched in stunned disbelief. Carol's comeback was the most incredible in pursuit history. From thirty-third to a top ten placement!

Still, there was more to go. She struggled to catch up with the final grouping she could see. Ahead there were three more in tight formation. For the final stadium entrance the crowd was treated to two straightaways of about two hundred meters each, just as in the men's races. By the final one hundred fifty Carol had joined them. Although the medals had already been won, the crowd roared their approval as the four women battled for pride alone.

It appeared to all that it was simply a matter of momentum that the others could not hold off Carol, and at the finish line, she prevailed. She finished fifth, the highest in American women Nordic history! Though her 10K time was the fastest of the day, her poor time in the 5K classic prevented her from medalling in the women's pursuit. She passed twenty-eight skiers, a feat unheard of in pursuit history.

Her final sprint left her small band of supporters delirious. "Car-ol! Car-ol! Car-ol!" they chanted in unison. Exhausted, Carol acknowledged their appreciation with a weak wave in their direction. Yes, she skied the race of her life, but in her moment of recognition, she knew it was Jules who put the rubber on the road.

Lisa, having press credentials, was able to rush to her side within the corral.

"Great race, Carol!"

"Thanks," she exhaled, gasping for more oxygen. "Man, I'm ready for a beer."

"Sounds great! I'm buying, after what you just did!"

"You're on." More deep breaths. "Let me get situated first." She eagerly accepted a liter bottle of Naya spring water. "I guess I owe Ichabod a kiss, eh? I'd hate to know what I would have agreed to for a medal." She laughed at the thought.

"I'll tell you what, Carol. I'll kiss him too," Lisa laughed.

"I gotta get a picture of that!" She thought to herself for a moment. "Lisa, do you think we should ask him to come along?" Then she added, whispering, "Please, please, please say no!"

"Well, Carol, skip the foreplay and get your kiss over with. While you're changing I'll find out what I need to know for now. There'll be a lot of time later to get the rest." Lisa was ready to finally join in the party, and Carol was definitely the one to be with.

"Okay! Let's go then!"

Carol skated over to Jules, who was patiently waiting for her arrival.

"Dinky, that is some bitching glide wax you got, my man." And as promised, she planted a big kiss on his right cheek.

Jules turned a crimson red, and laughed, "Well, it's not really wax, it is a perfluorinated compound with a molecular density which allows – "

Carol interrupted his treatise. "Dinky. I'm a skier, okay? I hate science. All this stuff is wax to me. The only difference is that this stuff is your wax. Got it? But, I admit it's good, real good. Well, in fact it's the finest wax I have ever used."

She expected a compliment from him on her skiing in return, but instead he stood there wringing his hands, and in a quick little rhythm his body was swaying from side to side like a pendulum, his feet alternating in little steps in place.

"Jules, do you need to go to the bathroom?" Carol asked him pointedly.

"Actually yes, Ms. Fabiano. I do, and have needed to for quite some time now."

"Well, do you want me take you there by the hand?" she asked sardonically, then she gratuitously added, "Dinky, you need to get a life." She said it as if she knew him all of her life. She withheld additional commentary for the moment, not wanting to embarrass her chemist further.

Finally, Jules quit his stepping, and stooped over to collect his belongings to take with him.

"Dinky, just leave it all here. I'm not going to steal it."

"Okay," Dinky answered, reluctantly removing his knapsack.

As he trudged off to the port-a-john, Carol shook her head slowly. "So, these are the people who make our waxes." The newly arrived Lisa interrupted the thought from developing further.

"Ever wonder what is in that bag of his?" she asked, smiling.

"Probably peanut butter and jelly sandwiches for lunch," Carol said, only half in jest.

Lisa found her remark hilarious. It was too fitting. They both ended up laughing together until Jules' return. Carol informed Jules she had to get changed, but not to worry, her coach would speak to him after all the other racers finished. She pointed out Beth for him. Jules applied his field glasses, nodding his approval. He assured her he would gladly wait for the chance to speak with her coach.

As Carol skated away, Lisa asked him, "Jules, how much did it cost to develop your waxes?"

"They are not waxes. They are compounds. Environmentally safe compounds developed for cold base bonding and durability."

"Okay...and...?" she replied, flipping her right palm up, urging him to answer her question.

"Well, my glide compounds came to...I have the bill right here in my backpack. Uh, $54.11. My grip compounds, well they cost a lot more...let me see...ah! Here we are...$63.27!"

"For one application?" she asked in alarm.

Jules looked at her aghast. "What Ms. Nelson? No! Heaven's no! That was the cost for everything. I bought too much in hindsight, because some formulas were discarded. But I have more than a year's supply right here with me," he emphasized. "I brought enough to supply an entire Olympic team. But I guess it is a little late for that notion," he said as an afterthought.

Lisa was already thinking of Tim's upcoming classic leg in the relays. "Your uh, grip wax...er, compound. Does that work as well as your glide product?"

"Well, I have to be honest. I didn't want to spend so much of my calendar earnings on it, but I had to. I just couldn't get it right for $55.00."

"Well, what did the extra eight and a quarter do for you?" Lisa asked, doing some quick math in her head.

"Um, $8.27, Ms. Nelson. Not to be picky, but accuracy is my life. I have found it to be a marked improvement, actually. With my grip compound I have been able to decrease drag in the kick zone in classic skis by, oh, conservatively, a little over ten percent."

"Ten percent! What are you talking about?" Lisa knew enough about cross-country skiing that the wax zone involved thirty to over fifty centimeters of the ski's base. Jules' claim, if true, would indeed be "a marked improvement."

"Well, Ms. Nelson, this is twenty-first century, uh, stuff," he said, arms folded across his chest defensively. "But remember, my percentages are only comparisons to products, not performance. I am not talking about time. These figures cannot be interpreted to mean a skier will enjoy a ten percent improvement in speed. We are talking mere seconds of improvement in a 10K race."

"How do you explain Carol, then?"

"I guess we both got lucky."

"Jules?"

"Yes?"

"Do me a favor. When Carol's coach gets here, make sure you ask her how to get a hold of the men's coach. His name is Leonard Franz. He will want to learn of your compounds. Here is my room number over at the Airlane Hotel. Call me there or leave a message. Don't let anyone else know about your compounds, okay? By the way, where are you staying?" she asked as a back-up. She should have asked this obvious question to Tim a week ago.

"I'm staying at one of the dorm rooms at Confederation College." The rooms had been made available for the Games during a break for the students, having been arranged long before.

"What's going on over there?" she wondered.

"Why? Is something supposed to be going on?" he replied, mystified.

"Never mind." IT'S ONLY THE OLYMPICS! she felt like screaming. She imagined Jules back at his dorm room eating peanut butter and jelly sandwiches in front of a Bunsen burner, reliving his glory days as an undergrad. And she thought she was bored. "Anyhow, Jules, let's get together again tomorrow. You find out about Coach Franz and I'll get you in touch with him, got it?"

Jules nodded eagerly, wringing his mittened hands in nervous excitement. Lisa felt free to leave as Coach Simmons arrived for her introduction. She saw that Carol was ready to go celebrate, and said her good-byes quickly. The party was waiting.

Meanwhile, the Europeans huddled once again, like spokes on a wheel. Rumors of an American technological breakthrough which began unfounded with the men's surprisingly strong performances, now solidified into an established fact. Fabiano's feat was all the corroboration they needed. In hindsight, they realized there could be no other valid explanation.

The only real surprise to their informant was that it took them so long to finally accept the truth. The Europeans were hardly prepared to capitulate. Whatever technology was responsible for the Americans unjustifiable intrusion into their domain needed to be exposed. The Italians, the Finns, the Russians, and the Scandinavians had found a common threat in the former friendly sleeping giant. All they needed was proof that the standards approved by the International Federation of Skiing – the FIS – set forth to ensure fair competition were being violated in these Games. It was time to burst the American bubble before it got bigger. After Fabiano's performance, they dared not risk an upset in one more race, especially in the upcoming relays.

Before she even crossed the finish line, it was agreed by the IOC that her skis would be confiscated for an analysis. They had been assured by a reliable source that in no way would they suffer the slightest embarrassment for doing so.

More than just national pride was at stake. Each quadrennial it was becoming less demeaning to suggest that money had everything to do with the Games. The Europeans, too, had their version of X-Tek Ski, Inc.'s, their Ultima glides, Kickback grips, and X-Tek skis – and they paid skiers from the elite Nordic powers handsomely for the endorsement of their products. As a result, nearly every nation and every great skier was irrevocably beholden to a variety of corporate sponsors. After all, it was the Olympics. There was no better time to advertise.

And, behind it all was no stranger to these Games. If there was anything their snitch – Mitchell Henry Hawk Plank – understood, it was the need for rules. And for Plank, rule number one was to ask, what is in it for me? And the second was similar: If your enemy was to get twice that of your greatest desire, wish to go blind in one eye.

So, while Lisa and Carol were anonymously drinking drafts at the Stanley Hotel twenty kilometers away on the banks of the Kaministikwia River, unbeknownst to them a rapidly assembled field of experts were on their way from Austria to cut a cross section into her skis. Two more from Italy and Norway scheduled flights to Thunder Bay to take scrapings from the base. Her record shattering skis would soon resemble the waste left over from a tool and die shop.

And without authorization, the scorned Hawk Plank was convening a hastily arranged press conference to explain what they were about to find out, and to tell all who would listen the real reasons why the Americans were succeeding in his absence. Suddenly, the American media became *very* interested.

Chapter Thirty-Six

WHEN TIM ARRIVED to Franz's room, upon seeing the skis, he asked, "Is this the so-called junk?" He handled an attractive pair delicately. "Man, do these ski as sweet as they feel?"

"I don't know. Ask Plank."

"Plank?"

"Yes sir. Remember the good glide you mentioned? What he used in Anchorage is right here before your very eyes – $7.5 million worth, engineered and designed by the best ForesTek's money could buy."

"Why haven't I seen Cane using them, then?"

"Would you believe he doesn't even know about them?"

"I know about them!" came a firm voice from near the opened door. It was Cane. He stepped in and with open eyes saw his father's project for the first time. He ran the palm of his hand along the base of the ski. "So this is what my father thinks I need. Well, like I told him, I'm not buying it . Not this time. Not any more."

"Cane!" exclaimed the confused Coach Franz.

"Don't worry Coach. I know everything. It's all about Dad. How he's going to come to my rescue. Well, the rest of you can use these skis if you like, but I'm not. I doubt that you will either after you hear the whole story. I thought about telling all of you since the phone call in Marathon. But now I can't put it off any longer. Can you get Phil and Jer' to come up, too?"

"Sure. No problem," said Tim, taken aback by yet another indication of maturation developing in Cane. He spoke with authority, with assurance. Five minutes later the Keagan boys arrived and Cane told them all he learned from his father. About the skis in Anchorage, about Gannon and Kranwitz and Scarborough. About the night in Seattle where he prayed for the first time, and that he did not want to lie in court. Most importantly, he accepted the fact his attitude was not conducive to the team effort Coach Franz preached about and how six weeks ago he vowed to give his all to the Games. He decided the morning after Anchorage when Coach Franz showed him the pain and glory of discipline that he was capable of doing things in his own life. If only his father was not always in the way of an instructor giving the positive push, perhaps he could have avoided his fate. But now, he had to account for himself. If he would agree to use his father's skis, it would prove to be a no-win situation. If he lost, he would be forever blamed. If he won, his father would take all the credit. It would be a medal for Dad and for X-Tek skis, and for Cane another chance to remain daddy's dependent little boy.

When he had finished the Keagans came to the seated Paulson, and surrounded him and patted him on the shoulders and back. Paulson stood up and battling back tears in his eyes, said, "Will you forgive me?"

There was no need to vote on that, or on his father's promise and threat. No debate. No testing. No X-Tek skis. It was one for all and all for one.

"I'll call Paulson myself," said Tim. "It is only fitting that I do. It's my turn."

"Wait!" said Franz. "One thing you need to know is that Paulson warned us that if we don't use them he'll find someone who will."

"Sounds like my dad all right," said Cane. He laughed, "I hope they work like they did for Plank."

Everyone laughed. Perhaps they were something special, but no one could deny that so far they've proved nothing.

Tim dialed the number.

"Mr. Paulson? Tim Keagan from the Olympic team. Yes...So, these skis sure look nice. Huh? No, we haven't tried them out...No, not tomorrow, either...No, it's not looking like we're interested...Is Cane here? Oh yes. Yes, he agrees with us. In fact it was his idea...Why? Why? No, you can't speak with him. Why? Because I'm not done talking to you. You know Mr. Paulson, what you tried to do to me and my boys was about the lowest thing that I've ever come across in this sport. But now I understand why. It's because you don't know the first thing about what it is to be a team. It is not about the gifted. It is not about advantage. It is not even about winning...What?...Yeah, it is about a combined effort, Mr. Paulson, and you decided several weeks ago you didn't care to be a part of it. In fact, you worked against it. Didn't you ever hear the story of the Little Red Hen?...Oh, we're going to pay? We're going to get our what kicked? Tsk tsk tsk, Mr. Paulson. Do you eat with that same mouth? Well, it's time to say good-bye, Mr. Paulson. Oh, Coach Franz informs me that you can pick up your skis down in the lobby. Oh, I don't think we are going to be sorry, Mr. Paulson. We didn't get to be where we are by feeling sorry for ourselves. But you'll probably never get this far to realize that fact, will you?"

He held his hand over the mouth piece. "Cane, do you want to talk to him?"

"Sure, why not?"

He walked over to Keagan, picking up the phone. Suddenly, his angry father could be heard in a garbled voice throughout the room. The tirade went on for several minutes. Cane stood listening, one arm folded across his chest.

Finally, he said, "Yeah, Dad. Are you done? No we're not...Well, go ahead. Do what you gotta do. Bye." He hung up the phone.

"What did he say?" asked Jerry

"Before or after he threatened to cut me out of my inheritance? It doesn't matter what he says. It's our decision, together, right team?"

Not a minute passed and the phone rang again.

"Don't answer it. It's just my father again."

It was too late. Coach Franz wanted to put his two cents worth in as well.

"Hello!" he shouted angrily. Suddenly, his attitude took a turn for the better. "Oh, I'm sorry. Beth? How are you? What! Carol took fifth in the pursuit?"

Everyone in the room heard it in disbelief. She informed Franz about the mystery wax. "Was it an X-Tek Ski, Inc. product?" he asked. She didn't know but she highly doubted Jules was involved in the scenario Franz described, but he could find out for himself. She would be over in thirty minutes.

Chapter Thirty-Seven

AT THE SAME time at the Stanley Hotel, Carol and Lisa had exhausted the subject of wax and of skiing. Inexorably the topic changed to the "m" word. Men. And specifically men who ski.

Carol wasn't very familiar with Tim Keagan or his sons, although she did note they were hunks. They seemed kind of clannish, although it was tough to make a judgment call. Perhaps, they were just more devoted to the sport. Nothing was known about Tim's earlier days, and Carol was surprised to hear that at one time he was the nation's rising star immediately after the days of Koch, because Plank had been dominant for so long.

She knew of Cane, of course. Everyone knew of Cane. The women on the circuit were attracted to him. He had everything. Good looking, tall, blond, very rich, muscular, and during practice, one of the great skiers in America over the past three years. He had earned his share of notoriety. But often he had that look in his eyes, that something in his life had gone awry – but didn't know what it was. It was always one step forward and two steps back.

Back at the Valhalla, Beth introduced the newest addition of the US Nordic Olympic Team to Coach Franz, et al, the one and only Jules Dinkel. His gawky demeanor and appearance gave her outlandish tale a sort of immediate and visceral credibility to the technology-wary quintet.

At practice the following morning, it was agreed that the men, too, would sample his wares. Of special interest to Tim were his claims concerning his grip wax compound. Such an improvement in area of the base devoted to the kick zone would make his classic skis the virtual equivalent of skate skis for double-poling purposes, which over time proved to be Tim Keagan's greatest advantage in competition.

The next morning they were to learn that in resisting the temptation of the evil of X-Tek skis, their reward for so doing would not disappoint. Jules' compounds passed every test.

Still in Seattle, the unaware Stu Weinberg had not yet heard from Lisa. He found it hard to believe that the Keagans were using X-Tek skis, though many in the media were reporting it as fact. Now Cane, yeah, he could see Cane using them. In fact, he would believe anything about Cane given his dealings with his old man. If nothing else the once staid sport was garnering the type of notoriety that attracted the media like flies.

Coach Franz's denials seemed less than candid given the fact his own skier was the son of the parent company's CEO. Most intriguing, he would not deny having met with Cane Paulson, Sr. about his products. Carol Fabiano's obscene gesture in response to their incessant accusations seemed to the thundering herd of reporters the type of adoptive admission the American public "deserved" to see for themselves on televised newscasts from coast to coast. Cane Paulson's attorneys insisted that the CEO was out of town and unavailable for comment. And Tim Keagan's unequivocal denials were rebutted by four-time Olympian Hawk Plank's revised theory of conspiracy. The tale was full of potential Olympic infamy and, in a Games where the entire American contingent had not earned even one bronze medal, the unfolding drama was elevated to the status of an answered prayer for the American media giants.

Cane Paulson, Sr. did not know what in the dickens was going on. He was truly in a fix. All the speculation was semi-flattering, but not a wit of it was true.

And the ignored and oblivious Jules? Well, he knew less about the controversy than Plank did of him, which was nothing. The secret of

Jules remained intact, as though the perfect diversion had been arranged. The ironic thing was that there was nothing discovered in the analysis of Carol Fabiano's skis to indicate they violated any rule promulgated by the governing board of the FIS or by the IOC. In stages, their findings were released. The construction and composition of the alleged X-Tek skis did not appear to be "revolutionary" in any sense. The chemical analysis of her base compounds revealed "nothing out of the ordinary." Finally, the FIS admitted the skis she used were manufactured by Madshus, just as she claimed from the beginning. But there remained a catch – even if the skis and base products did not violate any rule as far as the technology employed, the IOC took the unusual, if not extraordinary mid-Olympic position that X-Tek products, if they did exist, and even if found to be "acceptable" as defined within the FIS code, "must be universally available" to all the other teams competing in the events. Such a position, after all, only made sense. Competition is premised upon the performance of individuals being paramount, not products, so free choice and equal opportunity were appropriately deemed vital. Most astonishing of all to a bewildered American press, it was Coach Franz, the US representative to the committee who motioned for the proposal's adoption! The Europeans were flabbergasted as well. In effect, Franz craftily check-mated Cane Sr. once and for all. No one else could use what his team had already rejected on principled terms.

As the controversy expanded to rumors beyond supposition one thing became clear. X-Tek skis could not be provided to all twenty teams competing in the Games. The company simply was not in that stage of ready production. They could have been, but Paulson's attorneys failed to advise him that the Olympic Committee might be interested in fairness.

X-Tek skis, in effect, were dead on arrival. Little did Plank know that the entire American contingent could not have been made happier, now that those same skis could not be used by another team to defeat them.

Afterwards the in-house issue of Jules' wax arose. The US men and women were assembled to discuss the implications of the rule change.

Was it sportsmanlike to usurp the entire product's availability? Did they have a duty to share their good fortune with the competition? Would any medals or victories be forever tainted? Not surprisingly, the contestants looked to Tim Keagan, the erstwhile lawyer and defender of the faith.

Without an instant's hesitation he said he "didn't care and whatever you decided is okay with me," and that, "he would not lose one minute sleep over the decision and neither should anyone else. I just want to ski."

"I might!" exclaimed Cane. "How is this different from my father's stuff?"

"How can you say such a thing?" Phillip was a little more agitated and a lot more prepared to take sides. He knew enough about court-room advocacy from his father's profession, and felt constrained to put on his case. He continued.

"This woman will confirm beyond any doubt that Jules Dinkle's product was made available to each and every team – in fact to each and every contestant – prior to and during each race in these Games." He looked admiringly at Lisa. "Is that not a fact, so help you God?"

"It is indeed. I will swear to it on a Bible."

He called in Jules.

"This man, who developed these amazing products will attest to and confirm that his compounds have been made with one hundred percent universally available materials, and that attempts to market his products have been met by rejection after rejection after rejection by these Games' participants and by the very companies supplying the rest of the Olympic field." He looked upon Jules with a sound confidence he reserved only for the saintly. "Are these no longer hypothetical statements, but in fact, true to the best of the data you have obtained, so help you God?"

"There is no flaw in your analysis that I am able to detect. And I must add that my compounds pose no threat to either the consumer or to the environment. Further, this assertion includes both the manufacture and the application of the resulting product, which in fact, have been offered for use – without cost – to each and every contestant in these Games, as confirmed by Ms. Nelson."

"My next witness, Carol Fabiano." He paused for her to stand before her peers. "Ms. Fabiano, do you now or have you ever been associated with, or used products of any manufacturer in violation of the rules and regulations as defined by the IOC and /or the FIS?"

"Never, and my Uncle Vincenzo would like to meet those who say I have in some dark alley of St. Paul. I can further swear that until I myself risked all the acclaim I earned in these Games before trying Jules' wax..." much laughter interrupted the once upon a time also-ran, "this good, decent, and humble man," she raised her voice as if preaching, "was subject to ridicule, scorn, and humiliation. And now the world wants us to apologize? I think not! Let us look at the facts." She went through the myriad of lies. The so-called Keagan conspiracy. The "Cane Junior" connection. The Plank allegations. The list went on and on. The whole world was certain the Americans were using X-Tek products, and credited a lie for their best showing ever at a Winter Olympics. And the men's team hadn't even used Jules' wax yet!

"Finally, the world stood by and waited for the results of the tests which destroyed a pair of my favorite skis. In humiliation and shame, they were compelled to admit their pigheadedness and beg my forgiveness. For no X-Tek Ski product was involved. And what did they say of Jules' wax? Verbatim," she pulled out an excerpted statement. "We cannot detect any substance in the sample which would indicate grounds for disqualification under the strictest interpretation of all applicable governing rules. In summary, our analyses failed to disclose the presence of any substance not already found in ski base preparations already available and in use for these Games." She paused. "But you know what really hoses me off? I skied my butt off in that race and no one is giving me any credit!"

The whole room arose in unison, applauding loudly and cheering. They were tired of their abilities being ignored. All, except Cane.

Jules said weakly as the din wore down. "Carol is correct. My compounds do not make skis self-propelling mechanisms. They do not necessarily make the ski or the skier faster. All that is accomplished is a completely uniform base bonding for glide and extraordinary durability without the application of heat. My grip compound is basically a concentrated version of what is already in use. I tried to tell them..."

Before a vote was taken, Tim asked if any further discussion was necessary.

Slowly, Cane raised his hand.

"I'm sorry, but I disagree, Tim. It is not fair. Although everything that has been said here is true, and it would not be unfair to proceed as such, we know that Jules' wax is our choice. We know that Jules has only enough of it for our team. We also know that though Jules had been hawking his products, nobody really understood. No one who has credibility – my apologies to Jules – has publicly endorsed Jules' products."

"Even if we did, and everyone else decided to switch, we do not have enough to give them," Beth Simmons protested.

"Uh, Coach," Jules reminded her, "for $200 Canadian, I can buy the necessary elements right here in Thunder Bay and overnight I can supply the entire field and then some. So, if they want some, they will have it. I promise, provided of course I am paid in advance."

Lisa smiled to herself. He does have a Bunsen burner back in his room!

Franz removed his wallet. "Here's $200. Buy what you need and prepare it."

"What will that accomplish?" asked Lisa, a little concerned about the train coming to a halt.

"What if we get a medal?" asked Cane. "Later, like it always happens, they discover we used an unmarketable product. They won't give us credit. They'll put an asterisk next to our names. That's why I turned down my father with his X-Tek line of skis and products. Look at Carol! It's just like she says. She skied her butt off and everyone who knows about Jules' wax is giving that all the credit. If I can get a medal I want to earn it on my own. I think we all feel that way, really."

Jules looked down and then rose up again to speak. "I acknowledge the valid points Cane raises. The last thing I want to do is to leave any of you with a sense of shame should you accomplish your lives goals, and then later be forced to defend yourselves the rest of it for using my compounds, as if you have done something unethical. You have all trained hard and got here without me and my research and I watched all of you race. I believe Cane, Jerry, Mr. Keagan, and Phillip can win their race without any advantage my compounds might deliver. We must take into account what he says. Cane is right. I should wait and try again next ..."

"I can't believe this talk. We can't abandon Jules! Didn't he train and prepare for these Olympics, too? Doesn't he belong here as much as any one of us? Perhaps he cannot ski like us, but does that preclude him from the role he has earned just as much as any one of us?" Phil demanded of them.

"Yeah!" joined in Carol. "Just because he is smarter than their scientists shouldn't stop us. And even though he skis in knickers awaiting the arrival of some kind of weird bird there in New England doesn't mean he is any less worthy than us to represent America. This is his Olympics, too! As much as ours!"

Jerry chimed in, "Cane is right. Dad is right. Carol and Phil are right, too. But one thing is clear. This is the Olympics to use Jules' compounds. Not four years from now. Not next year. Now. Phil's right. Jules, no less than anyone of us, deserves his day in the sun. And if we win with his compounds, so be it. I don't see the Norwegians or the Italians waxing our skis, do you? In fact, they huddle together in their secret places before the race so no one knows what they are doing. They have a paid staff to do it for them. They have never offered us any of their secrets, have they? And don't think they don't have some."

Everyone looked at each other and nodded, for it was indeed one of the hallmarks of competition that the practice of waxing was a more closely guarded secret then any other aspect of racing.

Coach Franz, who was standing with one leg resting on the seat of a chair in the corner, slowly moved to the center of the room, one arm crossing the other bent ninety degrees, with his chin resting in his right hand.

"My friends. Jules' compounds, like it or not – and Jules we do indeed like them, believe me, that's why we are here – Jules' compounds, ladies and gentlemen, are already part of Olympic history. We can't undo what Carol accomplished two days ago. I have made it my rule not to endorse products and my skiers are free to use any products they wish to. It seems to me that we can combine the concerns of Cane with our desire to use Jules' products, ethically. This is not the discovery of the hydrogen bomb, mind you. This Olympics is not about war. It is about excellence. The people we race against understand a code of survival, of brotherhood, of sisterhood. Except when racing, we are friends, after all. We understand and strive to live – and to demonstrate to others – a better way of life. We accept what has been dealt us, and manage and cope with the elements, be it blizzard or sunshine.

"All we can do with the situation we are now confronted with is choose to be totally honest. If we are, we shall avoid that asterisk Cane perceptively brought up. Those who choose not to accept what we tell them is true can only blame themselves for their doubt. And in the generations that follow they will call us not only champions, but prophets. And not just prophets, but venerable.

"So then what are we required to do? If they do not believe Carol, if they do not believe Jules, if they do not believe us, but instead continue to put false hope in the Planks who lurk about them, fueling their lack of faith in us as athletes and as honest competitors, all we can do to convince them they are wrong is to outperform them. Make them pay. We are here to win if we can.

"If we choose to do less than this, instead of veneration we would properly be remembered with eternal ridicule. We have been thrust into a situation where we are left with no choice but to blaze a trail, or to cower from it and pretend any victory we may achieve in the absence of leadership will somehow make the medals we may win more precious. It will not. It is no sin to choose wisely. History will not hold us in contempt if we act intelligently. If we succeed, those who follow in our footsteps will prove us worthy of emulation. History will vindicate us. We will have been made worthy of competing in these Games; we will have been made proper ambassadors for the ages.

"I suggest to those who wish to use Jules' compounds, to do so. Along with Beth and Carol, I will espouse his products with sincerity, without remuneration, without hyperbole. Honestly. The products and their application can be made available to all upon request. I suggest Jules' current supply be reserved for immediate glide testing and be made available for our competition to test them. At this meeting's conclusion we will disseminate this information to the coaches personally and post it at the media center. Jules, so history may record we have maintained the Olympic ideal, if you could, please prepare more product, okay? We would not wish to be the only team left out."

Everyone laughed. They suspected no one was about to try some alleged compound invented by an alleged Jules Dinkel.

"Are there any objections?" He looked around. He looked at Cane. "How about you, Cane?"

Cane sat silently, rubbing his eyes. Coach Franz could not remember seeing Cane so disconcerted since Anchorage. In Cane's mind, he was back in Seattle, being told to lie. He was in denial; worse, in prolepsis. The ultimate failure awaited and he needed an excuse. Jules' wax would just make things worse.

"Ladies, Gentlemen," Franz exhorted the rest. "We must ski the race of the day and only the day of the race. Jules' compounds are good, but we only get to the finish line on our own. So let's get out of here and prepare for the revolution."

The room rose together, ostensibly united and upbeat. But compared to the rest, Cane remained in a funk.

Franz and the Keagans were fully aware of the signals exuding from him. He was starting to look like the old Cane. The pre-Olympic Cane. His father's Cane. After the meeting concluded, Franz, Cane, and his teammates remained.

"Cane, just what is the problem?" said Franz, perplexed. Now was not the time for second guessing. Everything was going their way for once.

Cane thought about his answer.

"You guys are really serious about winning, aren't you?"

No one answered. Their silence was an obvious affirmation to the allegation. More than ever the Keagans and Franz smelled a medal.

He continued. "You don't think I can win without Jules' magic wax, do you? You think I need a crutch or I can't win, right?"

"Well, Cane why do you think we are going to use it, too?" asked Jerry. "Maybe we can win without it. Maybe we can't win with it. But it's better, that's all."

"You want to build a lead for me. You're afraid I'll choke again. Isn't that really what all this is about? You're just like my father."

Tim responded, "So what is wrong with wanting to win?"

"All this talk about teamwork is just a put on. If I don't win it's all my fault." he laughed sarcastically. "And then where will you be? That's what I thought." He got up to leave. "If we don't win, I am the odd man out, eh?" he said with a sneer. "Who is my brother? Where is my father?"

"Cane!" called Franz. "That's not it! Not at all!"

"Never mind , Coach. I got to get away," and he stormed out the door, slamming it, disappearing into Thunder Bay, a town turned upside down, just like his life all of a sudden, just like the day he was having. There was something far more slippery going on than the debate over Jules' glide compounds. It was the realization that in two days he would be skiing head-to-head against the best of the best of the best. And they expected him to do something he had never done.

"Cane!" Franz hollered in futility. "You can't go on blaming everyone..."

Cane hurried away all the more. Their efforts to catch him before leaving were not successful. He was last seen driving his rental south to what was touted as the "World's Biggest Party." And that was one Olympic claim that more than lived up to expectations.

"What was that all about?" Tim asked.

"I'm afraid we may have seen the resurrection of the old Cane before our very eyes," Franz said in a complete understatement.

"But why? Yesterday he was a changed man. That's what he told us," Jerry whined.

"Today is a new day. Unfortunately, this behavior is hardly out of the ordinary for someone in his situation." Franz said.

"What has gotten into him? Jules' wax isn't that big a deal is it?" asked Jerry.

"Nothing. Everything. Who knows?" Franz sank back into his soft chair, lowering his head into his opened palms. He continued, looking up slowly. "Maybe I should not have told him before the meeting that I've made him our leg man."

"What are you talking about?" asked Phillip.

"I reconfigured the team. Cane's the leg man," Franz reiterated.

The Keagans were too stunned to protest immediately.

Finally Tim responded in a surprisingly calm voice, "Len, you can't be serious."

"I thought about it over and over and over again, Tim. Cane was our best uphill skater in training and he can outsprint Jerry. He is what we need in the fourth leg. Plus Phil has been better in the classic races here than Cane."

"Okay, that's true." Tim agreed. "But Jerry is much faster over 10K. Shouldn't he be our leg man?"

Franz exhaled heavily. "Yes, he should. I know it's a gamble. But I just have a good feeling about the three of you skiing in a chain."

"So start off with Paulson." Phil suggested.

"Absolutely not!" insisted Franz. "Listen. If anything can work, this will. We need a good start from Tim. With the Europeans so evenly matched I just have to believe they are going to reconfigure their teams in order to shake things up. That is why I want Jerry in the third leg. We can't afford to be out of the race after twenty or thirty kilometers. We have no other choice."

Tim seemed strangely resigned to the change. Maybe he knew it would lessen the pressure on his sons. He only put up a pro forma protest. "Well, it is probably too late to change your mind, isn't it?" he said to Franz.

Franz would have smiled but for Cane's disappearance. It was exactly the response he had hoped to hear from Tim.

"Now it all makes sense," Jerry concluded, in reference to Cane's outbursts. "Well, let's get out and find him before it's too late."

"Where?" asked Tim, staring out the window down Arthur Street, full of business after business, block after block, for four kilometers. Balmoral Street lay between, providing access to scores more of bars, nightclubs, and Olympic-sized parties, in scores more locations interspersed throughout the sprawling city. Thunder Bay was not Seattle, but it was not Traverse City either. With a population topping 120,000 and twice that with the Olympic crush, Cane would not be found by strangers tracking him down or by referring to the yellow page directory for guidance.

"We won't find him if he doesn't want us to," said Franz. "Hopefully, I'm wrong about where he is at mentally. One thing is for sure – if he does go to a bar, his drinking won't be a lesson in moderation."

Heads reluctantly nodded.

"Well, where do we start?" Tim reiterated.

Franz knew he was dealing with a potentially dangerous situation. One he didn't understand. He was thinking about the night in Anchorage. Perhaps he should have referred him to a professional. Even if he was wrong for not doing so, did Cane have to wait unit now to snap? He was doing so well. What concerned Franz was not that he might return drunk, but that after getting drunk, he might not return at all. Suddenly, the 4x10K meant nothing to him. But he had no solution.

"I don't have any idea. Maybe we're just overemphasizing it all. Let's give him twenty-four hours and I'm sure we'll see a different Cane." Of that he was certain. "I just can't see chasing him down at this point. You guys need to stay focused. I think Cane's just focusing in his own way. I'm sorry I brought it up at all. He'll be okay," he lied. He was the parent calming the children in a catastrophe.

"We have to do something," insisted Jerry.

"Then pray," he told his suddenly anxious team. "And let me do the worrying."

Chapter Thirty-Eight

TRAFFIC MOVED AT a snail's pace. And Cane was in the middle of it all. Cane tapped out a rhythm on the steering wheel of his rental. He wasn't about to turn back. He would have himself maybe just a couple beers, and then maybe later just a couple more. He looked around at all the festivities going on in the streets of Thunder Bay. God! It was good to see people capable of enjoying these Olympics! He wanted some of that. Just a little for now, and a lot more later.

He just wanted to assure himself that no matter what happened Saturday, women would still love his body and hair and his new thin blond goatee. He just wanted to practice that smile of his so it wouldn't fade in defeat. Because it was bound to happen. It always just does.

As Cane proceeded in the direction of the big lake south on Arthur Street, a being of light, who had just descended from the heavens, was halted by the traffic signal at the intersection facing east on Highway 61. This being of light instantly recognized him and told the cab driver to catch up with him. As they both approached Balmoral Street, the cab pulled alongside. The back seat window rolled down, the passenger letting in the frigid air.

"Cane! Hey, Cane! Cane!" emanated white plumes of speech. Cane lifted his head, as if rising from a trance-like sleep, hearing the muffled commotion through his closed window. It was Gavin Smith, who had just flown in from Traverse City via Minneapolis.

Cane's frozen expression slowly began to thaw. And he forced himself to present a more pleasant appearance. He rolled down his window at the light. "Gavin Smith. What a surprise," he said, flatly.

"Hey, pull over. Okay?"

"All right," he answered in resignation. Molecules were being rearranged. A new stimulus had been introduced. The eye of the hurricane.

Gavin picked up on the affectation he had seen and heard so many, many, many times before.

"Where are you going?" he asked.

"Nowhere. Nowhere in particular. Why?"

Cane knew he was being studied by Gavin's sober observation. He was instantly relieved he had not gotten drunk. He could mask his intentions. Maybe Gavin would leave.

"Well, I just got into town. Want to come with me for a cup of coffee?"

Cane smirked, and forced himself not to shake his head. He looked up the road. So many opportunities. But he had not yet succumbed. He sighed heavily. How could he say no? Just as Gavin picked up on his front, Cane picked up on Gavin's. It was like the stroke of midnight; the ball was over.

"Sure," he reluctantly huffed. In his mind, expletives exploded. The devil had been put back into hell for now, and it hated where it knew it must return.

"How about that place?" Gavin said, pointing ahead.

"Fine," Cane agreed. Right next to the bar he had in mind. It figures. Expletives faded into numbness. "Maybe I better try hot chocolate instead though."

Gavin smiled.

Cane smiled back, bemused by the turn of events. He may as well surrender to propitiation.

"What are you doing here?" he asked, without receiving the obvious answer.

Gavin asked if could catch a ride back to the hotel. Cane assured him it would be no problem. The luggage was moved to the rental from the cab. The cabbie thanked Gavin for the $5 Canadian tip, made possible by Gannon, et al, and disappeared into a late afternoon snow squall.

The small talk disappeared as Gavin convinced himself that Cane needed to understand what Gavin understood.

"You know Cane, when I heard you say you were going nowhere, nowhere in particular, guess what I thought?"

"What?"

Gavin stirred his coffee and sipped some. He chuckled. "I thought that you might be going out to a club and..."

Cane gulped some hot chocolate. Too hot. He grabbed for his glass of water. "And get wasted? Give up on the team? Why would you think that?" he asked, his eyes darting side to side, nervously.

"It's okay. It's okay. Cane, if you were, that wouldn't change things, you know. I've seen a lot worse than this, Cane. Trust me. I saw so many kids waste their lives growing up in Flint. Black, white. Traverse City, Flint. It is all the same, really. I just hoped you were one who turned the corner."

"So you think I'm a drug addict or an alcoholic, is that it?" Cane asked, indignant.

"That's not my call. Cane, we're all addicts of some kind to one degree or another, aren't we? You. Me. Coach Franz. Everyone. Whether or not you are, you still can't live tomorrow today. Do you know what I mean?"

"Well, that has been kind of my problem today," Cane answered.

Gavin laughed. "It's just the biggest thing that has ever happened to you, isn't it? And you expected to handle all this on your own?" He paused. "Cane, you're part of this team. You can't let them down now. Not after all you've been through."

"I feel like I'm just hanging on, you know?" Cane revealed a litany of stress. Everything that seemed set in Traverse City has slowly unraveled. His dad's intervention. X-Tek Skis. Plank. Dinky. Accusations. Carol's great pursuit race. But now they insisted on high expectations. The Keagans and Franz are thinking gold! And worst of all – worst of all – Franz has him skiing the final leg in a nationwide broadcast!

Cane continued.

"Gavin, you know I'm not the best skier on this team. Each one of the Keagans is better than me. Why is Franz setting me up? They're going to televise this race live in America for the first time. What if we're in contention? And they're sure to be talking all about Jules' glide wax. Tim Keagan told me he's afraid I'll choke again." He began talking in wider and wider circles.

"Whoa. Whoa. Whoa! Cane! Stop. Stop. Listen. Listen!" he paused until he had Cane's entire attention. "So what?" Silence. "Cane, look out this window. Just look out this window." Outside the snow continued to fall. It was dusk now. Cars were driving past, south on Arthur, slowly. Snow piled up aside ruts in the roadway. "Looks kind of ugly, doesn't it?"

"Yeah."

Gavin turned to a waitress, with a request. "Don't take this away. We'll be right back." Then to Cane, "Come outside with me."

They both exited the coffee house. Outside they stood in the middle of the parking lot. "Stand here. Close your eyes. How do you feel?" Gavin asked.

"Cold."

"Okay. Keep your eyes closed, but tilt your head back. More. As far as you can."

"What is this, a sobriety test?" Cane obeyed anyhow, until he was face up to the sky. Snow was falling gently, but persistently on his face.

"How do you feel now?"

Cane laughed. "How am I supposed to feel?"

"Open your eyes."

Cane did.

"What do you see?"

Out of the black, gray, and amber sky came thousands, millions, billions, of big snow flakes, falling slowly like little frozen parachutes, fractiously trying to defy gravity.

"Snow?" Cane offered.

"Cane, you're a real poet. Come on, don't you see something bigger at work?" Gavin said to the upturned chin.

"Nature? God?" Cane returned.

"Good. Good. Very good. Let's stick with answer two for a minute. Let's go back inside."

The waitress saw them return, stopping her gossip with the other young women about the cute blond skier.

"So, what was that all about?" Cane asked.

"Let's see. Cold, snow, nature, God. Those were your answers right? Why complicate things, Cane? Just get through the day."

"Right. It's so easy," Cane replied, unimpressed.

Gavin returned a look, a loving scowl. "Why do you want to make it harder? Me, I make things simple. I break them down everyday. Yes, I have pains. I suffer disappointments. But I quit feeling sorry for myself and I do what I can do. I don't worry about what I can't do. Do you think I am half the attorney Gannon or Kranwitz or Scarborough were? But I get places in spite of my limitations. I am never less than honest. And I have faith in something bigger. That God up there, out there, and in here," he said, indicating within him, as well. "And you know what my God has never once told me?"

"What?"

"To doubt doing what is right. And that is why I am here with you instead of my best friend, right now. I won't let you tear down nineteen years of his reconstruction. You want to feel sorry for someone? Listen to Keagan's story."

For the first time Cane heard the unlikely sojourn of Tim Keagan. Jerry and Phil had it rough too, compared to him. Finally, Gavin talked about their Olympic dream.

"This is the one solid hope that brought him back to life. He is more scared than you are of failure. He won't be back, but maybe you will. You made a decision several weeks ago that this time things would turn out different. And they have. Don't give in now."

Cane sat pensively.

"Let's get going Gavin. So where are you staying?"

"Darned if I know."

"Well, what's the name of the hotel?"

"Like I said, darned if I know."

"You mean you came all this way without reservations?"

"Well I couldn't get any this late in the Olympics, now could I?"

"Gavin!" he exclaimed, then added. "You attorneys are all the same." He stared at the momentary vagabond. "Well, you probably saved me from leaving one room empty in this town for tonight. So you can stay with me one night anyhow. You don't snore do you?"

"Uh. There are two beds in the room aren't there?"

"Yeth, Gavin." Cane replied, drooping a wrist. "Next thing I know you'll be taking my dog."

Gavin laughed. "I'm just kidding, Cane. I have a room. Tim called me the minute someone left town early. Same place he's staying at, the Valhalla."

"Good. That's where we all are. One big happy mixed up integrated dysfunctional extended American family."

"Well, I'm pleased to know I'm from a normal American home," Gavin noticed.

"You haven't met everyone in the family yet, my man. Wait until you get a load of Jules!" Cane laughed perniciously.

Gavin didn't get it, but he laughed alongside the strapping leg man, anyhow. The molecules inside Cane's head were again gripping instead of skating.

On the way back to the Valhalla, Gavin entertained Cane with a long monologue about his one and only adventure in Nordic racing.

"One year Keagan got me to ski in a twelve kilometer citizen race. I never saw so many white butts in all my life. Men, women, and children of all ages passing me. A few took a double take at the pudgy black dude sweating like a July day who had no business being in anything other than suits tailored for the courtroom. It didn't take long before the crowd at the mass start thinned out and I found myself skiing some lonely stretches of that hardwood forest. Well, I was on skis...I don't know if I should call what I was doing skiing.

"At about the 7.5K mark, I thought I wouldn't finish. I came upon an elderly white bearded man. He must have been seventy or seventy-five and, like me, skied slowly in the classic style although with more grace. 'First race?' he turned and asked me in a measured voice. 'Yes!' I yelled ahead, as if he was one hundred meters away, not the five he was, in a voice of total exhaustion. 'Well, you're doing a fine job, a mighty fine job.'

"I laugh when I think of that moment because there I was, nearly in last place, and the guy I'm trying to pass is comforting me. But his comment made me so proud, I actually saw things suddenly in a brighter light, and I even began to pick up my pace a little. As I approached his side I thought to ask him, 'How many times for you, sir?' I deferred to his age. He shocked me by answering, 'First time, just like you. Want to ski together?'

"Nothing much was said between us for the next five kilometers to the finish, but I have always remembered how easy it seemed. The only thing of significance I recall is what he said about skiing. Now that I think about it, maybe he referred to everything. He said, 'when the fun is over, it is time to quit.' Man, that sent goose pimples up and down my spine that day. Because I heard in that one simple line a perfect diagnosis of why people fail to accomplish things set before them. Well, it described more than that. It described alcoholism. Pessimism. Unaccountability. Every evil. Every sin. Every bad habit. Any excess."

Gavin's story must have struck a chord, because Cane became as silent as the North that cold snowy night. What Cane was going to do that night in Thunder Bay before Gavin crashed his party was not about having fun. And he realized it.

"Did you ever hear how I got started in cross-country skiing, Gavin?"

"No."

He told Gavin the story of his feat at Mount Rainier and about the drinking afterwards. "You know, that remains my most vivid recollection in this sport." He told him about Coach Franz having to wipe away a tear after he heard how his father handled the situation. "Who knows where I would be today if I hadn't wasted so many years in between?"

Gavin laughed, heartened to know Cane had shared so much of himself that evening. "Well, Cane, you are in the Olympics, after all. What better place can you be than where you are at now?"

Cane saw the humor in it too. "Well, I mean how good could I have been."

"Someday maybe you can look back and maybe you will know, Cane. But maybe you won't need to. After all, it's not like you lack the opportunity to find out right here."

"Yeah, of course."

"Cane?"

"Yeah?"

"This time, when you come back down from Big Thunder, don't let the fun stop. Can you do that this Saturday?"

"I think so."

"One more thing. Decide in your heart to be that kind of champion. Do it tonight and don't relitigate the issue. Even if you guys lose, do it with class. And to help you – don't ever, ever underestimate the awesome power of God. I cannot tell you how to ski, or how to win, but I can tell you here is a God who delights in you, and is just waiting to answer your most fervent prayers. Let Him."

Cane brushed away a tear as he turned his head to walk to his room. Gavin just stood there, and then Cane turned back to him and practically squeezed the life out of the attorney in an embrace.

"Thanks, Gavin. Thank God you found me tonight."

"Yes. Thank God. You'll do just fine, Cane. Listen to that disciplinarian inside you. You will not be skiing alone anymore. We are all with you now."

"Can you let Coach Franz and my teammates know I'm okay?"

"You bet."

"Tell them this. You tell them if they want gold I found some at the bottom of the mine. And I can't wait to bring it up to them."

Cane walked on air down that hallway not waiting for any response. Finally, Gavin saw some of Tim Keagan in Cane Paulson. A man. A destiny. The talk, the walk of a champion, one who might relish the role of the anchor leg. Gavin became part of the team. Not quite a jewel perhaps, but at least a stepping stone.

Chapter Thirty-Nine

NAWARE, TIM SEEMED presciently collected under the circumstances. Perhaps it was because he had plenty of hurdles of his own. He talked to his sons at length that night Cane drove off. He mentioned how people wondered how at age forty-three he could be here.

"Actually," he said, "I'm a better skier for it. I've been asked the same question over and over and over again. I remind them of Maurilio DeZolt, but I'm no Maurilio." He talked of his regrets. He lived through an entire generation of great skiers against whom he never competed. His favorite? Vegard Ulvang, hands down. "He was not invincible, no one is. But Vegard never let a race get a way from him. He lined up to race like a Norwegian Kirk Gibson in the World Series of Ski. He never skied with anyone else's pace in mind. It was his attitude. You wanted him on your team, that was for sure. But dropping names or having heroes is of no real assistance now, so why belabor the point?" he said.

He had been described in the media as a private man, with painful memories, and it was surmised that this Olympics might provide him some redemption and solace. Perhaps. "I could just as easily produce another tale of woe, like that the Olympian Dan Jansen long suffered." He admitted of this possibility, but would gladly accept that risk. Why? Because it was unthinkable to live life otherwise.

Curiously, he was already talking beyond Saturday, about how some Judges really irked him. Saying nothing is more amusing to him than hearing some old has-been on the US Supreme Court trying to justify his most insane opinion. Saying those who refuse to retire at a decent age and stay on past the onset of senility out of political concerns regarding their potential successor are total hypocrites. "If their opinions had any lasting virtue, they would have generations of plagiarists quoting them," he noted. About the "Big Bears" of the world, where resulting justice was always incidental to their convenience. "When I hear that we in the US have the best system of justice in the world, I laugh my butt off. The only people I hear it from are the obviously guilty and their attorneys who play judges like fiddles and who deceive marginally literate jurors into acquittals. What differentiates us as a people from others is freedom and only freedom," he said with conviction. "But, that is changing. After all, we were all victims of 'the best system in the world.' That case of Plank's should never made it to any court. If there was any justice, Plank and the rest would all be in jail. How likely do you think that is?"

"Well, back to skiing," he said. Cane was right about Jules' products; life was not just about equal opportunities, but an equal chance at equal opportunity. "But remember a couple things," he said, "you can lead a horse to water, but you can't make it drink. You can't make a silk purse out of a sow's ear. There comes a point a soul just doesn't want to, or can't be saved. We can't take their skis and wax them for them. Belief is a subjective thing, far more important than any other factor."

Jerry and Phil did not know whether to bring up their mother. She was on their minds. Was she a part of all this? Phil just barely remembered her. Jerry thought of her only in an imaginary sense. Phil thought talking about Lisa might be a way to bring up the subject. Tim's whole being lit up at the mention of Lisa. So finally, Phil put it bluntly because he knew his father never responded like that at the sound of any other name. "Was mom like Lisa?"

Tim did not expect the question, and considering the time devoted to his answer it must have been important to him to find the right words with which to respond.

"What is the difference between a memory and a dream?"

Typically Irish, answering a question with a question. "One can't replace the need for the other. But your mother, my Nikola, she was my dream at one time. Lisa? Well, I know a lot less about her than Nikola." he laughed awkwardly, embarrassed to admit what he really felt for her.

"What I mean Dad, was our mom a winner, like Lisa seems to be? Was she a 'keeper'?" Jerry asked.

"Oh, yes. There is no doubt that I was a lucky man. She was beautiful; she was faithful. She was a good wife and the best mother. We had some hard times. We had arguments. Oh boy, I'm glad you don't remember them. Especially over skiing, I did it so much. The funny thing is the longer I live the more I realize how much she meant in such a little time. Don't think it was perfect. She was not exactly like Lisa, but maybe I just didn't see it. But that's irrelevant. We had you two boys on our hands. Diapers, bottles, naps, you name it," he laughed, remembering. "To her, you guys always came ahead of my skiing. That's for sure. It created some tension. I won't lie to you. But she was right. It has taken me twenty years to figure out that I was right, too. I know, because here we are, eh? I can hear Nikola say to me every time I whine or complain to myself about giving up my so-called best years of skiing after she died, 'So what's the problem? You should have waited until now to try to make the Olympics anyhow.' For her one Olympics would have been plenty, and if I was going to try to make the team with you boys when you got older, my skiing in between would have been considered a waste of time." He laughed again, because that is exactly how it came about. "I hope she is right."

Jerry smiled at Phil, because they were always happy when their father referred to their mother in the present tense, as if she were still alive and with them. But, it was time to bring something else up.

"Uh, Dad. How come you never remarried?" Jerry asked.

"Oh, I had my chances. But really, I haven't been prepared to go back through the memories. Every relationship has stages and there comes a point romance turns to reality, and I was too devoted to my dreams, you know?"

"Well, Dad, we just wondered if you've been waiting for us to give you the 'okay'. Well, it's okay with us if you do." Phil replied.

Tim laughed. "I assume your referring to Lisa. I hardly know her."

They shrugged their shoulders, innocently.

"Anyone you want, Dad." Jerry said, as if naive.

Suddenly, rapid knocking interrupted their discourse. It was Gavin! He happily informed them that Cane was not only secured, but relayed Cane's message as well. Jerry and Phil each let out an enthusiastic, arm pumping, "Yes!" Tim smiled weakly, nodded, and gave the wall his wistful Celtic gaze. Gavin picked up on his distance immediately and demanded him to call his "girlfriend." Tim smiled; Gavin knew what was happening. So Tim made one final date with Lisa that night, two days before the relays.

The next day the entire team met back at Big Thunder to watch the women's relays. Tim was still with Lisa, holding hands and looking almost too content.

But, it didn't escape anyone's notice that coaches from the top eight men's teams were on hand as well. Coach Franz exchanged small talk with them, and saw that many of them carried clipboards and charts. They were there to compare pre and post-Jules results of the American women's performances, as one final precaution. When he returned and told the quintet about it, Tim squeezed Lisa's hand just so much tighter. More snow began to fall.

As the race evolved, it became clear the American women as a team would not duplicate Carol Fabiano's individual feat. Beth Simmons in no way felt let down by her women. She could not have asked for more. They came to Thunder Bay prepared only to show up, and they entered the race with wildly fantastic hopes of medalling. Jules' compounds were not enough, however. They were expected to finish fifteenth out of the twenty teams before Jules, so ending up ninth was disheartening only because they were so close to a medal. Two minutes and fifty-seven seconds away to be exact. Still, no medal for America.

Most upsetting to Coach Simmons were the aftereffects. The American media treated them as though they had failed. But, in truth they succeeded in one most important sense. The other Nordic coaches were not lining up at Jules' door. The men would enjoy the same advantage they had. The Europeans didn't even bother to test Jules' wax. They were sure of their conclusion that Plank was a total liar, and that Jules was a stooge. At least they were half right.

The one fact they didn't know was that Coach Franz's team had yet to competitively use Jules' wax. They assumed wrongly, thinking they had. After they decided that Plank was a double agent of sorts, once having believed everything, they now believed nothing. Status quo had gotten them all their medals so far. It would be unwise to devote even one more minute to some fantasy.

Anyhow, there would be no asterisk. And after all the hype was put to rest, the men seemed relieved, and seemed motivated to ski better than ever.

Chapter Forty

O N THE NIGHT before the race, Cane retired to his room early. He removed his wallet from his pants. He checked the contents, twenties, tens, fives. Funny colors.

But what was that crumpled bill stuck in the corner? He opened it. Oh, that. Now I remember.

He sat on the bed. Oh, yeah. A Gideons Bible. Why not? He opened it reading a little here and there. Though he was raised as a nominal Christian, only the inscription 'IN GOD WE TRUST' had any significance in his father's home. He leafed further before finally settling in on the passage of Coach Franz's stick-it note. Phillipians 4: 8-13. He read the passages once slowly. Then again slower. Then again and again. Then he began to ingest the words as if addicted:

> "Finally, brethren, whatever things are true, whatever things are noble, whatever things are just, whatever things are pure, whatever things are lovely, whatever things are of good report, if there is any virtue and if there is anything praiseworthy, meditate on these things. The things which you learned and received and heard and saw in me, these do, and the God of peace will be with you."

Could he actually sleep tonight? He wondered about this man Paul. His words reminded him of Coach Franz.

When those words were committed to memory, he went further in the same letter to Timothy:

"But I rejoiced in the Lord greatly that now at last your care for me has flourished again. Though surely you did care. But you lacked opportunity. Not that I speak in regard to need, for I have learned in whatever state I am, to be content. I know how to be abased, and I know how to abound. Everywhere and in all things I have learned both to be full and hungry, both to abound and to suffer need. I can do all things through Christ who strengthens me."

He read no further. He had no need to. He understood. This was his life, past and present. And future.

He thought about his mother and especially his father. He wondered how they would receive the person he became at that moment. How would his father react if his son overcame dependence? He wondered if his dad would feel any pride at all, whether or not he deserved it. Cane wanted him to feel it, regardless. He wanted his father to feel the value of an accomplishment that cost him nothing. But if he didn't, it couldn't change his decision.

He had taken another step. So hard. But so light. There was God, in his life.

Chapter Forty-One

I T WAS "ALL THAT," covered live in America, in Canada, in the entirety of Europe, Russia, and Japan. Not even the race of races in Lillehammer had such coverage. It was weaker than a typically weak Winter Olympics for the Americans, so every hint of the possibility of a medal in anything was pounced on by the media, with trumped up expectations, which were down-played by every expert associated with Nordic skiing.

And when Jules' wax became the American's ski additive of choice, the networks quickly prepared a twenty minute presentation about the subject and its developer. It was a classic story, fitting for the Games and Jules instantly became a sort of "Eddie the Eagle" for the Thunder Bay Olympics, as Lisa thought he would.

They merely touched on the X-Tek Ski flap because the skiers provided nothing to fuel the issue. They were content to answer honestly that they, like everyone else, might look at other products after the Games. And why wasn't Cane involved?

"You would have to ask X-Tek Ski, Inc.," he replied factually and with no hint of duplicity. "I never knew of it until a few days ago."

They covered the histrionics of the lawsuit. The media commentators thankfully took a position in lock step with Coach Franz that judicial review in cases like theirs essentially permits unqualified judges to act as de facto coaches. But Franz added that the lawsuit was not resolved fairly as reported in the media. "This was an unforgivable

abuse of process, and nothing about the resolution of this case will
prevent the same thing from occurring again and again in the future.
In fact, I suspect it will get worse. The solution? It will be most difficult, because our courts have helped foster a communal sense of irresponsibility, as so many of us have come to think that lotteries, luck,
and lawsuits are the surest and easiest ways to wealth. We continually
punish the productive elements of our society for their success. Maybe
judges should have some real-life training in what it is like to be sued.
Maybe they would see things differently if they too had to put their
wealth and careers on the line every time someone filed a complaint
against them. It would just let judges know how bad it is for the rest
of us. Then maybe they would get the point." And as an afterthought,
he took a shot at the Gannons out there. "And isn't it reassuring to
know the sleaziest and most clever lawyers are all too often reputed to
be the best in the profession?"

The sideshows were alluring to the media. The Keagans' story topped
them all. It had all of the elements of the American romance, like a Frank
Capra movie. And they seized on the tale of the first three relay skiers
until a nation that was formally cross-country illiterate were suddenly in
front of their televisions rooting for these underdogs by the millions.

As Jules made one last exit to the port-a-john, Tim summoned his
teammates inside the tent serving as the Olympians' compound. For
the first time, Tim suggested he lead them in prayer. Their nerves were
such that only nods came in reply.

"Lord, you have been with us throughout. This we know today
more than ever. Let us glorify You for the grace You have given us, in
the name of the Father, the Son, and the Holy Spirit. Amen," he said,
crossing himself. It was simple and short, and said with a tense confidence appreciated by his younger teammates. Afterwards, each nervously tapped each other's gloved fist gently for good luck and unity.
And adrenaline flowed into all of them like a torrent.

Cane spoke the last words, with the same spirit. "Timothy,
Phillip, Gerald, Coach. Be at peace. All things are possible through
Him." He paused. "Do you believe in me?" They stared at him, as if
he was half-crazed.

"Cane?" Jerry uttered.

"Well, do you?"

"Yes," Jerry answered. Tim and Phil nodded the nod of no choice.

"Good, because I believe in you also. Now let's go out there and show them we have something more going for us than just Jules' wax, and He is with us now. I know because I can feel Him smiling." Tension was released in a unified shout, and after everyone nervously gathered their skis piled up against the fence just outside the tent, they gathered around Franz, putting their hands together in a circle.

The cameras focused in on them.

"Okay guys," Franz said, in a double entendre, "let's show them a little of our behinds."

OLYMPIC WINTER GAMES
Men's 4x10K Course Profile
Big Thunder, Thunder Bay, Ontario, Canada

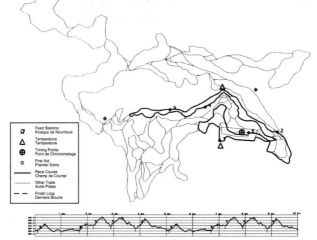

CLASSICAL TECHNIQUE

FREE TECHNIQUE

Chapter Forty-Two

IN THE MINUTE of silence before the gun, Tim lined up for his final thirty minutes of competitive racing. He looked skyward one last time. His life did not flash before him. He did not search for a sign. He did not think of Nikola. Or of Lisa. He gripped his poles tightly. He shuffled his skis back and forth slowly. His answer was within. He came to realize it always was. Thirty seconds. He looked back briefly at his sons, at Paulson, at Franz. This was his fate – their fate – our fate – to be here, this day, after all these days, months, and years. It was the right time, at last. Ten seconds! Total, eerie, silence. Tim's heart began racing...no looking back! He was here to ski fast. No! To ski the fastest! It was that simple. He felt light...strong...young!

BANG!

Twenty teams led by their starters sprinted out of the gates in their individual tracks, and began double-poling almost immediately. And Tim was not about to disappoint anyone, leaving the stadium abreast the Italians, Finns, Swedes, Norwegians, and Russians. These teams were the ones who were sure to challenge for the medals, and to lose contact with them meant death. The Germans, the Austrians, and the increasingly improved French were not far behind.

Finally the double-poling came to a halt as they approached the first of many steep climbs. It appeared as if every ski's tip was fastened to the tail of the one in front of the other.

Racing fans cheered crazily in a plethora of languages only a meter away, as the train of skiers chugged heavily up the hill. It was a 10K sprint, with rest coming only on long downhills, which instead demanded total mental acuity, little less exhausting in itself.

Jules was back, nervously wringing his hands, cheering for Tim Keagan. Though he would have provided the competition the great equalizer and the simple lesson of its application if only they had asked, he was clearly in the American camp, and indeed became their official team ski preparation official. It was all about rhythm, kick and glide, and kicking faster than anyone else.

What makes cross-country skiing the king of conditioning is that it requires a total body workout. Every muscle is implicated, and different combinations of muscles may be employed in the utilization of differing techniques, allowing for muscle recovery in the course of a race. It was a picture of artistic beauty to see the train of racers change technique in unison, following one another in lock step. And a revolution is set off when one makes the move to pick up the pace or attempt to take over the leader.

The weather was about average for February, -9°C, with the sun low in the southern sky. There was a slight wind from the west. The race would last approximately one and a half hours. With one thousand meters gone, the Nordic skiers were just beginning to sweat, their perspiration drying on contact immediately in the dry cold air wicking through their lycra suits.

The snowfall from the previous two days had been well packed for both classic and skating. It was clean, fresh snow, as fast as the track could be in a temperature in this range, significantly faster than conditions at or near -22°C, as in Lillehammer. Conditions were near perfect, and Keagan was chewing up the meters quickly. Everyone was.

The classic 10K trail, set apart from the 10K skating configuration, was groomed with two lanes of dual tracks throughout. The dense birch hardwood forest looked sparse, now locked in winter's grip. The trunks of the trees were buried with well over a meter of snow, making the bright uniforms of the contestants easily visible even in the distant high elevations that they compelled one another to sprint up in order to keep hopes of a medal alive.

At 1.7K Tim Keagan had held nothing back; still he remained only in fifth place, just ahead of the Italian, but only six or seven seconds from the leader. Essentially, there was no leader in this situation. Unless one can pull away, the leader is merely a pacesetter. He couldn't help but be satisfied with the pace because he had never skied faster or harder this early in a 10K. He did not appear to be struggling to keep up, but it was all he could do to stay even. To struggle meant to get out of rhythm, and rhythm is everything in cross-country.

Keagan's lungs were on fire; his only hope was that his younger counterparts were feeling the same. The pace exceeded any in his memory. His race in Anchorage seemed easy by comparison. The hills were more frequent and steeper, and the downhills were super fast; only then could a skier hope to suck in enough air to replenish oxygen necessary to keep up the hellish pace that the Finlander set.

Thousands of fans lined the edges of the trail – not like Lillehammer by any means where a significant percentage of the entire nation of Norway was on hand for that great race, but perhaps fifty thousand, which far exceeded any prior attendance record in North America for a cross-country event. And of course, the networks were on hand as well.

As Tim descended the other side of the long climb he saw Sweden in second, Russia third, Italy fourth. He had no interest in who followed him. They approached the 2.5K mark, where American television cameras were stationed. It was all going by so fast! But to his body every meter felt like ten. As soon as the chain of skiers passed the cameras, they expectorated one by one, ridding themselves of nasal fluids which build up so quickly and naggingly at this exhaustive pace in the frigid air. At the 4.1K mark, as they approached the next hill, a tall muscular Norwegian in his red, white, and blue suit moved to the left lane and picked up his tempo, passing Keagan.

Where is he going? thought Keagan. It was difficult to understand why he might pass on a hill when in a few hundred more meters they would all be reentering the stadium for the second 5K loop. His actions created consternation. Good God! Did he find the pace to slow? Tim remained behind the Italian, now in sixth place. When he got to the top of the hill, he saw a Norwegian TV crew. Maybe that explained the move.

More clearing of their passages as they descended the final hill into the stadium. The crowd was roaring furiously as the first grouping of six came double-poling into the stadium at the 5K mark. Here the lanes widened, an opportune time for anyone to make a move on the level surface. The Finlander was content to give way to the Russian and to the Swede and to the Norwegian. The Italian made a bid too, but fell back.

Now the Swede tried to pass the Russian, but the Russian picked up an even faster rhythm and staved off the attempt. It was now a sprint. The Norwegian got in behind the Swede. The Swede was obligated to move in behind the Russian. Now the Norwegian skied alongside the Russian and looked at him, contemplating taking the lead. The Russian had expended great energy holding off the Swede; he deferred to the graceful Norseman.

Roald Borgerson, the Norwegian, saw an opportunity to make the Russian pay further on the upcoming hill climb. He was determined to find out what the Swede and Russian had left. He plowed up the left lane on the hill, passing the quickly shuffling Russian in the first two hundred meters. The Swede tried to pass again and succeeded. But now Norway was already ten seconds ahead.

Fifteen seconds behind the Russian were the Italian, the Finlander, and Keagan. It was a critical stage of the race. The train had been split in two, and worse, the Norwegian was in danger of leaving them all in the wake of his pole plants making divots in the snow. This was not unexpected; Borgerson was the gold medalist in the 10K classic portion of the pursuit. He was the best of the lot. And he was skiing with the intent of giving his lesser accomplished teammates as big as lead as he could. Borgerson would not be looking back; that was his style, in the mold of Vegard Ulvang.

The Russian was broken, far more so than Keagan. He had made his move and had been rebuffed. The Swede was outdistancing him now.

The Finlander was still skiing well. His pace remained steady. He, like Keagan, and for the most part the Italian, skied in rhythm along with them, but now the 6.7K sign came and went. The leg was two-thirds complete. Keagan's time was 16:37. The Russian was now only fifty meters in front of them, but the Swede and Norwegian had already topped the hill. It was time to stop losing distance to the front runners. Keagan made his move to the left like before. The downhill flattened out just into the climb. On will alone, he bounded past the Italian, who then immediately pulled out behind him to join in passing the Finnish racer. The Italian was not about to concede. All three approached the Russian at the top of the massive climb. He had nothing left to match their momentum. Keagan took third place in a herringbone sprint to the top. The Finlander had been edged because he was blocked by the Russian. The Russian looked back quickly to see if more bad news approached from behind.

The American announcer was rabidly describing the move. At 7.1K, the US was in position to medal! Keagan could not shake the Italian or Finn despite increasing his tempo, which he had to do if he had any hopes of closing the gap between the Norwegian, the Swede, and himself. The Italian was content to ski on his heels, cutting wind resistance; so, too, the Finn in regard to the azure-clad Italian. Keagan fully understood their presence and strategy, but he had no desire to settle in like them. For his team's sake, he had to do better than ski strategically. He had to inspire. Down another hill. Up another, and back down again. Head down! Head down! Pole, kick, glide. Pole, kick, glide. Run. Run. Run. *"Hei! Hei! Hei!"* fans screamed. Yet, he was deaf to it all. All that needed to be said was in his head, the plain and simple affirmation that in less than five minutes his career would be over. Another giant climb beckoned. Jules' wax was superior. It was like bounding uphill on a paved road with track shoes on, the grip was so sure. Borgerson, though, seemed just as sure-footed. The gold medalist was close to cresting the hill. The Swede was halfway between. Keagan, glimpsing a sight of both, removed himself from the tracks and began yet another herringbone run up to the top. The Finn followed, passing the Italian. When Keagan reached the top he had gained several seconds on both the Swede and Norwegian, who, only because they had already descended the hill, looked to have an incredible advantage to the American viewing audience.

As he ran into one final herringbone climb on the next hill at 8.7K, Carol Fabiano screamed into his ear that he was seventeen seconds behind the lead. He had picked up only nineteen seconds in 2.6Ks of maximum effort. Before he reached bottom he began double-poling to ascend the next hill. He double-poled to the tip of the seventy-five meter incline, now beyond human exhaustion. His arms were awash in oxygen-poor blood, and heavily burdened by lactic acid. Down the hill he went, into a neat tuck resting the underside of his forearms across his aching thighs. He had separated himself into third alone and he could see the Swede now, only meters ahead, with less than a five second lead. Borgerson was already positioning himself for a wild double-pole sprint to the exchange. With less than five hundred meters remaining, to the astonishment of the huge contingent of North American fans, Keagan pulled into a tie with the Swede. Keagan continued to abuse his triceps and abdominals. He usurped every atom of power remaining to lift his heels from his parallel skis, passing the Swede, and now on the straightway entering the stadium only gold medalist Borgerson remained ahead of him, having a mere fifteen meter lead.

For all intents and purposes, the first leg was a tie. Still, Keagan pursued the Norwegian with heartrending momentum, fueled by an inexhaustible desire to push his son forward on the second leg.

Phil watched as his father climbed the bridge on the final approach to the arena, double-poling down the ramp which completed the 180 degree turn right in front of the main stands, filled with an awestruck throng of people. His abdominal muscles were so expended their tightness prevented Keagan from fully rising vertically, or filling his lung's chambers with crucially needed air. Instead, he leaned forward to increase his tempo. Fifty meters remained. The crowd roared, egged on by the Thunder Bay announcer who described the sprint with justifiable enthusiasm and shock.

Keagan caught Borgerson!

As Phil saw his father approach, the enormity of the moment sent shivers throughout his body. He had fantasized of this moment, but never really believed the old man could pull it off. Suddenly he felt totally unprepared; it was too good to be true. Worse than that. It was true! And the American media was sure to hype the moment. Could he too respond to his role? Whatever, he hadn't a clue.

"God, help me," he prayed, weakly whispering to himself, shuffling into the dual set track.

Tim touched off first!

After 10K, the Americans for the first and only time in history were in the lead in this event with a time of 24:02. Phil was off, double-poling, and so was the Norwegian. Tim collapsed to his knees and then fell on his elbows, and eventually to his stomach. He could not raise himself. His arms, his whole body, had cramped up.

Thirteen seconds later the Finnish 10K classic specialist double-poled in. Aside of him, the Italian. Twenty-seven seconds off the mark, the Russian touched off. Keagan's performance, tremendous though it was, merely kept hope alive. None of the six nations could be considered in any way out of the running.

Within the first kilometer the Swede had passed Phil and moved in comfortably behind the Norwegian who slowed the pace. It was a tactical move. He did not want to waste all his energy being the Swede's windbreaker. Though his decision allowed Phil to ski at a pace with them, all the others behind them were moving up. At 2K the Finn rejoined the train. At 2.7K someone had to make a move and pick up the pace. The Italian silver and Russian bronze medalist threatened to rejoin the grouping. The Swede wanted no part of a duel with his Russian counterpart. He sprinted to the outside track to pass. Phillip declined. The Finn joined behind the Swede. The Russian, seeing the ploy fifty meters back also leaped to the outside. The Italian skied desperately to catch Keagan. Keagan, panicked momentarily by the attempted coup, fell behind the Russian Konstantinov as he whooshed passed him.

Things were not going right, but there was a lot of race left. The Italian passed Phil on his right and then cut him off in the left, as he passed the Norwegian. Phil, in ten seconds time fell to sixth place, with the bronze and silver 10K classic medalists now in front of him.

I just got to give Jerry a chance, he thought to himself. I can't quit now. Phil's problem was not so much fatigue, but tempo. He had a longer, more loping technique than his father, utilizing the diagonal stride more frequently than double-poling. He gave up thoughts of strategy and decided he could only ski as hard as he could. He knew he would be skiing less than twenty minutes more. Let them provide the strategy. All I need to do is keep up and let Jerry catch up later, he thought. Soon he was fifty meters out of fifth. By the 5K mark he was one hundred meters back. And the Swede, Russian and Finn were toying with each other regarding the lead, twenty-five seconds up. Another 5K like this and the Americans were sure to go home medalless. Phil had lost nearly a minute to the Russian, half a minute to the Swede, and forty-five seconds to Finland. And he convinced himself he was skiing his best race. It wasn't nearly good enough.

"I thought he was a better skier then his father," said the newly arrived Stu Weinberg to Lisa, who had destroyed a manicure rooting for Tim. "I wonder what's wrong?"

The Americans silently perused their representative. How come he isn't double-poling like his father was? But on he went, very efficiently, very coolly, very deliberately, just not as fast, all alone in sixth place. The crowd was quiet as he passed in front of the stands. Where was his heart?

Further ahead lay a slight uphill leaving the stadium. Out of the corner of his eye he saw a fan at the turn focusing on him. He said nothing, but he looked familiar. As he approached the fan's location, he heard a normal, relaxed tone of voice, "What is the matter, Phillip? Do you think you have all the time in the world?"

Phil, sweating and breathing heavily, was about to return an expletive in reply, when the appearance of the young man changed. He was in a wheelchair. He refrained, but his ire had been raised. "Get bent!" he exhaled heavily. What did that guy know about an effort like this? He looked ahead to inspect the damage from the first 5K. Instead, he saw a blue banner draped over the plastic orange security fence inviting fans to visit the Terry Fox Monument. Why hadn't he seen it the first time around? He shook off the coincidence. Been there, done that, he thought to himself. He was out of answers. Everything he tried got him no closer to the pack moving on without him. He would make one final assault on the first major hill to try to rejoin the Norwegian and Italian. He no longer saw the others. At 6K came his final opportunity to make a play. He began bounding up the steep long hill. His legs felt heavy. His skis felt like cast iron sleds. I can't do it, he said to himself and he began to disintegrate, now wondering about the German, French, and Austrian team approaching him from behind. He continued trudging up the hill. At its top, an American television crew focused in upon him. He was much too much aware of it. He looked to his left to avoid eye contact with the camera. Another banner? St. Jude Children's Hospital? The Canadian Olympic Committee, in an effort to advance the legacy of Terry Fox, in conjunction with ABC, had agreed innocently enough to promote the world class charitable cancer research facility during this event. To Phil, the three encounters taken together were concentric; it was a message, a spiritual wake-up call and he felt a surge of great strength. The paraplegic. The handicapped Terry Fox and his courage; his unfinished marathon. St. Jude. He had heard of St. Jude in catechism classes at St. Francis in Traverse City. All these things convinced him not to give into his fatigue. Keagan, a Catholic, remembered the patron saint of hopeless cases. He prayed a prayer to the Saint to get him back into the race. Instantly, like a light bulb turning on, the red-head remembered he had the advantage of Jules' wax! He had forgotten all about it, and now he was inspired to race with a fresh confidence. He put his head down and carried on. He would not give in! His immediate goal was to send a message to the approaching trio to forget catching him. He picked up the pace, forcing his body to execute what he demanded from within.

At the 6.7K mark, though still in sixth, he was no longer tired. Unlike his father who skied over pain at this juncture, young Phil appeared strong. He had gotten his second wind and it was a hurricane. He exploded up the hill telling himself he would catch the Italian by its top. And to the Italian's surprise the American rushed past him there, like an insult. "Should have used Jules' wax. *Ciao.*" He said matter-offactly. The downhill was easy, too easy, and he was aching for more running, gliding, and pole planting. The next hill came. He dashed to the top, leaving the Norwegian stunned at the ferocity of his pace.

The American broadcast team suddenly found itself excited again, and embarrassingly scrambling for mea culpa's. They had maligned Phillip throughout the first six kilometers, but with three thousand meters left he was skiing more fluidly than his father had at this same point.

The Russian was on form though, leading the leg and skiing assertively. The Swede was steadily dropping behind, now fifty meters separated them. The Finn was twenty-five meters from the faltering Swede, and Keagan had sliced to within one hundred fifty meters of the Finn. Still, he was way behind the Russian, who held a commanding lead.

Keagan continued his charge, stabbing a herringbone run up another slope. As he reached the top he saw both the struggling Swede and Finn running doggedly up yet another impossible incline. He tucked and sped to the bottom, step-turning tightly into the climb, sprinting for twenty steps, and converting to a herringbone sprint half-way up the hill. The Finn looked back at the approaching American, taking one and a half steps for his one, and looking tough. The Finn attempted to pass the Swede who, like a cornered animal, gave a last fighting response to maintain second place. Keagan looked up briefly and saw the duel. It was not impressive. They clearly did not have the reserve he had and it was too late in the race to get one.

When they topped the slope at 8.3K, Keagan had halved their lead. He might pass them, but where was the Russian? Konstantinov was already preparing to climb the next hill. At least he was in sight now. Konstantinov was not charging the hill like before, but skiing deliberately – regenerating energy for the mass of fans awaiting his entrance.

Keagan's legs were just beginning to tighten, intractably. The sprinting and herringbones had produced a squeezing, vice-like sensation, in the muscles of his massive and powerful quadriceps. Blood was pooling in his thighs. Instead of giving in, it served as a reminder to him just how powerful his muscles were. He skied over the pain.

He had to. There was another sprint up the next hill – the one the Russian gave up, and then he double-poled into the next. He hoped to enter the stadium in time to see the Russian exchange. This descent was treacherous and mercurial, and at its end it deposited the skiers straight into the final climb. He sprinted to the left of the Finn and Swede. He would pass them both with 1.2K to go! Suddenly he saw and heard a half-crazed Gavin Smith screaming, "Konstantinov fell! Konstantinov fell! Go! Go! Go! Go! Hurry! *Hei! Hei! Hei!*"

Konstantinov was still one hundred meters ahead, but now grimacing in great pain, as he struggled to enter the stadium. Down the hill Keagan made the extreme right turn back toward the stadium, avoiding the oblong crater caused by the crash of the big Russian's body. He could see the Russian feebly poling up ahead, one red pole and one blue. Phil flew past the broken pole. The final descent had exacted a heavy toll from Konstantinov, who continued laboriously and courageously plodding along. His collarbone was broken and his right arm was virtually worthless. Still, the tough Russian carried on, gasping in unimaginable pain with every weak, abbreviated poling motion.

Now Keagan went exclusively into a double-poling technique, for the first significant time since the exchange. From here on, his arms and abdominals provided the primary means of propulsion, a muscle combination that he had conserved well. Konstantinov struggled toward the approach to the exchange, with Keagan in a full double-poling sprint only twenty meters back. The Finn and Swede were just entering the arena well back of Keagan now. Keagan caught the Russian in one final sprint and double-poled into the crazed final stretch. He would not be denied.

Lift heels. Pole! Pole! Pole! Pole! Lift heels. Pole! Pole! Pole! Pole! Lift! Pole! Lift! Faster! Faster! He was saying to himself inside. On the upstroke he saw Jerry only ten meters away! He stretched out his right arm. Twenty kilometers were in the books!

He tagged an already skating Jerry. The change in style from classic to freestyle was pronounced. Jerry sped off without hesitation, wanting the greatest possible lead from the exchange. As the Finn approached his teammate to touch off, the Swede poled in fifteen meters behind him.

One second. Two. Five. Seven. Eight. Nine. The ailing Russian approached the finish, deflated, and in extreme pain. The Finn steamed by, passing him just before the exchange. The Swede chugged in three seconds later.

The Italian and Norwegian were now in their double-pole sprint to the exchange, both about twenty seconds behind.

Jerry had been handed the most improbable of leads. The pace of the race accelerated appreciatively, especially here in the stadium while still on the flats. He knew he would be hunted down for the next 10Ks, but he had firmly decided not to be anyone's draft animal. He would not be part of providing anyone an aerodynamic edge.

His sprint out of the stadium served two purposes; the first to create the psychological anxiety that comes with an uneven start between competitors, but foremost was his desire to achieve tactical superiority. The Norwegians, since Lillehammer, had employed the great Bjorn Daehlie in the third slot, who invariably destroyed the competition, leaving leg man Thomas Alsgaard incredible advantages over the likes of the Fauners and Isometsaes of the world. It was similar to having Lou Gehrig batting before Babe Ruth. Well, in Daehlie's case, vice-versa. Though those greats weren't here, several of the teams employed the same strategy in these Games to avoid a duel with Italy's Marco Forletta in the final 10K .

Jerry was not only America's greatest freestyle Nordic skier, but the most intelligent. He had run through a variety of scenarios in advance of the race, and had a plan for each. This was a tactical race, and with six skiers crowding trails meant for two at the most, he did not want to be wasting energy trying to pass anyone if he didn't have to. He resolved not to relinquish the lead. He did not care if they kept up, he just wanted complete confidence that he had another gear to shift to and force all comers to exhaust themselves in the pursuit of him. He would not attack the hills now, not yet. Just a fast pace. He didn't want to get comfortable relaxing, either. Ninety-five percent was right. The Finn was tough, as they always are. He was on a mission from Helsinki. He would be no draft animal either. He was all alone in second, with the blue cross adorned across his white lycra top, lost in the blinding sun reflecting in the snow.

The Russian was rapidly ceding geography to the Italian and Norwegian. All was proper and fine at Big Thunder, except these Americans. The Norwegian and Italian didn't waste time drafting on the Russian. They V-2d by, on a rare fifty meter flat before their V-1 up the next monstrous hill. They liked the taste of gold, and to them Keagan was not a king. He wasn't even in their court. He would be dealt with harshly by the Triple Entente. It wasn't a question for any of them that he would be caught, but once they passed him, how deep they would bury him. Just to make certain all the old boys were represented, Sweden soon took its place west of Russia, eager to make its alliance with the others and destroy the infidel.

Tim Keagan watched the drama unfold. It was like watching a pod of orcas gather for the attack. Phil was finally catching his breath.

"Nice double-poling at the end," Tim said, in an understatement.

"Thanks, Dad."

"Well, what do you think Jerry will do?" he said looking up the mountain, concerned for the moment.

"He's going to give Cane a chance to win."

"How do you know?"

"It runs in the family."

Tim smiled. "Is that how got you here?"

Then Phil remembered his prayer. He looked for the handicapped man. Gone. He had to tell the truth.

"Faith in hopeless cases, Dad. That is what did it. I was dead out there. That and the snow being a little too slippery for Konstantinov."

"That's what its all about. It got me here too, you know."

They both laughed nervously and went back to worrying about Jerry.

Cane observed the undulations from the beginning, He possessed an air about him this day that both confused and calmed his teammates. It was as if he brought no expectations of their performances with him, yet he was confident about his upcoming role. Franz was now his constant companion and would be so until approximately five minutes before the exchange.

Franz was beyond expression. Pacing, twisting, checking his watch, checking the leader board. Praying silently. Cane interrupted all of it.

"Coach. Coach!"

Franz paced over quickly.

"Yeah, Cane? What do you want?"

"You remember when you took me out for that 40K skate in Anchorage?"

"Sure do Cane. I hope you ski a little faster than that today."

Cane laughed. "You know that was one of the hardest things I've ever done. And you did it so easy. There aren't too many sixty-year-olds in this world who could do what you did." He paused. "Coach, whatever happens today I need to thank you for all you've done."

"You're my man, Cane. In the end I put my chips on you, didn't I?"

"I wonder why."

"It has something to do with puking your guts out, I guess. So what are going to do out there today?"

Cane looked up the mountainous trail system, watching Jerry's lead increase and decrease with every downhill and uphill.

"You know what, Coach? I'm going to ski the race of the day." He smiled, nervously. So did Franz.

But Franz's attention refocused to Jerry. The 5K mark was upcoming. The undulating chase continued. On the flats Jerry's twenty meter lead looked fine to the American television audience, but his nine second advantage had disappeared. As Jerry entered the stadium with five nations in tow, Cane's nervous smile vanished. Another 5K like this and Franz's strategy will have failed. Jerry could not build a lead. It was a race of strategy, not of dominance. It was not Jerry's fault whatsoever. There was nothing more that he could do and everyone knew it. Cane silently walked to the fence to gather his Atomics.

The skating trail connected with the classic system only at the stadium portion of the course. Though the designers at Big Thunder created one of the world's finest viewer-friendly Nordic systems, it was still impossible to see everything that happened in Jerry's first five kilometers. The layout for the 10K skate was more difficult than the classic trail. In particular there existed an immense climb from the 7K to the 8K mark. Skating that particular uphill in these Games required reserves of inhuman endurance. And each skater had to climb it twice. At 7K into the third leg Keagan began to lap Greece, then Denmark, Slovenia, Spain, Belarus, Ukraine. The one kilometer climb loomed ahead and was on the mind of each and every competitor, rising in a steep pitch in that short span – steep – but not quite the Sleeping Bear. There is just no forgiveness skating uphill. In another 10K – in twenty-three more minutes – this climb would dictate who may medal and who may give up lifelong dreams. But for now the dreams of twenty-four skiers remained intact.

Jerry had improvised an intelligent strategy – to climb at less than a breakneck pace to 7.8K, where a very brief respite gives way to another half a kilometer of a far more benign climb of twenty meters more ending at approximately 8.7K. Between those two points, he had full intentions of punching it, before the huge descent and sprint to come in the final thirteen hundred kilometers.

Regardless of what Jerry could muster in the final three kilometers, Cane was beyond feeling butterflies. He was in the realm of the unconscious. He was now lining up against the world's first tier of great skiers for a 10K sprint. Cane's best ever world class finish came right here in the Olympics just days before. All of the others at one time had won at least one World Cup event. Coach Franz approached him for the final time.

"Cane. Cane! Okay, now Jerry's going to get in here with the lead," he spoke assuredly. "But don't think about that. You need to get into a pace, a strong pace. Keep with the others. Keep your head down. I don't want you looking up for anything. When you get passed, don't worry about it. Just stay with the leaders and your chance will come. Don't try to outthink them. Don't outrace them. Just stay up. At the end, you'll know what to do."

Cane nodded. His throat had never been so dry. "Coach, can you get me a drink of Vernors? I got some over there in the snow."

"Sure."

As he returned, Cane reached for the half-liter bottle. His hands were shaking so badly, Franz had to hold the bottle to his mouth for the first drink. Cane took a tentative sip.

"Take the darn thing and chug it down!" Franz commanded.

Cane did so, and by the time he emptied it, he had stopped shaking so horribly. He let out a big belch.

"Feel better, now?"

Cane, embarrassed slightly, found humor in the episode, giving a little nervous laugh, apparently more conscious of his surroundings. "Yeah. I'm feeling better."

In the distance, a minute form was seen ascending the final climb, skating furiously. Behind him the train of five responded in kind. Jerry, now in an all-out sprint, could not leave them in his furious wake.

Franz stayed at his leg man's side.

Cane looked up the hill one last time pensively. The lead was not commanding. He looked back at Coach Franz. He looked into the Coach's old brown eyes, splitting them like atoms with his, icy blue. He looked over to Tim and Phil who were pacing nervously, checking the times. Jerry had skied exceptionally well, and he had nothing to show for it. Less than nothing. He had lost time. He looked back at the lineup assembling against him. Franz saw it, and startled Cane by making light of what he was observing. He slapped Cane on the shoulder.

"You're just a boy. Just like all these other guys are. And anything is possible with the faith of a child. Don't you know that? You are just skiing with other boys today with hairier bodies and deeper voices. Not one of them is a god. They have all been beaten many times before getting here."

Cane looked up into the stands. There he saw his father. The one who covered up for him so many times.

"Cane?"

"Yeah, Coach?"

"Remember that story you told me about the first time you went out skiing? Be that little boy again. There is nothing you can't do."

Cane tried to respond but couldn't. His mouth was already dry again. His steely blue eyes met with Franz's one last time. He nodded.

It was time to leave Cane alone. He pushed Cane away from the corral gently, maybe too gently. In the end, he imparted no stirring words. And he walked back to Phil and Tim.

Cane nervously placed his hands under and through the spider web straps of his Exel poles. He snapped the race bindings on each ski twice to ensure they were properly secure. Cane still watched for his teammate, now less than a kilometer away. The course was leveling out again with about seven hundred fifty meters remaining.

Cane took shallow breaths, occasionally interspersed by a deep controlling draw of air; hands gripping and releasing; feet sliding back and forth. He looked over at Tim and Phil, who responded with a thumbs up. Jerry followed with a sign of the cross and pointed at Cane to do the same. His poles flailing wildly, Cane did so and weakly smiled back at Jerry, giving a thumbs up in return. Tim repeated the ritual, catching on and pointing up. He was smiling, too.

"What's the deal?" Franz asked looking up, seeing about half of the incident.

"Power, Coach. It's about power. Team power. Synergy," Tim Keagan replied.

"It's a God-thing, Coach," Phil added.

Cane looked up and took an extremely deep breath and let it out slowly. The camera focused on him. He looked one last time at the others lined up against him. It was an incredible sight, an unbelievable thing for an American to be found in this spot. What were they thinking? Had they prayed, too? There was nothing else to plan. He couldn't dictate the race. He had to ski the race of the day.

Jerry's final push produced only a thirty meter lead, the V-2 alternate stroke having been abandoned for the V-2, poling with each push-off , achieving an incredible speed of fifty kilometers per hour on the firmly packed white expressway. Fifty meters. Forty. Thirty. Fifteen. Jerry stormed into Cane, but tagged him softly, and as Cane skated on, yelled, "Pick me up, Cane! Go, buddy!" And Jerry collapsed too, resting his forearms across his thighs, bending over in exhaustion, before falling to the ground, completely spent.

Chapter Forty-Three

In just three hundred meters, all six fresh skiers were in a train, and Cane found himself the caboose.

Coach Franz stood and looking down, arms crossed, whispered to himself. "Don't lose contact, Cane. Please God, don't lose contact."

They began climbing the first of four major inclines with Cane at the back. A long downhill followed. No problem. The next kilometer was fairly flat. The lead skier, a Swede, now led them across the flats at an Olympic speed, clicking off the meters. Two kilometers had taken all of four minutes and thirty seconds. The next kilometer would not be so easy. It was The Hill, the same they would encounter in another 5K. Up they went in a V-1 hang-arm skate. Fans were lined up on both sides of the trails screaming passionately for their favorites.

The Russian first challenged and then overtook the Swede. The Finn challenged the Italian. The Norwegian followed the Finn. Cane slipped further back, quietly. He had been forgotten. His presence had been lost in a maze of skis and poles scrambling for traction on the slippery slope. The Keagans and Franz had seen it all before. But this time it was understandable. The clouds rolled in off the Great Lake. The day had turned gray. Just as it had been forecast. And to top it all off, at the bottom of a small spike, Cane fell, just like he did in Anchorage.

As Franz and the Keagans watched the nightmare unfold, they were interrupted by an approaching Jules Dinkel, muttering, "Oh, boy. Oh, boy." Jules began stepping into place like a pendulum once again, and wringing his hands.

They all looked at Jules and hung their heads. Cane was not coming though for their wax technician, either.

"Uh, guys?" he nervously blurted out. "Why aren't you using *those* skis?" he asked, pointing to a stack of three pair of Fischers and one of Atomics in the corner of the big tent erected as shelter for the participants and their staffs.

"Those are ours?" Phil exclaimed. "What are they doing there? We were told ours were over here!" he said, pointing to fence row outside the tent.

Jules was more nervous than ever. "You guys have been racing on your alternate skis! And I never applied my compounds to them!"

Just as Tim was about to demand how such a screw-up could have occurred, a skulking Hawk Plank sauntered into the midst of them, laden with credentials.

"Monsieur le Dinky Jou-elles! So glad to see you again! Oh. Did I put your skis in the wrong corner? *Quelle domage.*"

"Plank! You bastard!" Tim roared, charging his way. Franz and his sons instinctively restrained him. Jules was knocked down in the process.

Plank, secure for the time being, let out a vindictive laugh.

"No, no, no, no, no. You have me confused. I'm Jacques LaBrie. Don't you see?" he said, referring to fraudulently obtained plastic-coated credentials he fondled in his hand, draped from his neck. "Funny, how there is a price for everything. And I do mean everything, isn't there?"

"Why!" Tim raged, huffing from being held back.

"I guess it is my turn to talk finally, eh?" he laughed. "Let's just say I got real good at switching skis thanks to Cane's father. Let's just say I did it for the old man."

"Cane's father put you up to this?" Jerry exclaimed.

"No, not even he is that low. But I am. You see, I don't like being left out of anything by anyone. Paulson screwed me back in Grand Rapids. This is just pay-back time. Get it?" Plank answered.

"You are a sick man, Plank. You ought to be put away like the sick weasel you are!" shouted Phil.

"Weasel? Really. Tsk tsk. Well, it will never happen, boys. You see, I might as well be a figment of your imagination. I'm Jacques LaBrie, remember? I don't even exist."

"We have witnesses!" reminded Jerry.

"As did I. But that didn't seem to help me out a few weeks back. Did it boys?"

He paused for effect. "Anyhow, by then the damage will be done. No one is going to run this race over for any 'Jules' wax' on account of an alleged Jacques LaBrie." He laughed.

Plank glanced up at the trail at the innocently unaware Cane scrambling to his feet. "Isn't it funny that after all this drama you guys are skiing on placebos? Well, I wish I could stay for the grand finale, but I gotta fly! See you in the loser's circle!" He hustled away, confidently slipping back into the masses where he would savor his greatest Olympic moment.

The stunned Americans resigned themselves to an immobilizing disbelief, watching their countryman – the ex-Olympian – get away with the mass homicide of a dream.

The greatest of works can be destroyed so easily. As simply as waking up.

Chapter Forty-Four

H E STAYED UNMARRIED For nineteen years. More precisely uncommitted. Death of a spouse is so much more definitive than divorce, especially when children are involved.

If Nikola had lived, then out of spite he could have remarried. Perhaps more happiness would have ensued. But now after years of analysis in his law practice, in his observations of those who lived surrounding him in Traverse City, the only conclusion that made sense was that successful marriages are marathons, not relays.

He had seen marriages end for every, any, and for no cause at all. In court one need only recite the magic incantations that the objects of matrimony have been destroyed and there remained no reasonable likelihood that the marriage can be preserved. Sworn testimony by one party would suffice. Words uttered in court, with more conviction than vows taken weeks, months, years, decades, or half-centuries before in church. In the end, people who would quit defer to self, not to God.

When Tim visited his last memories of Nikola, with it always appeared the ghost, the presence, the juxtaposition of his near-affair girl. She was not the horrible person he thought her to be so long after Nikola's death. She simply remained in character. It was Tim who went off the deep end.

But if marriage proper is marathon-like, what could be said of his own with Nikola except that it was a sort of relay, where she handed off her life to his two sons. Indeed in them, possessed by her traits, another generation carried on her image, at least in the eyes of Tim. He laughed bitterly at his own self-pity. Such a short marriage. Nuts. He, in her life span, was aching for its convenient end. And when God saw fit to grant it on His own terms, all of a sudden there was merit in the vows he had taken! Suddenly, afterwards raising a family was more important than individual achievement. Nikola was right after all.

So as Cane fell further and further off the pace, Tim understood that his demise was not punishment, but redemption. He had earned another dose of reality. He had made it here. Be satisfied. His sons had skied well. Be proud. Cane had the toughest assignment. We could not have done better. Be honest. Be happy. Life is too short. It is now time to get on with it.

He wondered what Lisa was thinking. I had my fifteen, well, twenty-five minutes of fame, but now without a medal? He laughed, remembering the fantasy. I'm back at who I was before the Games. It seemed cruel in a way, a kind of death, really. Oh, there would be some who might remember that first leg. Quick! Name one American sprinter besides Jesse Owens and Carl Lewis on any relay team. And those people had won so much summer gold. Maybe all those others are forgotten because memories of them are diluted by expectations of gold. But here? Oh, the mother of all upsets! In the dead of winter with an American television audience unheard of for this unheralded sport and we gave them thirty kilometers of chance. Or so it seemed for the millions watching.

Tim could not help but feel sympathy for Cane. He would be penalized. He would be unmercifully sentenced as a loser by those who could not and would not understand.

He called a recovered Jerry and Phil to join him with Franz. They would defend Cane together. They would protect him from the ignorant who would presume him guilty. Looking back, it was a crazy notion. We were supposed to give him a big lead. How could we have been so naive, to think we had a chance?

They watched together as the 2K mark turned to three, and the Russian lead over Cane soared from one hundred meters to two. The Russian's first three kilometers were an incredible display of speed and power. Still, the others in the train hung on. All except for Cane. He was all alone, no longer even a caboose.

"Can he keep that up?" Phillip asked about the Russian.

"Easily, the next K is rest time," Jerry responded, noting the descending earth that awaited him.

"Maybe he'll fall, too." Tim opined.

He didn't. And neither did anyone else. Cane remained in sixth. To the world at large he was last.

Chapter Forty-Five

"Tell me, old dude. How do you do it? Where do you get your power at the end of a race? What is the secret to winning?"

It was Cane to Tim, a month ago, a sixty kilometer per hour west wind aging his face, peering into the infinite atop the mother of all dunes.

****

THE FALL HAD not induced slow-motion terror in Cane as it did in so many others observing the miscue. On the contrary, as Cane jumped up from his tumble, he felt an embarrassed rage. It was a little fall, caused by a lack of concentration. Only his feelings were hurt. He vowed to return to the pack. His tentativeness ceased, and his fall served to inspire temerity in him. He ferociously attacked the huge climb, all alone. There was one thing he could do, can do, will do. He will ski this race. This day.

As Cane began his descent from the 3.8K mark, he glanced down the mountain at the string of colors so vivid in comparison that now dull white snow and the cloudy horizon set before him, in line with his sight of vision. Screaming down an extremely long descent, he tucked tightly, his gloves holding the handles of his poles as a shield against his wind burned face. It was too early to quit and he was too far back to choke. He caught his breath on the long downhill. He had to close the gap, but could not do so here. In the stadium he resolved to sprint in a V-2 skate, kicking off sideways with each stab of his poles. His tempo would double, and he mentally blocked out the real possibility he would exhaust himself before returning to the pack. It was a desperate gamble, but what other choice did he have?

The fans were delirious watching the spectacle of five nations vying for the gold this late into the race, and when Cane heard the roar from the arena it motivated him further still. He wanted some of that, whatever it was. He began his sprint even before the hill flattened out, and when he entered the arena his appearance was strong. He was now only ten seconds behind the Italian in fifth! But had his sprint cost him too much energy for the upcoming climb?

"Go, Cane! Go! Go! You can do it!" yelled the Keagans, greatly lifted by their resurgent comrade, and he exited the stadium in a blur.

Forletta, the Italian, was a tremendous skater, and in the mold of his predecessor Silvio Fauner, the world's best sprinter. The Russian Chechnov wanted no part of him the second time around and neither did Heikkenen of Finland, Unger from Norway, or Sjoborg the Swede. Forletta would cherry pick as long as he could. The leaders clearly knew they had to wear out his sprint by continuing the exceedingly fast pace. When the first uphill of the final 5K arrived, attempts at passing one another was a foregone conclusion. The trail wasn't wide enough for more than one to pass at a time and Sjoborg was tired of the Italian on his tail. He moved out adjacent to Unger. Unger, no more desirous of having Forletta behind him, forced Heikkenen into a reluctant up-tempo, culling Chechnov out of the way.

Cane glanced up at the affray. He wanted to be part of it. He went into his unorthodox climb pattern once more, taking advantage of those above him expending valuable energy jockeying for position. This was easy compared to the Mother.

Heikkenen cut off Sjoborg at the last moment, but Chechnov wasn't about to wave the white flag. Now the four leaders were side by side and Forletta filled the void, in fifth place, only ten meters back.

Cane, closer now than any point since the 2K mark, was only fifteen meters back of the Italian, yet was no concern to any of them. They didn't even know he was still in the race.

Unger was getting desperate. Norway's collective memory had the pain of Fauner's Lillehammer leg permanently etched into it. He would not be victimized here in Thunder Bay. He squeezed in between the Swede and Finn. Heikkenen was forced to either pass Chechnov or move aside. He stepped it up. He had to pass at a cost higher than he preferred, but the Norwegian continued his assault on the leader. Heikkenen merged in front of Chechnov. Unger, stabbing the incline and pushing hard off each step and glide, moved up. Sjoborg followed, and stepped in front of Chechnov. Forletta, with every assault remained a bystander, fully realizing the fears expressed in the actions of the leaders.

Paulson did the same, conserving energy on a par with the Italian. The line-up resembled more the start of the race than the finish. No one was conceding the race.

Each skier topped the hill in single file again. Down a nice long slope, each skier moved slightly up on Unger who now absorbed the role of windbreaker. For the next 1.5K flatter land appeared, until the King of Climbs once again reemerged.

Franz looked on. "The only strategy left belongs to Forletta. He is resting, already preparing for his grand entrance."

"No, Coach," Tim said, "Forletta's in for a surprise. He has never been in a six man scramble. He thinks it is going to come down to a one-on-one. I don't think so. It's too crowded. I just hope Cane can move up before they top the next hill."

"I just hope he can get up that hill," said Phil.

"He will," assured Jerry. "But I think we found the daddy of those cubs back at 'the Mother,' if you know what I mean."

The four leaders stabbed the snow covered earth with more violence, and they approached the mountainside in dual tandems. And close behind cruised Forletta, whose patient style seemed docile by comparison. Forletta decided to test the leadership here, to see if he could break down the crowded field. His only concern was getting jammed-up. Tim was correct in his thinking. The Italian dashed to the outside of Heikkenen, and passed Chechnov too, filtering in behind Sjoborg. It was so easy.

Cane moved with him and Chechnov was stunned to find the American still in the race. But he couldn't match Cane's uphill technique the second time around. Sjoborg stayed even momentarily, but

Cane skipped in ahead of him. Forletta remained ahead of Cane. Incredibly the Americans were back in third!

Unger sensed the change, and charged harder than ever. Now things were getting real serious. The hill was only half climbed. Forletta kept pace, as if he was stalking Unger. After the steepest portion was completed, another kilometer of quick, steep uphills and downhills beckoned.

The six remained strung together. Unger slowed slightly, purposely, just to see Forletta's response. Forletta had had enough cat and mouse. He struck like a cobra, seizing the opportunity at once and moved to pass. Unger responded defensively to his own tactic; he did not expect Forletta to start his charge already! Chechnov dashed outside of Cane, and Heikkenen outside of Sjoborg, all panicked as if being chased by a lion. Forletta was the proximate cause. The six couldn't be squeezed any tighter. The pundits and announcers were astonished that after thirty-eight kilometers they could be so close to one another.

Chechnov skated in front of Cane, just ahead of the single track downhill segment. Forletta forced himself ahead of Unger. Only twelve hundred fifty meters remained! Several small spiked uphills remained, but the vast majority until the stadium was downhill. At the end, the field would encounter once again six hundred meters of level earth, with just one slight rise at the crossing of the elevated snow covered bridge, before doubling back at the halfway point, right in front of the stadium.

Unger passed Forletta again on a small spike. Sjoborg passed Chechnov. Heikkenen passed Cane. Sixth again! A quick downhill. Cane sighed deeply, and panted for air before the next spike. Cane charged past Heikkenen, and pulled even with Chechnov. Sjoborg pulled even with Forletta.

Cane was dizzy, almost passing out on the slight drop. His arms felt drained of blood, numb. His legs were taut from abuse, but on he went, forgetting all ahead, all behind, all beside. He was racing within himself with no other thought in mind. He was skiing his ultimate race and he knew it. The roar of the crowd was now able to be heard once again. They were nearing the end. Above the din, a single voice. He heard that voice before. That voice was right before. It echoed in his head over and over. A strong voice. "Cane, you can do it! Cane, you can do it!" Like a dream, suddenly, a golden path widened before him. The arena was blindingly white as the sun broke through the clouds. There was no time to slip his Briko's back over his eyes. He squinted one last time ahead, and unable to see the end, kept pushing forward.

Head down! Down! Balance! Skate! Push! Faster! Faster! he directed himself. The sun still shined brightly. He passed something, someone on his left. Something, someone on his right. An incline. The bridge! Two hundred fifty meters remained! V-2 uphill. V-2 down. V-2 ahead. Balance! Skate! Push! Poles! The crowd was screaming, deafening, vibrating the air. Where was he?

****

Tim squinted, still looking westward over Lake Michigan. "You're asking me? What have I ever won of any importance?"

"You beat me. That's enough by me." Cane replied.

Tim thought for a moment. He thought he understood what Cane wanted to know. "Okay, valid enough. You have the ability and the skill. You know the way. Still, there is no substitute for putting one ski ahead of the other. You need to be one. That is all."

"One? You mean one of them? One of you?" asked his confused teammate.

"No, Cane. You. Just be One. Capital O." Tim paused, and then looked at Cane right between his eyes.

Cane stared back at his teammate, poker-faced. Did he get it?

"Think about it," Tim concluded, and resumed his gaze toward the gray northwestern sky.

****

Soon Cane heard just four voices in front of him. "Go! Go! Go! Go!" Tim! Phil! Jerry! Franz!

Chapter Forty-Six

THUNDER BAY IS called the Land of the Sleeping Giant. Legend has it that off the Northwest shores of the greatest of the Great Lakes, Nanabijou, a formidable Ojibway giant, once stood guard over the Treasure of the Silver Islet. The silver hoard he protected remained secure off the shore of Thunder Bay for many generations, until one day a Sioux scout happened upon it. Knowing the value of his discovery, the Sioux brave paddled away to inform the white man, who might conquer Nanabijou and pay him a handsome reward in return.

As the raiders spied the island from a distance, the great treasure glistened and dazzled in the high noon-day sun, verifying for them the fantastic report received days before. As the antagonists approached the Islet's shores the sky blackened with the cry of the thunderbird. The waters of the mightiest of inland oceans roiled and stirred into a funnel-spout, and with the treasure, the great Ojibway giant disappeared into the maelstrom. Nanabijou laid down, face up, and became an island unto himself, burying the treasure in the unfathomable depths in his last sleep, guarding his silver forever.

But the screaming in this arena in the final sprint could wake the dead.

The Italian faltered ever so slightly. Unger poled hard. Fifty meters! Cane, snow blind, carried his momentum. Faster! Faster! He skied on heart alone toward the voices, straight on. More! Faster! One day! One race! Where is the finish? Where!

Suddenly he was tackled and caged by an octopus. Arms, flailing and hitting him. Hugging. Laughing. Screaming. Kissing. Grabbing. Lifting. Lifting!

The crowd was in a total daze, waiting for the results to be announced.

"*En premiere place, Les Etats Unis!* In first place, the United States of America!"

That was all many needed to hear. The fair contingent of American fans were going berserk! They stampeded over the rails to be part of the greatest moment in American Nordic history. The true fans, so long-suffering, could not be blamed for their ecstatic eruption, screaming their assent at the news. And the sky was blue again, and this day would not fade into night. The American's would leave Nanabijou's silver cache undisturbed.

"You did it Cane! Man, you did it! We won! You won! We won the gold! Gold, Cane!"

He was high above the Keagans, resting above the shoulders of Jerry and Phil. Tim was slapping Cane on the back, raising his right index finger – number one! America had won its first medal in these Games. Heavy metal – the gold!

Cane, high above his jubilant teammates, unzipped his turtleneck lycra top, removing a necklace. Raising it still higher he kissed the pendant. A gold cross. He waved his right hand around in several circles and then threw the necklace high into the air toward the crowd.

Outstretched hands clamored for the talisman, too small to be recognized for its significance from afar. It was time to share his promise. Cane had never been so intoxicated, nor the Keagans, nor Franz, nor Jules, who watched over the exasperated quintet with a scientist's curiosity.

"I know that feeling," Jules told a visitor form Norway.

"Oh?" said the Norwegian. "You ski?"

"That I do sir."

The Norwegian, his pride still freshly smarting by what just transpired, took a jab. "You look more like a herder of reindeer to me."

"Apparently a lot of your people thought that sir. If they wouldn't have, you would be knowing this feeling instead of me. But we won straight up without me. Anyhow, Merry Christmas," he said, and strode away toward the winners, like MacArthur retaking the Philippines, leaving a totally confused Norwegian behind.

When the jubilant team spotted Jules they lifted him high as well. They were not about to let "Jacques LaBrie" have the satisfaction of ruining anyone's day but his own.

The cameras descended en masse. Reporters. Microphones. Canadians. Americans. Who knows who.

For the moment the four Americans scurried about the compound shaking hands of their stunned competitors. All graciously received them, and in some ways, seemed relieved they had not lost to one another. All this way shared the shame, if there was any to be felt at all.

Carol Fabiano hustled together two of her St. Paulian girl friends. "Come on Sue! Laurie!" she said, looking on. "Let's go party with some studs!"

She watched the cameras encircle the jubilant victors. "There may never be another chance," she mused as she proceeded, undaunted none the less.

In the distance, Gavin watched the scene. He restrained his tears, but only for a moment, in awe of his friends' accomplishments. Many would never know of his intervention, but Cane knew, and that was all that mattered. Even so, he was only a part. He knew something bigger was involved and he had acknowledged it years ago. He just didn't happen to be at Arthur Street and Highway 61 by accident. It was fortune. He was hoarse from screaming. Every muscle in his body ached as if he skied the 4x10K himself due to the necessity of bounding from location to location along the course in the thigh deep snow during the race, yelling encouragement. Cane greeted him. Tim Keagan followed.

"Gavin. We did it! We did it!" Cane yelled.

Gavin embraced the tall kid. "You sure did Cane. You earned it my friend."

Tim followed. "Thanks partner for being here. I guess we proved our point in the forum that mattered most, eh?"

"Don't get me started on that 'eh?' business," he laughed. "I wonder what that dimwit Gannon's thinking now. You guys did a little better than thirteenth, eh?" he laughed.

Some reporters burst through the celebration, recognizing the attorney, "Mr. Smith! Anything you can add?"

"It's a great day for America, eh?" he laughed. "I'm so proud of these guys. I think you saw more than an upset today. This was the triumph of Olympic spirit." He grabbed Keagan and put his arm around his shoulder. "And this old duck here...I doubt we'll see the likes of him again. He got them started – and Cane over there – " he stopped, seeing him carrying on with the St. Paulians along with the Keagan boys, "well, it was a race for the ages, better than Lillehammer, eh?" he laughed again. "And Tim's boys? Well, being a Traverse City man, I wasn't the least surprised. I knew our day would come. I mean if we can put a white boy in the NBA...well, forget that analogy..." his voice trailed off, as the party engulfed the thought.

Cane had yet to see his father. His dad's greatest moment of fatherhood. But Cane had done it all on his own, rebuffing the support of his father. And this time – the first time – he thought of his father from a man's perspective. And not just as a man, but a man among men. The time had come.

He soon saw his father standing alone. Cane studied him, all bundled up, indistinguishable from dozens of others his age still roaming the grounds. Gray, weathered, small, cold, alone. So alone. Cane saw the old man like never before, and took great pity on the prodigal father. His dad wanted to be on top of the world today, but he didn't dare ask of Cane that favor. Cane, for his part, learned that he did not need to hear his father grovel as he once felt necessary. Still, not all had been rectified in Cane's moment of shocking triumph.

"Dad! Come here!" Cane called, in a disciplinary voice.

He obliged. He walked over, his head bowed. He looked up at Cane. There was a moment of tense silence.

"Well," Cane began, "I guess I won't have to wonder whether you would have been here if I would have blown it at the end one more time."

"Did I ever once abandon you when you lost?" his dad replied. "I know I don't belong here. I only came over because you asked. You proved you don't need me."

Cane thought. Maybe his father was always there. But he remembered the slap in Anchorage and so much more. Still, he was his father.

"Maybe I don't need you anymore, Dad. But, someday I'll want good memories of you." He looked over at Tim, Phil, and Jerry. So dignified and proud. "I want to start making them now. Do you know what I mean?"

His father looked that way too. In a moment he saw all that was missing in his life. He embraced Cane and began to sob like a baby. All his millions washed out in torrents to the sea, but he was still alive and so was his son. So was the hope they might reach shore together after all these years. Just getting home was the most important thing now.

"I promise I will start trying," he managed to blubber.

Cane looked into his father's eyes. He was sincere. It was neither a business transaction nor a favor. They were words from a father to a son, whose eyes had finally seen a man in his boy.

Cane squeezed his father tightly, but remained dry-eyed. This was another scene he hoped for. It was the start of another team; the beginning of another relay. Cane's steady voice finally faltered, "Dad, I only needed to show you..."

"No, Cane," his father answered, wiping his nose. "I wanted you for myself. I didn't know until today how little a medal is worth compared to a second chance to be a good father for my son. I know its hard to believe but that is what I was thinking, dying with you as you sprinted to the finish line. And when you won, all I could hope for was a chance to prove myself to you like you did to me today. Now go celebrate with your friends. I'll leave the light on for you back home. I hope you'll come back." He kissed his son, for the first time in Cane's memory, and said, "I want to give you those memories, Cane. I don't know how right now, but my father always told me when you don't know where to begin, start with yourself."

He began to collapse to his knees, but Cane held him up.

"Forgive me, son. I've been wrong at every turn."

Cane surprised him by laughing. "Dad. You can start by getting on your own two feet. We'll have lots of time figure out how to do the rest. But not today. Now go over there and apologize to my coach and my teammates while they're in a good mood, all right? That will be a good memory for all of us. And don't ruin their day doing it." Cane signalled to them that things were okay, as his father took the first few steps toward expiation. Cane smiled. Not bad. Two marvels in one day. He could get used to this real easy.

Cane's mother made her way to Cane. She basked in a mother's peace, unsurpassed in her son's twenty-seven years. She had endured.

"I knew you would win one day Cane. It is so wonderful that today is here." She wiped tears from her eyes with a tissue. Cane gave her a gold medal hug.

"I found something so wonderful, Mom. And I can hardly wait to tell you and Dad about it."

"Oh, your father and I know all about the dinky-do wax, Cane," she assured him. You could take Mother out of Mercer Island, but you couldn't take Mercer Island out of Mother.

Cane just smiled and winked to the onlooking Gavin Smith. There would be a lot of time later to explain that, too.

Franz was on a different plane, elevated to a new dimension. The Americans he knew would someday stir the pot had come through.

A reporter saw him standing alone.

"Coach! Coach! Coach! How did you feel with Cane Paulson out there on the last leg? Do you feel now you have been vindicated?" she asked.

"Where are you from, young lady?"

"I'm from the *Traverse City Record-Times*."

"Traverse City. I've heard of it," he laughed.

"Ever hear of the Keagans?" she joked.

"Your name?" he asked.

"Paula Phillips."

"Well, Paula I don't remember how I felt. Pretty empathetic. I would say. Vindicated? It was a great victory. But do you want to know the truth? This went way beyond vindication. This was a matter of grace. Do you understand what that means, Paula?"

"Grace? What about Jules' wax – er, compounds? There is a rumor starting that your team didn't use them after all."

"Yes, grace," he replied, ignoring her scoop. "An extension of time. Another opportunity. A gift, the love of God. Oh, don't write that down Paula. Your readers won't likely give it the attention it deserves. Write about what they had for breakfast today or dinner last night. Their poles or their equipment. The wind conditions. You know, those things we can quantify. It's just human nature to avoid the uncomfortable notion that we may actually have the ability to bend and shape events and circumstances by will alone. Jules didn't happen to be here accidentally. Belief in a end result made his appearance at these Games necessary for an accomplishment. We want to find logical explanations for miracles. I can tell you one clue. My men had faith – a combination of faiths. They were here to win the gold and nothing could stop them."

"You would go so far as to call this race a miracle?"

"Yes," Franz smiled at his wry testimonial. "You might write that we turned a little water into wine and then walked on it." He wryly smiled, amused at his own play on words. "Even if this feeling lasts only a day, let me tell you how good it feels to be a child again." Coach Franz glanced at his merry team. "There is a positive force out there, Paula. See it?"

"But what about the rumors...?" Paula asked Franz as he was leaving to rejoin his boys.

"Paula, the one thing I've learned in the past two months is you shouldn't put much stock in them."

His team beckoned him over and all four raised him high in the air. The darkhorse, with the spirit of a colt, rising high, clasped his gloved hands high in silent thanks, as he looked down with pride at his warriors. What they had just accomplished, the American public appreciated greatly. But the Nordic powers understood. They were truly victims of forces beyond human reason. They simply had been in the way of something even reality could not check.

And Lisa? Tim motioned for her to join him in the World's Biggest Party. It was happening in his heart. He hugged her so tightly, but so gently. Who was this man she had fallen for? He was a champion! Lisa hugged him in return, tighter than any man she would ever again. Something bigger than both of them was going on in this crazy life. It was the chapter she had waited for. And Tim? For him one story ended; and with the same ending, a new book had begun. But for the moment, this page was quite enough. There could never be another day like this day. It was heaven.

The hoopla carried on and splintered into chaotic episodes of relief and joy everywhere on the wide expanse of white-packed snow. It wasn't long before Tim and Cane found themselves together, awkwardly left alone, if only for a moment, though such a fuss whirled about everywhere surrounding them on their account.

Their eyes met, and they embraced. As equal as two men who ever lived. As heroes – as two men who understood just what is this notion of immortality, and the successful pursuit of it – to be remembered as men who came to fulfill the mission of their time. And to know the mission better than one's self.

Chapter Forty-Seven

THE MEXICAN BOY brought the "Big Bear" his daily paper only three days late. As he sat in the warm morning sun, reading glasses comically perched upon his nose, he saw a headline. "USA takes first Winter Games medal – Gold!"

"Humph! One medal! What's wrong with America today, anyhow?" he muttered to himself, not realizing that the USA has never been much of a Winter Games power. He turned to the sports section. "What's this?" he bellowed, a little louder.

He read on. Loud ear-piercing expletives issued.

"Jill! Tell me this can't be true!"

His secretary scurried over to his white pot-bellied side. She couldn't understand the concern.

"What?"

The Bear threw down the paper.

"What can't be true?" she repeated.

The Bear removed the glasses and set them on his soft, pale protruding middle. "I think I might be changing vacation destinations this summer, Jill."

"You mean the one to Seattle, Judge?"

"Yes, Jill."

Griffey just stared over the open blue sea. In his face he was feeling the winds of change. The Olympic Peninsula just didn't sound good anymore. And he shivered at the thought of his return to Michigan.

Chapter Forty-Eight

I N THE GAMES' final event, the Nordic marathon classic, no American medalled. Unfortunately, Jules had not yet had time to develop his compounds for 50K of high performance durability. Though the Americans were compelled to use the products of their competitors once again, all were ecstatic at the results as Jerry, Phil, and Cane placed seventh, tenth, and nineteenth respectively.

Maybe Jules had not homered after all. But he proved that an easy to apply cold-base bonding compound could work, and yet be produced economically, at a cost the average skier could afford.

And how did Tim finish? His marathon ended days before. He spent the final day holding hands with Lisa as they both watched his sons and teammate solidify the understanding that America had finally arrived.

Meantime, back in Seattle, Gannon was in high spirits, as usual.

"What's the matter Gannon, didn't you hear about the Michigan boys winning the gold?" an associate baited him at their bi-weekly staff meeting.

"I couldn't be happier, boy and girls. Do you realize what this means for X-Tek, and therefore us?" He raised his right hand rubbing his thumb back and forth against his finger tips. "*Mucho de niro. Beaucoup d'argent.* We get them coming in and we get them going out." He laughed. "I love this job!"

"X-Tek had nothing to do with it," he was reminded.

"Not this year, but that's the great thing about the future, it's so full of ... opportunity!" he stressed. "I'm going to get Paulson out of this cross-country business and into the real money. Downhill, people. Alpine. Snowboarding. That's were the money is at."

Suddenly a courier came rushing into the room.

"Sorry, Mr. Gannon. But I was told this package must be delivered for the meeting this morning." He plopped the overnight letter onto the table and exited submissively.

"Speak of the devil," he beamed. "A correspondence from Mercer Island. The home of our gold medalist, gang." He smiled even more broadly. As he struggled to open the tightly sealed express letter, he casually tossed out typical agency earnings for the commercial representation of such an athlete. "This particular one will be gloriously magnified, I assure you all," he confidently asserted. America had but one set of Olympic heroes from Thunder Bay and Cane's finish would exalt him above them all.

"Well, what does it say?" Scarborough asked.

Kranwitz leaned over Gannon's shoulder.

Gannon's expression turned sour.

"You read it," he told Kranwitz. "Little snot," he muttered.

"Woe to you, teachers of the law, you hypocrites!" Kranwitz announced with flair. "You blind fools! Which is greater: the gold or the temple that makes the gold sacred? You blind guides! You strain at a gnat but swallow a camel, neglecting the more important matters of the law, justice, mercy, and faithfulness. You snakes! You brood of vipers!" Kranwitz was laughing so hard he came to tears as he read along, "You travel over the land and sea to win a single convert and when he becomes one, you make him twice as much a son of hell as you are! On the outside you appear to be ..."

"Okay. Okay! Enough!" Gannon cut him short, "We get the point." He paused again. "We are such an oppressed class," he chuckled, finding humor in his own remark. "Okay, what's next on the agenda?" he asked, hardly skipping a beat.

Scarborough hesitantly raised his hand.

"Is this a good time to inform you that I succeeded in getting all the equity out of the widow Robinson's home?"

Kranwitz interrupted a response, still scanning the missive, "P.S., he writes, God loves you...Ha! Ha! Ha! Ah, one more thing," he paused before revealing the sender's identity. "Typed in capitals," his voice cracked, "re...re...ah-hummm!" He cleared his pipeline of so many damnable lies. "REPENT!" he blurted out loudly, quite unintentionally. An embarrassed silence prevailed, if only for a split second too long. When he recovered, in a low tone he said, "Signed, Cane Paulson Jr...All right!" he shouted, several volumes louder than his call for salvation, "Who really sent this?"

"Well, even if it is really Junior's writing, the real money is still in our corner," reminded Gannon.

Another knock came.

A different courier.

Another missive.

Another Paulson.

Another headache.

An Olympic sized migraine, followed by the requisite wailing and gnashing. It was so...biblical.

Chapter Forty-Nine

THE EEL SLITHERED out of town before the presentation of medals.

Plank was a man without a future. He had humiliated too many important people at Thunder Bay. Only two months earlier he was considered America's premier skier, but now he was a pariah. He was once the heir apparent to Franz's job, but from now on he would be remembered disdainfully, as a representative of the olden days, when America was a third rate nation in the sport. He was reduced to utter meaninglessness, not even worthy of being sued for all of his misrepresentations and defamations. He would go home and live with his mother, that is what he would do, he whimpered to himself.

And never go out in the cold again.

Chapter Fifty

STU WEINBERG RODE the crest of the wave. His April issue ushered in the rebirth of a Nordic craze in America, not seen since the hey-day following Bill Koch's silver. Advertisers hounded him for space. Subscriptions following the February issue skyrocketed. And with each winter issue, readers were assured, at least one article would be devoted to the stars and to the notable amateurs of the sport of cross-country skiing. A sport which above all, readers were informed, exists not only to make the season bearable, but "yearnable."

And his prizewriter, Lisa Nelson, would stay with the magazine, but she would remain behind by the waters which wind their way to the Atlantic all the way from Thunder Bay and beyond. From the Land of the Sleeping Giant to the Land of the Sleeping Bear, perhaps a few molecules of that deep Olympic winter's snow atop Big Thunder would trickle down into that great freshwater basin, and eventually lap at the sandy shores of Lake Michigan, the glorious vision she looked upon from her word processor in Glen Arbor. She found a new contentment, away from the chain of her answering machine and men she would rather not be reminded of. She could not resist the compelling story. The story of love. But could he? He who could wait twenty years for what he really desired, while her biological clock ticked away?

Chapter Fifty-One

PHILLIP MADE GOOD on a silent promise to visit Memphis, Tennessee, after the Games ended. And although he didn't have any St. Jude stories of virtue to share with the kids, they all listened intently to the true story of brave Terry Fox.

Jerry tagged along with Phil. There, a dying child waved him to her side. Jerry stroked the girl's thinning hair gently. "Am I going to die, mister?"

"How old are you, little girl?"

"Seven."

"Seven! I thought you were at least eight! Are you sure you are not eight?"

"No, I'm just seven! Dummy!"

Jerry smiled.

"What's your name?"

"Nikola."

"What a pretty name. That was my mother's name."

"Where is she? Is she in heaven?"

"Can I sit down here, Nikola?" he said, referring to the front of her bed.

"Yeah!"

"Do you want to know about my mother?"

"I think so."

"My mother died before I was even two years old. I don't even remember her. But my Daddy told me she was really nice. I wonder what it is like to have a mother. Do you have one?"

"It is so good, Mister! I can't imagine not having a mommy!"

"Nikola. Guess what I found in the snow one day?" he changed the subject.

"What? What did you find?"

He removed a necklace. A gold cross. It was Cane's. "Something for you. Do you like it?"

"Yes!"

"Can I give it to you?"

"Yes!"

He gently draped it around her neck.

"You know what?"

"What?"

"The boy who wore that before me got better. Maybe it will work for you too."

"How do you know? You found it in the snow!"

"I saw the person who put it there."

"Why would he throw it away?"

"I guess he had to make room for a bigger necklace. The one God gave him when he got better."

"Was it a miracle he got better?"

Jerry looked into her pale blue eyes which looked so prominent in her shrunken face. He stroked her light brown hairs again.

"Oh, yes Nikola. I promise you. Miracles happen all the time. I am not lying about that."

"Will I get better, too?"

"I hope so. I want to come back and see you again someday. But I don't want to see you here. I want to see you at your house, okay?"

"Okay, Mister."

"My name is Jerry. Jerry Keagan. I'm a skier, did you know that?"

"Okay. Jerry the skier."

"Well, I have to go now, Nikola. Take care of your necklace, okay?"

"I sure will, Jerry the skier. You know what?"

"What Nikola?"

"I think you're a pretty cool guy. And if I don't get better, I'm going to tell your mom all about you up there," she said, pointing to the heavens.

Jerry returned to her side, patted her head, and nodded. But, he had to leave. The pain was too real. He had to leave little Nikola the memory of strength and confidence.

"Okay, Nikola. I think you're super-cool yourself. And I'm going to tell your mother how super cool you are, too. Good-bye Nikola."

"Good-bye Jerry, the good skier."

Chapter Fifty-Two

T HE FOUR SKIERS and their coach were invited to visit the White House later that same week. It was May now and recognition for their achievement was long overdue. Tim prevailed upon his sons to consider a visit to Baltimore in their itinerary.

"Baltimore?" Jerry asked.

"Yes, I always have wanted to watch a game at Camden Yards and the Tigers will be in town that week." Baseball. His summer mistress.

And so on their way to see the President, they stopped at the surprisingly vibrant city by the Cheasapeake Bay.

At 7:00 a.m. the day of their visit, Jerry woke to the bright sunshine illuminating the city. Reluctant to flip on the television so early in the day, he flipped through a visitor's guide. After five minutes or so, he had to wake Phillip, saying there is something he needed to see.

"What?" he growled. Could that clock be right? "At seven o'clock?" he scowled.

"Just get dressed and come with me."

They took the elevator down from the eleventh floor and walked up to Baltimore Street away from the Lord Baltimore Raddison Plaza. Past Park Street, past Howard, past Eutaw. Turning right on Paca, walking past Fayette and Lexington, to Saratoga.

"Why are we here?" Phil complained once more.

"Don't you see?"

St. Jude Shrine.

"Don't you think we're overdoing it, Jerry?"

"Never mind. I just thought you might want to visit the 'nation-wide center of his devotions'," he dutifully informed his older broth-er, tossing him a copy of the Official Baltimore Quick Guide.

"You're so Catholic," bemoaned Phil. "So, why are we here this time?" he asked, giving in reluctantly, as was his habit.

"I'm going inside to light a candle."

"All right, I'll come in with you. One more time," he relented. Phil wondered if too many miracles came his way, hopelessness might cease.

***

The reunion was special. Franz, Paulson, and the Keagans were graciously received. They were all celebrities of sorts now, and the President's praise of them and their accomplishments left them col-lectively self-conscious. But her words fairly represented a nation's pride in them. They were as popular as any cross-country skiers could ever hope to be. The President was curious if Tim would consider sending her Chief of Staff his resume, as she anticipated a vacancy in the US District Court in Grand Rapids soon, winking at a radiant Lisa Nelson in the process.

After the ceremony, the five caught up with one another. Cane informed them all that he had traded in the craziness of his Generation-X lifestyle for the functional chaos of Italianism, as he continued dating his tag-along Carol Fabiano, who as the astute Madam President earlier opined, deserved to be there on her own accord. Jerry and Phil were still fantasizing about the Cheery Queen, Cane was informed, and that she had a younger sister, who was even better looking, which reduced the threat of any internecine warfare. Franz, with his wife Lauren, informed them they could cross Washington D.C. off their list of places to go, but would still call Minneapolis their home. He planned to visit Thunder Bay again later that summer. Cane said they all could definitely expect to hear from him soon for a big reunion in the Northwest. He told them to bring Gavin along, as there could be some serious business on the agenda. He had some skis he would like the Keagan brothers to try out, using Jules' new and improved compounds his father agreed to test-market.

"Most of all, I want you to know I miss you guys, and you are always welcome to drop in on me," he told them, and embraced them one by one.

As Cane turned to leave, Jerry called out to him.

Cane looked back as Jerry ran up to him.

In a soft voice Jerry said, "You know, what you did... well, I don't think any of us could have done it. I wanted you to know that. How did you come back after you fell?"

Cane smiled, and threw an arm around his teammate.

"You know Jerry. I wondered about that, too. But the only answer I keep getting is the same one."

"What is it?"

He looked over toward the White House, and then looked right into Jerry's eyes.

"I didn't." He paused until he had Jerry's complete attention. *"We did."* He smiled at Jerry and said, "Think about it." He embraced the young star once again, laughing, "Your father will know what I mean."

To which Jerry responded, "Let's do it all again in four, eh?"

"You betcha', Jer. Keep the old dude healthy for me now, okay?"

After more hearty good-byes and firm promises to get together regularly, the Keagans returned home to Traverse City. The pond-hopper glided into the Cherry Capital Airport late that same evening. It was May tenth, and it was snowing. Significantly. Oh, Michigan.

Chapter Fifty-Three

THE NEXT MORNING Jerry once again greeted the break of day. The ground was covered with nearly ten centimeters of snow. But he knew it was the last breath of winter. He resisted the thought of actually putting on skis and going around the yard for a couple laps. Instead he opted to check the mail that no one remembered to bring in the night before.

One letter attracted his attention. A plain envelope, addressed simply to The Keagans, Olympic skiers, Traverse City, MI. Not even a zip code.

He opened the letter. In neat handwriting, he read its contents:

"Dear Mr. Keagan and sons:

Many years ago I had the occasion to visit your community. Until by fate I happened upon your recent interview during the Olympics, I had no idea of the significance of my time there.

I was travelling south from Petoskey on US 31 on that awful day. I, we, had no business being on wheels that day. Out of sheer nerves I forced myself to stop at a gas station just south of a place called Elk Rapids, for coffee and sympathy. There I met a women with such a pleasant disposition, who saw my concern.

"You look scared to death," she said.

"I have never seen anything like that out there," I said. I

recall even today that great fear I felt inside.

"You shouldn't worry. Just drive carefully," she told me.

I asked her why she was out that day. And she told me that her husband was skiing in a big race, and that she couldn't bring her two boys with her to see it. But she told me to remember her husband's name because I would hear it again because he was going to win an Olympic gold medal. And I'll never forget that look because she said it without a shred of pretense.

We conversed some more. Although I really hadn't an interest in the topic so much, she was after all, very attractive, and I had no yearning desire to go back into the storm. I asked her about her boys, and she said they were a lot like her husband, and I asked flippantly if I should listen for their names as well. She said I wouldn't have to, because wherever they were she would be right there with them, and I would remember them that way. But, when they won their gold she would take her share out of them.

I said you really must love your husband to come out on a day like this to watch him, and she just smiled and said, "Even in the best of marriages there are days like this, but above the storm the sun always shines. If you are patient enough, the clouds always disappear." I couldn't stay in the station forever, so I said my good-byes to her. She wished me good luck on my journey and I wished her the same, and she replied, "That's okay, mine is almost over."

She left the station behind me and I continued south. I don't know how far back Nikola was. She could have been only two meters back, the visibility was so poor. I never prayed so much as on that stretch of road that day. Suddenly out of a cloud a truck came at me head on, passing a dark image filling the other lane. He swerved. I swerved. Somehow I escaped without a scratch. After I caught my breath I turned around and drove back home, unaware of the tragedy that escaped my notice. Her prophecies came true, after all. But her words on that day meant more to me than you will ever know. Her brief synopsis of married life made me reconsider all my attitudes I had about it at the time and my impatience to get to places I didn't need to be. If I had been aware of my responsibility I would have come to your aid so much sooner, and of hers on that sad day. I hope you can forgive me for my sin of omission. And especially I pray that somewhere in this last report you and your family may find some words of solace and of continued hope. I admire your great achievement in Thunder Bay. My prayers were with you all the way.

I hope also it is not a disappointment to you that I choose to remain anonymous. All this concerning Nikola is true and perhaps because I choose to remain a mystery it will attach credibility to my words, and to some facts you would never have known otherwise. God's love be with you."

To Jerry the letter was exciting as a note from his own mother.
"Dad! Phil! You gotta read this letter we got!"
Phil meandered down the staircase. He was up anyhow. Jerry handed him the letter and Phil studied the contents.
"Incredible."
"I'll say. Do you think it is true?"
"Let's ask Dad what he thinks."
Tim's forehead furrowed tightly as he read the opening phrase. "I have to have my glasses," he said. He rarely resorted to glasses. He was digesting content, but looking for inconsistencies. But it all fit into place. The attendant remembered seeing her there. But did she talk to anyone? He studied it closer. He went over it again. And again.

All this concerning Nikola is true...Why would she reiterate that? He looked at the letter one last time...the occasion to visit?...turned around and drove back home? Attitudes? Married life? Reconsidered. Places I didn't need to be...there was something peculiar about the handwriting. It seemed ...!
"Jerry?" he asked calmly, masking a racing heart.

"Yeah, Dad?"

"Where is the envelope?" A diversion. A long pause, as he asked himself why.

"Right here, Dad."

Only a postmark. Indianapolis, Indiana. So that is where she ended up, he thought.

It was all too bizarre, but it explained everything. It was an accident after all! Now he had no doubt. She would not invent a story to conform to her change of character. No, not her. But why couldn't she have told him sooner? No matter. He understood. A saint's prophecy should be left undisturbed. More heapings of guilt would not have changed the past; it could only have confused each of their quests for redemption. And it was time. His indulgence had been granted; his last burden lifted. He was free!

As Jerry and Phil stood over him, his nod was cut short as the phone rang. Tim smiled. "It's Lisa." He lifted the receiver. "Good morning, my love...No no no. No more skiing, Lisa. Not this year," he laughed, as if his mood had changed like the weather. It was different; relieved, relaxed. "You know, Lisa, I've been thinking, the only thing I want to see in white for a while is...would you...come over here so I can do this right?"

The boys could hear from the other end an excited completion of his proposal, followed by a pause. The corners of Tim's mouth evolved into a kind of boyish grin. Their father was smiling. No, he was beaming!

"Yes! I will! Yes, I'm serious! Now! I'm here waiting! Yes, I do, too! Okay! Okay! We will talk about all that when you get here." He hung up the phone as gently as it had been answered.

He looked at his sons, still standing there, silent. They had become such men.

He knew that they understood enough about all that had just occurred. He looked away, not knowing where to begin. He was so happy! So completely!

"Uh, you know, Lisa thinks the women's team could use a couple of Keagans, too." he said, looking down momentarily. How did she hear about that one?

Phil and Jerry looked at each other. They smiled together, innocently.

"There is nothing wrong with that, Dad," Phil replied.

Tim stared out the picture window from the kitchen table. In the distance he saw a flag unfurl in a strong south wind. The clouds above began to thin, giving way to the proper season. The snow disappeared into the green grass like a thief into the night.

Tim rose and placed an arm around each son, and hugged them tightly. For some sins, one can and must repay. For others, there can only be forgiveness. And it must be accepted, as accepting as Jesus. He buried his face into their shoulders, until his tears finally turned into a period. There was, after all, only One Great Thing.

"I love you, my sons."

Chapter Fifty-Four

Epilogue

As THE DAY had just begun to break, a pair of footsteps picked up their pace. Turning a sharp corner, one foot found a piece of broken pavement. A stumble. A near fall. The runner grimaced. A sprain. With just two blocks to go, he hobbled on as quietly as he could, onto the pier in a stagger-step run.

Only a Newfie, thought the waiting cameraman.

But the runner would not let a recording of this mistake mock his deed. Wincing in pain, the Canadian who fantasized so long for this moment forced himself to resume an even pace. As he reached the shores of the Atlantic, the flame representing the better side of mankind burning brightly in the torch proudly held high, he looked back and threw a kiss toward Thunder Bay.

Mrs. Lauren Franz clasped the hand of the man who ushered in a new era. Her nomadic husband divined that though the flame may disappear from view, it would not cease to make plain infinite numbers of pathways rising to meet men and women who possess a clear destination.

The relay was complete. The Spirit passed into the hands of the Eternal. The Marathon of Hope found its destination resolved, not at some distant shore, but at a point inseparable from its origin. For there shall remain forever that first step taken in triumph which imparts inspiration to this day, not in the form of longevity, but in abundance of light.

As Mrs. Franz was about to wish her husband a happy birthday, a shadow passed before the rising sun. She looked up to see three...no wait! Just two white birds circling contentedly, higher and higher, toward the heavens. Like the little girl, whose recovery half a continent away left a team of specialists scratching their heads, they had come home again at last.

All received welcome in Newfoundland.

ADDITIONAL INFORMATION

If you are unable to obtain a copy of *Kickländ*, or if you would like to contact the author or publisher, please use the following address:

Hayes and Hyde Press
1210 W. Hyde Rd.
St. Johns, Michigan 48879
U.S.A.